COLD MOON HOME

AN ABBY SILVERNALE MYSTERY

JULIA POMEROY

CARROLL & GRAF PUBLISHERS
NEW YORK

COLD MOON HOME

Carroll & Graf Publishers
An Imprint of Avalon Publishing Group, Inc.
245 West 17th Street
11th Floor
New York, NY 10011

AVALON
publishing group incorporated

First Carroll & Graf edition 2007

Library of Congress Cataloging-in-Publication Data is available.

ISBN-10: 0-7867-1981-8
ISBN-13: 978-0-78671-981-5

9 8 7 6 5 4 3 2

Book design by Maria Elias

Printed in the United States of America
Distributed by Publishers Group West

To my husband, John, with love

ACKNOWLEDGMENTS

Any liberties taken with institutions or places are solely my responsibility, as are any errors; on that note, I'd like to thank Commissioner Paul Mossman, from the Department of Social Services in Hudson. Any similarity in this book to people living or dead is purely coincidental, except for the usual guys, and they know who they are.

There are two men I've thought of a lot lately: my father, Liv Pomeroy, OSS veteran, reporter, foreign serviceman, inventor, and traveler, who has such courage in the face of his worst enemy, old age; and George Rickey, whose beautiful kinetic sculptures I borrowed for Norman Smith (along with his cane and work ethic). George was generous to a fault and a true gentleman; I was fortunate to know him, if only for a short time.

Heartfelt thanks and affection to all the smart people at Carroll & Graf—Will Balliett, Wendie Carr, and Shaun Dillon in particular. They make a great team. A big thank-you to my wonderful agent, Richard Parks, and to my patient readers, Phyllis, John, Anne and Dale. As always, to Jarrett and

Algy, the former for her notes on the ending, both for being who they are. And Francesca, for all she does in Cortona.

Eugene, you made it out of Bazra—thank god and I love you. Now where's that Rolex from Kuwait City?

Finally, I want to say that it was a real pleasure to work with Michele Slung, my editor—who is clear-thinking, smart, and disciplined. The way I'd like to be.

CHAPTER ONE

Abby lived alone, so she couldn't allow herself to get easily spooked. But she had to admit that sometimes, late at night, the InnBetween made her nervous. When the people who usually filled it had gone, when all that human business—the shouting and hustling, cooking, laughing, arguing and eating—was over, the silence that followed was carved out of something solid. There were times when it even seemed to breathe.

It was a Saturday at the beginning of September, and it was one of those nights. Abby had stayed late to do the tallies and lock up. By midnight, she'd closed out the cash register and credit card machine; by twelve ten she'd finished the paperwork.

Downstairs, she made sure the bar was wiped clean, the shelves restocked, the beer cooler filled. The floor was sticky with spilled soda and the air stuffy with the smell of beer, but the day man would take care of that.

After turning off all the lights except the bulb that hung from the ceiling in the back hall, she took the front stairs up to the main dining room.

Behind her, the ice machine suddenly started buzzing. Abby couldn't help it—she glanced behind her, down into the dark shadows of the underground barroom. Nothing, of course. But she was glad Dan the dishwasher was still in the kitchen, scrubbing the pots, listening to his Christian radio station. He would be there well after she was gone, getting the work areas clean for the prep staff's arrival in the late morning. With him close by, she could keep the jitters in check.

Upstairs, she pulled on her windbreaker and looked over the main dining room one last time. The chairs were upside down on the tables; the room was silent and dark. Everything was in order.

In the kitchen, the cooks were long gone. They had put away the food and scrubbed the counters and cutting boards. The floor, its high-traffic areas covered in thick, perforated black rubber mats, was littered with lettuce leaves, chunks of bread, orange peel, and smashed tomato slices; it glistened with cooking oil and other spills. The smell was a combination of grease and sweat, with a harsh overlay of bleach.

"'night, Dan," she called out.

He didn't answer. He couldn't hear over the running water and the radio. She knocked lightly on the wall and, when he looked up, waved good-bye. He raised a hand and nodded.

She pulled open the back door and picked up the brick that kept it from closing all the way. It swung shut and locked automatically behind her. Standing under the yellow pool of light from the corner streetlight, she took a deep breath and zipped up her jacket; even though August was barely over, the temperature had dropped fifteen degrees since her shift began that afternoon. The night air felt damp and chilly.

Abby was bone tired. It had been a long, busy night. The County Fair ("Every Labor Day Weekend, Rain or Shine") was still going on at the edge of town, and she could see the glow of the lights from the fairgrounds. At the InnBetween, they'd done one hundred and thirty covers, and the small of her back hurt from being on her feet.

There were more cars than usual on Main Street, and as she crossed it to get to the Dollar Store parking lot, she went through her jacket pockets, looking for the keys to her blue and white Bronco. When she didn't find them, she put her cracked brown leather purse on the rusted hood of her car and unzipped it. She took out her wallet, address book, notepad, and sunglasses, and moved aside a fistful of loose paper money—singles, tens, and three or four twenties, her tips for the evening. Underneath, amongst the change and lipsticks, she found her keys.

Outside the village border, the darkness swallowed her up; there was no moon, and the combination of humidity and condensation created a thick, dense fog on the tree-shrouded road. A few miles down, her windshield began to cloud, and she turned on the heat, hoping to dry it out.

Her mind was drifting back to the shift that had just ended when suddenly the weak lights caught a movement to her right. A face appeared out of the blackness on the side of the dirt road, within a foot of the car. Abby yelled, veered to the left and slammed her foot on the brake. She cut back quickly to the right to avoid the narrow shoulder, skidded a few feet, and promptly stalled. It felt like it was all over before it happened.

She turned and looked back, thinking she might have imagined the face. Maybe it was a tree branch waving in front of the car. But no, someone was there, swaying, as if hurt.

"Oh, no," Abby groaned, and jumped out of the car. "Are you okay?" she called out, as she ran back. No answer.

When she reached the person, she saw it was a woman wearing a black fur coat, which was probably why Abby had only seen a flash of white face in the darkness.

"Are you hurt?" she repeated fearfully, touching the woman's arm. She couldn't see her face very well, but she was sturdily built, shorter than Abby's 5-foot-8-inch frame.

The woman pointed toward the dark embankment on the other side of the road.

Abby looked, and caught a glimpse of something reflected off her headlights. She walked across the narrow dirt road and looked down. There, steeply angled and wedged into the trees, was a small dark-colored sports car.

"Christ," Abby said. She looked at the woman, who had limped across the road and was standing next to her. "Was there anyone in the car with you?" Abby asked.

"Just me," the woman whispered, shaking her head slowly.

"Good. Great."

"But I need my things, the keys—"

With a glance at her own vehicle, parked askew in the center of the road and lighting up a section of the woods, Abby scrambled and slid down the embankment until she reached the car. It was a dark Miata, freshly dented where the right front side had glanced off a thick tree. The driver's door was open, as if the woman had thrown herself out. The car was empty except for a large gold leather handbag on the floor in front of the passenger seat. Abby reached in and pulled it out. The keys were in the ignition, and she took them, shutting the driver's door when she was done. She put the purse on her shoulder and clambered up the hill, grabbing hold of weeds and saplings whenever she lost traction.

The woman was nowhere in sight. "Crap," Abby muttered, panting. She went to her car and threw the purse into the back seat.

"Did you get my keys?" asked a voice. The woman was sitting in the passenger seat, the fur coat wrapped tightly around her.

"Oh, there you are," Abby said. She slid into the driver's seat, leaving the door open so the overhead light stayed on and she could look at the stranger. "Here," she said, handing her the keys.

Abby guessed she was about forty. She had no makeup on, and her hair looked dark red under the interior light. It was matted and tangled, and she had a cut on her forehead, right by the hairline. It had already crusted over and was starting to swell.

"That must hurt. What happened?" Abby asked.

The woman took a breath. "A deer crossed the road in front of me—I swerved, and suddenly, there I was, in the damn trees. I lost my pretty new slipper," she added, her chin trembling.

Abby wondered if she was in shock. She glanced down. One plump foot, toenails painted a bright red, was bare and stuck with mud and pieces of brown and red leaves. The other was wedged into a muddy sheepskin mule. Abby herself had never owned a pair of mules, but she was pretty sure that was what they were called. Delicate, fluffy slip-ons with little wedge heels. Mules. Half-breed donkeys. Strange footwear for a midnight drive in the country. And even stranger were the pink ruffled pajamas Abby could see sticking out from under the black coat.

Abby opened her mouth to say something, then changed her mind. She shut the car door. It was none of her business, and she just wanted to go home and get into bed. "Where am I taking you?"

Her passenger paused, as if she had to think about where she lived. "Bantam Center. My father's house."

Abby nodded and started the engine. At least she was facing in the right direction. In total, there were five Bantams. Abby worked and lived in the Village of Bantam, an old railroad and tavern town and the biggest and busiest of the Bantams. The others, each with a distinct personality of its own, were West Bantam, North Bantam, Old Bantam, and, finally, Bantam Center.

Bantam Center was one wide main road, flanked by generously built farmhouses sitting back from the road, with fields of flat farm land behind them. Luckily, it was only about ten minutes from Abby's house.

She swallowed her exhaustion. "That's a nice car," she remarked as they proceeded down the dark road.

"Oh, damn, damn the car. Oh, to hell with him, I'll pay for the fucking repairs, he'll get over it," the woman said angrily, as if she were arguing with herself. She turned to Abby: "It's not my car, it's Mitch's. Can I use your cell phone? I left mine at home."

"Nope. I don't have one. There's no service here anyway." Abby Silvernale worked long hours at the restaurant and then usually went straight home. She didn't have much use for a cell phone and didn't want the bills.

"Damn—I'll have to get a tow truck or something."

Abby shrugged. "Good thing you didn't hit that tree head-on. You could be dead."

"I know that." She looked at Abby with a frown, as if such thoughts were unsuitable.

Abby wondered if the woman had been drinking.

"So, who are you?" The question was abrupt.

Abby didn't feel much like talking, but the darkness around them created a sort of awkward intimacy. "Abby Silvernale. And you?"

"Germaine LeClair. What do you do?"

"I wait tables. At the InnBetween."

"The InnBetween? On the circle?"

"That's the one."

"I remember it. I used to live here a long time ago. I mean, a *looong* time ago."

Abby nodded. "Yeah. It was called that in the seventies and early eighties, I guess. The last people who owned it named it Chez Nous. Dulcie renamed it the InnBetween when she bought it."

"Dulcie?"

"My boss."

"A waitress—that must be interesting."

Abby glanced at her, wondering if the woman was being patronizing, but it was too dark to see her face. "Can be. Can also be a dead end. What do you do?" she asked.

"Oh, I'm a travel writer."

Yeah, she was probably being patronizing.

"What d'you write?" Abby asked.

"I just wrote a book about fixing up a farm house in Tuscany."

Abby tried not to sound impressed. "Oh. One of those."

"No, it's not like that. It's different," Germaine LeClair said with a note of irritation in her voice.

"I'm sure it is."

A coolness descended in the car. Abby took advantage of it. Silence was easier than small talk.

Five minutes later, they turned onto the main road of Bantam Center. Most of the houses were dark, though a few upstairs windows were lit, throwing soft lights on porches and front yards.

"It's that one," Germaine said, gesturing to a mailbox on the right. The house was a large black silhouette, barely distinguishable from the night sky. Abby could see neither color nor details. Behind it, an undersized ornamental streetlight spread a flat circle of yellow.

As she turned in, her headlights lit up a section of dark siding and flower beds, and she felt gravel crunching under her tires. There were no lights on in the front of the house, though there was a faint glow from somewhere downstairs and to the back. About twenty feet away from the house, on the other side of the little streetlight, was a separate and smaller structure. It had probably been built as a carriage house or shed. It had a large picture window facing the driveway. A lamp was lit inside the room, creating a dramatic pyramid of white; in the light sat a person, head bowed, back to the window.

"Here you are," Abby said as brightly as she could manage, turning partway to her passenger.

The woman, however, didn't move. She stared at the picture window and the person sitting in it. Abby followed her gaze, then looked back at her, wondering how drunk she really was.

"You're here," she repeated.

Her passenger turned to her, her expression agitated, the matted hair and blood-encrusted cut adding to a sort of desperate air about her. "I'll be right back. Five minutes. Will you wait for me?"

"Whoa, whoa. What do you mean, wait for you?"

"Please. Don't leave."

"I'm going home. I can't—"

Germaine LeClair didn't respond. She opened the passenger door, eyes on the picture window.

Abby was too tired to make sense of it. "What's going on?" and then, with a flash of alarm said, "What are we doing here?"

Germaine pointed a finger at Abby. "Please. Please. Don't leave." Without waiting for a response, she climbed out of the car and ran, now barefoot, toward the carriage house.

With a groan, Abby slumped into her seat. What the hell had she gotten herself into? This woman might be violent or delusional or both. If so, whoever was sitting inside the outbuilding was about to get a nasty surprise when she appeared, leaves hanging off her like a middle-aged Ophelia. With an effort, Abby climbed out of the car. She jogged after her. "Stop!" she said, trying to project a whisper.

But Germaine waved at her to go away and continued to the door of the smaller building. She began to turn the handle. Abby backed up and ran around to the front, so she was closer to the picture window and could see in, without herself being seen. From her new perspective, she realized that the person inside had white hair and shoulders stooped with age. She felt a wave of panic. Had she put an old person at risk? The woman hadn't seemed dangerous, she said to herself, already making excuses.

Suddenly, the figure in the picture window looked up and to the left. It was an old man. He must have heard the door opening because he pushed back the stool he was sitting on and slowly stood. He was small: standing, he wasn't more than a foot taller than he'd been when he was sitting. He reached for something, and Abby saw it was a cane. He leaned on it, still staring at the entrance. Oh, god, not just an old man, but a small, frail old man. Abby moved to the right, and she could now see Germaine framed in the doorway, her red hair backlit by the little streetlight and sticking out around her, her coat open to reveal the pink ruffled pajamas.

She started to speak, but Abby couldn't hear what she was saying.

The old man said something in response.

Germaine listened, then spoke again. Her reply seemed more agitated.

He now raised his cane and pointed it at Germaine, who put her hand in her pocket, reaching for something. Abby wondered what kind of a peace offering would work in a situation like this.

However, when Germaine drew her hand out of her pocket, Abby saw with disbelief and horror that she was holding a small pistol. Slowly, she raised her arm and pointed the barrel at the old man. Her lips were moving.

Abby felt the adrenaline rush into her head and ears, drowning out sound and will. Each of the seconds that followed stretched to the length of a short lifetime, in which things should happen, but nothing did. She knew she should do something, but she couldn't. She didn't move. She just stood there in the dark, staring, her mouth open.

Real time was restored by the old man. While Germaine stood there, holding the gun, he began moving toward her, thrashing his stick from side to side like a blind man looking for a tree in the desert. The expression on Germaine's face changed to one of shock and surprise. Her arm with the gun dropped down. They were no more than twenty feet apart to begin with, so the old man came at her quickly.

When the heavy cane must have been close enough to create a breeze on her face, she leaped back, arms pulled up and away from him. Abby heard her scream as she backed out of the doorway. Once clear of the entrance, she turned and ran.

Abby followed Germaine, who was running back to the car. By the time Abby climbed in, Germaine had done up her seat belt and was sitting there, panting and crying.

"Are you crazy? Where's that gun?" Abby said, kneeling on her seat, reaching for the woman's hands. They were empty. Leaning over her, she grabbed at the sides of her coat, looking for pockets. Abby's adrenaline rush was starting to make her tremble.

All she could think was that she had to get this person away from the house, away from the elderly person inside. She put the car in gear and backed out. Stopping for a moment, she looked back at the shed. The old man's outline was visible. He was standing up by the picture window, peering out into the night. One hand was up, shielding his eyes from the light. Abby wondered how much he could see. The thought crossed her mind that she should go in and make sure he was okay, but she felt it was more important to get her passenger out of here.

"I'm taking you to the police," she snapped, her knuckles white on the steering wheel. "Where's the gun? What did you do with it?"

"I would never have used it. I just wanted to scare him," Germaine said through her tears.

"Where is it, damn it?"

"I don't know, I must've dropped it somewhere," she whimpered.

Abby drove quickly, while her passenger sat hiccoughing and wet-faced. Her compassion level was lower than low. Let her stew in it. She had threatened someone at gunpoint in the middle of the night. Abby was still absorbing the fact that she'd just been part of some kind of assault. What if she'd shot him? Abby would be an accomplice.

Finally, when they were about a mile out of Bantam, she couldn't help herself. "Who was he?"

"He's my father, but he didn't know I was in town."

"That was really your father? You pulled a gun on your *father?*"

Germaine sniffed and wiped her nose with her hand. "Yes, well, I haven't seen him in a long time. I guess I startled him."

In disbelief Abby said: "Startled him? You said hello with a gun. In the middle of the night."

They drove into the village. They went around the dark traffic circle, past the InnBetween, with its three levels of wraparound porches. The streetlight on the corner projected the pattern of the railings on the painted brickwork. It felt like hours had passed—not just forty minutes—since she had stood under that light and zipped up her jacket. The building was dark, except for a faint glow from the kitchen. The thought of Dan and his Christian music helped anchor her.

Abby pulled up in front of the Lacey Memorial, the columned building that housed the village clerk, the mayor's office, and the police station. Let the cops deal with this. However, the entire building was dark and shut down. There wasn't one cruiser in the reserved parking.

Abby said in frustration: "Now what do I do with you? God, why didn't you just call him, go during the day like a regular person?"

Germaine answered defensively: "I was nervous about seeing him, so I thought that I'd be better off going late."

"At one A.M.?"

"He always keeps late hours."

"This is crazy. Christ, I can't believe I drove you there so you could do that." She thought for a second. "Where are you really staying?" she asked coldly.

"Spencerville, I'm staying with friends in Spencerville."

Great. Spencerville was ten minutes on the other side of Bantam. But Abby didn't know what else to do with her.

They turned up Main Street, and drove past the movie theater, the pet grooming shop, the Carlson building, and Victor's Café, where Abby usually had her morning coffee. Everything was dark and shut down.

She crossed the railroad tracks and when she came to the only streetlight in town, she took a left. They headed east to Spencerville.

"Where am I taking you?" Abby asked. "Into the village?"

"No, before you get to town, on the left. Bunson Road." They rode in silence for the next five minutes. Finally, Germaine sighed heavily. "There, that's it. Turn here."

On Bunson Road, it was the second house on the right. Even though it was night, Abby could see it was a carefully renovated colonial. Abby pulled into a well-lit circular driveway in front of a red door with polished brasswork.

As soon as they came to a stop, Germaine heaved herself out of the car and slammed the door so hard Abby thought she heard bite-sized chunks of rust breaking off the sides of her precious old vehicle.

"Hey, take it easy!" Abby protested.

Germaine began walking barefoot to the front door. Abby could see wet leaves still hanging from the hem of her fur.

She remembered the woman's handbag, which she'd thrown on the backseat. She leaned across to open the passenger door and called out: "Wait!" and held up the bag. Germaine turned, then limped back to retrieve it.

As she reached into the car to take it, Abby moved it a few inches out of her reach. "I want you to ring the bell and get the owner of the house downstairs. I want to make sure they know who you are before I leave you here."

Germaine took an ineffectual swipe at the large bag. "It's really none of your business."

"I wish."

Germaine put her hand on the seatback to give herself support. "I'm sorry, this was all a spur-of-the-moment thing. I'd gone to bed, but then I lay there and thought, why not now? Just get up and do it. So I did."

"Why the *gun?*"

Germaine leaned further in, resting one knee on the seat, her face close and fierce. "You want to know why? I'll tell you why. Because he killed my mother. I know that, I just can't prove it. So I thought I would scare him into admitting it. It was a really stupid idea, I admit it. I'll never do it again, I promise. You have to believe me. Now, can I have my purse?"

Abby ignored the request. "What do you mean, killed her?"

"Killed her. Made her die. He did something to her, I just don't know what. Give me my bag," Germaine said, and snatched it out of Abby's hand.

"Hey," Abby said, "don't forget this," and she picked up the single matted sheepskin mule from the floor of the passenger's seat.

Germaine grabbed it and shoved it into her handbag. "Thanks for the ride," she answered, and shut the car door harder than the first time.

"Ring that bell or I'm going to start with the horn," Abby said through the open window.

Germaine gave her a black look, but at the door she pushed the bell. Abby sat and waited, her car idling noisily. Finally, a light went on inside and a woman in a robe opened the front door. She looked at the car, talked for a second with Germaine, and then let her in. Germaine never glanced back at Abby.

As she drove slowly back into Bantam, Abby hoped she had done the right thing. She had probably let her tiredness get in the way. She should have used the restaurant phone, called the police, and handed Germaine over. She wondered if she was still a danger to the old man she claimed was her father. He had certainly seemed able to take care of himself. God, she wouldn't want to be in Germaine's shoes—her mules—angry, drinking, driving around at night with a gun.

But thoughts of the problematic situation she'd found herself in dissolved as she got closer to home, and as Abby drove up her rutted dirt driveway, all she could think about was letting her dogs out and getting into her bed.

The trailer was lit briefly by her headlights before she turned into the little parking area next to it. The dark honeysuckle that grew next to the door looked like a wide tear in the wall. She could hear her two dogs barking, one deep and the other high, with a yappy frequency. Home. Abby yawned until her jaw felt it would dislocate. She turned off the engine and rested her forehead on the steering wheel before climbing out, her legs stiff and leaden. As she unlocked her door and stood to one side, so that the white pit bull and the tiny gray mutt could rush by her, she could already feel the cool caress of her sheets against her skin.

Which brought to mind the pink pajamas. She'd handled things badly. She hadn't found out about the gun: was it Germaine's, and if so, did she have a permit—though, hell, there was no permit that allowed you to go to someone's house and threaten them. Most important of all, had it been loaded?

Abby wondered if she would ever see her again. She sincerely hoped not. The evening could have ended in the emergency room, the woman's head split open with a cane. Or the old man shot to death. Anyway, it was over, and no longer something she had to worry about: right now, all that mattered was sleep. She'd think about it properly in the morning.

In bed at last, the silence around her was restful; all she could hear was the soft, intermittent hum of her refrigerator. She shut her eyes and let her muscles relax into the mattress. Anyway, she couldn't be responsible for every nut job wandering the countryside. Even though, a little voice said, she had given the nut job a ride, watched her pull a gun, then driven her home.

Abby rolled over and shut out the chatter. Nothing had come of it. It was no longer her problem. Her responsibilities were showing up for work, paying her bills, and looking after her dogs. It was a pretty basic life, and she liked it just fine.

CHAPTER TWO

The next morning, Abby overslept and was ten minutes late for her job interview. Each fall her boss, Dulcie, who was also her good friend, was forced to cut back on the wait staff hours. She stingily doled out shifts, doing her best to treat everyone fairly, but somehow ensuring that no one made enough money to survive. After Labor Day, weekenders would begin to spend more time in the city, and seasonal renters would pack up and leave. Those left behind ate out less, either to save money for the holidays or because home seemed cozier. Whatever the reason, by the end of September the number of covers each night at the InnBetween fell away dramatically. So, early in the month, Abby and many of the other waiters started looking for second jobs. Or, at least, began to think about looking for second jobs.

The week before, out of the blue, a neighbor had called her. Paul Becker's father-in-law suffered from Alzheimer's; he and his wife, Maddie, were looking for someone to stay with him about three mornings a week and go over his mail with him.

"He gets confused about the letters. He thinks we're hiding them from him, so we thought an outside person for a few days a week would put his mind at ease," said Paul. "Come and meet him. See if you hit it off."

Dull, but Abby would make enough money to pay a few bills.

Abby dressed quickly in a pair of worn but respectable dark blue trousers and a clean white shirt. She usually wore jeans, even though they bored her and she had a pair of red leather sneakers she liked to work in. In her closet, in a box, she had a pair of stiletto heels in a soft green leather, but she never went out with them on. Once in a while she wore them around the trailer.

She didn't have a full-length mirror, so before putting on her only pair of conservative black loafers, she stood on her bed to see how she looked in the mirror over her dresser. Presentable. She turned, trying to see if the pants clung to her behind. They didn't seem to. Couldn't ask for much more. She stepped off the bed, trampolining her small gray dog, Rick, who was resting there. He looked at her briefly, coldly, and shut his eyes again.

She drove down her hill, past the old Silvernale farmhouse left to her by her husband, who had died two and a half years before. The truth was, Jonah had put a shotgun to his head. Behind the house. Abby thought about him every time she looked at it. The two images, house and body, were indelibly linked, as though the heat of the pain had melted them into each other. The pain had eventually eased, but the images could never be separated.

Because of that, she no longer lived there. Instead, she rented the farmhouse to Lloyd and Doreen, who had cows and used the pastures. Abby herself lived on the hilltop behind the farmhouse in her trailer. It was an ugly little place, but since it was on her own land, it was affordable.

Abby called it a double-wide trailer but it was, in fact, two loaf-shaped trailers that had been riveted together by the previous owner, after he used a blowtorch to cut through the walls. The back trailer was the bedroom and bathroom, and the front was the kitchen/living room, with a small entrance way. The whole thing was about 16 by 20 feet and was set on a cement slab. The man had put it together for his daughter and son-in-law, so that they could live on the edge of his property in Copake; they had used it for fifteen years, never paid a penny in rent. According to the man, they had upped and gone south one day, without so much as a thank-you.

Which is how Abby had bought it for a song. It was tinny, and when it snowed heavily she had to use a ladder to get on the roof and shovel, but she didn't mind. It sat in a pasture at the top of the hill, with beautiful views of at least two distant mountain ranges, depending on the weather. And it was hers. Unfortunately, it was sided in mustard-yellow vinyl, but she didn't want to paint it, believing that would start a cycle of upkeep that she was not prepared to set in motion. Better to let it age gracelessly.

Which was sort of the way she felt about herself. Recently turned thirty-two, which meant she was nearly thirty-three, she waited tables and had odd jobs here and there. If you asked her for a personal inventory, she'd have to think a moment. Then, the answer would go: she had all her teeth, and they were pretty straight, except for a gap between the front two. As a child she could squirt water about three feet through that gap. And there was her hair. Brown, thick, shoulder-length. When it was clean and shining, it was her best asset. As far as her body went, she could eat whatever she wanted without putting on weight, but some of that was because of her job, always moving. Her eyes were green, which she liked. She didn't care much for her looks, though she appreciated the clear skin. Privately, she would have liked sharper cheekbones.

But all in all, she had nothing to complain about.

She had friends, but no bosom buddies. Why was that? Wasn't she trying hard enough? She had moved to the area when she was sixteen, so you'd think she'd have some roots, know plenty of people who wished her well, wanted to have her over for dinner, include her in their lives. But she didn't make friends easily, and her only family, her parents, had moved to Arizona years ago, selling their house and coming back only once to visit her and Jonah when they'd first moved into the farmhouse.

When she thought of Jonah, she couldn't see his face as clearly as she used to. She could picture his mouth, and his eyebrows. His blond hair. She remembered his nose, straight but with a scar across the bridge where he'd run into barbed wire as a seven-year-old, but she had trouble conjuring up his entire face. Poor Jonah. Who would remember him if she didn't?

She turned left on River Street. The old man lived ten minutes' drive from Abby. She was tempted to go back and see if the abandoned Miata was still there, but she didn't have time; she was heading to Bantam Center, which was in the opposite direction.

Afterward, she was surprised at how slow she'd been to ask herself if the old man she had an appointment with and Germaine's father were one and the same. When she saw the driveway, following the instructions she'd been given, she finally paid attention. The house turned out to be dark gray with blue trim. It looked shabbier by daylight. But the shed behind the house, and the ornamental streetlight that lit the path between it and the main building, were just as she remembered them. So was the picture window.

Abby had hoped to forget all about Germaine LeClair. But apparently that was not meant to be. Did this mean Maddie Becker and Germaine were sisters?

Paul Becker's green Taurus was already there. Abby pulled in next to it. She wondered if she should come clean right away, or not mention last night. She wanted the job. Maybe, if no harm had come of it, she should let it go. Germaine had been drunk and upset. It was highly unlikely she would do something like that again. If Abby could find the gun, she could forget it ever happened.

As she walked up the short path to the front door, Abby noticed that the flowerbeds were sprung with weeds, and the narrow siding on the house was peeling, showing a lighter gray color underneath. She knocked on the door. Paul opened it immediately, frowning. He was a stork of a man, thin as a rail, stooped, serious, bald, with a fringe of gray hair. His ear hair, however, was dense and bushy, giving the impression of a black pipe cleaner stuck into one long, rubbery ear and coming out the other. He taught engineering at SUNY Albany. Abby wondered if his students drew little caricatures of him on the borders of their notebooks. *She* would have.

He seemed surprised to see her, which was strange because he had made the appointment. Maybe he was the one with memory loss. She started to apologize for being late, when he held his index finger upright against his lips, admonishing her to silence. He stepped outside, pulling the front door closed behind him.

He walked back down the path without saying anything, and Abby followed him, her spirits sinking. When he reached his car, he turned to her: "He had a bad night. He's napping. I'll give him ten more minutes, and then we can wake him up and the two of you can meet."

Abby knew more about his bad night than Paul did. She also recognized an opportunity for escape. "Maybe I should come back tomorrow, when he's feeling better."

Paul shook his head and kept shaking it, to get his point across. "No, no, today is fine. He just needs a few more minutes."

To show that he meant what he said, he leaned against his car, crossed his long, thin arms, and brought one elongated leg over the other in a classic position of repose.

For the next ten minutes he leaned without moving. Abby was once more reminded of a stork, motionless in a body of water, supported by one long thin leg. She stood in front of him, digging little patterns into the white gravel with the tip of her shoe. The scuffed black leather turned gray while she and Paul talked about his father-in-law, Norman, his illness, health insurance and institutional care in general, and the likelihood of a cure for Alzheimer's. It wasn't a lively conversation, and she didn't have much to contribute. She finally lowered herself to the edge of a spent peony bed, beaten down by the sheer grimness of the subject.

Eventually, Paul looked at his watch and pushed himself off from his car. "Time to wake him up. You wait in the hallway. I'll go in first, then when he's awake and alert, I'll call you in."

She sat on a long bench while Paul headed through an archway into what she presumed was the living room. Before he disappeared from sight, she saw his head flick forward nervously. The front hall was overheated, the air smelling closed-in and slightly sour. A staircase led to an upper floor, turning midway at a small landing. To her left was a room that seemed to be used as an office.

Abby could hear everything that happened in the next room. Obviously, his father-in-law was still asleep, because she listened to Paul clear his throat, then say in a loud, chipper voice, "Norman, time to get up, it's nearly lunchtime."

There was no reply. Then a loud crack, which she could swear was a jaw snapping shut. A sleep-encrusted voice barked, "Who the hell are you?"

Abby thought she heard a soft protest from Paul, but it was drowned out.

"How dare you? How dare you walk uninvited into my house? Get the hell out!" Then a shuffling sound, and the voice took on a constricted sound as if the speaker were struggling to stand. "I'll call the police. How dare you? I've never heard of such a thing! Get the hell out, I said."

And sure enough, Paul popped out again, his face red and blotchy. "Jesus Christ, the old bastard," he whispered. He waved her away. "Quick, quick! Before he finds you here."

They both scuttled out the front door. Abby wanted to keep running down the driveway and out to the road.

Outside, Paul looked defeated. Abby felt sorry for him, but said with relief: "I guess we'll have to try again another day, right?"

He looked at her in surprise. "No, he'll be fine. We'll go back in, in a few minutes. He won't remember anything."

Abby sat back down next to the peony bed. Paul sat in his car with the door open, and began rifling through papers.

"Tell me," Abby asked, "does Maddie have any other siblings?"

"Two sisters."

"Two. That's nice for her. Do they live nearby?"

Paul sighed, not in the mood to talk anymore. "One lives in Woodstock, and the other travels."

She assumed the latter was Germaine. She understood why the woman had been attacked with a cane. Not only had she drawn a gun, but if the old man hadn't seen her for a number of years, there was a good chance he had no idea who she was. Which made Abby feel less concerned about confessing to Paul that she'd brought her to the house the night before. Maybe Norman didn't remember the incident, which sort of meant it hadn't happened. In a way.

"What about Maddie's mother? Is she dead?"

Paul looked up at her impatiently. "Yes, Wanda died more than twenty years ago." He watched her to see if she would ask anything else.

She thought she might as well. "What did she die of?"

"Cancer."

Five more minutes dragged by. Abby thought about the restaurant, and wondered what specials George the cook was making that night. She hoped they included one of her favorites, pasta with asparagus. She was in the mood for asparagus.

Paul climbed out of his car. "Okay, let's try again."

They walked to the front door, and this time Paul rapped loudly on it before turning the handle. "Hello! Norman! You in?" he called out through the open door.

"Yes?" The same voice called out from the next room.

"It's Paul, Maddie's husband. I've brought someone to meet you. May we come in?"

Silence.

They waited without breathing, in guilty partnership. Then a slow, shuffling step, and the little old man from the night before appeared in the arched doorway. He had a round head covered in wispy white hair. He looked frail, and his thick corduroy trousers had stains on them. He walked with the help of the gnarled hardwood cane, smoothed and polished to a high gloss. It looked a lot more innocuous than it had the night before. His body was bent over, as if gravity were trying to pull him forcibly into the ground. His ears were large and stood out from his head, giving him a gnomelike appearance, and behind thick lenses in black frames his eyes were a very pale, washed-out blue.

"Of course, Paul. Come in, come in."

He turned, and walked slowly back the way he had come, through the archway. Abby and Paul followed him. His white hair was flattened in the back, probably from sleeping on it. Paul tried to slow his long nervous stride to accommodate the short shuffling steps of his father-in-law. He looked as if he were dancing on coals. Abby followed behind.

They were now in a large area that was living room on the left, and dining area on the right. Directly in front of them was a massive brick fireplace. Probably to increase the size of the room, the walls on either side of it had been removed, leaving it freestanding, its chimney disappearing into the ceiling above. The room extended to include the kitchen beyond. In the living room area, the space was brightly lit by tall casement windows that gave out on a garden. There was a long couch against the wall immediately to Abby's left, and a couple of armchairs across from it, separated by a low coffee table. On the right side of the room, a large dining table took up most of the space. Abby noticed that the ceiling over the table seemed to be decorated with a low-hanging blanket of small pieces of bent metal. Unthinking, Abby walked over and reached up to touch it.

"Don't do that," snapped Paul, glancing nervously at Norman.

Abby pulled back her hand.

"That's all right. She can touch it." Norman came over to the table, and reached up. She noticed that his hands seemed large, out of proportion to the rest of his body. Gently, he tapped one of the small, metal pieces. The movement passed like a ripple through the steel pieces until the whole blanket was moving ever so gently. The pieces bowed and twinkled, the small motion setting them going as if there was nothing that would ever stop them.

"Wow," she said.

"Do you like it?" Norman asked.

"It's beautiful."

"I made that in 'sixty-seven." His look of pleasure at her compliment slowly dissolved. He frowned, unsure. "I think it was 'sixty-seven."

Paul stepped forward. "Norman, this is Abby. Abby Silvernale. Abby, Norman Smith. Abby heard you were looking for a secretary. She's very interested in the position."

"Oh, good, good. Would you like tea? We should have tea."

They sat on the low, plaid couch, drinking from china cups. Prompted by Paul, Norman discussed his mail.

"There is a lot to do," he told Abby. "What I need is an amanuensis."

Abby looked in puzzlement at Paul, who rolled his eyes and sighed in impatience.

"Right. An amanuensis." He pronounced it ah-man-you-en-sis. "It means a helper, or secretary." And to Norman he raised his voice: "That's what she is, Norman. The new amanuensis."

The old man nodded. "Good, good. Write down your hours, would you, my dear? Leave them where I can see them. My memory isn't what it used to be."

"Write it big. And make sure to put your name and phone number," Paul said out of the side of his mouth.

They drank their tea in silence, and when they were done, Paul rose, saying, "Well, Norman, we'll leave you to your work."

Norman stood slowly and said to Abby, "You must come back again some time."

"She will. She's going to help you with your mail, right, Norman? Remember?" Paul reminded him.

Norman shot him a sharp look. "Of course I do. Do you think I'm stupid?"

Paul blushed angrily. "No, no."

In the entryway he patted her shoulder. "That went wonderfully," he whispered. "Smart of you to admire his mobile."

Abby shrugged. "I didn't know it was his."

Paul glanced nervously back toward the arched doorway. "Right. Well, thanks for coming. I won't keep you."

She said good-bye to him at the front door and took her time walking to the car and getting inside.

What she really wanted was to look for the gun. Germaine must have dropped it somewhere between the shed and the front of the house, where Abby had been parked.

Sitting in the driver's seat, she fiddled with the radio, opened and shut the glove compartment, made a show of looking through her purse. But when she glanced up, Paul was still there.

At last she ran out of delaying tactics and was forced to start the engine and back out of the driveway.

She'd get another chance, she said to herself, when Paul wasn't there.

As she drove back toward Bantam, she wondered if, by the time she found herself in Norman's condition, they would have legalized some kind of doctor-assisted suicide in New York State. Though being vulnerable to grudge-bearing relatives like Germaine was worse than memory loss. Abby thought of her in her pink pajamas, on the warpath about a death that had happened twenty years before. Why wait until now to make accusations, especially when it seemed as if the man she was accusing would soon forget his own name?

CHAPTER THREE

It was Sunday of Labor Day weekend and every table was taken at the InnBetween, both upstairs and down. There were people waiting outside, standing in little groups, and Abby could see their hungry, irritated faces at the long windows. The street level put them lower than the seated diners, so they seemed like the drowning in *Titanic,* the ones who wouldn't make it into a lifeboat and would have to be beaten away with oars. Abby knew not to make eye contact, or they would start gesturing, pointing to their watches or even to their open mouths. As if they hoped a waiter would open a window and tip a spoonful of something hot into them to keep them going.

Inside, customers were reaching other levels of irritation: the victorious glow of getting a table can only last so long. Sooner or later they would need bread, water, alcohol. The most obvious signs were laid aside menus, frowns, tapping fingers. Abby tried to pick out the unhappiest and deal with them as quickly as possible.

The truth was, Abby always enjoyed a rush. Whether it was the adrenaline or the focus, busy evenings were usually easier than slow ones. On a slow night, each time a customer walked in the door you had to pull yourself up by your bootstraps or, to move on to another metaphor, make like a cheap whore and fake energy and enthusiasm. On a slow night, your limbs were heavy, and you felt lethargic, clumsy. You were more likely to break dishes or snap at the other waiters. You dragged yourself through the long evening, wondering if it would ever end, and knowing that if you were lucky, you'd go home with twenty dollars in tips. Also, like the cheap whore.

But on a busy night, look out. The food was steaming, flying through the swinging door, and the kitchen was a burning, hissing, crashing symphony of dangerous coordination. On a busy night, you worked like a machine, sidestepping other waiters with a quarter of an inch to spare. You took orders, delivered hot plates, poured wine, brought bread, and cleared tables, all with a dancer's restraint. You calculated, you consolidated, you picked up this, returned that, dodged, weaved. You were light, fast. On fire.

Just when the evening was slowing down, the door opened and Germaine LeClair walked in. She was with two of the InnBetween's regular customers, known to the staff as Mr. and Mrs. Merlot. Suzie Helder was the woman who had opened the door for Germaine the night before, though Abby hadn't recognized her at the time.

Gone was Germaine's leaf-dotted black fur and dirty pink ruffles. The change was startling. Whereas someone else of her stature and build might have appeared dumpy, she looked voluptuous, her clothes fitted to her full curves. She was glossy and bright, laughing with her friends.

Abby watched Becca seat them at a table on the porch. The porch was enclosed, but it had big windows and was a little quieter than the main dining room, so some people preferred it. The Merlots immediately ordered their usual bottle of medium-priced California wine. No surprise there. It wasn't Abby's station—she was working the other side of the room—but she saw Becca carrying the bottle out to the table.

Abby was clearing her last tables when Becca pulled her aside. Becca was a pretty, slender brunette in her early twenties, with a sweet, rather nasal voice. She was the gentlest member of the staff, and she suffered from low self-esteem. One slow night in early spring, the staff had passed around a notepad in which each person was required to draw a self-portrait. Becca's person was short and dumpy. Cat, a waitress who had been known to chase a customer down the street to return a tip if she didn't think it was big enough, said in amazement, "You have a terrible body-image, Becca." To which Becca replied, with a sad nod, "I know. It's my thighs, isn't it?"

Tonight Becca was looking at Abby with that same expression. "Can you deal with the woman at A4? She's with the Merlots, and she says I brought her the wrong pasta."

"Did you?"

"No, no, she wanted the rotini, and that's what she got. But she says it's not real rotini. Keeps raggin' me about it," Becca said glumly.

Abby sighed. She often stood in for Dulcie, especially when strong-arming was needed. Maybe because they had a very young staff and Abby, thirty-two and a five-year veteran of the restaurant, had natural seniority. She had started working there soon after Dulcie first bought the building at auction from the bank; the previous owners had skipped town, owing a large and mushrooming amount in back sales tax.

"I'll take care of it," she told Becca. Abby hated arguing with people, but it ticked her off to see anyone picking on Becca, who wouldn't hurt a fly—literally—as she was a vegetarian. Which to Abby made her seem somehow more delicate than the rest of the staff. "I know who she is. I'll deal with her."

Abby went out to the porch, and walked toward A4. The Merlots had their backs to her so she could see Germaine, who was talking earnestly to them. She looked very different from the last time they met, makeup enhancing her eyes and cheeks, the red of the wine in the glass in front of her catching and reflecting the red in her lips and in her shining helmet of dark red hair. Abby revised her estimate of her age. She now put her in her late thirties. Her eyes were sparkling, and she was wearing an emerald green top in some shimmery material. The only trace of her accident was a small Band-Aid on her forehead.

The offending plate of rotini was sitting in front of her, and at least half of it seemed to be gone. Obviously one of those complainers who eat the food, then say it isn't properly cooked. Abby felt a little more iron enter her soul.

Her smile widened. "Hello, Germaine. Remember me? I'm Abby."

Germaine looked up at Abby. Suddenly she broke into a big smile. "Oh, god! It's you!" She looked truly excited to see her, and her sincerity took Abby off guard. "Suzie, this is the woman who saved me last night, when I went into the ditch!"

No mention of the visit to her father.

"I should have known it was Abby. She's fabulous," said Mrs. Merlot, as if Abby were standing in a different room.

"Abby, these are my friends, Suzie and Mitch Helder," Germaine said with a flourish.

Abby merely nodded. "How's the car?"

Mitch gave a bark of laughter.

"I'm buying it from Mitch," Germaine explained. "Seems only fair."

"I guess so," Abby smiled, though it seemed a little extreme to her. But Mitch looked pleased. Anyway, it was no concern of hers. "Becca tells me you're not happy with your pasta. Maybe I can help."

Germaine looked up at her, pleadingly. "The waitress thought I was complaining, but I wasn't, really." The fullness in her face gave her a girlish quality. Her thick hair was cut in bangs, emphasizing the impression she gave of being a large child. "The pasta is delicious, isn't it?" She looked for support from both the Merlots, who nodded approvingly at her, as if encouraging their oversized little girl to speak for herself. "I was just trying to explain to our waitress that in Italy, rotini aren't quite this shape. They're more extended. Fatter. But these are delicious! I love them! No, you can't take them away!" She put her arm around the plate, dramatically.

Abby hesitated, unsure of what to say next. "Well, as long as you're happy with them. I suppose all those pasta companies make the shapes a little differently. If that's it, I'll get back to work. Nice seeing you again."

She turned to go, and heard Germaine say: "These can't be Italian."

Abby turned around, and Germaine looked up at her guiltily. As if they were playing *Mother, may I?* Abby wanted to yell: "Freeze!"

Instead she said: "We're in upstate New York, not Rome. Our chef is second-generation Italian, from Brooklyn. But the pasta's straight from Italy. I'll get you the box."

Germaine shook her head vehemently: "Oh, no, no! I'm so sorry! But I just came back from Italy, and I'm obsessed."

"No big deal. Enjoy the rest of your meal." As she walked quickly away, she promised herself that the next time she saw someone by the side of the road in the middle of the night, she would drive on by. Especially if they were wearing a fur coat and pajamas.

An hour later, she saw the Merlots and their guest go out the front door. They were the last customers, so she was looking forward to locking the door after them. However, just as she was about to close the door, Germaine popped her head back in.

"Oh, it's you, great. I just wanted to say one thing. I'm sorry if I was a bitch tonight. And also," she added, dropping her voice, "you know all that ranting about my father?"

Abby looked at her. "Yes, I remember perfectly."

Germaine smiled ingratiatingly. "Forget about it, okay? It's just crazy talk. Forget it, please."

"I'm trying," Abby answered. "Goodnight." She took the door handle firmly, and started to close it. Germaine looked slightly put out, but she removed the part of her body that was blocking the door and was gone.

CHAPTER FOUR

It was her first day as Norman Smith's "amanuensis" and Abby was nervous. She had looked up the word in her old dictionary. The definition was: "an assistant who takes dictation or copies something already written; secretary: now a somewhat jocular usage." She looked up *jocular*, just to be sure, and found it to be "joking, humorous, full of fun." Interesting. When she'd first heard it, it hadn't made her laugh. She turned to the front pages of the dictionary. First published in 1952, latest edition 1972. That explained it. The word was once used regularly, then became so rare and quaint it seemed funny. Now we don't even get the joke.

Three days had gone by since she had met Norman Smith, and the morning was wet and dreary, which she took to be a bad sign. She wondered whether he'd throw her out or offer her tea. After all, she had seen that frail old man attack his daughter with a cane and eject his own son-in-law; if he could do that to family, what would he do to a stranger?

When she pulled into the driveway of his house, a red, late-model Honda

Civic was there ahead of her. Paul's wife, Maddie, was sitting in the driver's seat reading a letter, and when she saw Abby, she climbed out. Abby liked Maddie. She was a small woman of about forty with prematurely gray hair cut into a tidy bob, and today she was wearing a gray sweater set and neat brown pants, their creases sharp. She looked frail. Her skin was pale, her lips and cheeks bloodless and waxy. Even though she looked as if she might have trouble walking to the corner store, Maddie worked full time as a social worker in Pittsfield, ran in the local marathon, and volunteered at the Humane Society. Abby decided long ago that Maddie was in great physical shape, but her heart didn't bother pumping blood to her face or skin surface, finding it an inefficient use of energy. She was nothing like her sister Germaine, that was for sure.

Maddie had called the night before to say she would meet Abby at her father's and show her where everything was kept, explain his routine, give her a list of numbers to call in case of emergency, and so on.

"I'm glad you're here," Abby said nervously, adjusting her dark blue pants. The button at the waist had fallen off so she'd had to use a safety pin. She made sure her white shirt covered the front closure as she followed Maddie to the door.

Maddie glanced at her. "Relax. He's looking forward to seeing you. I've mentioned you a number of times over the weekend. He has a pile of letters he wants to go over, so that will take you most of the morning."

Inside the house, everything was quiet.

"Norman?" Maddie called out. Abby found it interesting that she called him by his first name. She wondered if she always had, or just as an adult.

No answer. "Hmm."

They walked through the living room into the kitchen. Pinned to the wall next to the phone were emergency numbers, under it pill bottles and containers. There were a few clean dishes in the drying rack, but otherwise everything looked spotless and uncluttered.

"He has a housekeeper. She comes every morning, helps him with breakfast, does some cleaning, and prepares and gives him lunch. Then she comes back in the evening and gives him supper. Works pretty well."

"What's her name?"

"Saranda. From Senegal," she added, as if to explain the exotic name.

As they walked out of the kitchen, down a few stone steps and into the back yard Abby asked Maddie: "You have a couple of sisters, right?"

Without looking at her, Maddie nodded. "Sort of. Adopted."

Abby took a moment to absorb that fact. "Do they come often to visit Norman?"

Maddie stopped. "Why do you want to know?"

Abby watched her carefully. "I met one of them the other night. Germaine."

Maddie glanced at her. "Really? Where?"

Abby took the coward's path and omitted half the truth. "At the restaurant. She's staying with friends in Spencerville."

Abby expected Maddie to show more interest, but she said nothing and continued along the flagstone path that went to the smaller building. Abby could see the picture window as they approached. They crossed the twenty yards from the house to the small outbuilding, which in daylight looked about the size of a double garage. Maddie gestured to it with both hands, as if presenting something.

"Here's where he works."

Abby nodded. To their left and behind both buildings was a large flat pasture, about eight acres in size and hedged by large, mature trees. At the far edge of the field Abby saw another building. A big angular gray structure, dingy with age and overgrown. It was incongruous in the rural setting. Abby could just make out a dirt track that led off to it, beginning on the far side of the work shed.

"What's that?" Abby asked, pointing at the building.

"That's the old studio. We used to call it the Metal Building. Basically storage now."

"Big place."

Maddie nodded. "Big place, big pieces. He hasn't made one in years." A large, gray cat appeared out of nowhere and trotted next to them as they walked up to the door. On it, a small sign, handwritten in a wobbly script, read:

Do not Enter—Private
By appointment only

Maddie knocked firmly on the door and opened it. The cat darted in front of her, beating her in through the door. Abby followed them both inside.

The room they walked into ran the full width of the shed, though not as deep. She had only seen it from the outside. At the back was a short corridor that ended in a closed door. On it was another handmade sign:

Gallery
By invitation only

The walls were Sheetrocked but unpainted. The space was a real workroom, planks on the floor, tools hanging on the walls, shelves piled with dusty supplies of metal in strips, coils, and small sheets. Plastic bins on the floor held more usable scraps and found objects, such as hubcaps and rusted signs. Abby saw an old toaster sticking out of one of them.

There were windows on both sides, though on the left they were small, and obstructed by shelving. A small cot was nestled in the left corner, curtained by an old army blanket tacked to a wooden beam. Across the room, the work area was arranged in front of the large window, obviously to take advantage of the northern light. On the bench were attached various vices and small cutting tools. Norman sat hunched over at the table, his back to the light. A cassette player/radio that had been new twenty years earlier was on the shelf under the window. A Bach piece was playing, climbing and interweaving in the still room.

"Norman," Maddie spoke in a loud voice, as if she had to break through a barrier with her voice. It seemed a pity to interrupt the old man, so hard at work.

He looked up, startled, and stared at them, his pale blue eyes large behind his thick lenses. After a few seconds delay, he smiled with pleasure.

"Well, hello, hello. Is that Maddie?" Abby was relieved he recognized his daughter. "Well, what a surprise! What are you doing here?"

Maddie nodded at him. "I brought Abby Silvernale. Abby is going to do some secretarial work for you, remember?"

"I didn't know that," he answered reproachfully, "but I'm glad to hear it. I have needed an amanuensis for some time now."

And so began Abby's first day with Norman Smith. They worked in the main house, in a downstairs parlor that had been set up as an office. She read his letters to him, slowly and carefully. If he had trouble understanding, she read them again. She typed out his answers. One of his letters was from an old friend, mentioning Wanda, Norman's wife, and a weekend they had all spent together forty-five years before. They had eaten a picnic lunch by a nearby lake and Wanda had drawn his portrait.

"So, Wanda was an artist, too?" Abby asked, after she had finished reading. She thought she might get Norman to talk about his wife. But he frowned.

"Wanda, an artist? No, no. She drew on napkins." He pushed the letter aside with one large finger. "I won't answer that letter. Silly." He pointed at the pile of circulars, bills and junk mail. "Read another one."

Throughout the morning, Abby could hear the housekeeper, Saranda, moving around in the rest of the house, sometimes the kitchen, other times upstairs, the vacuum cleaner roaring as it was dragged and bumped across the floor. Occasionally Abby would sneak a look at her watch, but the time moved at a snail's pace, leaving a trail behind.

By lunchtime she was worn out. Norman, on the other hand, seemed peaceful and relaxed. In the kitchen, the housekeeper poured out a steaming bowl of soup for his lunch, and his eyes brightened when he saw it. Saranda was a large woman, tall and full-figured. Her face was wide at the cheek-bones, and her dark skin gleaming and flawless. Her hair was cut short and she wore a loose skirt, a print of daisies against a dark blue background, and a man's blue shirt, sleeves rolled up. Her expression was stern, and she seemed to have no time for chit-chat. Norman seemed very comfortable with her, happy to follow her terse instructions and take his place at the table. After lunch he was to go back out to his studio and work, and the prospect seemed to soothe him.

"Good-bye, Norman," Abby said, when she was ready to leave. "I left my hours on your desk, so you'll know when I'm coming back."

He looked up from his soup, and smiled sweetly. "Good-bye, my dear."

Abby left by the kitchen door and stood in the backyard, breathing in the crisp air, enjoying the light on the leaves, still green and lush with summer. A breeze seemed to have blown the clouds out of the sky, leaving the day bright and clear. Once more she noticed the gray building in the far end of the field. She wondered if it was the age of the artist that had rendered the building obsolete, or if Norman's work had simply changed direction. What had Maddie said? "Big place, big pieces."

She started to walk around the house to the front, where she had left her car. She glanced back at the kitchen, but Saranda was nowhere in sight.

It was a perfect opportunity to look for the gun. She walked to the door of the shed, and stood over the flower beds next to it, spreading the plants aside with her foot so she could see between them. When she found nothing, she went down on one knee and spread the greenery with her hands, occasionally glancing over her shoulder to see if anyone was watching her. After she had looked through all the beds on both sides of the door, she stood, stretching out her knees. She went back to what she was doing, and followed the flowerbeds around the length of the shed, carefully poking through the flowers and weeds to make sure she hadn't missed anything.

Nothing. No gun. She had already spent too long looking. She would have to continue another day.

She walked slowly to her car. Maybe she had missed it. She tried to re-create the scene, trying to picture Germaine's hands. Had she thrown her arms up in the air? She might have flung it quite a distance. Abby should have done something about it right away, she should have reported it. As she started her car, she asked herself what she was doing. But she couldn't come up with a quick answer. Or even a slow one.

CHAPTER FIVE

It was hunger that made Abby go to the restaurant that night. Or so she told herself. She wasn't on the schedule, but the truth was, she was lonely. After leaving Norman's, she had driven up the steep dirt driveway to her mustard-yellow trailer with its distant view of the Catskills and the Heldebergs. She made a sandwich and ate it sitting outside on her metal porch chair, her feet on a milk crate she had borrowed two years ago from the restaurant. Between bites, she rested her sandwich on her lap. The dogs sat next to her, and occasionally she handed them each a scrap of cheese or ham. They watched Lloyd's cows in the next field, who chewed the grass and watched them back.

After her day with Norman she felt sad, though she wasn't sure why. It occurred to her that maybe it was close contact with old age. Instead of making her feel young and full of potential, the day had left her with the cloudy understanding that the few threadbare decades she had left would gallop by before she could figure out a way to make them count. At least he had family. She would be dependent on strangers.

It was about seven o'clock when Abby parked by the Dollar Store and walked over to the InnBetween. A small sign taped to the inside of one of the front windows caught her eye:

DISHWASHER WANTED
Inquire Within

Surprised, she stopped in front of it and stared. Behind the sign, a table of four was eating. They watched her curiously. Abby ignored them.

The only dishwasher they had was Dan. Dan loved them, and they loved Dan. So maybe Dulcie had decided to get him an assistant. When she got inside, Dulcie was standing by the cash register, going over some figures. Dulcie was a tall, thick-limbed blonde of Scandinavian descent, who favored shapeless, ankle-length floral print dresses with dropped waistlines. She always came to work with her thin, white-blonde hair loose. During the course of the day, she usually pulled it back with found objects, like pieces of string or wire. Abby had seen it held up with garbage ties, a latex glove, and, once, even knotted and stuck with a carrot.

Dulcie looked up at Abby. Her expression was darkly serious, as if there'd been a death in the family. Her hair was loose. Either it was too early to tie it back, or she was too upset to look for something to use.

"What's with the sign?" Abby asked, concerned. Though Dulcie was the boss, Abby had alternated between acting as muscle and confidante for the older woman, helping her when she could, protecting her from people she didn't like dealing with, and shielding her from situations she wanted to avoid.

Dulcie shook her head. "Dan's leaving."

"Dan? Our Dan? What d'you mean, he's leaving?" Abby fired back, stunned.

"Something to do with disability," Dulcie answered, her face pale and owlish.

Dulcie was often overworked and tired, which was no surprise, given that she was a single mother of three and owner of the InnBetween. But today she seemed overwhelmed.

Abby didn't want to believe what she was hearing. "He can't leave us. What'll we do? When did he tell you?"

"When I got in." Dulcie went back to her notepad but seemed unable to focus on what she was doing. She looked at Abby. "You talk to him. He listens to you."

Abby pushed through the swing door into the prep kitchen. Dan was at his machine, long apron covering his chest and legs. His sleeves were rolled up, and she could see the bottom of one of his tattoos peeking out from under the cuff. The ankles and feet of a pinup girl. Dan had been in the Merchant Marine, and he had old school tattoos to show for it. When he saw Abby he smiled. He couldn't leave, she thought, he was one of them.

"Good woman comin' through," he said, his usual greeting.

"Dan, what's going on? Is it true? Dulcie says you're leaving," she said, no time for rituals.

"Don't want to, but I can't stay on. I'm gonna lose my disability if I do." He pointed the sprayer he was holding at a plate of encrusted food. Abby watched a lump of mashed potatoes slide into the stainless steel bed of the washer, knocking a chunk of meatloaf ahead of it.

"I got this lung condition, and I got the disability, but I can't work or they'll cut it off."

"That's no problem, Dulcie can pay you off the books," Abby said hopefully.

Henry, who doubled as both waiter and bartender, came in carrying a pile of dirty plates. "Back!" Abby moved aside and he slid them with a crash onto the counter to Dan's right.

Dan took a plate off the top of the stack and began spraying it. "Already is. But if anyone finds out, I'm up a creek." He placed the dish in the washing rack and reached for another.

"Dan, what're we going to do without you?" Abby said. She wanted to whine and stamp her foot.

"You'll find someone. You found me, didn't you?"

"No one will report you, you can—"

"Hey, I can't lose that check," he said softly, looking at her, making her pay attention. "Anyways, Abby, I'm tired. I could use some nights at home."

She closed her mouth, and nodded wordlessly. It was a nasty job. Plates piled up high, thick with food, and he had to scrape away at them, wash them, do the pots, hour after hour up to his elbows in a greasy, steaming stew. And when the restaurant closed, it was Dan who stayed alone to sweep and mop the work areas, leaving everything ready for the next day. It wasn't easy to find someone who could stand it night after night, who would show up and keep showing up for longer than three weeks.

Abby knew what lay ahead. They had been through half a dozen people in the months before he came to their door. Students, each lasting about a week; a poet, who worked one shift and then over the phone told Dulcie she could go fuck herself; a laid-off book editor, who came to work on time but was understandably depressed and worked under a bitter and suicidal cloud. There were many nights when Dulcie and Abby had to take turns at the large commercial machine, moving from there into the kitchen to scrub the bottomless stack of sauté pans the cooks threw into the deep, stainless steel sinks.

Finally she nodded. "We're really going to miss you, Dan. And not just because of the dishes."

In the dining room, Dulcie whispered to her: "No luck, right?"

"He's sick and he doesn't want to stay here every night till two A.M., shoveling crud, scrubbing pans, mopping, and hauling heavy rubber mats." Abby shrugged. "The man's crazy."

"I've put ads in the local papers," Dulcie said, sadly.

Abby nodded. Soon the parade would begin. She patted Dulcie's arm. "We'll find someone decent. We always do."

Dulcie smiled sweetly at her, her deep dimples appearing like last-minute gifts. "I hope so."

An hour later, Abby was sitting at the bar arguing with Henry about wine. Henry was Dulcie's in-house bad boy. He was twenty-four, beautiful in a Latino/Aztec way, dark hair and eyes, high cheekbones, and a slightly curved nose. He loved the restaurant business and said he wanted to be a wine steward when he grew up, but at the moment he was too busy sowing his seed wherever the wind would take it. At the restaurant, each tablecloth was covered with a sheet of butcher paper, with a little glass of crayons placed in the center of the table. As far as she could tell, Henry considered this nothing more than a means of facilitating the exchange of phone numbers with attractive female customers. That was when he waited tables. When he was bartending, he kept a Sharpie on hand and used the cocktail napkins.

Dulcie, their all-natural earth mother owner, cold-bloodedly encouraged this because she believed in the Double Bait Theory: if the bartender was a good-looking man, he would attract women to the bar, who in their turn would attract men. Bait for the bait. It might have worked fine in a real bar, but at the InnBetween the bar was down in the basement, and was only about ten feet long. It was a glorified service bar, the misconceived brain-child of the previous owner, who thought bars should be small and hidden and cozy. Not Abby's idea of a good bar. She liked a bar you could see from the street, where you could peer in the window and find out ahead of time if it was deserted or elbow-to-elbow in desperately lonely drunks. Or, worse, if the person you hated most in the world was sitting next to the only empty barstool.

That evening, there was no one else sitting at the bar with Abby. The restaurant was busy, most tables taken, but no one was waiting for a table, which was one of the chief reasons people sat at the bar. She and Henry were arguing about French versus California wines. She didn't know much about either, except that she liked some of each, and Henry had pretensions but very few hard facts. Their ignorance, however, wasn't getting in their way.

"Wait, I'm out of Tanqueray," Henry interrupted. "I'll be back." Henry had been organizing his stock while they bickered, and now he went out through the door behind the bar. "But you know I'm right," he called out to her as he climbed the back stairs.

Abby closed her eyes and enjoyed the hum of voices, letting it wash over her like an ocean breeze.

"Abby, my savior!"

Startled, she opened her eyes.

Smiling at her, her arms open wide like a ring master at the Greatest Show on Earth, or an old friend expecting a hug, was Germaine LeClair. She was wearing a dark green skirt made of crushed velvet, and above it an embroidered white peasant blouse. Her reddish hair glinted under the low lights of the bar.

"Hello, Germaine," Abby said diffidently.

Germaine adjusted her skirt. She was wearing strappy black sandals with dangerously high heels. She hung her purse, a red leather square, on the back of her chair and raised herself onto the stool.

She was vivid, even more so than when Abby had last seen her. She laid her hand on Abby's.

"You're an insider, Abby," she said. "What do I have to do to get a drink around here?"

Abby stood up and moved behind the bar. "What can I get you?"

"You're an angel. I'm so, *so* exhausted, I've been thinking about a Stoli and tonic all day. Suzie and I have been cleaning out her daughter's room. God, what a mess."

"Her kid's in college, right?" Abby took a glass from the shelf behind her, and filled it with ice.

"Gone to Spain," she said. "Junior year abroad. Suzie is *devastated*."

"Must be hard." Abby poured out the vodka, then used the gun to fill the glass with tonic. Germaine was watching the glass the way a cat watches a small, wounded animal. If she had a tail it would have twitched. Slice of lemon, a cocktail napkin on the bar, and the clinking, icy glass on top of it.

"Oh, God bless you," Germaine sighed, and took a long drink.

"How long have you had your farmhouse in Italy?" Abby asked, leaning on the bar. Henry appeared in the doorway behind her in time to hear her question.

"You have a farmhouse in Italy? Rockin'. Can I come stay?" he interrupted, subtle as usual.

Germaine smiled at him. "Sure, but you've got to earn your keep."

Henry's grin spread wide. "I can do that," he answered, his voice sounding constricted.

Germaine kept eye contact with him long enough to make Abby squirm, then laughed.

"What are you doing behind my bar?" Henry turned to Abby, testosterone obviously surging.

"Just picking up the slack, boyo. Henry hangs out in the kitchen," she said to Germaine, "eating scraps." She returned to her barstool.

"Henry," Germaine asked in a low voice, "am I allowed to eat at the bar?"

Without taking his eyes off her, Henry whipped out a menu from under the counter and laid it in front of her. "Of course," he answered. "You can eat anything you want."

Germaine raised her eyebrows suggestively at him then looked down at the menu. Abby watched her concentrate, her eyes squinting. Probably needed glasses, she thought, but was too vain to wear them.

"Fried calamari. I love fried calamari."

Henry tore himself away from her and turned to Abby. "You want something to eat, too?"

"Yeah, if it's not too much trouble," she said, letting the sarcasm fall heavily. He didn't notice, but she was too hungry to make anything of it. "I'll have the mushroom ravioli." She couldn't sit next to fried calamari and eat a dinner salad.

"Mmm, that sounds so good. Maybe I should switch." Germaine looked as if she could taste the differences between the two dishes.

"The ravioli's good," Abby volunteered. "But I don't know what it tastes like in Italy," she added, remembering the rotini. She didn't want to encourage this woman, and then be blamed if the dish didn't taste like the real thing.

"Oh, okay. I'll stick with the calamari."

Henry left, and they heard him running up the back stairs.

CHAPTER SIX

Abby didn't waste time. She lowered her voice. "I looked for the gun today, but it wasn't there," she said, watching Germaine carefully.

Germaine glanced guiltily around the room. "God, don't talk about that here."

"I couldn't find it anywhere in the bushes around the house." Abby said, keeping her voice down. "You have to remember where you dropped it."

"No, no, I can't. God. You're creeping me out."

"*I'm* creeping *you* out? You're the one who had it. Where'd you get it? Is it yours?"

Germaine looked at her horror, as if Abby were suggesting she eat cockroaches. "No, it's not mine. I don't have guns."

Abby felt a grudging respect for her. The woman had a hell of a nerve.

"It belongs to Mitch."

"Have you told him you took it?"

"No, not yet. I will. When the moment's right."

Abby rubbed a hand over her eyes. "God, what a mess. I should go to the chief."

"Are you kidding?" Germaine said anxiously. "You're making a big deal out of nothing. The gun was empty, no bullets. It's still sitting in a flower bed there, and no one's going to find it till next spring. Take it easy, Abby. God. If you get the police involved, it'll turn into a huge ordeal. Mitch'll get into trouble, too."

Abby didn't say anything. She let the silence gather between them, then said, "You didn't ask why I was over at your father's house."

"I thought you were looking for the, ah, you know," Germaine said, lightly.

"Not really. I was working there."

Germaine looked startled. "Working? Doing what?"

"As it turns out, I've been hired as his secretary."

"His secretary?" Germaine repeated, staring at Abby.

"Actually, his amanuensis."

Germaine laughed humorlessly. "Of course. His amanuensis. That's funny."

"Really?" Abby said, thinking of *jocular.*

Germaine asked: "When did that happen? When did he hire you?"

"The same morning I met you, just about eight hours later. Funny little world, huh? And I started work today."

Germaine looked at her with fascination. "What specifically do you do for him?"

"Read his letters, help him answer them."

"But I thought you worked here."

"We're going into the slow season. But I don't want to talk about me. I want to hear about you and him."

"Why should I tell you anything?"

Abby considered the question. "Because I saved you, remember? And I saw you wave a gun at him."

"I told you, it wasn't loaded."

"Start with your two sisters."

Germaine was defiant. "Only one real one."

"Oh, right, you were adopted."

"When I was ten and Athena eight."

"So how old was Maddie?"

"Maddie? I think she was six. Yes, six. She was the baby of the house."

"So, how was it?"

"Why do you want to know?"

"Come on. Having to become part of a brand new family, suddenly having a third sister. That can't have been easy."

Germaine sighed. She realized Abby was determined to make her talk. "First we were fostered. The adoption became final when I was twelve."

"How were they, as parents?"

"Wanda was a kind woman. Norman was always busy in the studio, we never saw him. No time for any of us."

"Was that difficult?"

"We didn't think much of it; I don't think we really cared. Wanda was the one that mattered to us. We loved her. So, yes, it was fine."

"What were you doing at his house the other night?"

Germaine smirked. "He's senile, he doesn't know anyone anymore. It wasn't my fault that he wigged out."

Abby ignored the blatant untruth. "What happened with your own family that you had to go into foster care?"

"Jeez, you're making me pay for the other night, aren't you?"

Abby nodded. "Yup."

Germaine shrugged, defeated. "I'll tell you everything, and then we'll be even. My mother was an alcoholic. No father. The last time I ever saw her was the day we went to Norman and Wanda's."

Abby felt a small flush of remorse for prying into what must be a painful past. But not enough to stop. "Go on."

Germaine shook her head. "She had problems—mental problems. She died soon after in a crash."

"A car crash? Had she been drinking?"

Germaine didn't answer and stared into the mirrored back bar. Then, with a visible effort, she came back to the present. She looked at Abby with an unreadable expression.

Abby kept going. "So, why did you say that Norman killed your mother? And when you say 'mother,' do you mean your biological mother, or Wanda?"

"Wanda. Always Wanda. My bio mother was a crazy bitch."

They could hear heavy footsteps on the back stairs, and Henry appeared carrying two plates, one piled high with crisp, golden calamari, and the other laid out with steaming ravioli, the creamy sauce drizzled across them.

"Yay!" squealed Germaine, her troubled past forgotten. She clapped her hands, and looked as if she might bounce up and down in her chair. That would've made Henry really happy. As he put the plates in front of them, he kept a close eye on the top of her drawstring blouse. Abby focused on her ravioli. She wasn't going to bounce up and down, but the smell of the food made her swallow in anticipation.

By nine, Abby was still on her first drink, and Germaine on her third vodka. She and Henry had moved past light flirtation and were filling the air with heavy-handed innuendoes. Abby excused herself and took both empty plates up the back stairs. Dan was at the dishwasher, and she put them down next to him.

"How's it going, Dan-the-Man?"

"Good woman, coming through," he replied, his eyes on his job. Abby went into the kitchen and stopped at the high, stainless steel counter and warming table that divided the line from the rest of the room. George, the head cook, and his sidekick, Sandy, had their backs to her.

"Evening, O great ones."

"Yo, Abby," said George, glancing over his shoulder at her as he flipped some sliced peppers in a small frying pan. They hissed as they landed, and he gave them a shake and grabbed two plates off the high stack in front of him. He used tongs to retrieve two crisp, golden chicken halves from the grill and tenderly placed them on the plates.

"Good evening, Abby," said Sandy, his voice high. He was neatly arranging a thick slice of meatloaf on a plate, next to a mound of fluffy-looking mashed potatoes. Abby remembered the mashed leftovers from earlier in the evening, sliding down into the sink.

"You weren't workin' tonight, were you, babe?" asked George, his eyes on his work.

"Nah. Came in because I was hungry."

"So, who's the hot number Henry's got lined up at the bar?" George always knew what was going on.

"A writer. New in town. And old enough to be his mother."

George laughed coarsely. "Shit, man, he don't care."

Sandy just shook his head. His back seemed tense with disapproval. Just then, Henry bounced in and slammed an order down on the high shelf. "Order in!" he yelled.

"Easy does it, big boy," George said, shaking his head.

"She wants me," Henry said, grinning at Abby. "And I'm gonna make her proud tonight."

Abby snorted. "The two of you have already been having eye sex down there. No need to actually do it."

"What you got there, my man?" George asked without turning around.

"A hard-on," answered Henry.

"Oh, please," Sandy burst out. "What's the order?"

"Oh, yeah. Cheeseburger medium, with Fromunda cheese."

Sandy turned, looking upset. "What's Fromunda cheese? We don't have any—"

Henry's eyes lit up. He gripped his crotch. "It's from undah here," then he moved his hand to his armpit, "and undah here—" With a burst of laughter, he left the room. Abby found herself smiling against her will, and even George was shaking his head, chuckling. Sandy looked disgusted. "Idiot," he hissed.

Within an hour, the dining room had emptied of customers. Abby went in to start putting up chairs and found Dulcie sitting at a table talking to someone. The man's back was to Abby so she couldn't see his face, but it was a big back. Dulcie had an application form in front of her, and she looked unhappy. She noticed Abby and gave her a pleading look. Abby walked over, but when she realized who Dulcie's companion was, she stopped. It was Bailey, their local drunk. Reluctantly, she approached the table.

"Hey, Dulcie. Bailey, hello. What brings you here?"

The man was about six-four; she knew because she had stood near him enough times when she had to evict him from the restaurant. His reputation was not good—a child beater, a wife beater, and a beater of anyone who crossed him. He had a mean glint in his eye when he was drunk and a hard look when he was sober.

"Bailey was applying for the dishwashing position," Dulcie said nervously. She hated dealing with him, and Abby usually took care of it.

"Great," she said, in a takeover tone. "We'll keep your application, and let you know. We've still got a lot of people to see."

Bailey looked at her with his predator's eyes. "Yeah, sure. But I want the job, I can start anytime. I'll start tonight."

"That's good to know, but we have a dishwasher tonight. And so many people to interview. The phone's been ringing off the hook. A lot of factors to take into account."

Bailey shot her a slow, venomous look. He was about to speak, when Germaine walked up the staircase from the bar. The luminous green of her skirt was like a beacon in the low light of the dining room. It caught Bailey's eye. "Now that's a woman," he said, as if Abby and Dulcie had been applying for the job and had received extremely low ratings.

"Abby, I've been looking for you," Germaine said, unaware of the tension she was walking into. "I think I might rent an apartment in Bantam, what d'you think?" She stopped and looked at the three of them. The only sign that she had had a drink too many was her head swaying gently on her neck. It made her red hair move from side to side and added a vulnerable girlishness to her.

Abby walked over to her and put an arm through hers. "Germaine, I need to talk to you."

"You know, Abby, I feel a little woozy. Too much vodka."

To Bailey, this must've seemed like proof that he was looking at his soul mate. His chair scraped noisily on the wooden floor when he stood up. He looked fixedly at Germaine. "Let me buy you another one."

Germaine, too drunk to read the man in front of her, smiled sexily at him. "Sure, I'd like that."

Bailey's lips pulled back in a rare and unlovable smile, his discolored teeth a testament to the fact that they never saw daylight. He moved toward her, interview forgotten, his body lumbering and huge. Germaine looked dismayed but seemed helpless. Abby wondered what she could do to put an end to the little love dance.

"Bailey, forget it. I'm taking her home," she said quickly, trying to deflect him.

"I always knew you were a dyke," he snarled at her. "Fuck you, the lady wants a drink. Come on, gorgeous, let's go—"

"You've got to be kidding," Abby said, pulling on Germaine's arm. "Bailey, I warn you, I'm calling the cops—"

But Bailey knew what he wanted, and he took Germaine's other arm in his left hand and put his right arm around her waist. He pulled.

Dulcie, who had been frozen in her seat, finally leaped up. She ran to the kitchen door, swung it open, and called out:

"George, come quick! Henry! Bailey's grabbing a customer!"

Henry ran out, chewing, and George followed him. Sandy appeared in the doorway. Henry, a gleeful look on his face, grabbed a chair by the back and pointed the legs at Bailey. He began to use it as a weapon to poke him, even as Bailey was still trying to yank Germaine out of Abby's grip.

George, who had played football in college and had the bullish neck to go with it, grabbed Henry's chair and pushed it away. "Stop that!" he shouted. "Everyone, relax!" When no one seemed to pay attention, he bellowed: "Bailey, what the hell, man, let her go!"

The movement in the room slowed and then came to a halt. Bailey and Abby stopped pulling and slowly released Germaine, who looked dazed. George lowered his voice. "This is ridiculous, guys. Bailey, my man, what the fuck're you doing? You can't force the lady to go with you."

Everyone in town liked and knew George, and he had obviously, somewhere down the line, even found time for Bailey. The huge man looked at him. "I'm not forcin' her, she wants a drink, and the little bitch over there won't let her."

"Bailey," George said. "Go home. Now. Before I change my mind and call the cops on you."

Bailey shook his head as if to clear the debris rattling around in it. He moved slowly toward the door. Just before opening it he turned around, his inflamed eyes searching the group until they found the terrified Dulcie, and said: "About that job, I'm serious, lady, I can start anytime."

"I'll let you know," Dulcie answered in a whisper.

He pulled the door open and walked out. Everyone watched him as he stumbled down the front steps to the sidewalk.

"George, you should've let me beat the shit out of him," Henry said.

George rolled his eyes. "He would've made chili out of you. He's strong as a bull, worked construction for twenty years."

Germaine looked at him, her eyes wide. "Really?"

Abby started turning chairs over and putting them on the tables. "I'm going to drive you home, Germaine."

"Yeah, they say he fell off a beam—" Henry joined Abby putting the chairs away.

Abby let out an exasperated sound. "I am so sick of that guy, every time anyone mentions his name, they always say, yeah, and he fell off a high beam, and has an iron pin in his leg a foot long, blah blah blah. Who gives a shit. He's just a mean drunk. Oh, and Dulcie, if you give him a job, I'm quitting."

CHAPTER SEVEN

Once again, Abby found herself driving Germaine to Spencerville. This time, the woman was leaning back on the headrest, breathing heavily, asleep. When Abby pulled into the circular driveway, she had to shake her passenger to wake her up.

"Oh, are we there? That was fast." She didn't move, and her eyes stayed shut.

"Germaine," Abby said, "you've got to be a little more discriminating, okay?"

Germaine sighed, and looked sleepily at Abby. "I know."

Abby snorted. "I hope so."

"Tell me about George. He's your cook?"

"Forget George," Abby snapped. "He's married. Happily. With kids."

"Okay, okay."

"You better go now, I've got to get home to my dogs." Abby jerked her head to the right, indicating that Germaine should get out.

"Of course," Germaine said as she opened the door, slowly maneuvered her high heels down to the ground, "you have people to get home to."

She had teetered half way up the path, when she suddenly stopped. "I forgot, I have something for you!" she said, turning back to the car. She opened her red purse and pulled out a book. "Here. My book." She handed it in through the open window.

"Oh, thanks," Abby said.

Germaine waved the words away. "Bridget," she said in a stage whisper. "That was her name—Bridget. Isn't that a sweet name?"

Abby was confused. "Who's Bridget?"

"My real mother."

"Oh. I thought you said she was a crazy bitch."

"So?"

Abby shook her head. "Yes, it's a lovely name. Good night, Germaine."

Germaine nodded obediently. "Thanks, Abby. What would I do without you?"

"You'd be fine. Go, go." Abby made a shooing gesture.

"Wait, I want to ask you something," Germaine said.

Abby sighed, wondering when she would ever get home. "Okay."

Germaine now spoke soberly through the open window. "You're working for Norman now, you're with him a lot. You might come across something, anything. You know. Or maybe, just ask him outright. Ask him how she died. Casually. And if you can't do that, just look around, see if you find out anything."

Abby couldn't help laughing. "Germaine, he's my boss. He's a sick old man. I can't spy on him. Or say, 'oh, by the way, how did you actually kill your wife?'"

Germaine backtracked. "I don't mean that, or for you to spy on him. Just find out what happened. What was going on when she died."

"Why do you think he did something to her? Paul said she died of cancer. He must've learned that from Maddie."

Germaine opened the car door and, to Abby's dismay, sat back down on the passenger seat. "It would be so easy to make people think that."

"Okay," Abby said, crossing her arms. "So tell me why you think something happened to her. You weren't home, right?"

Germaine shook her head sadly. "No, I was away at college."

"Go on."

"She was really unhappy. He was mean to her."

"Was he abusive?"

Germaine shook her head. "I don't know. I spoke to her the week before she died. If she'd had cancer, she would have told me, I know it."

"What did she say?"

"She said Norman was breaking her heart."

"Those were her words?"

"Pretty much."

"Did you believe her?"

Germaine groaned and threw her head back against the seat. "Sort of. I guess I thought she was being dramatic."

Huh, thought Abby. So that's where Germaine got it from.

"What happened next?"

"Nothing. I got off the phone. Later that night, I called Athena. She said it was nothing, Wanda was going through a rough patch. Menopause, or something. But she promised to keep a close watch." Germaine rubbed at something on the palm of her hand. To Abby it seemed a slightly studied gesture, like many of Germaine's moves. "But what could she do? She was a junior in high school, she was busy. How could she know what was going on?"

Abby felt sorry for her. Regardless of her melodramatic style, she obviously felt a lot of guilt about her adoptive mother. "So then what?"

Germaine stopped fidgeting and looked at Abby, straight on. "So nothing. Things came up, I called a few weeks later and she was dead. Even the funeral was over and done with."

"That seems pretty harsh. What reason did they give for not calling you?"

Germaine blew air out of her nose. "Athena said Norman didn't want me to come. She said she tried calling my dorm room, but I was always out. Finally she gave up." She gave a huge yawn, covering her mouth with her hand. Talking had seemed to relax her.

"None of this makes sense. Why did you wait so long, if you really think something bad happened to her?"

Germaine paused before speaking. "I didn't. I just recently got some new information. I'm trying to figure it out."

"What information?" Abby asked.

Germaine glanced back at the house. The night was overcast, so there was no moon or stars to brighten the heavy blackness around them. The windows of the house were dark, but Germaine turned her back to them as if she were afraid someone was watching. Her behavior was overly theatrical, but the mood was catching and Abby shivered. She couldn't help glancing around.

Germaine lowered her voice. "I got a letter." She pulled her wallet out of her red bag, opened it and out of a side pocket, she slid a folded piece of paper. "Unsigned, so I don't know who sent it. Take a look." She handed it to Abby. "It's a little beat up, but you can still read it."

Abby unfolded the paper. It was written on a plain piece of typing paper that looked as if it had originally been folded in thirds. The creases were old and fraying.

"How long have you had this?" Abby asked.

"I got it around Christmastime last year in Italy. It was forwarded to me, but it had originally been mailed from Belgium. It must have been lying around in some Italian warehouse somewhere, because the Belgian post-mark looked like August."

Abby turned on the overhead light so she could read it. "So it was sent about a year ago."

The note was short and hand-written. It was in capital letters.

WHAT REALLY HAPPENED TO WANDA?
WHEN NORMAN DIES YOUR CHANCE OF FINDING OUT DIES WITH HIM.

Germaine watched Abby read it.

Abby looked at her. "Do you think it's for real? It sounds sort of reme-dial, you know, 'woo!' scary. What would be the point of writing this?"

Germaine shrugged. "Could it be that someone's afraid to tell the truth, so they want me to do it for them?" she said. "I mean, that's one solution."

"Maybe. It could also be that there's someone out there who has no idea what he's talking about but is trying to stir up trouble. Or maybe it's a sick joke."

"No, I believe it," Germaine said. "I think it's someone who knows I'll shake things up."

"Hmm. I still don't understand why Norman was so angry at you when Wanda died."

Germaine shrugged. "Because I wouldn't stay at home and take classes at a community college. I couldn't wait to get away, but he wanted me to live at home and look after him."

Abby was puzzled. "He let Maddie go to boarding school. Why not you? You were older. I thought parents always wanted their kids to go to college."

Germaine gave a bitter little smile. "Yes, but I was adopted. To him, Athena and I were just one notch up from servants. Maddie got to go, but we were supposed to stay and mind him and Wanda. Polish his lousy sculptures." She fell silent.

Abby couldn't help yawning. She was beat. She looked at Germaine, and saw that her eyes were starting to close.

"Oh, no. Germaine, wake up," she said, giving her a shake. "Time to go to bed."

Germaine sat up with a start and blinked blindly at Abby. She nodded, got out of the car and walked unsteadily up the path. Without looking back, she fumbled with the door, opened it, and went inside.

Abby was about to turn the key in the ignition, when she remembered the book. She turned on the overhead light, picked it up, and looked at the cover. The words *Tuscany, My Heart* ran across the top in flowery lettering; *by Germaine LeClair*, also in flowery script. It looked more like a novel than a factual account. In spite of herself, Abby was touched. The cover showed a villa, pink stone, vines climbing up the walls. Romantic. A romantic novel made sense in a way, coming from the needy creature Abby had just watched wobble up her pathway. Abby opened the book, and on the title page Germaine had penned:

To Abby, who saved my life!
Affectionately, Germaine

With a sigh, Abby dropped the book on the seat next to her and turned off the overhead. Time to go home. Her people needed to be let out so they could pee on the bushes.

CHAPTER EIGHT

Two days later a stranger was washing dishes. His back was to Abby when she walked into the prep kitchen at the start of her shift. Without saying a word, Abby turned around and went looking for Dulcie.

"You're just trying him out, right?" she asked her boss, who was standing on a chair in the dining room, writing specials on the large, ornate mirror that hung on one of the walls.

Dulcie looked down at her. "Oh. Hi, Abby. Do you mean Fritz?"

"Fritz?" Abby made it sound like a floor cleaning product.

"Shh, Abby," Dulcie whispered, leaning a hand on Abby's shoulder and climbing carefully down off her perch. "He'll hear you." She looked at Abby innocently. "He's very well qualified. He's worked at a number of places in Placid, he loves restaurant work, he knows the machine, he's okay with the hours—so, let's hope." She gestured to the words on the mirror. "What do you think? Legible?"

"I just think we should try out a lot of people first—"

Dulcie interrupted her. "Abby, you've got to trust me on this. I have a really good feeling about him. You'll see."

Reluctantly, Abby nodded. Dulcie's instincts were no better than anyone else's, but she was the boss and they needed a dishwasher. She went back into the kitchen.

"Hi, Fritz, I'm Abby," she said, loud enough to be heard over the thunder of the machine.

Fritz turned around at the sound of her voice. After a second's delay, he pulled off one of his rubber gloves and offered her his hand.

He was in his thirties and short, maybe five-foot-six. Her first impression was that he looked like a pirate. His head was covered in a bright bandana, red chilies against a yellow background, and he was swarthy-looking—with dark eyes and lashes, a hawklike nose, cheekbones covered with a five o'clock shadow. Gold hoop earrings. The impression was slightly weakened by a chin that receded gently into his neck, creating a pouch of fat under it. He was broad in the chest and shoulders and short-legged, like someone who had taken up weight-lifting to compensate for his lack in stature. He wore the usual checked restaurant pants and white apron over a t-shirt.

She shook the proffered hand. His grip was warm and moist, his smile friendly. "Hey, Abby. I've heard about you."

"Welcome." Abby added. "Anything I can help you with, just let me know."

"Appreciate it." He winked at her, put his glove back on and turned back to the machine.

That evening, Abby worked upstairs. The Bantam Business Alliance had rented the downstairs, with a cash bar and free wine and hors d'oeuvres. Sort of a networking happy hour for working Main Street, rowdy and convivial, where everyone knew everyone, and no one got stuck with the bill. The laughter and conversation traveled up the staircase, and for once the main dining room was the duller of the two floors. Occasionally, one of the upstairs diners would descend to use the bathroom, and stay longer than they needed to, talking to friends. They would eventually climb the stairs, still chatting with someone below them and calling down one last word or sentence, before breaking the connection and leaving the fun behind.

Upstairs, the crowd was thin but steady. It was a Wednesday, so Cat and Abby were working three stations. They had divided them up as fairly as possible, and were having no trouble staying on top of things.

When Franklin Van Renesse, a local lawyer, came in, he asked Abby to save him a table in her station. Then he went downstairs long enough to get a glass of wine and shake a few hands.

"I'd rather sit down and eat a meal than try to stand and talk, eating bite-size pieces of overhandled food," he answered, when she asked him why he wasn't joining the noisy crowd at the bar.

"Such a snob."

He shrugged. "What can I say? I'm just an old stick-in-the-mud. I know what I like."

She looked at him and shook her head. Far from old, he was in his early forties, and given the usual white-bread look of the clientele, his skin color made him exotic, adding to his natural appeal. She had become friends with Franklin over the last six months, though she had known him longer. She had always found him kind and generous, and she valued their friendship, though she sometimes wondered why it had never seemed to occur to either of them to move it in another direction. Maybe they were both afraid they would screw it up and be left with nothing.

She brought him his salad and looked around. The six tables she was responsible for were all eating and talking. She pulled out the chair opposite him, and sat down.

"How's work these days?"

Most of Franklin's work was criminal defense, though like any small-town lawyer, he had to be flexible, filling the slow time with closings and estate work.

"Busy. Want some?" He offered her his fork, handle first, and his plate of lettuce and arugula.

"No thanks." She picked up a slice of crusty bread from the basket, tore off a bite-size piece and put it in her mouth. "Guess what? I have a day job." She chewed the bread.

He looked at her, interested.

"I work for an old man with Alzheimer's. A sculptor named Norman Smith."

Franklin nodded. "Sure. He was pretty big in his day, you know."

"I wondered about that. I should Google him."

Before Franklin could say anything, Abby noticed movement at the front door. Someone was coming in. "I better go," she said, standing up. She pushed the chair in and wiped her crumbs from the butcher paper.

The new arrival stood inside the front door, waiting to be seated. It was Germaine, red hair reflecting the light, wearing a pair of floating black pants and a copper-colored top.

"Hi, Germaine. Everything okay?" Abby asked.

"Fine, sweetie. Just fine." She looked around the room.

"You alone?" Abby asked her.

Germaine held up her index finger. "I don't know."

Gracefully, she sidestepped Abby and walked over to Franklin's table. She put a hand on his shoulder. "Franklin Van Renesse, isn't it?"

He looked up, and when he saw her he stood up quickly, his chair legs catching on the floor. "Yes, yes," he stammered, all his cool gone.

"We met the other day, on Main Street. I'm Suzie Helder's friend, Germaine LeClair." She dimpled at him, widening her eyes.

"Of course I remember."

And then, just like that, Germaine said: "Are you here alone? May I join you?"

And Franklin answered: "That would be wonderful." He pulled out Abby's chair for her. And, abracadabra, they were on a date.

Abby was in shock. There she was, talking with *her* friend Franklin, and this bimbo, this *mega* bimbo, came along and inhaled him. And he seemed to be loving it. Men had no shame.

She took two dishes from under the warmer for delivery to another table, and after she had dropped them off and picked up a credit card at a third table, she saw Germaine say something, and she watched as they both laughed. Then their heads moved closer, and he said something. And again they both laughed. Abby couldn't remember seeing Franklin so animated. He certainly didn't get like that around her, Abby thought.

"Watch your back!" Cat was right behind her, trying to pass between two tables."Sorry," Abby said, stopping in front of the cash register with the credit card. Cat delivered her plates to a nearby table then came and stood next to her.

She leaned close so she could whisper. "Franklin's gettin' lucky tonight, is my guess."

"Please." Abby rolled her eyes.

"Oh, stop it, she's incredibly sexy. Have you seen Henry when she comes in? And he's half her age."

"Come on. He'd do anyone," Abby said meanly. She dragged the credit card too quickly through the machine. It didn't register. "Shit." She dragged it again.

"You're just jealous 'cause someone else wants him." Cat tidied up the pile of paid checks.

"Bullshit." The printer started clacking as the receipt came through.

"You are. You're being possessive. Stop it."

Abby ripped the receipt out of the printer and stapled it to the check. Grabbing the credit card she turned to her.

"Why would I be possessive?"

Cat raised her eyebrows. "I don't know, my dear. Just don't poison her soup, okay?"

"Yeah, well, she's not getting soup. She's ordered the ravioli. That should turn him off, watching her oink out."

"Are you kidding? As she licks that cream off her lips? Nope, the mushroom rav is a clincher. Sorry, babe." Smirking, Cat headed back to the tables.

Sure enough, when Germaine slurped down her order, Abby didn't see Franklin turn away in disgust. In fact, she saw Germaine feeding him one off her fork. He took it in his mouth delicately, keeping eye contact with her all the while. Germaine mimicked his mouth movements the way a mother does when feeding her baby, and that just seemed to lock the two of them in a little tighter. Abby stood by the cash register and saw it all.

Cat, who was walking by with some dirty plates, followed her gaze.

"Oh, jeez, let them alone. They're having fun."

"They're disgusting."

"Listen to yourself. What *is* your problem? As far as I can see, Franklin lives like a goddamn monk. Give him a break."

Abby took a deep breath. Cat was right. She hated to admit it, but she was being irrational, territorial. He was her friend and Germaine was moving in. But it was the way she did it, all curvy and playful. Like an otter. Sliding around him, over him. And he was eating it up. Literally. Abby glanced at them. Against her will, she liked Germaine, but she saw no reason to trust her. A picture of her in her black fur, pistol in hand, flashed through her mind.

At the table, Germaine was saying something, and Franklin was nodding. Cat was right, they were having fun together. And Franklin could take care of himself.

Still, she looked around to see who was watching him make a fool of himself. At that moment, however, she was the only one who seemed to care what he was up to. With an effort, Abby forced herself to stop keeping track of every move they made. She left the check on their table, and barely saw them argue over it. She took Franklin's credit card when he was ready, and when the time came, she didn't see them leave. So she didn't know if they left all cuddly, or if they said good-bye at the front door. It was not her concern, she told herself firmly as she cleared their empty table, which was covered with crumbs, splashes of cream sauce, and wine. They hadn't even had time to draw on the butcher paper, she thought with a snort.

Later that night, Fritz took off his bandana and, to the staff's surprise, they discovered his head was shaved clean. When Abby walked past him, she noticed that he had a series of little tattoos on his scalp, raindrops that started on his crown and went down the back of his neck and disappeared into the collar of his shirt. Eventually, while leaving off a stack of plates, she noticed that the drops had tails.

"Cat, you see the tadpoles on Fritz's head?" she said a little later, when she and Cat were clearing a table together.

Cat looked at her with a world-weary expression. "Those little fellas are not tadpoles."

"Yes, they are—"

"They're sperm."

"You're kidding! Who would do that?" Abby demanded.

"Fritz, I guess."

"What a dick," Abby shook her head.

"Exactly. A spermhead," Cat answered.

"And that, dearly beloved," Abby concluded, "is how the dishwasher got his name."

Cat snickered. Abby smiled too, at last superior to someone. Anyone who would permanently ink sperm on their scalp had to be even dumber than she was. Yeah.

CHAPTER NINE

Working with Norman was a lousy way to find out anything about Wanda's life, much less her death. Norman never brought her up in conversation, there were no pictures of her, and Abby saw no letters written to Norman that mentioned her. It wasn't part of Abby's job to read his files, so she had no reason to go through his personal papers looking for information.

She did look him up online, however. She discovered that he had pieces in museums in Japan and Australia, on university campuses across the country and in private collections in England, Germany and France. She followed one link that led her to a biography. She read that Norman Smith was born in Toledo, Ohio, in 1913. He had studied engineering at the University of Ohio; after graduating and moving to New York, he began taking classes at the Art Students League.

Three years later, Norman took a job teaching painting at a private school in Connecticut. During the war years, and thanks to his degree in engineering, he was employed by the army doing research at a base in the Midwest.

He started making metal pieces in the late sixties. They gradually became larger, and more ambitious. His success grew. He was very prolific up until the early eighties, and then it was as if he had dropped off the face of the earth.

Abby typed the name Wanda Smith into the search engine but came up with nothing.

She decided to put it all on a back burner. It had waited for twenty years. It could wait a little longer.

It seemed to Abby that the unexpected advantage of a failing memory is that you can be thrilled and surprised by the same thing, over and over again. On her mornings with Norman, they would gradually go through the mail, and if there was nothing new, they would revisit letters Norman had read before. To each letter, he would carefully dictate, in an antiquated prose, his reply. Abby would then type them all out and bring them back to Norman for slow and laborious signatures.

A few days into her job, a letter came to him from a man in Berlin who was building a collection of shoes donated by artists. He planned to open a shoe museum and would be most grateful for a pair of Norman's work shoes for his collection.

"Does he need new shoes?" asked Norman, confused by the request.

"No, I don't think so, Norman," Abby answered, reading the letter through once more. "He wants *artists'* shoes, shoes you've worked in. Something really worn."

"I see," he nodded. "Well, we should be able to find something." He reached for his cane and stood up. Slowly, painstakingly, they went upstairs. He sat on his bed, giving her directions while she looked through his closet, but all they found was a second pair of everyday brown leather lace-ups, worn but not ready to be given away. Finally, he rose.

"I know where they are, I know exactly where they are." They made their way back downstairs. In the kitchen, Norman started opening drawers, looking for something. When he didn't find what he wanted, he slammed each drawer shut. Saranda came into the kitchen. She was holding a feather duster.

"What're you looking for, Norman? You scared me, all this crashing about in here." She didn't look the least bit scared, just annoyed.

"I want the key to the studio, my shoes are there." He kept opening drawers, but now he was no longer looking, just opening and slamming.

"The studio's not locked, you know that," Saranda chided him.

"I don't mean the small studio, I mean the other one. That one." And he jabbed a finger out the window, across the field.

"No, you can't go there."

He looked hard at her, and lowered his voice. "Oh, but I can."

Saranda stared back at him, considering how to handle him. She looked at Abby, maybe for support, but Abby kept her expression neutral. "Well, I suppose so, but mind that path, and look out for rusty nails," she added, shaking the feather duster at him for emphasis.

"I'm not going to work there, my dear woman. I just want my shoes. This young person can come with me, can't you?" he asked, addressing the last question to Abby. She guessed that, for the moment, he had forgotten who she was.

"Of course," Abby nodded at him, then turned to his housekeeper. "We'll be careful, Saranda." Abby felt as if the housekeeper was Norman's mother, big and powerful; without her approval they couldn't go out and play. "I'll drive over in my car, if you'd like," she added.

Saranda shrugged her shoulders, unconvinced, and turned away. Abby thought she was giving up on them, because she walked to the kitchen door and started to close it. But hanging on a hook behind the door was a lanyard, with a key ring on one end. She picked it off the hook and handed it to Norman.

"Aha," he crowed victoriously.

Saranda smiled reluctantly, a small smile. She shook her head a second time.

"Be back in half an hour for your soup, you hear me?" she barked, reclaiming her authority.

It took them a few minutes to get into the Bronco. It was a little high for Norman, and Abby had to hoist him in. Once he was in and buckled, she gave him his cane, ran around the car, and climbed in behind the wheel.

The backyard next to the work shed was largely edged in flower beds, now choked with weeds. Abby followed the narrow track that began where the flowers ended behind the shed, and cut across the flat field. The field was in a slow process of becoming woods, dotted with saplings and thorny bushes. The tire tracks themselves were still relatively clear, though the growth in the center of the dirt road was high. It scraped against the car noisily. Abby drove slowly so Norman wouldn't be bounced around too much. In a few minutes they were across the field, in a small parking area still sparsely covered in gravel.

After she'd helped him out of the car, she looked at the building in front of them. Norman stood next to her, as if he too had never seen it before. It was at least thirty feet high, and somewhat wider. It was built of unpainted cinderblock, the gray of the cement darkened and blotchy with age. Weeds grew high around the edges of the building, and on the right front corner a trumpet vine had grown, clinging victoriously to the rough walls and softening the harsh, block-like appearance of the structure. It still had a number of bright crimson blossoms on it. Dark green tendrils waved and hung down over a small light green metal door, the color dulled by dirt and a rash of rust. Directly in front of where Abby stood with Norman was a pair of oversized iron doors, built on runners like the sliding doors of a barn. Abby guessed that they were for moving huge objects or vehicles in and out. Abby could see, on the left side of the building, two large propane tanks against the wall. Tall casement windows in iron frames, set in the wall at a height of about fifteen feet, ran at regular intervals around as much of the building as she could see. Between these windows, the walls were made of factory-size glass blocks. Both windows and glass blocks were dirty, filmed over in a thick gauze of brown neglect.

The key Saranda had given her fitted into the green door, and when she turned it in the lock and worked the handle, the door moved an inch, then jammed. Something had shifted over the years. Abby had to push it hard to open it wide enough to pass through. The metal screeched as it scraped again the floor.

Inside, she was hit by the cold. Damp and deep, it was flavored with a smell of mildew mixed with rust and machine oil. The light that filtered through the dirty window panes cast an underwater glow over the space in front of them. Abby saw, in the pale, filtered light, a cavernous space open to the roof. When her eyes had adjusted to the gloom, she saw, parked to one side, a small tractor and various large pieces of what appeared to be antiquated machinery. Against the back wall, an iron staircase went up to a closed mezzanine. Long worktables were built into the right side and the back wall under the mezzanine, with shelving above them as far up as the casement windows. On the left wall was mounted what looked like a big industrial space heater. The center of the room was covered in large, spiky shapes, heaped on the poured concrete floor. Looking closer, she realized they were metal: cut, welded, and bent steel in what appeared to be abstract or geometric forms. They were in a pile, as if discarded carelessly or in a hurry. She guessed this was a cemetery of Norman's work, maybe the useless pieces, the ones that had failed. She saw more shapes on shelves and hanging from hooks on the wall. Twisted, and sharp-edged, covered with a film of dirt, they looked abandoned and fleshless, like skeletons in a looted crypt.

"Aha!" Norman sounded as if he finally understood the answer to something that had been puzzling him for a long time. She looked over at him. He was staring around the room, an expression of distaste turning down the corners of mouth.

"How long since you've been in here, Norman?"

"Is this my work?" he asked, pointing with his cane at the pile in the middle of the floor. She couldn't tell if he was referring to the metal pieces, or the disorder.

"I don't know. Has it been a long time since you've made big pieces like this?"

"I think so. They moved, did you know that?"

Again, she was unsure of his meaning. "You moved them here?"

"No, no," he snapped. "There's a special word for them. Air makes them move. Some of them like this, and some like that," he illustrated with vertical and horizontal arm movements. "Blades. I called them blades. The wizard of air."

"What's that? What's the wizard of air?"

"I don't know who, but someone called me that. I think."

"I like that. The wizard of air. You made magic." If she hadn't seen the beautiful piece over the dining room table, she would have had trouble believing that anything in this filthy pile of discarded metal had moved, unless it was hauled away by a junkman. "Did you leave this studio in a hurry?"

"I don't think so." He lifted his free hand to his mouth, covering it. "I don't know. Maybe. After they all left, I didn't work here anymore." He looked at her, his expression confused. "Why did we come here?"

"We wanted to find your work shoes."

"Nonsense," he said, confidence returning. "I don't need any other shoes, these are fine." He tapped the ones he was wearing with the tip of his cane.

"Well, maybe we should go home then," Abby said, sorry to leave so soon, but at the same time concerned that Norman might trip on something and hurt himself. And there was no point in explaining why they were looking for shoes.

"No, first I want to go upstairs," he said, gesturing with his cane to the iron staircase.

It was steep and unsafe looking, with narrow steps made of grillwork and no risers. "Norman, it looks dangerous."

"Don't be ridiculous, I've done it a thousand times. If I chose, I could run up it. You don't believe me, do you? I can tell you don't. Watch me, I can run up it."

"Oh, no, please, I believe you, really, I do. I just think that—"

Ignoring her, the old man walked to the foot of the stairs, held on to the railing with his right hand and put his cane on the bottom step. The tip went through one of the patterned holes.

"Oh, god, look at the time, Norman. It's lunchtime. Saranda must be worried about you."

"I don't care about Saranda," he said. It was as if he could smell her anxiety and took strength from it. "I'm going upstairs." He put his right foot on the step, then his left. He was up one. He looked at her, his expression victorious, his eyes fierce with determination. He took another step.

Abby knew there was nothing she could do, other than grab him by the ankles. She exhaled and turned away. "I give up. Go ahead. But I'm going to go back to the house for lunch. Hot soup. Come when you're ready, okay?" and she walked to the entrance. When she was at the door, she turned partway and sneaked a look at him. He took another step, the metal clanging. Three steps up, and his hand was gripping the painted iron railing, the knuckles white through his thin, bloodless skin. Abby was afraid she had really mishandled the situation. She didn't know what to do.

She glanced longingly outside. The sun was shining. She couldn't wait to leave the gloom of the studio.

Just then, the light from the door was blocked. Abby, startled, realized there was someone standing in the doorway, backlit by bright sunlight. She couldn't see who it was. "Who's that?" she asked, taking a step backwards.

"Abby?" said the shadowy person. "Ah. Didn't mean to startle you. It's Paul, Paul Becker. Where's Norman?"

Abby gestured to the staircase, embarrassed that her ninety-two-year-old charge was controlling her like a two-year-old.

Paul didn't say anything when he saw Norman.

To Abby's surprise, he walked casually over to the pile of discarded metal, squatted down next to it, and started moving pieces around. The noise was loud and jarring, and Norman looked over. "What's going on?"

"Oh, hello, Norman," said their visitor, looking up at the old man. "It's Paul, Maddie's husband. I just stopped by to see you, but now that I'm out here, I think I'll look for a three-foot circle."

"Why do you want one?" Norman asked suspiciously.

"Remember when we took the big sculptures down?"

Norman started to turn on the staircase. Abby watched nervously as he positioned his cane and slowly made it back down one step, then the second. Once on solid ground, he came toward Paul. "Did you take them down?"

Paul kept sorting through the metal pieces. Without looking up he said: "You and I did it together. We took them all down, one by one, from this field."

"Why?"

Paul looked up at him. "It was what you wanted. A clean start, I remember you saying."

Norman nodded slowly. "You used to work for me, isn't that right?"

Abby was interested.

"Yes, I did. Here, in the Metal Building," Paul said, standing up and dusting off his knees.

"How long ago was that?" Norman asked.

Abby was surprised that Paul Becker had worked for Norman. He'd seemed to have very little rapport with him on her initial visit to the house. She was curious. "Yes. When was it?"

He glanced again at Norman, and then at her. "Well, when I was a boy I worked here one summer, and then the year before I went to school, so, gosh, it must've been well over twenty years ago, wouldn't you say, Norman?"

Norman smiled and nodded. "Yes, yes. And in Paris."

"No, no, not Paris. Just here. Oh, Norman, I have a message for you. Saranda sent me out here to tell you that lunch is ready."

"Lovely, lovely. What are we waiting for? Let's go."

He led the way out of the building, and Abby followed Paul, gratefully pulling the green door closed behind her. Paul helped Norman into Abby's car.

After he closed the passenger door, Abby lowered her voice. "He worked in Paris?"

"No, he had an agent there, years ago, and used to go pretty regularly. But he never worked there."

Abby nodded, not surprised. "Tell me something, what was it like here, when he worked at the Metal Building? I mean, it's not a subject he talks about much, and I wondered . . ."

Paul turned his back to the car so Norman couldn't hear him. "Well now, let me see, there's not much I can tell you. By the time I was here, most of his staff had moved on. Wanda had died the year before. He wasn't selling much. I wasn't that interested in the work, honestly, just in saving money for school. God, he could be surly," Paul snorted. "I wish I'd talked him out of taking down all those pieces. There were eight or nine of them. Glorious. His later stuff wasn't like his old work. Not much life to it."

"So when did you meet Maddie?"

"That first summer."

"And you started dating then?"

"No, no. He," Paul made a sideways movement of his head in Norman's direction, "wouldn't have allowed it. But by the summer after, he had loosened up."

"Why does he never talk about Wanda?"

"Painful, I would guess."

"I see."

"Well, I'd better go. I have an afternoon class."

"Do you want a ride back to the house?"

"No, no, I need the walk."

With a wave, Paul strode off, his long legs making fast headway across the bumpy field. When Abby got into the car next to Norman, he tapped his cane on the floor and said: "Kinetic."

Abby was puzzled. "Kinetic?"

He nodded impatiently. "The sculptures. That's the word. Kinetic." And with an irritated nod of his head he added: "Hurry, you're making me late for lunch."

CHAPTER TEN

On Monday nights, Abby went bowling. She liked it. She wasn't a bowler by passion or skill, but it was something she had stumbled her way into during the summer, therapy to help a friend. She first met Mike Testarossa when he was looking for his runaway daughter. A man in his fifties, he was the plumber for the InnBetween, a chunky bulldog of a man who had turned to Abby for help. He was a good bowler, and at the end of July he had started giving her lessons. She asked him to do it because she thought it would get him out more. He agreed, but only because he thought it would get her out more. They formed a team, joined by his assistant Sean Kenna, his old school friend Sally deCintio making up a fourth. The league games began in September. Abby felt like the anchor, the one bowler who could be counted on to keep them firmly tied to the bottom of the league. But she was learning. The week before, she had kept the ball out of the gutter. Mostly.

Abby always made sure to arrive early at the Lanes, and this Monday was no different. She didn't have her own ball and there was only one alley ball she liked, so she had to get there in time to claim it. It was lighter than the others and the finger holes weren't too big. It was dark green and had the name "Vicky" printed on it in script. She sometimes wondered about Vicky but didn't ask too many questions in case she found the woman. Vicky might decide to take her bowling ball home with her if she knew someone was using it. Next stop was the shoes, piled like kindling on a single shelf behind the counter. The ones she preferred were pink-and-beige, and she liked to think they also belonged to Vicky. Another reason not to find the woman.

On this particular night, Mike and Sally arrived soon after she did. He carried a cracked green-and-tan, thirty-year-old bowling bag with a plastic handle. It matched his physique—no frills, stocky and serviceable. Sally's bag matched her makeup—in bright pinks and blues, strong and plastic-coated. The two of them had been married to other people, and now each had one child and both were single. They had also been in the same high school production of *Damn Yankees,* something that Abby couldn't help thinking about whenever she saw them together. Tonight, Sally wore black spandex leggings and a blue, tunic-length shirt with a red satin appliqué of a bowler on it. The shoulders had pads with an eighties heft to them, and her red hair was teased and piled up around a blue ribbon.

The machines started up to allow the teams to practice, and up and down the cavernous, low-ceilinged hall the balls rolled and thundered down the alleys, pins crashed, and the old machines that reset them whined. Mike reminded Abby to concentrate on keeping her foot perpendicular to the fault line and swing her arm straight. "Reach toward the little arrows, Abby," he added.

"Got it. This week's going to be better, I feel it," Abby said, starting to tense up already.

"Hey, Sal," she heard a familiar voice behind her. Sean Kenna. Abby made a point of not turning around. She held the ball up to her chest and tried to visualize her throw.

"Hello, handsome," she heard Sally say, followed by a kissing sound.

"Hey, Mike, how's it going? Can you believe it? I just finished up the Hillsdale job."

Abby walked forward, swung her arm hard, and let the ball go, hoping for the best. She watched as it bounced on the alley, rolled away on a gradual diagonal, and knocked down one pin on the far right.

Sure enough, Sean wasn't going to let it pass.

"Abby, ouch! Mike, you've got to get her to stop twisting her body."

"Shut up, Sean," she said, turning to look at him when she was sure her cheeks would no longer give her away.

And so the evening began. Sally kept score, and Mike, Sean, and Abby drank draught beers they bought at the bar. They all bought raffle tickets, three for two dollars, and ate French fries. Her three teammates knew everyone, because the Lanes on league nights was a Bantam stronghold. No weekenders, no city people, no visitors. Abby knew that one team was made up of the folks that worked at the hardware store, another a car dealership on the outskirts of town; she recognized a school bus driver and always said hello to the woman who answered phones at the vet's office. No, there wasn't much crossover with the InnBetween customer pool.

Sean talked easily to the other men and flirted with the women, who laughed at anything he said. Abby tried to ignore him, though there were times when she had trouble keeping her eyes away. His dark good looks and lean frame stood out against the sturdy, family types in the barnlike room. Her favorite moments were when he was up there bowling. Then, she could sit on their vinyl bench seat and stare. When he was done, he would turn around and catch her looking. Yes, she liked Monday night bowling. Even though she sucked.

By eight forty-five they had finished up their third game and were putting away their gear.

"Definite improvement, Abby," nodded Mike. "You've got to keep your shoulders square to the foul line, and line up your ball with the second arrow from the right, aim for it, and go."

"He's right, honey," said Sally, pushing her hairdo higher up on her head, as if it were threatening to slip. "And don't forget, you've got potential. Truly. In a few months, you're gonna be really good."

"Thanks, Sally," Abby laughed and shook her head as she took off her shoes. "But I'm not feeling the potential, you know?"

Sean was sitting next to her, undoing his laces. She watched him pull off his two-tone shoes. Catching her gaze he said in a low voice: "I'll sell you my shoes, it'll help. Trust me, anything will help you."

Caught unawares, Abby gave a burst of laughter. Mike glanced over at them. Sally narrowed her eyes, wondering what she'd missed.

In the parking lot, the four teammates said good-bye, promising to meet up in a week. Abby left the lot first.

By the time Abby got home it was a little after nine, and the dogs were gratifyingly happy to see her. She quickly made her bed and picked up the clothes lying on her bedroom floor. Then she went through her tiny kitchen/living room, straightening up. Just as she was finishing, she heard a vehicle whining up the steep driveway. She gave a last look in the bathroom mirror and went to the door.

When she opened it, Sean Kenna was standing in the doorway, hands in his pockets.

"Could I use your telephone, ma'am? My truck broke down just outside your door, and I don't have one of them little carryin' phones."

"Sorry, I don't have a telephone," Abby answered.

"You don't? Well, ma'am, I'm a plumber, maybe I can fix your—"

She put her hands on his neck and kissed him, and their teeth touched because they were both smiling. Then she pulled him inside, and he freed one hand long enough to shut the front door behind himself.

It was a ritual. They always left the lanes in separate cars. When he showed up at her house, they would get down to what had propelled them through two hours of beer and small talk. Yes, bowling was their foreplay, and by the time Sean arrived at her door there was no time to waste.

"You're such a lousy bowler," Sean mumbled into her neck, "it should be a real turn off."

Abby helped him pull off his shirt. "I just pretend to be bad, to make you feel like a bigger man. That's how I get what I want," Abby said.

Usually Sean left before dawn, which suited Abby fine. She didn't need him to stay longer. She didn't need him at all, she told herself. But by Thursday, she began to look forward to Monday, and by Saturday, all she could think about was going to the Lanes. The whole idea of bowling had taken on an erotic meaning for her. It occurred to her that this was how people became fetishists. Maybe instead of high heels, she'd become one of those people who could reach orgasm only when wearing bowling shoes.

Abby had first met Sean the summer before, but early on in their charged relationship, Abby had decided it wasn't going to work. She felt she was too recently a widow to be able to handle a relationship. So she broke it off.

The first time the team gathered at the Lanes, Sean and Abby ignored each other for the entire two hours. When Sean appeared at her house later that night, Abby told him to go away, but he touched her arm with one finger, and she instantly felt her insides turn to hot, slow liquid. A human lava lamp with legs, is how she thought of herself around him.

Tonight, Abby allowed herself to enjoy being with him. She allowed herself to luxuriate in his body, with its smell and warmth, its hard curves and angles. It was a rich feeling, even though she knew that the moment the last shiver of pleasure was over, the separation would begin, slowly and unavoidably, wider and wider, until the following Monday when they would begin the evening as if they barely knew each other. And she guessed that one Monday, for whatever reason, it would stay that way.

When they were done, she lay back in his arms, forcing herself to delay the usual quick disconnection. Sean stroked her hair gently and kissed her temple. She closed her eyes, allowing herself to drift off to sleep.

When she opened them, Sean was reading a book with his free hand. *Tuscany, My Heart,* to be precise.

Abby yawned. "You're not going to like that. It's a book about polishing tiles, bonding with the colorful locals, and eating spaghetti."

"I don't think so."

"Well, something along those lines. I know, the author gave it to me."

"You're kidding." He turned the book over and looked at the cover. "Germaine LeClair. She lives around here?"

"Just visiting friends. She hangs out at the restaurant."

"Listen to this . . ." Sean started reading:

"Today I have an appointment with a man I know only as Sabatini, the iron-worker. I have a delicate wrought-iron balcony, but a section of it must've broken off many years ago."

"See?" Abby interrupted. "Broken house parts, I told you."

"Quiet. Listen.

"It is bakingly hot this afternoon," he read on, *"and I am upstairs in my bedroom resting, wearing only a pair of lace panties. I hear a car engine coming up my driveway. I rise, pull a loose dress over my head, and stand barefoot at my window. I see a small Fiat truck with a closed cab. A utility truck. It raises a cloud of dust behind it. The flies buzz lazily in the dark shadows of the window and the heat makes my dress stick to my breasts."*

"You're kidding!" said Abby. Sean ignored her.

"Slowly, I go downstairs and stand outside, waiting for him. Sabatini, if it is he—"

" 'If it is he!' What's that!"

"Shut up, Abby. This is serious shit.

"Sabatini, if it is he, gets out of his truck. He is in his twenties, and breathtakingly handsome."

"I like this.

"When he turns around to lift out his toolbox, I can see that his work shirt is wet with sweat and his dark hair curls damply at the nape of his neck. He carries the heavy metal box toward me, and I can see the muscles in his forearm straining."

"I should've known," Abby said, sitting up on one elbow. "Germaine would never write about fixing tiles."

"Don't interrupt." Sean continued to read:

"Ciao," I say.

"Buongiorno, Signora LaClara. So' Sabatini." I gather he is introducing himself, so I smile and hold out my hand. He is forced to put down his toolbox and extend his own hand, and I can feel the hardened skin of his palm, the fingers swollen and toughened by labor. I feel my body respond to the touch, to the hard masculinity of his hand.

"Madonna, quanto fa caldo." He looks at me, waiting to see if I understand. I nod, uncaring, knowing it won't matter. He continues, "Very 'ot."

"Ah, si." I grab the front of my dress and pull it deliberately and repeatedly away from my body, as if it will help me cool down. He glances down at my full breasts, and

"Does she have big breasts?" Sean looked up from the book, suddenly interested in what Abby had to say.

"No, she's a flat-chested bag of bones. Read."

Sean looked at her suspiciously, then back at the page. *"—my full breasts and then quickly up at my face, to see if I am displeased by his attention. What he sees on my face obviously reassures him. He looks down again, and this time I see the tip of his tongue slip out of his mouth and run over his lips."*

"Okay, okay," Abby interrupted again, this time grabbing the book out of Sean's hands. He tried to snatch it back, but she wedged it under her body.

"You are asking for tro-bell, Miss Silvernalee-o! I am Sabatini, the Iron Man," Sean said with a phony accent, his eyes squinting dangerously.

Abby giggled as he lunged at her. "Stop!" She pushed him away. "I want to see if it's all like this."

Abby pulled the book out from underneath her, and leafed through the pages. "Oh, wow, listen to this:

"He wrapped my legs around him, and thrust hard. I could feel the unforgiving stone of the garden wall under my naked cheeks." Ouch. Don't they have scorpions there? Hey, this is a different guy, this one's name is Domenico." She flipped through a few more pages. "Listen, listen:

The brambles grew around the clearing by the old well like the guardians of Sleeping Beauty's castle, the branches thick and brown, covered with lethal spines. Domenico used his curved scythe to hack at them, the blade so sharp they separated cleanly from the trunks. He used the rake to pull the tangled mass over to the side. When he finally cleared a path, he took me by the hand and led me into the small, dark clearing. He took off his sweat-stained shirt and threw it on the ground. I sat down on it and looked up at him. Slowly, he undid his—"

Abby shut the book, holding it with both hands. "That's it. No more."

Sean turned on his side to face her. "Why not? It's fun, come on, read some more."

Abby frowned. "I can't believe this stuff really happened to her, so what's going on? What kind of a book is this?"

"Maybe it's what she wanted to happen. Come here—" and he leaned over and gave her a slow kiss. She pushed him away. "Sorry," she said, but she didn't sound as if she meant it.

"Okay," he replied, rolling away from her. He sat up. Abby pulled the sheet up over her, suddenly self-conscious.

"I was hoping we would start something new, something we could call Sabatini Sex," he said, looking at her with a smile, trying to lighten the moment.

Abby laughed, though it felt forced. She sat up, crossing her legs, holding the sheet around her chest.

Sean stroked her hair. "Abby, let's have dinner together one night, at the InnBetween."

"Why?" she asked.

He shook his head at her deliberate obtuseness. "Ah, because I like you, because I would like to come out of hiding, you know, take our relationship public."

"What relationship?" said Abby, and jumped up from the bed, picking up her T-shirt from the floor and pulling it over her head. "We bowl and have sex."

"Well, that's better than most couples," Sean answered. "And now I want to have a meal with you at the InnBetween."

"Oh, god, no. Are you kidding? I can't have everybody at work knowing about us. I'll never hear the end of it." She pulled on her underpants and looked around for her jeans. She found them in a heap on the floor and pulled them on.

"The end of what? It's not like they're going to suddenly know you're a child molester or something."

Fully dressed, Abby sat on the bed next to him. She put a hand on his thigh. "I like things the way they are."

Sean covered her hand with his. "I do too. It's fun. But it doesn't have to, you know, end here. We can eat, go to the movies, maybe even hang out with friends."

Abby twisted her mouth up to one side. "Let me think about it, okay?"

Sean stood up and began putting his clothes on. Abby watched him, a feeling of panic tightening her throat.

When he was ready and had his car keys in his hand he said: "You've got to stop taking yourself so seriously, Abby. I just wanted to go out to dinner. Hey, can I borrow your friend's book? I'd like to read the whole thing. I need the company."

Abby shrugged, and Sean picked up the book from the bed. "Oh, and thanks for everything," he said, gesturing to the bed. "See you next Monday."

And he left. Which was supposed to be the way she liked it.

After the sound of his truck's engine had died away, Abby slowly stood up. She moved into her little living area, and sat on her couch. She pulled her legs up under her. Her clock said it was twelve-thirty. She stared ahead of her, wondering if she would ever find out what she wanted from life. Or if anything would ever make sense to her. Or if it even mattered if it made sense to her. I mean, if a tree falls in the forest, etc. etc. As long as she did her work and showed up on time, what difference would it make to anyone?

She thought about Germaine. What mattered to her? She thought of her driving around in her pajamas, thinking about her mother, threatening her father. She envied her—she wrote a book about sex with strangers, she drank too much, she was impulsive. But she wasn't afraid. She would never have turned Sean down. She would have slurped food with him in public and enjoyed it.

If she brought Sean to dinner, she would be out here for everyone to see, just like Franklin had been, the night he ate with Germaine. Everyone would know their business, just like she knew everyone else's. And people would think of them as a couple. And that scared her. What was wrong with her? I mean, she could get naked with the guy, but she wouldn't eat with him in public?

CHAPTER ELEVEN

The next morning, Abby had just finished brushing her teeth when the phone rang.

"Abby," Germaine said, not wasting her time in hellos, "today's your lucky day."

"How did you get my number?"

"From directory assistance. Anyway, I'm going to Woodstock to see my sister today. You can come, too."

"What if I don't want to come?" Abby asked, distrustful of Germaine's motives, even though she was intrigued at the thought of meeting the third sister.

"It's a nice day, we'll put the roof down."

"Germaine, I have to work today."

"I'll get you back in plenty of time, trust me. Athena and I can't spend too long together. So, I'll meet you in an hour. At Victor's. Don't be late."

By eleven, with a cup of Victor's strong coffee in her hands, Abby was sitting in the passenger seat of the dented blue Miata, heading south on the New York State Thruway. Sure enough, the canvas roof was down, and her hair was whipping around her face like weeds in a hurricane. Germaine was looking like a sixties movie star, a peach silk scarf tied around her head and large sunglasses covering a third of her face.

Abby held her hair off her face long enough to glance nervously at the speedometer. The Bronco had trouble going over fifty, and Germaine's little car was cruising at eighty. Abby wasn't used to speed.

"My sister's going to love you," Germaine looked over at her.

"I don't see why. Keep your eye on the road."

"No, really. Athena will like anyone who spends time with Norman. And you're a straight shooter."

"She likes straight shooters?"

"She should."

Abby digested this piece of information. "Well, as far as that goes, I'd say you're more of a shooter."

"Really?" Germaine said, ignoring the reference. She was in the passing lane, coming up fast behind a black and yellow tractor-trailer. When it looked as if they were going to drive under it, she pulled into the right lane.

Abby said: "So what's with your family?"

"What do you mean?"

"You're sisters, but you don't see Maddie, and other than that surprise attack the other night, you never go to visit Norman. What's the deal?"

"I know," Germaine said. "It was a stupid move, especially that late, but I swear, he used to work till all hours, and it was always his best time—" She stopped talking long enough to pull back into the passing lane and accelerate hard past a large white SUV.

Abby didn't rush her. Arriving alive seemed more important than understanding Germaine's thought processes. As soon as they'd returned to a somewhat more reasonable speed, Germaine said: "I didn't mean to do that thing, you know, with the gun. I started to say hello to him, but he wouldn't listen. He told me to get out and went for his cane, so I thought if I pulled out the gun, it would make him stand still and listen to me. But it was like he didn't see it, he just came after me."

"What did you say that set him off? Did you accuse him of killing Wanda?"

"No, of course not! All I said was: 'Norman, hi, I'm your daughter Germaine, remember me?' That's when he grabbed that stick, pointed it at me and started to run me down, saying, 'Get out of here, out, out!' I don't know what he was upset about. You saw the rest. He was on a rampage. I had no choice. I backed out of the door and ran."

Abby remembered the scene: Germaine, backlit by the outside light, her red hair sticking up around her head, the blood on her forehead and her black fur coat.

"Let's back up. How did you drive into the ditch?" Abby asked. "Don't say it was a deer—I'm not buying that one. Was it alcohol, or was it something else?"

"I don't do drugs, if that's what you mean." Germaine was indignant. "Just a couple of drinks. I'm surprised you weren't on my case about it then."

"I wasn't thinking about it. It was late, I was tired. And you were armed."

"Well, lucky for me you found me. You've become my best friend here, so I feel bad I didn't tell you the truth." Abby wasn't sure, since the glasses covered Germaine's eyes, but it sounded as if she was beginning to cry.

"Hey, hey, stop that," she said, worried. "You're driving, remember?"

When they reached Woodstock, they drove through the village, then down a side road, made narrow by the tall evergreens that grew along it. After about half a mile, Germaine turned onto a short, surfaced driveway. She pulled up in front of a simple, two-story house sided in natural cedar, the trim and windows a freshly painted dark green, the front door giving on to a deep porch with steps leading down from it. The land immediately around the house was cleared, bordered by a rough split-rail fence. Growing up against the fence were rose bushes, the blooms long gone, the leaves turning brown. In front of the porch was a bed of late-blooming mums; they added rich, dark reds and yellows to the warmth of the wood siding. All the flower beds that bordered the house were cleaned and mulched. Abby could see little metal signs stuck in the ground, she assumed to identify each sleeping plant. The trees circling the split rail fence were wolf maples and oaks, interspersed with tall pine trees. It seemed as if the fence were holding them at bay, keeping them from the neat and colorful area that surrounded the house.

Abby followed Germaine up the front steps and waited to one side while she opened the screen and knocked. Within minutes a tall thin woman wearing jeans and a soft, fuzzy sweater opened the door. She had wavy brown hair down to her waist. She stood staring at Germaine for a second before taking in who she was.

"Gerry, I don't believe it!" she said, and threw her arms around her sister. "Oh, my god, oh, my god!"

Abby watched as they hugged, separated, then started all over again. They seemed to care deeply about each other, but it was clear they hadn't seen each other in a long time. Finally Germaine, flushed and beaming, gestured to Abby.

"Teeny, this is Abby, a friend from Bantam. Abby, meet my little sister, Athena."

Abby smiled and shook her hand; she noticed Athena's eyebrows, which were dark and dramatic against her pale skin. She had sharp cheekbones, and her mouth kept moving, nervously, even when she wasn't speaking. When she did, her voice was deep, her speech clipped and clear. "Come in, both of you, come in," she said, opening the front door wide.

Before Abby could cross the threshold, however, Athena glanced at her sneakers. She herself was wearing slippers.

"Shall I take them off?" Abby asked, pointing to her feet.

"If you don't mind," Athena said with some relief.

Germaine was already standing in the hall. "My shoes are clean," she said, "and I can't take them off, I'll be too short."

Athena looked as if she were about to say something, but didn't. She led them into a center hallway, with wide board floors and walls painted a rich, buttery yellow. Abby noticed a stencil that ran around the room, below the crown molding. It seemed to be of round-faced cherubs.

Abby and Germaine followed Athena through a doorway to the right. The living room ran from the front of the house to the back, with windows on three sides. It was a large, warm room. A comfortable-looking cinnamon-colored couch faced a generous, brick fireplace, two saddle-yellow leather club chairs precisely arranged on either side of it. A pen-and-ink drawing hung over the carved mantle. It was of a woman, probably Athena, sitting in front of striped wallpaper, one strap of her camisole or blouse falling off a thin shoulder. As Abby moved further in the room, she was surprised to see a Christmas tree dominating the far end of the long room. It was covered in ornaments and topped by an angel with spread wings. Even the lights were lit.

"Wow," Abby said, "Christmas! Already!"

Athena laughed as she turned an ornament so it faced the room. "I know, everyone thinks I'm crazy, but I love Christmas. It's my favorite time of the year, so I start a little early."

Germaine shook her head. "Early is Thanksgiving, not September."

"Hey, I'm nearly thirty-nine, I can do what I want. And I'm an artist, so people cut me a little slack."

"You're an artist?" Abby asked with interest. "A sculptor?"

"No, god forbid. Musician."

"Why do you think she lives in Woodstock?" Germaine said. "There's a guitarist under every bush here. I bet her entire band lives within a three-mile radius, right?" she said, looking at her sister.

"True. Oh, Gerry, I can't believe you're here. Come on, let's have tea." Athena led the way through a door near the massive fir tree.

"Goody. Ground bark root sweetened with bee turds," Germaine said grumpily as she followed her sister out of the room. "Do you have any vodka?"

Abby lingered for a moment in the welcoming room. She went over to the tree, responding instinctively to the pull of childhood. She touched the nearest branch and put her nose next to it, looking to breathe in that tangy, resinous smell. To her surprise, nothing. She pinched the spiny twig and looked more closely. She moved her hand back, shocked. Plastic. It was like stroking a lover's skin, only to discover it was vinyl. Looking up the length of the tree, she could now see an unnatural symmetry in its fullness and rich dark color. It was a good tree, but still fake. Then she realized that, of course, if you're going to have a tree starting in September, it had better be plastic or it would be brown by Halloween and a bare skeleton by Thanksgiving.

"You discovered my secret, didn't you?" Athena was in the doorway, watching Abby.

"I guess it has to be synthetic to last as long as you need it." Abby was proud she'd thought of the word "synthetic." It seemed more sensitive than "fake."

"I considered having two trees, but that seemed environmentally wasteful. This one'll last for years. You'd probably have been fooled if I'd used some pine scent. You want tea?"

"Sure." Abby followed her out of the room across the hall into the kitchen, which was large and cozy, a homey mixture of old cabinetry and new appliances. Abby noticed a neat arrangement of photographs stuck to the large refrigerator. They seemed to be mostly of Athena and a little boy. Athena laughing, holding the boy; Athena playing the piano with the boy at about sixteen; one of him as a young man, his face thin and his dark hair pulled back in a ponytail.

Abby took a seat at a rough-hewn, rectangular table in the middle of the room. Germaine sat opposite her, looking fidgety. No hardworking men to come on to, Abby thought to herself. Nothing to drink.

Athena poured them each a cup of tea in what looked like hand-fired mugs, and handed around a plate of cookies. Abby took one and had a bite. It was bland and wholesome. She put it down and listened while Athena and Germaine caught up.

Athena didn't know about the Italian farmhouse. "You bought a house in Italy? How did you manage that?" Athena exclaimed, sitting down.

Germaine looked slightly defensive. "I've been teaching English as a foreign language for years, barely taking vacations, tutoring in the summer. I had a nest egg."

"That's right, I forgot. The difference between you and me is Cal. He's my nest egg."

"Cal?" Abby asked.

Athena turned to her and said with some surprise in her voice: "My son. Didn't she tell you I have a son?"

"How is Cal?" Germaine asked swiftly, smiling brightly at her sister.

"He's great. He tours with me sometimes."

"Does he have a girlfriend? Or boyfriend?" Germaine asked.

"He's straight, thank you very much," Athena said, "and no, no girl-friend at the moment, but he's had plenty."

"I just thought, you know, he might be a bit of a mama's boy," Germaine teased.

Abby watched her in surprise. What was she trying to do, start something? She hadn't seen her sister in years, as far as Abby could tell, and there she was, trying to get a rise.

"Well, he's not. But even if he were gay, it wouldn't matter to me," Athena said stiffly. She changed the subject. "So, tell me more about Italy. Why so far away? What about the people you're close to?"

Germaine didn't answer right away. "Like who, for example?"

There was an uncomfortable tension building, Abby realized, and she wasn't sure where it had come from. Maybe this was the reason they didn't visit a lot.

"Athena," she said, thinking she could distract them and learn something at the same time, "tell me about Norman. Was he a good father?"

The tall woman looked at her, blankly. "How do you know about Norman?" she asked.

"I work three mornings a week for him."

Athena seemed confused. "Really? You work for Norman? Gerry, why didn't you tell me?"

"I didn't think of it," Germaine answered. Abby thought she looked pleased.

"What work do you do for him?"

"Amanuensis."

"Of course." Athena nodded. She looked at Abby as if she were seeing her for the first time. She turned to her sister. "How is he?"

"I haven't seen him," Germaine answered.

"Really?" Athena said to Abby, as if she didn't believe Germaine.

Abby wasn't sure how to answer. Germaine interjected: "When did *you* last visit?"

"I don't know. A long time ago."

"But you're so close," Germaine said. "It's an easy drive."

"Oh, well," Athena shrugged.

Germaine started to say something, then just rolled her eyes.

The tension was firming and taking shape. Abby thought she should get her questions in while she could. "Tell me more about him," she encouraged Athena.

"I worshipped him when I was little. He was always good to us," Athena said, selecting a thick strand of hair from the back of her head. She held it in front of her with one hand and twirled the end with the other. It looked like a steady habit. Her mouth moved nervously.

Germaine snorted. "Who are you kidding? He barely spoke to us."

Athena nodded. "I know, but that's because he was always working. It's not like he was mean or anything. He just didn't have the time. But he took us in, didn't he? He cared about us." She laughed suddenly. "I remember the day we moved in. It was on Maddie's birthday, remember? She thought we were presents."

Germaine snorted again. "Yeah, she tried to send us back, the little brat."

Athena nodded. "I remember Wanda telling her, 'These are your new sisters, they're here to love you and keep you company.'"

"Right, and him just watching, not saying a word. God, what an awful day."

Athena shook her head. "I loved it. I was so happy to be there. I was so happy to be in a family, with a real house. A father and a mother."

Abby watched first one woman, then the other. They were a good-looking pair, though the angularity of Athena's face made her seem older than her sister, not younger.

"Have you kept in touch with Maddie at all?" Abby asked Athena.

"Once a year I send her and Norman Christmas cards. Naturally." She laughed wryly, at herself. "But I never hear from them. I know she's busy. And Norman, well, he's Norman. By the way, how is he?"

"He's pretty good, I think. But he's ninety-two. His memory is deteriorating and, according to Maddie, he has Alzheimer's. So I guess it'll just get worse."

Athena nodded, listening, her expression revealing little. Then she said, "It's too bad, but I'm getting together with some of the band members in a little while. If I'd known you were coming, I'd have cancelled."

"No, no problem," Germaine said. "Abby has to get back to work anyway."

"Oh, to Norman's?" Athena asked politely.

"My other job. I work at a restaurant."

Athena smiled and nodded, uninterested. She picked up her mug and took it to the sink. Abby picked up her bitten cookie, and looked for a garbage can. When she couldn't find one, she slid it into her pocket. She took the plate and put it on the counter.

Germaine pushed the chairs under the table. "The whole thing was pretty pathetic, in a way," she said, her mind still on the events of their childhood. "But we were lucky. Wanda was a good mother. It was a decent home, they fed us, sent us to school, didn't molest us. I mean, things could've been a lot worse, right?" She looked at Athena.

"Definitely," Athena nodded.

Germaine now stared hard at her sister. "But I still don't understand why."

Athena stared back, a frown forming. "Why what?"

"Why you sent me the letter."

"What letter?"

"Oh, come on, Teeny. This letter."

Always theatrical, Germaine pulled a piece of paper out of her skirt pocket and held it in the air. Abby recognized the dog-eared anonymous letter. Germaine opened it with a flourish:

"'What really happened to Wanda?'" she read. "'When Norman dies, your chance of finding out dies with him.'"

"What the hell's *that?*" Athena asked.

"A little note I got nearly a year ago," Germaine said. "I know I've been slow to respond, but I think you were even slower to write it. Maybe twenty years too slow."

"I don't know what you're talking about. I never sent you that. Let me see it."

Athena reached for it, but Germaine kept it out of her reach. "Oh no, no, you can look, but not with your hands." She held it up for Athena to see, about three feet from her face. Athena went to a counter and came back with a pair of glasses. She put them on and peered at the note.

"Why the hell would I send you this? It's bullshit," she said, looking past the note at her sister.

"You wanted to get me all worked up. And you succeeded."

"I've never seen it before. I wouldn't be surprised if you wrote it yourself." Athena put her glasses down, grabbed Germaine's mug and Abby's and took them to the sink. She put them in too roughly. There was a sound of breaking pottery. "Damn!" she said. "Look what you made me do."

"Have you ever wondered why?" Germaine asked her sister, her eyes bright.

"Why what?" Athena asked.

"Why they did it. Why they took us in."

The sisters looked at each other. The silence grew.

"I mean," Germaine went on, "he only cared about his work, Wanda cared about him, and Maddie was perfectly okay with being an only child. Years after I left home, I used to wonder if he was our real father. Maybe he and our mother had been lovers and he had no choice, he had to—"

"Shut up! That's a nasty idea!" Athena snapped.

"Why?" Germaine asked. "Why's it nasty? Maybe that was it. He was our biological father. It would certainly explain why he took us in. Though if that's true, he should have shown us a little more love."

The three women formed a triangle in the room, but Abby could have disappeared in a puff of smoke, and Germaine and Athena wouldn't have noticed.

Athena's eyes filled with sudden tears. "You always saw the worst in him! You just see the ugliness everywhere! I know why they did it. Because for the first time he was making money, and they wanted to give back. Taking us in, giving us a roof over our heads, educating us, was their way of contributing. And it worked! If we'd stayed with Mom, we'd have been killed in that damn car, or we'd be hookers or drug addicts by now!"

Athena wiped her eyes and walked quickly out of the room. Abby and Germaine listened to her footsteps as she ran up the stairs.

"Oh, *please*. What a drama queen," said Germaine flatly.

When Athena didn't return, they let themselves out.

They drove in silence for a while until Germaine said, her voice taking on the sing-song of mimicry, "Oh, Cal, he's my nest egg." And then in her regular voice: "She always tries to make me feel inadequate—with her perfect home and her perfect child. If I didn't like the kid I'd hate him."

"Who's the boy's father?" Abby asked.

"A musician she shacked up with for a while in Austin. Long out of the picture."

"You made up that whole thing about the note, didn't you?"

Germaine turned to look at her in surprise. "No, I swear."

"Do you really think Athena sent it?"

Germaine shrugged. "She's the only one who knows what happened to our mother. I figured she's too afraid to do anything herself, so she's trying to get me going. That would be typical."

"But then why not just write to you directly?"

"I have no idea."

"Hmm. Well, I'm sure there are things about your life that she's envious of," Abby said, trying to be nice.

"I didn't say I was envious," Germaine said in a clipped voice.

Abby gave up. For the first time in her life, she was glad she didn't have a sister.

When there was no vehicle close behind them, she took the half-eaten oatmeal cookie out of her pocket, and threw it out the back of the Miata. She watched it hit the road and fly into pieces.

CHAPTER TWELVE

I'm working on a new piece," Norman said, as he shuffled slowly into the office, leaning on his cane. "It is evolving. In my head."

Abby looked up. He was late, and she was leafing through an old catalog from a show of his sculptures. The date on the book was 1975. Before he came in, she had skimmed the essay at the front, but it didn't mean much to her. She had been studying photos of the thin, shining towers of stainless steel, some topped by hoops and others by blades. Even though the reproductions were washed out and lifeless, his creations looked elegant and strange, even beautiful, like an alien population of giant praying mantises. She tried to imagine them moving.

"The idea came to me last night in a dream," he continued. "It requires pianos."

"Pianos?"

"Please, don't repeat everything I say. Pianos, hanging pianos."

After he sat down, Abby picked up the letters that were on the desk. "Shall we go over the mail?"

"I should hope so," Norman replied, sounding petulant.

Abby read the top one. "Here's one from California."

"I know no one in California. I don't want to read it. Is it lunchtime?" he asked.

"Nearly. Saranda will be ready for you soon." Abby took a breath then dove in. "Norman, I met a woman who said she is your daughter."

"Yes, Madeleine. She's a good child."

"Yes, I know Maddie, but this is another woman. Her name is Germaine. Does that sound familiar to you?"

"Germaine?" he asked, frowning.

"Yes. Germaine LeClair. She says she's your adopted daughter."

"Germaine. It sounds familiar. Oh, yes, yes, I think so. Of course. The orphans."

"Orphans?"

"My dear, of course they were orphans. They had no family—they were bound to be orphans. I can't remember their names."

"One is Germaine, and the other is—"

The old man looked down at the desk and tapped his fingers on it. "Germaine. Yes. Do you know her?"

"I do. I also met the other one, Athena. Do you remember her?"

Norman didn't answer. He kept tapping his fingers, louder and louder.

Abby continued: "Would you like to see Germaine? She's living in Bantam at the moment. I could invite her over. I'm sure she'd love to see you."

He stopped tapping. "Is she the fat one?"

Surprised, Abby found herself defending Germaine: "Well, she's curvy. Not fat."

"She was a fat little girl. She up and went away, just when I could have used her help. She'll get nothing from me, as I told her the last time I saw her."

"When was that?"

"When was what?"

"When did you see her last?"

"I chased her away. Now, it's time for us to get back to work, young lady." He resumed tapping the table with his fingers.

Dreading more dull letters, on impulse Abby said: "I've been looking at this catalog. It's from a show of yours."

The tapping ended abruptly. He looked at the book. "A show? What show?"

"Of your work," Abby said, handing him the catalog. "Back in 1975. Beautiful pieces. They were big, weren't they? I wish I could've seen them."

Norman opened the catalog and leafed slowly through it. "I don't know what this is."

"It was a show of your work, your sculpture. I think it took place, here, in the back field."

Norman nodded slowly, still squinting at the soft cover book. "I see. Well, if you like this, we could do it again."

Abby nodded. "With the pieces you're working on now. We could invite friends, have some wine and cheese."

"Yes. Maddie could come and, if she insisted, she could bring her husband, that tall man, What's-his-name."

"Paul. He used to work for you," Abby prompted.

Norman's eyes brightened. "Yes. I would like that, a show. We could have it in the Metal Building."

"Yes," Abby repeated, now with a little less confidence than the first time. "We should talk to Maddie, I think."

"That'd probably be wise," she said, with relief. "She can decide if it's a good idea."

He frowned. "I don't need anyone telling me what to do. My life doesn't hang on anyone's approval."

"No, of course not," Abby agreed, sensing trouble.

"I have decided. I will have a show. Now we need to plan it."

"But—"

"Don't say but—"

"I wasn't, I just want to be sure that—"

Norman pushed his chair back and stood up, outrage in every line of his bent body. "I won't put up with any more of this. I have work to do. You are a fool, a stupid fool."

Abby was taken aback. "Why, what did I do?"

He looked at her with something like loathing. "How dare you ask me, after what you've done? You disgust me, Wanda. You have ruined everything with your self-indulgent greed. I want you to get out, now." And he gestured angrily to the door.

Abby stood up and pushed her chair back. "That's not fair," she said. She was offended. And shocked at his venom. She walked out of the room and kept going, out the front door. She wanted to get in her car, leave, and never come back.

Once she was outside, she started to cool down. It wasn't his fault, it was the disease making him behave so erratically. She wondered if she should just head home for the day or go back in and pretend nothing had happened. He had obviously confused her with Wanda. What had she said or done to trigger that? She thought back over their conversation. Could it have been the mention of a show? Or could it have been the fact that she tried to change his mind? What did he say to her? "You have ruined everything?" Strong words.

She heard Saranda in the kitchen. She wanted to speak to her, so she walked around the side of the house and let herself into the kitchen, keeping an eye out for Norman. He was nowhere in sight. In the kitchen, Saranda was stirring a pot on the stove.

She stood in the doorway. "Saranda, Norman's mad at me."

The housekeeper took a bowl out of the cabinet. She laughed. "So? He'll get over it. Faster than most."

"I know but, wow, he gets ugly. Tell me, how long have you worked for him?"

Saranda gave another stir and looked up from what she was doing. "Oh, going on seven years now."

"That's a long time. When did his wife die, do you know?"

The woman shook her head. "I'd have to believe it was back in the eighties. Before my time. I know he'd been alone for some time here, managing. Maddie hired me when she noticed he was getting forgetful and missing meals."

Abby walked over to the list of emergency numbers pinned next to the wall phone.

"Have you met his doctor?" She looked at the list. "Doctor Melikovski?"

"Yes, I have."

"Has he been Norman's doctor for a long time?"

"Let me think. Maybe five years now? Something like that."

Abby nodded thoughtfully. "You don't know who his doctor was before that, do you?"

"Hmm, hmm." Saranda stopped what she was doing, trying to remember. "I don't recall his name. He had an office in Pittsfield, I know that for a fact. Oh, my lord, I remember the fuss Norman made when the poor man said he was going to retire. He did not want a new doctor. No, sir."

"He was used to him, right?"

"He said no one else would look after him right."

Saranda went back to her chores. Abby watched her for about half a minute, then pushed off from the counter. "I'm going for a walk across the field. I'll be back in ten minutes."

She let herself quietly out the kitchen door and circled behind the shed to the rough dirt road out to the Metal Building.

She admitted to herself that she had pushed Norman. His memory was too unstable for him to be questioned like that; when he didn't remember something, he became confused and lashed out at the nearest warm body. Also, it was clear he didn't like to be defied, probably never had. She should have just backed off. Funny, the way he had called her Wanda. Something had obviously happened with his wife that had angered him. Maybe she'd had an affair. Which might explain why he was still angry at her. Poor woman, dead for all these years, and still unforgiven.

When she reached the gray, deserted building, she realized what it reminded her of: an old abandoned gas station, the kind you might see on a country road. A place where people had once filled up their tanks or pulled their cars in for repairs; men had welded, run machinery, and done whatever they needed to do. The kind of place that now, for whatever reason, sat empty, hinges rusting, its tanks maybe leaching pollutants into the soil, the weeds growing up around the sides of the building hiding old tires rotting in the weather. You had to be careful walking around a building like that—there could be sharp things left behind in the tall grass.

When she got back, Norman was sitting at his desk. In front of him lay a yellow legal pad and the old catalog of his show. With his left hand he was holding a pencil in the sharpener attached to his desk, and slowly cranking the handle with his right.

"We have a lot of work to do," he said, taking the pencil out and examining it. It was obviously not sharp enough, because he put it back into the hole of the sharpener, with some difficulty, and resumed turning the handle.

"The mural will be the background for the show. As soon as my amanuensis finds the drawings, I will begin. I will also need an assistant."

"The mural?" Abby asked, blankly.

Norman grew irritated at her slowness. "Yes, the mural. I never finished it. The drawings are filed. I will need them."

Before the moment could go sour, Abby stood. "I'll call Maddie now. Maybe I can catch her before she leaves for work. I'm sure she'll tell me where to find what you need." To forestall any other instructions, she walked quickly out of the room. She'd call Maddie from the kitchen phone. She heard the sharpening of the pencil start up again.

To her relief, Maddie answered after the second ring.

"I'm glad you're still there," Abby said.

"What's wrong? Did something happen?" Maddie asked, her voice tight.

"No, no, everything's fine, I just need to know something about a mural. Did he ever start one?"

"He did, right after the war. At a college in the Midwest. That's where he met my mother. She was a student of his."

"He said he never got to finish it."

"Oh, he finished it. It's still there."

"Well, he wants me to find the drawings for it. He wants to redo it here. He said you'd know where they are."

Maddie thought for a minute. "I guess it's not such a bad idea. It would give him something to do."

"He wants it to be the background for a show. The mural."

Maddie sighed. "A show? Listen, we'll talk more later. I'm late for work as it is."

"Wait!" Abby said, before she could hand up. "The drawings, where would I find them?"

"Look in the filing cabinet to your right when you first go into his office. It's the wide one. There are lots of letters and drawings, all filed by date. Let's see, try anytime after nineteen forty-nine. And before 'fifty-one. It's somewhere in there."

"What am I looking for?"

Maddie spoke impatiently, and for a minute she sounded like her father. "Drawings, from a sketch pad. You know. About twelve inches by eighteen. There are probably about ten of them. I've got to go." And she hung up.

"Wait—" Abby said to a dial tone.

Back in the office, Abby said brightly to Norman: "Okay! I think I know where to find the drawings."

He looked at her uncertainly.

Just then, Saranda stuck her head in the office. "Soup's on, Norman," she said.

"Good, good," he said, nodding at her.

"Norman, I'll look for them," Abby said, "while you're having lunch. How's that?"

"Splendid. Thank you." He looked relieved to be off the hook. Carefully, he got to his feet. He left the room, leaning on his cane.

She pulled open the top drawer of the filing cabinet, and started to read the headings of the files. Most of them seemed to be names, and when she randomly pulled one partially out, and glanced at the contents, she saw they were letters. Looking at the first one, labeled Roland, Jeremy, she saw it was written in an elegant, sloping hand. The date was April 12, 1939. It began:

"My dear Nephew," and the bulk of the letter seemed to be family news and trivia, a birth, an illness, and the writer's own state of health. He seemed to have pains in his legs. It was signed, "affectionately, Uncle Jeremy."

Abby pushed the file back in and glanced at the door, making sure she was alone. This might be her only chance. She began leafing through the files, looking for both the mural drawings and for Smith, Wanda. But there was nothing. Not under S, nor under W. She shut the drawer. Maddie had said that the files Abby was looking for were listed by year, so Abby opened the next one. Here, too, seemed to be nothing but letters—no Wanda, and no drawings. The correspondence seemed to be mostly business related—buyers, collectors, and some family. Abby found nothing of interest, even after looking through all the drawers.

It was then that Abby remembered Maddie had told her to look for a wide file. Next to the tall cabinet she had just gone through was a lower piece of furniture, one that Abby would have described more as a chest of drawers than a filing cabinet. She realized it was probably storage designed for an architect or a draughtsman.

She pulled the top drawer open by its two widely spaced handles. Inside were three worn portfolios of different sizes. Abby gently lifted out the first one. On the cover, written in black ink, was the year 1942. The one underneath it was labeled 1945. Still not what she was looking for. She closed the drawer and pulled open the one beneath it.

Someone had taken care to organize Norman's work, and it took Abby only a few more minutes to find the mural drawings. They were all together, though some were pencil sketches, while others were watercolors. The style was the kind that glorified the workingman, and reminded Abby of Soviet stamps she'd once seen. Muscled men and women, their sex barely distinguishable, sleeves rolled up, proudly working machinery and factory assembly lines. The colors were rich browns, reds, and blues.

When she'd found what appeared to be all of them, Abby laid them out for Norman on the dining room table. She went into the kitchen and told him what she had done.

"Thank you, my dear. I will look them over carefully this evening."

He seemed to have put the whole morning behind him. Just as she was walking out the kitchen door, Saranda stopped her. "Abby, I got it. Jaspers. Remember him, Norman? Dr. Jaspers?"

Norman finished swallowing and nodded. "Yes. Dr. Jaspers. He was a good friend." His expression grew sad. "He must be dead now, along with everyone else I know." He stirred his soup and took another mouthful.

Abby waited to see if he was going to say anything else, and when he didn't, she went back into his office.

She found a leather-bound phone book and flipped to the letter J. Sure enough, he was under Jaspers, Morris. She copied the information down on a scrap of paper: phone number, and his home address, 21 Minerva Road, Pittsfield. She hesitated for a moment, then picked up the receiver and dialed the number. After three rings a woman answered.

"Hello?"

"Hi," Abby said, "is Dr. Jaspers there?"

"Who?" said the voice. Not a good sign.

"I'm looking for Morris Jaspers. Until a few years ago, he used to have this phone number."

"Oh, Morris. Of course. I'm hard of hearing, so you have to speak slowly. He just stepped out for a minute. I'm a friend of his."

"Wonderful. I wanted to visit him. I'll just pop over then."

"You do that, darling. Who should I say is calling?"

"Abby. I'll explain when I get there."

"Good. He'll like that. He doesn't get many visitors."

"Thanks. Okay, then. Good-bye. Oh, it's Twenty-one Minerva, right?"

"What?" The old woman made it sound like a duck quacking.

"His address is Twenty-one Minerva Road, correct?"

"No, no. Not any more. This is Yorkshire Villages."

"Yorkshire Villages? Where's that?"

"In Lenox. Where are you calling from?"

"Bantam, New York."

"Oh," she said, sounding disappointed. "Is it a long drive?"

"No. I'll be over soon."

"Lovely. I'll tell him you're coming. But get here before five. At five, we go down to supper."

"I will."

"Abby, right?"

"Right."

"Good. I won't forget."

CHAPTER THIRTEEN

Yorkshire Villages was a sprawling, white edifice overlooking Route 7, the main road that traveled north-south through the western end of Berkshire County. Small semidetached cottages were dotted around the main building, which Abby supposed loosely justified the Villages part of the name. She parked in the visitors' area and walked through the main entrance. A small bus was slowly unloading its elderly passengers. She made it to the door just as they began a slow conga line into the building, some with walkers and canes. It would have been tacky to dodge between them to get to the head of the line, so she held the door politely.

Once inside, she easily found an open door marked Office. A portly man was on the phone, and when he saw her he held up his index finger to signal that he was nearly done.

"What can I do for you?" he asked hopefully, once he hung up.

"I'm looking for Dr. Morris Jaspers," she asked.

"Oh, good. Are you family?" he asked, friendly but protective.

"No, but I work for an old friend of his, and was hoping to see Morris," she answered politely.

"Let's see, he's in two nineteen. Top of the stairs, at the end of the hall on your left."

Three women were sitting at a table in the dining room. They watched her walk up the carpeted staircase. Along the corridor, each room had a removable name plate in a small holder attached to the door. Abby wondered how often each one was replaced. What the turnover was. Some of the doors had decorations on them, paper flowers or American flags. Two nineteen was the last door. Abby knocked.

She didn't have to wait long before she was greeted by a tall, thin man with a bulbous forehead and sparse, white hair combed close to his head. He had a strong nose, and thin lips that were curved downward, sunken between pendulous jowls. His eyes were half hidden under hanging lids. Behind him, Abby saw a large double window with a view of woods.

"Dr. Jaspers? I'm Abby Silvernale. How are you?" She held out her hand, and he shook it somewhat reluctantly.

"Fine, thank you. I don't mean to sound rude, but do I know you?" he asked. A polite way of asking who the hell she was.

"I work for Norman Smith."

"Norman Smith! Good lord, I hope you're not bringing me bad news," he asked, still not throwing the door open and asking her in.

Abby smiled, trying to soften him up. "No, not at all. Actually, I came to pick your brain."

"I don't understand," he asked.

Time to cut to the chase. "Would you mind if I came in?"

Reluctantly, he moved aside. "No, no. But I don't have much time."

A small table divided the cooking area from a shipshape little sitting room, with a television faced by two comfortable armchairs covered in a dark green fabric. Against the wall was a large bookshelf that housed books interspersed with a few pieces of what looked like handmade pottery. It was a welcoming and comfortable space.

"This is nice," Abby said admiringly. "I like compact spaces."

"Thank you," said her host, responding to the genuine warmth of her voice. "It's not bad. The hardest part was deciding what was important enough to keep. One collects so much in life, don't you think?"

"Have you lived here long?"

Jaspers led her into the sitting room and gestured to one of the chairs. "Have a seat." He sat down across from her. "About a year. I had a house with a few acres, but when my wife died, it all seemed too much for me. Now, how can I help you?"

Abby cleared her throat. "Well, I work for Norman, going through his mail, answering letters, and so on. He has Alzheimer's, as you may know." The doctor nodded. Abby continued. "There seem to be certain issues that set him off and get him upset, and I'm trying to understand why. So I can be more helpful when these moments happen."

The old man pursed his lips, making the deep grooves around his mouth temporarily disappear. "What issues in particular? I haven't been his doctor in a number of years, but I still can't discuss his medical history with you. Not without his permission."

Abby nodded. "Of course. I really only have one question. About his wife, Wanda. He seems to hate any mention of her, and I feel a little uncomfortable discussing it with Maddie."

"Wanda? Wanda died years ago. Let me think, it must have been in the early or mid eighties."

"Would you mind telling me how she died?"

He looked at her, then seemed to make a decision. "I can't see any reason why it would matter now." While he thought, he ran his hand over his large forehead and back over his head, smoothing the already flattened strands of white hair. "She had cancer. Unnecessary, really. Cervical cancer, which could have been avoided if she'd taken better care of herself."

"How do you mean?"

"It's caused by a virus, you should know that." He frowned at Abby. "Do you have regular check-ups?"

Abby tried to remember the last time she'd been to a gynecologist. "Yes, of course," she said. She'd make an appointment soon, she promised herself.

"Well, do it," he said, as if he could read her mind. "They even have a vaccine now, so you have no excuse. Is that all you wanted to know?"

Abby thought. "Did she die at home?"

"Yes, she died in her own bed."

"He waited too long before bringing her in?"

"Not on purpose. It was a sticky situation. She refused any help. I tried to treat her at home, and she saw me for a while. But by the end she refused to see me, refused even to talk to me on the phone. Poor man. He went through a lot."

"He seems so angry at her. Still."

With a sigh, Jaspers said: "Wanda Smith had a serious drinking problem during the last years of her life. I wanted to put her someplace where she could be treated, but Norman wouldn't allow it."

"Why is that?"

"I think he believed with his help and support, she could conquer it." Dr. Jaspers looked uncomfortable. "And she was difficult."

"Was it the cancer that actually killed her?"

The doctor rubbed his jaw. His bloodhound eyes looked sadly at her. "In the end, it was pneumonia, not cancer, that killed her. The woman was in terrible shape, physically."

"From the drinking?"

"That was part of it, no question. And she was malnourished—thin as a rail. I think she'd been starving herself."

Abby walked down the hallway. Starved herself to death? Did she go on a hunger strike? Or had it been a slow suicide? If so, why? Had Norman really tried to help her, or had he fooled Morris Jaspers?

She thought of Wanda, refusing medical treatment. Was it so she could be near Norman? Was that real love? Abby had no idea. She glanced to her left, into the dining room. The three women were still sitting there. She raised a hand and waved at them. They waved back, and watched her till she walked out the front door.

CHAPTER FOURTEEN

That night the women's bathroom flooded. Everything was running smoothly until a customer came upstairs, found Dulcie, and whispered to her that the downstairs floor was wet. The cause seemed to be some kind of overflow in the ladies' toilet.

Dulcie did her best to appear calm. "Oh, thank you. I'm sure it's nothing. We'll take care of it."

Dulcie found Abby in the prep kitchen, scooping ice cream. "Abby, the women's toilet is flooded, I need you."

Abby put the scoop back into its holder and closed the chest freezer. She thought for a moment. "Okay. Fritz," she said, turning to the dishwasher across the room, "you get the bucket and mop. I'll go downstairs and start with the plunger. Becca and Henry can cover the floor and—"

"Hold up," interrupted Fritz. "Dulcie, I'll handle this, okay?"

Dulcie smiled sweetly. "Don't worry, Abby can—"

He turned to her, and Abby was shocked to hear a sharp edge in his voice when he spoke to her friend. "I said, I'll handle it." And then, when he caught Abby staring at him, he added, "You should be thanking me. You lovely ladies get to keep going, business as usual."

"Wonderful, Fritz," Dulcie said, glancing quickly at Abby.

But Abby ignored him. She went downstairs to assess the damage. Sure enough, the floor was wet and there was an unpleasant smell, not the kind you want floating up into your diners' noses. Standing in the doorway, she could see that the toilet was backed up and dirty water was flowing over the top of the bowl. She took hold of the plunger.

Fritz arrived, with a clang of the metal pail. "Hey, get off your high horse, Abby," he said. He looked at her. "What are you, one of these women who don't need men for anything? Here, give it to me." He held out his hand for the plunger.

She held it away from him. "Why'd you talk to Dulcie like that?"

"Like what? What're you talking about?"

"You know what I mean."

"You've hated me from the day I walked in, haven't you?" he said. "Why? What did I ever do to you?"

Abby felt a twinge of guilt. She hadn't liked him. And maybe she'd imagined the meanness in his voice when he spoke to Dulcie. With a shrug, she handed him the plunger.

Once he had it in his hand, however, he deliberately rubbed it against her leg.

"What're you doing!" she said, jumping out of the way.

He laughed and, holding the plunger with both hands, started working the toilet. The water slopped over the edge.

"Slow down," Abby said, "you're making a mess."

"Shut up. When I need your opinion, I'll ask for it," he said, breathing hard.

"I've done this before," Abby said. "There's something stuck. You're going to have to reach in there," she added with a certain amount of pleasure.

With a hiss of irritation, Fritz put on one of his dishwashing gloves that was tucked into his waistband and reached in. He felt around.

"Bingo," he said as he pulled out a black pen. In was a cheap Bic. The wait staff used black Bic pens, taken from a supply box under the cash register. It would be easy for one to fall out of the short black aprons they wore tied around their waists.

Immediately, the toilet gave a satisfied belch and started to drain, the water level steadily sinking. Fritz held up the pen, flicking it around so droplets of the dirty water flew at Abby.

"You fucker!" she snapped, wiping off her arm.

Dulcie walked in just in time to hear her. "Abby!" she said, shocked.

Fritz shook his head in mock sadness. "Nothing I do makes Abby happy. But, look, I found the problem, darlin'."

With a shiver of disgust, Abby washed her arm in the sink before going upstairs.

When Fritz reappeared, he pointedly ignored her and went back to work. A few minutes later, Abby noticed him take Dulcie aside and whisper to her. Dulcie nodded as he spoke, a frown creating a crease between her eyebrows.

She called Abby over. "I need to find out who's responsible. I want everyone in here for a minute."

"Dulcie," Abby protested, "no one did it on purpose—"

"I never said they did, but I have to deal with this."

Abby shot a look at Fritz, who'd gone back to his dishes. "His idea, right?"

Dulcie took Abby's wrist and pulled her to the staircase landing, out of earshot. "No, it was mine. I'm the boss, this is my restaurant. I want to know who dropped a pen into the damned toilet."

"Fine," Abby yanked her wrist out of Dulcie's grip. She went slamming through the swing door. She collected the other two waitresses and brought them back to Dulcie.

"Okay, we're here. Now what?"

Dulcie, looking defiant, said: "I'm sorry, but I need to see if everyone has the pens they started the shift with."

Becca stuck her hands into her short black apron, feeling around beneath the checks. She pulled out two. "Yup. This is all I had. Can I go now?"

Dulcie nodded. "Thanks."

Cat pulled out three. "I like to have three. I forget them at people's tables and they take them home."

Dulcie nodded again, and Becca went out through the swing door. Dulcie turned to Abby. "What about you? How many did you start with?"

"Christ, I can't believe this, Dulcie. Let me see—I started with two and I have two left, okay?" Abby reached in her apron with both hands, grabbed one pen, then felt around for the second one. Nothing. She squeezed her remaining blank checks in case it was nestled amongst them. No pen. She looked up at Dulcie and then shot a look at Fritz. He was watching her. Smiling, the bastard.

Abby shrugged and said to Dulcie. "I guess it was me. What're you going to do, dock my pay? Down from three bucks to two-fifty?"

Dulcie frowned at her tone. "I just want you to be more careful, that's all."

Abby nodded. "I will, trust me. I'll be much more careful." She looked over at Fritz. "But you should be careful, too, Dulcie." She meant to give an ominous ring to her voice, but it came out sounding merely petty. She saw Fritz's smug grin widen.

Chapter Fifteen

The next morning, Abby was on the road by eight-thirty. In Hudson, she stopped at a flat, ugly building on the upper end of Warren Street, which turned out to be the Social Security office. The department she was looking for, Social Services, had moved out of the building a number of years before.

The elderly security guard gave her a copy of a hand-drawn map. "I'm new here. But this should do it," he said to her in a kindly voice.

Back in her car, she followed the map, crossed the railroad tracks and drove out of the old part of town. Eventually she found the long, lonely driveway that circled up through a stand of trees, into a field. The building was a squat, dirty yellow structure, the large parking area spreading to one side. She understood why they had moved to a large empty field—it was a sea of cars. Looking for somewhere to park, Abby drove past rows of spaces reserved for city officials and employees, their claims staked with large aggressive signs. Obviously, this was not an organization that needed to seduce and win over its customer base.

Finally, she found an empty space and pulled in next to a battered, dark green sedan. The rust on the Bronco was around the wheel wells and the edges of the body, but the rust on the green sedan was in patches, like spreading skin lesions. Abby liked her rust better.

A young woman was trying to shut the driver's door. The locking mechanism seemed to have seized up and each time she slammed it, it bounced back out with equal force. She was dressed in a skirt over leggings, heavy black lace-up boots, and a turtleneck sweater. Her black hair was streaked with premature gray and tied back in a pink ribbon.

Abby watched her for a few slams, and then went to the back of her Bronco and pulled out a can of WD-40. "Here, try this," she suggested, holding it out to the woman before she could bounce the door on its hinges one more time.

She looked at the can and then at Abby. "Awesome."

"Squirt it on, let it sit, then try jiggling the handle. It usually does the trick."

"Thanks. I should have some of my own, with this junker."

"I don't go anywhere without it. When you're done," Abby added, "just put it in the back there. I always leave it unlocked."

She glanced back as she headed to the main entrance of the DSS. The woman was knowledgeably attaching the tiny straw to top of the dispenser. Abby wondered what she was there for. She watched the woman lean down and spray the oil into the lock of the car. Abby pulled the door open and went inside.

The inside matched the outside of the building, the same dingy yellow. It was functional and shabby, like a waiting room in a third world airport. At least half of the plastic seats were taken, and to Abby's left was a glass-fronted reception booth. A tiny, ancient African-American woman stood in front of one window, her chin barely past the height of the counter. A robust, rosy-cheeked young white woman, about seven months pregnant, stood with her elbows on the counter at the other window.

Abby wondered how long she'd have to wait. The woman at the window told the elderly black lady to take a seat and promised that someone would call her name. She nodded, turned away from the window and walked slowly to one of the chairs.

"Yes?" asked the woman behind the window, summoning Abby.

Abby stepped up to the glass. "I am looking for information from an old file."

"What kind of a file?" the clerk asked, an edge of impatience to her voice.

"Two girls who were put into foster care about thirty years ago."

"And you're one of the girls," she said, as if Abby were trying to hide the truth.

"No, no, I'm a friend," she explained.

The woman shook her head. "We can't give out information about one of our placements. That's confidential."

Abby nodded. "Okay, if I come back with a woman who was taken from her mother and put in foster care when she was a girl, and she wants to see her file, will you show it to her?"

The clerk shrugged her shoulders. "It depends. She can put in a request, but there are no guarantees. Depends on the wishes of the biological parents, the age of the child when she was put in care, and so on. It's our job to protect the children. Come back with the woman, and we'll see."

Abby nodded. "Thanks."

She turned to go. The pregnant girl was standing by the door, talking to a man in a leather jacket who was holding two small children. She took the youngest from him and hitched him on her hip. She started whispering to him as she bounced him up and down. The little boy watched Abby as she left, his chin resting on his mother's shoulder.

When Abby got out to her car, the oil can was neatly replaced in the box in the back of her Bronco, and the door of the neighboring sedan was neatly closed, as if it had never given its owner any problems.

Abby drove north out of Hudson. Outside Bantam, she turned east toward Spencerville. At the Merlots' crisp white house she pulled up behind Germaine's dented car.

She rang the doorbell.

When she opened the door, Germaine had a mug in her hand and was wearing a robe. Fluffy slippers, reminiscent of the defunct mules, peeked out from under the hem. "Well, hello there, Abby," she said happily. "Come on in!"

"No, I just stopped for a second. I just wanted to tell you that we, that you and I," she said, "have to go down to Hudson together. Tuesday morning if you're not doing anything."

"Oh, goody, I'm free. Shopping? Lunch?"

"No, sorry. No shopping. No lunch. We're going to the Department of Social Services."

Germaine frowned. "Why? I don't want to go there."

"Because," Abby said, "I can't do it without you."

"Do what?"

"Access your adoption file."

"What're you talking about? Why do we need to do that? I don't want to."

"You do, you really do."

Germaine stepped outside and closed the door behind her. She looked unhappy. "No, I don't."

"Come on, Germaine. Wouldn't you like to know why your mother gave you up to Norman and Wanda, two people who had never taken in kids before? Personally, I don't think they were being civic-minded, whatever Athena wants to believe. Most people who want to give back, they donate to the Red Cross, their church, or an animal shelter. They don't take on two little girls they don't know."

"Why not?" Germaine said. "Those were different times. People didn't make such a big deal about it then, not like they do now. And, you know, we saw our mother quite a bit, at least at first."

Abby looked hard at her. "You saw your mother? That's not what you said. You said you never saw her again after you went to live with the Smiths."

"Did I? I don't remember. Maybe I exaggerated. I mean, I didn't see her often, or for very long, but she did come by a few times."

"Why would you lie about that?"

"It made you feel sorry for me, didn't it?"

"You are a bullshitter."

Germaine gave a chortle of laughter, and took a sip from her mug.

"Look," Abby continued, letting that thread go, "you should be curious about the people who took you under their roof. About your mother."

Germaine shrugged. "Water under the bridge. What good is it going to do me? To dig up all that old stuff? And why do you care?"

Abby wanted to take her by the ear and twist hard. "You're the one who wanted me to believe that Norman killed your mother. Twenty years later, it's definitely water under the bridge—but now *I'm* interested. Something happened then, and I want to know what it was. It's got to do with Wanda. So I want to know why she and Norman took you in."

"For god's sake, Abby! Is it so damn hard to believe they did it out of the goodness of their hearts?" Germaine snapped.

Abby looked at her. "Yes, it is. And you were the one who got Athena all bent out of shape by saying they did it because Norman was really your biological father."

Germaine sighed impatiently. "I said that because I knew it would upset her, that's all. Okay, I'll go to Hudson with you. Christ. But you'll see, there's not going to be anything there."

She started walking back to the house. "Shit," she said over her shoulder, "now you've taken all the fun out of the day for me."

Abby felt murderous. "Hey, you're the one accusing an old man of murder, to his face even, and now when the time comes to do anything about it, you get cold feet." She started walking to her car. "I'll pick you up Tuesday at nine. Right here."

Germaine turned and shouted back at her: "No, I'll need coffee to go. Nine-thirty. At Victor's."

CHAPTER SIXTEEN

Tuesday morning was cool and bright. She picked Germaine up in front of the café and had to listen to her complain about the Bronco's shocks for the next half hour. When they finally made the turn into the long, winding driveway to the Department of Social Services, Germaine became silent.

The yellow building came into view, and Abby heard her whimper, "What *is* this horrible place! I don't want to go in there, Abby."

"Come on, it's not as bad as it seems, really. It's just ugly, that's all."

When they finally found a parking place in the sprawling lot, Germaine climbed out of the truck and groaned as she rubbed the small of her back and twisted her spine from side to side.

Two men were standing outside the front door, smoking, talking intensely. They both had long, greasy hair, and their clothing was layered and threadbare. It was hard to tell their age. One had a full beard, and the other a face that hadn't been shaved in a good while.

As Abby and Germaine walked toward them, Germaine grabbed Abby's hand nervously.

Before they reached the door, the bearded man reached for the handle and pulled the door open. He held it for the two women, without pausing in his conversation or breaking eye contact with his companion.

"Thank you," Germaine said in surprise, standing in the cloud of smoke, but the men didn't respond.

Behind the counter, Abby saw that the same clerk she had dealt with on her first visit.

Standing behind the second window was another woman. She looked familiar, and then Abby remembered. She had lent her the can of WD-40 the week before. The woman with the rusted green sedan. She was scribbling on a piece of paper, her expression serious.

Abby grabbed Germaine's arm and walked quickly over to the second window.

"What can I do for you?" Rusted Sedan said, looking at her wearily, as if she'd much rather not know.

"Hi. Ever get your car door fixed?" Abby said.

The young woman looked at her sharply, as if seeing her for the first time. Abby watched recognition dawn. "Oh, sure, you're the one who gave me the oil! Hey, thanks."

Abby shrugged in her friendliest way. "Happy to help."

"You know, I haven't had any problems since. I think the lock was just hungry, you know?"

Abby laughed. "I do. I know well. Just feed it once in a while, and it keeps going for miles."

"I'm Reesa, by the way," the young woman said.

"I'm Abby, and this is Germaine," Abby said, pulling Germaine up to the counter.

Still smiling, the woman put her hands flat on the counter. "So, how can I help you?" she said, sounding as if she really meant it.

"Well," Abby began, leaning her elbows on the counter, "I came in a few days ago, trying to look into an old case file. I was told, quite rightly, that you can't discuss old files with me, but that if someone who was involved with the case came in, you could look into it."

The woman nodded. "Okay. What do you mean by, 'involved with the case'?"

Germaine spoke up. "It's me. I was put in foster care when I was ten. With my little sister. I'd like to see the file."

Reesa nodded, slowly. "I'll need to take some information. Put in a request." She looked Germaine over, assessing her age and the relative age of the files. "It may take a while to locate."

"Not so, I'm sure you'll be fast," Germaine said sweetly, tapping three red-painted fingernails of her right hand on the desk, in unison. Her thumb and pinkie remained in the air, undecided.

Abby put a hand over the tapping fingers.

"Great," said Reesa. "Let's start the paperwork." She walked over to a filing cabinet against a wall, and pulled out a thick form from one of the drawers.

"Fine." Germaine tossed her hair over her shoulder. "What do you need to know? Name, rank, and serial number, I assume."

Reesa looked at her. "Name, for a start."

"Germaine LeClair. Actually," and she shot an embarrassed look at Abby, "it's probably under Gubinek."

"What?" Abby said, unable to contain herself.

Germaine lowered her voice. "You are not allowed to repeat it. That was Bridget's name. We were Gubinek until Norman adopted us, then we became Smith." Turning back to the woman behind the desk, she added, "My sister was Athena Gubinek. She's a musician now, Athena Smith. Do you think she'd have had any kind of a career if she'd called herself Athena Gubinek?"

"It makes no never mind to me," said Reesa, writing. "You could call yourself Queen Elizabeth for all I care."

"I thought about it, believe me," muttered Germaine.

"Okay. Your mother's name?"

"Bridget Gubinek."

"Father?"

"Gubinek, I assume. But I have no idea what his first name was. None."

"Do you know when you were placed in foster care?"

"I was ten. It was 1974."

"Two years before the Bicentennial," the woman said with a smile, as she wrote.

"Whoopee," Germaine said under her breath.

Reesa looked up from the paper, her expression encouraging. "Do you by any chance know the date?"

Germaine shook her head. "No."

Abby suddenly remembered something Athena had said. "It was Maddie's birthday, right? She thought you were her presents."

Germaine looked at her, nodding slowly. To Abby's dismay, her eyes filled with tears. "That's right. Her birthday's in February. The fifteenth. It was the fifteenth of February, 1974."

Germaine was quiet for much of the drive home, limiting her complaints to grunts when the shocks bounced them too hard. Reesa had promised to call Germaine as soon as her file was located. Everything from the mid-seventies was still in paper files, none of it computerized, so she warned them it might take some time to unearth. And when she found it, she would need to get approval to let Germaine look at some or any part of it. It varied from case to case.

"How did you decide on the name LeClair?" Abby asked as they drove into Bantam.

"After Wanda died I decided I needed to make a break, legally. I would have gone back to Gubinek, but it's so damn depressing and ugly. And LeClair seemed perfect. It would have been a much better name for us. Just think—Bridget, Athena, and Germaine LeClair. The LeClair women. Compare that to, what, the Gubinek Gals? Ugh."

"Did LeClair have any special meaning?"

"To me it did," she said, sounding embarrassed. "But you can't tell anyone. I bought a slip about that time, I think it was at Macy's. Yes, it was Macy's. Ivory silk, and slinky! Oh, I loved that slip, I felt like a movie star in it."

Abby didn't see it coming. "So?"

"The label said *Lingerie by LeClair.*"

"Are you serious? You named yourself after *underwear?*"

"Why not?" Germaine snapped. "Would it make more sense to you if I'd lasted a month in some shitty little marriage to a guy named LeClair?"

CHAPTER SEVENTEEN

Athena and I want to see Norman." It was a quiet midweek evening, and Abby was bartending. Germaine was sitting across from her, leaning on the bar, nursing her usual Stoli and tonic.

"You mean, another armed midnight raid?"

"No, this time I want to do it right. Maybe we could take him out to dinner or something, or go over for tea. What do you think?"

Abby was curious. "Since when are you and Athena all buddy-buddy?"

"Oh, we're fine, we've talked. Maybe I got a little carried away. So? What d'you think?"

The mystery of sisters, Abby thought. "It's not my show, Germaine. Call Maddie—she's in charge. Just don't try to do it behind her back."

Germaine looked at her thoughtfully. "That's a good idea. It's time to be a grown-up, right?'

"Yup."

"That's why I have a huge favor to ask you," Germaine said, after a pause.

"No," Abby answered, flatly.

"How can you say that? You don't know what I want!"

"I don't, but I bet it's something I don't want to do."

"It's nothing big, I swear."

"You said it was huge."

"Please, Abby."

"Christ. Okay, what?"

"Will you ask Maddie? If Athena and I can take Norman out to dinner?"

"No. Absolutely not." Abby went to the wall phone by the bar, picked up the receiver and dialed.

Maddie picked it up on the first ring. "Hello?" She sounded hoarse, as if she'd been sleeping.

"Hi, Maddie, it's Abby. Is this a good time?"

When Germaine heard Maddie's name, she started making shaking her head emphatically, and cutting both her hands sideways through the air, so they crossed each other. All she needed was earmuffs, and she could get a job directing airplane traffic.

Maddie cleared her throat. "Let me get a glass of water."

Abby gave Germaine a nasty smile. Germaine slumped down.

"Much better," Maddie said when she got back. She sounded more alert. "I'm listening."

"Good. We have to talk about your dad's show."

Germaine relaxed visibly.

"You're right." Maddie let out a slow breath. "Hey, how did the idea of a show come up in the first place?" Abby thought she heard a hint of suspicion in her voice.

"It's my fault, I guess. I'd been looking through a catalog of one he had way back when, and—"

"And that set him off." Maddie sounded resigned.

"I guess I encouraged him. I mean, I thought it might be fun for him if he had something small, you know, just to show the stuff he's working on now. But then it escalated. He wants to revive his big pieces, use the Metal Building."

"God."

"I'm sorry. Maybe he'll forget all about it."

"Let's hope."

"I won't mention it. But I just wanted you to know."

"Okay. Thanks. Otherwise, everything's okay?"

"Yup, everything's fine. Oh, just one more thing."

Germaine sat up nervously.

"Someone here wants to talk to you." Without waiting for an answer, Abby thrust the phone at Germaine, who threw her hands back as if the receiver were of molten lava. Abby shook her head at her in disgust and brought the receiver back to her own ear.

"Abby? What's going on?" Maddie asked.

"As you know, your sister Germaine is in town." Abby half expected her to ask: "Who?" But there was silence from the other end.

"Maddie?"

"I heard you. What does she want?"

Abby felt a surge of irritation. How had she gotten herself involved with this family? What happened to, "Great, how's she doing, that long lost sister of mine?"

"I don't know. But I thought you might like to talk to her. Here she is." And without waiting for a response, she grabbed Germaine's hand and forced the receiver into it.

Germaine, knowing she was beaten, brought it slowly to her face. "Hello? Maddie?"

Abby began meticulously polishing one end of the bar as she listened to the stilted conversation between the sisters. They sounded like people who barely knew each other. It didn't take Germaine long to get to the point.

"Athena and I would both like to see him, but we didn't want to just show up,"—here she shot Abby a look—"without running it by you. Actually, we thought it might be fun to take him out to dinner. Maybe the Inn-Between, on a night that Abby's working."

Abby heard Maddie's voice, and watched as Germaine nodded obediently. "That would be fine, if you'd prefer it. Sure, sure." Pause. "I'll tell Athena. Perfect. Sure, here's Abby."

She gave Abby back the receiver.

"Hey, Maddie," Abby said.

"That was a surprise."

"I think Norman would enjoy it," Abby said, though she wasn't at all convinced of it.

"Maybe. I just don't want him getting upset."

"Why would he get upset?" Abby was curious.

"Wouldn't you, if some complete stranger claimed to be your daughter?"

"But—"

"He won't remember either of them, and it'll confuse him."

"I'll help. We'll plan it properly."

"Just let me know when it's happening, okay?"

"Sure."

"Thanks. Is that it?"

"Yes, it is."

"Goodnight, then." And she hung up.

Abby stared at the phone and then at Germaine. What had happened to make Maddie so cold? She had hardly sounded like herself. She put the receiver on the hook. "You know, I went to see Dr. Jaspers today."

"Who's—oh, wasn't he Norman's doctor?"

"Yup. And Wanda's."

"Oh. Is he still practicing?"

"No," Abby answered. "But I wanted to talk to him."

Germaine's stared hard at her. "So? What did Norman do to her?"

Abby watched Germaine. "Well, he doesn't accuse Norman of killing her."

"He's just defending him."

"That's not the impression I got. He believes she killed herself. Jaspers says she refused to get treatment."

Germaine shook her head in disgust. "That's a lie."

"Why do you say that?"

"Because Wanda loved us, she loved Norman. She wouldn't have tried to hurt herself. She didn't want to leave us."

"How would you know? You weren't even there. Did you know she was an alcoholic?"

Germaine sat up angrily. "That's not true!"

Abby was surprised at her vehemence, and though she thought Germaine was being naïve, she didn't want to argue with her. She was beginning to get a picture of Wanda's death; it wasn't pretty, but it didn't sound as if it had been Norman's fault.

The dinner out with Norman might be a good idea. If Germaine actually spent some time with him, she might see him for what he really was: a tired and confused old man. And if she understood how uncertain his memory was, she might even forgive him. She watched as Germaine took another long swallow from her glass. Somehow, it all sounded too good to be true.

CHAPTER EIGHTEEN

The nights were getting longer, encroaching on the cool days. Germaine's plan for a cozy dinner for three with Athena and Norman was blown out of the water the day after the phone call. Maddie called Abby, and said she'd thought more about it. Norman, she'd decided, would be confused and unhappy without familiar faces. So she and Paul would be joining the group. And as soon as Athena found out that Paul and Maddie were coming, she insisted that Cal be included. She wanted him to get to know his grandfather, and she knew the old man would feel the same way. Anyway, why should her son miss all the fun? That was how she put it, the fun. Abby was reminded of the "jocular" amanuensis.

The reservation for six, under the name of Smith, was set for the first Sunday night in October. Fall Sunday dinners were usually quiet at the Inn-Between, so Norman wouldn't have to put up with too much noise and confusion.

Germaine and Athena had permission to pick him up, as originally planned, though Maddie insisted she would be at the house to see him off. While she waited for the convoy to arrive, Abby carefully set the best table in her section. She made sure it didn't wobble, and she found a little vase of silk flowers on a shelf in the office, which she placed in the middle of the table.

The departure must have gone smoothly, because the Miata arrived only a few minutes after six-thirty, with Athena following behind in her own car. Abby was surprised to see Norman sitting in the front seat of the small car, looking like a slightly malignant troll; he must have chosen it over Athena's more sedate ride.

Together, the sisters helped him out of the low seat and walked him up the steps of the restaurant.

Germaine was obviously nervous. "I need you to suggest food to him, okay, something that you think he might like," she whispered to Abby, after she'd helped her father take off his overcoat.

Abby nodded. "I think he'd like the meatloaf. It's old fashioned and comes with mashed potatoes," she reassured her.

Cal arrived next. He wore jeans and a sweatshirt. His long hair was in a bun. Abby hoped the hairdo wouldn't confuse Norman, making him think his grandson was a young woman. Cal looked as uncomfortable as if he were in a tuxedo.

Maddie and Paul came in last. Not having seen each other for so long, they all hugged and said polite things to each other. Abby watched, interested. Though the hostility was put away, their interactions were stiff and forced. Paul embarrassed Cal by calling him "the secret nephew" and wanting to sit next to him; Cal looked anxiously at his mother, hoping she would save him, but Athena missed it—she was too focused on Norman. She smiled nervously when Maddie graciously insisted that the two sisters sit on either side of Norman, saying: "I see him all the time. He'll probably be glad for a change."

Everything started well. The ordering of food and wine went smoothly enough. Norman seemed to accept without question that Abby, his amanuensis, was waiting on him. She explained the menu to him and, with her help, he decided on the meatloaf.

The restaurant was quiet, so she was able to keep an eye on the table. The group settled quickly into its various dynamics. Germaine was working as hard as she could to please and entertain the old man. She agreed with everything he said and laughed hard at anything that seemed light-hearted. Which wasn't much. Athena wore an anxious, generic smile that only slipped a few times. Paul focused on his food and drink, ordering refills whenever he ran the risk of getting low on either bread and butter or martinis. Maddie sipped her gin and tonic and watched her sisters. She seemed to have little to say.

Cal reached for the crayons as soon as he sat down, and started drawing a multicolored octopuslike creature, with tentacles that stretched to the center of the table. He stayed focused and bent over his work, looking up politely only when called on. Occasionally, Paul would lean over and say something to him in a low voice and follow it with a laugh. Abby guessed these comments were awkward attempts at small talk. They only managed to make Cal look uncomfortable.

"Cal's a wonderful and talented musician," Athena said brightly to Norman. Her face looked stretched thin with tension.

Norman looked at Athena in confusion. He didn't seem to know who she was talking about. She gestured to her son. Norman's pale blue eyes turned to the young man. He watched him draw. "Do they mind when you paint on the table?"

Cal answered with a shrug. "They like it okay, I guess. They gave us crayons."

Norman nodded. "I painted a mural, once, you know. I never had a chance to finish it."

A silence fell on the table. Abby, who was clearing a nearby table, worked even more slowly so she could hear.

"What happened to it?"

Norman looked at the young man as if he didn't really understand the question. "I have the drawings for it. I am going to continue the work where I left off."

"That's a good idea," Athena chimed in, trying to show support.

He ignored her. "She," he said, pointing a large finger at Abby, who was still clearing up the next table, "is going to go through my papers and find the drawings for the mural." It was as if he knew she was listening in.

Abby played along. After all, she *had* been eavesdropping. "Good idea. I'll find them next time I'm in." She didn't want to say that she'd already given them to Norman.

"Where are they?" asked Cal.

"How should I know?" he answered, making a dismissive gesture with one hand. "They're archived somewhere. Wanda will know. She put them away. Taking care of things like that is Wanda's job."

Just then, a customer at one of Abby's other tables knocked a full glass of wine onto his own lap. There were a few moments of jumping up, mopping, and clearing, and Abby went to get fresh napkins and paper towels.

When everything was settled and the damp customer had a new glass of wine and clean table linens, she glanced over at the Smith table.

At first she thought Norman was holding Germaine's hand, and she was touched. But Germaine's face told a different story. She looked on the verge of tears. Maddie sat with a hand shielding her closed eyes, simultaneously rubbing her temples with her thumb on one side, and her middle finger on the other.

Abby hurried over. Norman's food was unfinished, and she now realized he was holding Germaine's wrist not affectionately but gripping it with a white-knuckled fist. Germaine was twisting her arm, trying to break loose.

"Norman, Norman, hello, how was your meal?" Abby asked brightly, trying to divert his attention.

"I insist on going home," Norman said loudly. Germaine broke free of his grip, and started rubbing her wrist.

"Would you like to see the dessert menu, Norman? Anyone? How about you, Maddie?" Abby continued, noticing the red marks that encircled Germaine's forearm.

"No thanks, Abby. I think we're done," Maddie answered, a resigned tone to her voice.

Norman said, his voice now sharp with anger: "I am going home. Who is driving me home?"

"Norman, what's wrong?" Abby asked, dropping any pretense of normality. "Is everything okay?"

"No, it is not." His expression was fierce. "This woman, this armed intruder, was prying into my past, into my private life."

"Norman," Germaine said, tears in her eyes, "I'm your daughter, I wasn't prying! I was asking about Wanda, she was a mother to me!"

"Be that as it may, her death is no business of yours!"

The nearby diners fell silent.

But Germaine didn't notice. In her mind, she and Norman were the only people in the room. "Why not? I cared about her, and no one even told me when she died, no one even sent me a fucking postcard!"

"How dare you! How dare you speak that way to me!" Norman threw his napkin down on his plate of food and, in a motion that twenty years before would have been swift and dramatic, slowly, tremblingly, rose to his feet. His chair tipped back and fell with a crash on the wooden floor. For a moment, the old man teetered there and Abby was afraid he would follow it over.

She grabbed his elbow to give him support. "Let me get your cane, Norman," she said, her voice as calm as she could make it.

Suddenly, all the anger seemed to ebb out of his body. He said, in a voice now soft and frail: "I need to go home, I don't know why I came here."

"Of course, we'll get you home. Germaine, would you get Norman his coat?"

"Yes, of course," she said.

Everyone else at the table stood up. Maddie heaved a sigh. "Norman, Paul and I'll drive you home, okay?"

Germaine brought his coat. "Can I take you home?" He allowed her to help him into it, but said coldly: "No, I want Maddie."

Germaine's expression showed her old familiar resentment. "Fine."

"Paul," Maddie said, "will you walk Norman outside? I'm just going to settle up with Abby, and I'll be right out."

Paul nodded obediently and offered his arm to his father-in-law. Together they made their way slowly to the door.

"What happened?" Abby asked Maddie.

"I don't really know. He's so unpredictable. It could have been something she said, but maybe not." She turned to her sister. "But I don't think you should see him anymore, Germaine," she added. "It isn't good for him."

Germaine sat back down at the table with Athena and Cal. Maddie followed Abby to the cash register and stood next to her, waiting for the bill.

"She means well, I'm positive," Abby said, glancing at her.

"You think so?" was Maddie's answer, as she handed Abby a credit card. "I don't know. Maybe. But it's my job to protect him."

She signed quickly and was gone.

At the table, Germaine was crying. Athena was patting her hand, and the octopus Cal had been drawing on the butcher paper was spreading to the place next to them, around the base of Paul's empty martini glass.

CHAPTER NINETEEN

Abby went home early and was asleep by midnight. She woke to a scraping at her window; the dogs heard it the same second she did and bounded up in a frenzy of barking. Abby, confused with sleep, her heart racing, tried to avoid their scrabbling claws. They leaped off the bed and threw themselves at the wall below the dark glass of the window. Abby slid out of bed and groped around for the flashlight she kept on her dresser. Without turning on any interior lights, she stood to one side of the window and shone the light through the pane. It was hard to see past the reflection, but if she concentrated she could follow the strong beam as it cut through the darkness outside the trailer.

Nothing.

Suddenly, with a bang, a white hand slapped against the dark glass. Abby jumped, her insides turning to water. It was a ghostly starfish stuck to the pane, so close she could see the lines on the palm. She jerked back, and the hand disappeared.

A second later the dogs, knowing something she didn't, galloped out of the bedroom. She heard them at the front door. There was a crash. Clutching the flashlight, Abby walked softly after them. Was her front door open? Had someone just broken in? But the door was closed, and on quick inspection, the windows were the way she had left them.

"Rick, Delilah, shut up!" she said, trying to hear over the cacophony of their barks and growls. For a moment they obeyed her, and in that space Abby heard a voice:

"Come *on,* let me in!"

The dogs, unconvinced, renewed their racket with even more energy. Abby walked cautiously to the front door, pushing them out of the way.

"Who is it?" she called, putting her mouth close to the frame.

"Let me in, Abby, it's me, Germaine!" the voice called out plaintively.

Abby leaned her head against the wall, waiting for her heart to slow down. She was going to kill this woman.

She flipped the switch that turned on the outside light and looked out the peephole. There was Germaine, in her black fur coat. Through the fish-eye lens, she looked like a night creature from Madagascar, her eyes wide and slightly buggy in the harsh, overhead light.

Abby watched her mouth move, and heard her words.

"I had such a hard time finding your house. I tried calling you, but there's no service around here. And then I tripped."

Abby kept watching Germaine, while she fidgeted and stamped her feet. She wanted to leave the door locked and go back to bed, but she knew she couldn't. Germaine would never go away. Abby unlocked the door.

"Thanks," Germaine said as she walked in. She noticed Abby's T-shirt and underwear. "You're undressed!"

Germaine, on the other hand, was wearing the same maroon dress she'd had on at dinner.

"It's bedtime, I was sleeping, Germaine. How did you find me?"

"It wasn't easy, believe me. I had to call Dulcie, and then I stopped at that farmhouse at the bottom of the hill. It took them forever to come to the door."

Abby thought of her tenants, who got up with the sun. "What are you doing here? Is there something wrong?"

Germaine shrugged carelessly. "I'm okay."

"Have you been home at all tonight?"

"No, not yet. It's only one A.M., for heaven's sake," she said dismissively.

"What have you been doing?" Abby sat heavily on the edge of her desk chair. The seat was cold on her bare skin.

"Well, first, I had a drink at the bar with Athena and Cal."

"That's good." Abby yawned.

"It was a blast, as you can imagine. Athena was really upset, more than me, in fact."

"I hope Cal drove her home."

"No, they had separate cars. But she was okay to drive." Germaine looked curiously around the small living room. "This is so familiar. I used to live in a place just like this, with my mother and sister."

Right, Abby thought. It's the middle of the night and she's going to go sentimental on me. She had had enough. "You need to go home, Germaine. It's late."

"I just wanted a little company, that's all. That was a shitty family reunion. You saw. So I was hoping I could, you know, hang out here for a little while."

She looked at Abby, her expression a mix of defiance and need, a combination that seemed to curdle on contact, making her look indifferent.

Abby simply had no energy for dissecting her visitor's feelings. "Listen, if you want, you can spend the night here. The love seat unfolds. I've just got to get back to bed, okay? So try to sleep yourself, and we'll talk in the morning, I swear."

Germaine waved a hand, as if none of it meant much to her. "No, no, I'll go. I just wanted to have a drink and talk it out, you know. I'll be okay."

She turned to the door, and started to leave. She hesitated. Turned back. "He hates me, doesn't he? I just wish I knew why."

Abby sighed. "You mean Norman?"

Germaine nodded.

"You can't force him to tell you things he can't remember. Or to feel things that have, I don't know, evaporated. Now go home, get some sleep. Think about the future, to hell with the past. Anyway, I thought you hated him."

"Yeah. I need to remember that."

Just as she was shepherding Germaine out, the phone rang.

"What the hell? It's too late," she said, picking up the phone in her little living room area. "Hello?"

"Yes, hello?" said a reedy voice.

"Norman?" She glanced at Germaine, who was watching her with interest. "Is everything all right?"

"There is someone in the house. A thief."

Abby forced herself to think clearly. "Okay Norman, I'm going to hang up and call the police. Stay right where you are. As soon as I've called the police, I'll come over. I'm hanging up now, okay?"

"Hurry," he quavered. And the line went dead.

"Germaine—"

"What's wrong?"

"Where did you just come from?"

"That's none of your business."

"You'd better not have just been at Norman's," Abby said, as she dialed 911.

By the time Abby arrived at the old man's house, a police car was parked in the driveway. Two officers were standing in the doorway, and past them she could see a small, bent outline.

"Norman, is everything all right?" she called out. The policemen turned toward her and watched her walk to the front steps of the house.

"Who's that?" Norman asked. He sounded tired.

"It's Abby," she said and added, reluctantly, "the amanuensis."

"Oh, good. Then we're fine. You may go now, officers." He waved his cane at them.

As the two men came down the stairs, Abby stopped them. "Is everything okay? Did you check the house?"

"Yes, ma'am." The first one, whose name tag she couldn't read in the dark, nodded. "We went through the whole house, and the outbuilding. No sign of intruders. Were you the party that called it in?"

Abby shook her head wearily. "Just me. No party."

The officer looked at her. "I'll need you to answer some questions."

Ten minutes later, Abby watched the police cruiser drive away. The sound of the engine grew fainter, until there was nothing but the chirpings and rustlings of the night around her. Reluctantly, she opened the door and went inside. The hall was dark, but Abby could see a light coming from the kitchen. She found Norman sitting at the wooden table.

"Did those men finally leave? I've been waiting for you. You have to help me find something. It's very important."

"Can't it wait until tomorrow, Norman?" Abby asked. The house felt eerily unfamiliar at night and she wanted to go home.

"It *is* tomorrow, young lady. I don't have time to waste."

He led her to his office and slowly fumbled on the wall until he located the switch that turned on the overhead light. Abby was shocked to see drawers pulled open, files tipped out, stray papers spread on the floor.

"God, what happened here?" she asked.

"We need to find the picture, my picture," said Norman, his voice becoming more agitated as he looked around the room, as if he too were seeing the mess for the first time.

Abby took a deep breath. "Okay, okay," she said, pushing aside files with her foot so that she could pull out one of the chairs. "Here, sit down, Norman."

With seeming relief, he sank down into it and leaned his cane against the desk. He rested both hands on his lap, loosely, the fingers curled, the palms slightly up. His face was contorted with worry.

"Let me tidy up a little, then you can explain what you're looking for," Abby said, as she putting folders on the desk. "I'll figure out where they belong next time I come to work."

When she was done, she sat on the second chair and looked at Norman. "Tell me about the picture."

Slowly, he put his fingertips to his forehead and shut his eyes. The overhead lights cast deep shadows under his strong fingers, creating prison bars on his face. The bare windows were rectangular pools of black night behind him. Abby's tiredness had turned into an acidic buzz of nerves, and she had to force herself to sit still.

"Norman?"

"A picture of Wanda," he said, finally. "That's what I want." He looked up at her. "Can you find it?"

Abby needed to know more. "I'll try. Is it a photograph?"

Norman paused. "No, I think not." He spoke slowly, carefully.

"Okay. Not a photograph, therefore a painting or a drawing. I'm pretty good at that now. Maddie showed me where things are, remember? I had to find the drawings for the mural."

Norman nodded, watching her.

"So, I'm going to guess that, if it's a drawing, we might find it here," and she pointed to the draughtsman's dresser.

"Aha," said Norman.

Abby began looking through the drawers. She tried to remember the years. Maddie said Norman and Wanda had first met after the war, about 1949. The files were well organized, and she went back to where she had found the drawings for the murals, which had been stored in their own file. She picked out the portfolio that was chronologically next in line and opened it on her lap. At the top of the pile of loose drawings was a charcoal of a tiny cottage on a hill. The wind was blowing the branches of a tree that stood about ten feet from the structure. A small stone wall followed the curves of the hill, and encircled about an acre of land around the little house. The view behind the hill was of a flat plain, with distant hills on the horizon. Abby now saw that within the low wall were rows of gravestones, many of them tilted, some cracked. Looking more closely, Abby realized the cottage was a small church.

She passed it to Norman, for the time being forgetting the hour or the darkness blanketing the house. "Look at this, it's wonderful."

He peered at it. "I did this?"

Abby shrugged. "I don't know." She looked at the next sheet of paper, which was turned facedown. Something was penciled on it. She looked closely. In a small, neat script it said:

Wanda, April 16, '49. N. S.

She turned it over.

It was a charcoal nude. The figure was a female, reclining. She was outdoors, because Abby saw grass and what looked like a tree trunk behind her. The model, who seemed young—her breasts were small and pointed and her body slight—was lying with one knee up and the other bent so her thighs were open. Her head was to one side, her face covered by one arm. The other was flung wide. The artist must have been sitting on the ground below her feet, so that his point of view was directly up, between her splayed legs. There was no question as to where the viewer's eye was intended to go.

Abby blushed. She felt a prudish desire to turn the drawing over again. She realized that her feeling stemmed partially from a confused sense that Norman was no longer a man, but a child, and that in some way she had to shield him from adult things. Which was silly, she said to herself, as he was the one who, according to the initials, had drawn the girl in the first place. And if anyone was intruding, it was her. After all, this girl had once been his wife.

"Is this what you were looking for, Norman?" she asked. She stood, holding the open portfolio and placing the drawing on the desk next to him.

Norman turned his chair around. "Aha," he said again, but this time with more energy. Carefully, he lifted the drawing and peered closely at it, as if fascinated. "I wonder who this is," he murmured more to himself than Abby. He looked up. "Did I draw this?" he asked.

"You initialed it in nineteen forty-nine. And the name is Wanda. I bet this was the year you met her," Abby said.

"Could be. I haven't thought of back then for a long time." He put the drawing on the desk, and looked at it, a hand on each side of it. "She was very beautiful and very young, I think, don't you?" With a surprising flash of humor, he added, "Younger than she should have been, no doubt." And he released a long, slow sigh that to Abby's ears sounded full of regret.

"Is that the picture you were looking for?" Abby asked.

Norman looked confused. "Maybe. I think so."

Abby was happy to settle for that. She stood up. "Good. I'll leave it here."

Norman picked up his cane and rose from his chair. "Thank you. I have come to depend on your help."

"Thanks, Norman," Abby answered, touched and surprised.

"One last thing." He walked to the door. "Come with me."

"Norman, I'm sure it can wait till morning. I'm tired. And you need some sleep."

"This cannot wait." Not even trying to smother a groan, Abby followed Norman as he walked through the living room. At the door to the basement he stopped and looked at her.

He pulled the door wide open and carefully flipped the light switch. "Please, after you."

Abby had been down to the basement once, during her first tour of the house with Maddie. It ran the length of the house, and about twenty years earlier had been turned into a serviceable space, with wine racks lining one wall and utilities—furnace and hot water—along the other. The walls were bare stone—the original foundation of the house—and the floor was poured concrete. The only windows were high rectangles, and during the day they spread a pale, gloomy light across the gray space.

Reluctantly, Abby started down. It crossed her mind that he might push her down the stairs and lock her in.

But she made it to the bottom, and slowly, one step at a time, Norman followed her, his cane ticking a syncopated rhythm.

Abby was not surprised to discover that by night the basement was even colder and more dismal than by day. It was lit by evenly placed fluorescent strips. There was a pungent smell of cat feces coming from a litter box pushed under the stairs, and even in the poor light Abby could see that it was lumpy with turds, a sprinkling of litter surrounding it. The powerful combination of sight and smell made her gag.

"God, Norman, I forgot you have a cat." Abby pulled the collar of her T-shirt up over her nose and mouth. It helped a little.

"I do, I do," he answered. There was an urgency about him she found a little unnerving. "His name is Monsieur Hulot. He is very shy. It is because of him that we always leave the basement door open."

"Who's supposed to clean the litter box?"

"I don't concern myself with these things." Unfazed by the smell, the old man tapped his way to the far end of the basement, past the furnace. He stopped and turned to Abby, using his cane to indicate a space about twenty by ten.

"I am going to put an apartment right here," he said, contained excitement in his voice.

"Why here?" Abby asked. The smell from the far end of the room was making her feel slightly queasy, and her exhaustion didn't help.

"For you. You will live here, free of charge. Over there," he added, pointing to the dark corner under the stairs that housed the litter box, "will be your office."

For a moment Abby was speechless, awed by the blend of sheer lunacy and logic in his presentation. Then she felt a white anger that she had been woken up and dragged down here so she could listen to an arrogant old man's plans to store her in his basement; and finally the anger was followed by a small wedge of compassion. He had no idea how crazy he sounded. She forced herself to speak calmly.

"Thank you, Norman, for the offer, but I have a home."

"That may be so, but it would suit me to have you near at hand. Sometimes I need to work at odd hours."

"But I don't want to live in a basement," she insisted, anger beginning to flare. It felt as if the damp stone walls were beginning to close in on her, and she felt a flash of panic, as if he could change her mind through sheer force of will.

"Maybe we could put in French doors. To make it brighter," he conceded, but she could tell he was just saying it to placate her, as if she were being a sissy.

She took a deep breath which she immediately regretted. "Can we go upstairs and talk about it? It stinks down here."

"This is where I was imprisoned, you know," he said, his voice filling with the promise of ghost story.

Abby looked at him in surprise. "Imprisoned?"

"Yes," he said, nodding slowly, tapping the cement floor with his cane. "The Holy Fathers. They threw me down the stairs and slammed the door. I can remember hearing the key turning in the lock. I begged and cried through the door, I pleaded with them to forgive whatever they thought I had done, but they walked away. I could hear their footsteps on the floor above me. They felt no pity—nothing. They steeled their hearts against me."

Abby was about to say something, but Norman ignored her.

"During my imprisonment, they fed me only enough to keep me alive. I wanted to die. Why did they do it? I may never know. I always believed the command came from the Vatican. That is why I have insisted in my will that, after I go, nothing of mine be given to anyone in Holy Orders."

Abby wondered what had caused him to imagine such an elaborate and paranoid conspiracy. She waited for him to continue, and when he seemed to be done she nodded. "Let's get out of here, Norman," she said gently.

"Why certainly. Go ahead, my dear, after you," he said, and graciously let Abby lead the way out of the basement. "And we can start work tomorrow. You must call a man who can do these things in the morning."

"The contractor," Abby said as she started up the stairs.

"Yes, I must change my will," he said.

Abby glanced down at him in surprise, but decided to let that last unexpected comment pass. If she asked him about it, it was likely to lead back to the Holy Fathers. When she reached the top of the steps, she went to the kitchen door and threw it open. She stood on the back step gulping in the cool night air, its smell fresh and clean with a touch of wood smoke from someone's distant fire.

"Norman, I need to go home," she said.

He shook his head. "I have something to tell you, something important."

Abby took him by the arm and guided him to the foot of the stairs. "When you remember, make a note of it. I promise, I'll be here first thing in the morning, and you can tell me then. Get some sleep, okay, Norman? You'll feel so much better."

Later that night, with dawn was only a few hours away, Abby dreamed she was standing in a low-ceilinged house. She had something draped over her shoulders, something heavy that irritated her skin and made her itch. She tried to crane her neck to see it, but when she turned, it moved with her, staying out of sight. She tried and tried, and eventually she succeeded in grabbing a corner of it. She pulled it around so she could take a close look.

It was an animal skin. Short, caramel-colored hairs. She turned it so she could see the underside. It had been dried and treated, and from what she could guess by feel, seemed to be in the original splayed-out shape.

Abby tried to pull it off, but it seemed to be attached to her shoulders. She yanked hard at it. It wouldn't dislodge. It was stiff and uncomfortable against her back. With every move she made, each time she felt it against her, she was becoming more repulsed by it. She was desperate to get it off her.

And then, to her relief, she noticed she was standing next to a sort of armoire, or wooden cupboard. She knew what she had to do. She maneuvered the end of the skin—the deer's head was still attached—between the doors of the armoire, wedging the head inside. With the skin anchored firmly in the cupboard, she moved away sharply from it, expecting the skin to be wrenched from her back.

But it held firm. She pulled harder, straining away from the heavy piece of furniture, putting all her strength into it.

But instead of the deerskin coming free, the armoire began moving. To her horror, she was dragging it behind her, massive and dark, like a tall, legless monster. It moved and rocked on its feet, and started to tilt toward her. Knowing she was about to be crushed under it, she screamed and tried to run, panic taking over.

Abby woke with a loud shout, sweating and thrashing. She kicked off the bedding and lay still, her heart thumping in her chest, the sweat cooling her body. She knew dreams couldn't kill you. Still, she had a terrible taste in her mouth. Something rotten, like old flesh.

CHAPTER TWENTY

J ust as she was getting ready to get up and get dressed, Abby had a call from Maddie to tell her she was taking Norman to the doctor that day for his regular visit. She apologized for not remembering to tell her the week before, but it meant Abby could stay home. Gratefully, Abby put the phone down, rolled over, and went back to sleep.

On Wednesday morning, she left home at a quarter to nine. There was a bite in the air, and the leaves were dying beautifully, in red, yellow, and copper. Each time the wind gusted, a few would detach from the mother tree and twirl or swing to the ground. River Street was covered with a damp layer of brilliant vegetation.

Saranda's car wasn't parked at Norman's house. The housekeeper's husband sometimes dropped her off, then picked her up at the end of her shift. After emptying the mailbox, Abby walked slowly around to the kitchen door, glancing through the letters and circulars.

She let herself in, expecting to see Saranda. But the kitchen was empty, and she closed the door quietly behind her. Norman's breakfast dishes were untouched and she noticed a note on the small square table. It was written in block letters. Abby picked it up.

NORMAN,

I AM NOT COMING IN ON WEDNESDAY MORNING. I HAVE TO PICK UP A FRIEND AT THE AIRPORT. I WILL COME AT LUNCH. ABBY WILL BE HERE AT 9 AND CAN HELP YOU GET BREAKFAST.

SARANDA

Abby knew it was standard operating procedure to put everything in writing, so that Norman could be reminded of it frequently over the course of the day. Where was he?

It occurred to her that he might be sitting impatiently waiting for her in his office. She walked through the living room, and as she passed into the front hall she cleared her throat and said: "Norman, good morning! It's Abby, I brought the mail!"

As if making a stage entrance, she walked with a confident stride into the office. However, his chair was empty.

She stood still for a minute. Had she forgotten something? Was Maddie taking him somewhere again this morning? She put his mail on his desk and sorted it into neat piles. The mess from the other night was still visible— piles of papers where she had stacked them. If Norman was upstairs, asleep, which now seemed very likely, then this was a perfect time to put everything back where it belonged. Quickly, Abby sorted everything into stacks and refiled them as best she could.

When she was done, she went softly up the stairs and, making as little noise as possible so as not to wake him, she peered into his bedroom. To her surprise, it was empty. So were the other two bedrooms.

What if he'd fallen in the shower? Abby was worried. His bathroom door was ajar, so she took a look inside. To her relief, he wasn't there, lying unconscious in the tub, or propped up on the toilet. She tried to quiet her imagination.

Downstairs again, she went out to the work shed. But he wasn't there, either. She glanced out into the field toward the Metal Building, to see if he was taking a walk. No sign of him.

Back in the kitchen, she knew it was time to call Maddie. She had taken the phone off the wall and was beginning to dial when something she had seen earlier made her pause. She couldn't remember what it was, but some part of her brain had registered information that was important.

Carefully, she put the receiver back on the hook. She walked slowly back into the living room. She looked around the room. Windows, closed. She noticed something she'd missed before. A bunched up blanket on the floor by the couch, partially hidden from view by the long, low coffee table. And before she actually understood, she knew. Her stomach lurched hard, as if she was in an elevator going down too fast.

She walked quickly to the coffee table and pulled it aside. There was Norman, face down on the floor, wearing his heavy corduroys and a thread-bare sweater. His white hair was flattened at the back of his head, as it did when he'd slept on it. His right arm was extended, and his left folded, as if he were about to do a one-armed pushup. His feet were turned neatly inward.

"Norman, Norman, are you okay?" she asked stupidly. She knelt next to him and touched his hand. It was cold and dry. She looked for a pulse but couldn't find one. She gently tried to roll him over, but his right arm stopped her. She pushed it in next to his body and, with two hands, managed to roll him over. His face was darkened, as if he had a tan. His eyes were partially open. His mouth was slack, his cheeks sunken into his face. He was lifeless. Dead.

Abby moved away from the body. She stood, sick and afraid.

If he was dead, she shouldn't have touched the body. But she had to, to find out, right? What should she do now? Her brain seemed to be moving sluggishly. She tried to pull herself together. She should call Maddie, then 911. No, the other way around. 911 first.

A woman answered the phone, and Abby gave her all the information she could. She had to struggle to remember where she was, where Norman lived.

Maddie next. The phone rang and for a moment she was afraid that no one would answer. Finally, Maddie picked up, her voice abrupt.

"Yes?"

"Maddie, it's Abby. I have some bad news. I'm sorry. You need to come here, to your dad's."

"Is he hurt?" And when Abby didn't answer, said: "He's dead, isn't he? Oh, god, I'm coming." And she hung up.

Abby went slowly back into the living room. She sat on one of the chairs opposite Norman, hunched forward, her hands between her knees. He looked tiny and flattened, as if he'd had something sucked out of him.

The mobile over the dining table began tinkling. It was moving and rippling like a blanket of silver shards. How could that be, in such a still place? Abby didn't move, only her eyes traveled around the room, through to the kitchen. There was no movement anywhere. She swallowed. Maybe there was a window open, and a sudden breeze had started it going. She forced herself to breath. Yes, that must be it. Norman had designed his pieces to be very sensitive to air currents. She made herself stand and walk into the kitchen. Sure enough, the back door was open. She must have forgotten to close it after going to the shed. She shut the door and went back into the living room. She sat down again, willing the paramedics to arrive.

Norman's cane was leaning against the wall next to the door. She guessed he had been taking a nap on the couch when he had either tried to sit up and fallen, or rolled over in his sleep. Could a fall like that have killed him? Abby wanted to open a window, but she was afraid to change or touch anything.

Abby waited. Norman waited with her.

The distant whine of the ambulance flooded her with relief. She stood up and went out the front door.

An hour later, Abby stood next to Maddie as she signed forms that allowed the ambulance to drive away with her father's body. Abby put an arm around her when she started to sob, her body heaving with the strain.

"I don't know why I'm so upset," she said, her eyes red-rimmed and wet.

"It was his time, right?" and she started to laugh, an edge of hysteria to her voice.

Abby nodded, glad she wasn't really expected to answer.

Paul arrived a few minutes later and Abby relinquished the job of comfort giver. "I'll be taking off now, Maddie, if there's nothing else I can do," she said, awkwardly.

"No, nothing. Go. Thanks. For everything," Maddie said, with a final shudder and sniff. "Oh, wait, there is one thing I need you to do for me, Abby," she added, blowing her nose, already beginning to recover her balance. "I know it's a lot to ask, but would you please call Germaine and Athena? I can't face telling them."

Abby couldn't deny Maddie, not now. She nodded. "Sure, I'd be glad to," she said, trying to sound as if she meant it. With a last look at the house, she left.

CHAPTER TWENTY-ONE

Abby drove slowly home. The sky was overcast. She thought it might be a good day just to hide out. Go home, climb under the covers, and read a book. Or simply lie there. Not answer the phone. Do nothing. But when she walked in her door and saw the flashing light on her answering machine, she made the mistake of pushing the play button. There was only one message, but it was from Germaine.

"Abby, I'm brilliant. I found a house in Bantam. Did I tell you, I'm going to stay here for the winter? I'll explain when I see you. Anyway, it's right on Findlay Street, and they say I can move in immediately. I need you to look at it with me. I'm meeting the broker at noon, number one eighty-seven. Don't be late!" No phone number. Abby looked at her watch. Already ten past twelve. Where had the morning gone? Under normal circumstances, she wouldn't consider meeting her. But these were not normal circumstances, and she'd promised Maddie she'd be the one to tell Germaine. With a sigh she headed back to her car.

As she drove into town, she wondered about Germaine's decision to stay. In the board game of life, it seemed surprising to Abby that Bantam carried more points than Tuscany, given that across the Atlantic Germaine had a charming stone farmhouse waiting for her, completely fitted out down to the espresso spoons. And extremely friendly neighbors and handymen. But maybe the handsome African-American lawyer with the gentle eyes had something to do with it. And maybe it was a good thing she was telling Germaine about her father now, before she signed a lease, in case Norman was the reason she had decided to stay.

Number 187 Findlay was a narrow house, not as pretty as some of the Victorians on the tree-lined street, but clean and well kept in a spare, low-maintenance, rental kind of way. The plantings around the building were large rubbery shrubs. The siding on the house was vinyl, good for covering old wood and keeping in heat. The color of the house was an inoffensive beige. The front door, also beige, was open, and Germaine's car was one of those parked along the curb. Abby walked up the flagstone path.

She stood in the foyer, looking around, listening for voices. The front entrance led down a narrow hallway. There was one door immediately to Abby's left, and one at the end of the hall. A narrow staircase hugged the wall on the right. The floor was carpeted in a speckled green deep shag, knotted and discolored, and there were flattened shapes on it indicating where furniture had once stood. No doubt a scientist would be able to read, in the carpet's battered and uncleanable depths, a detailed history of every tenant for the last twenty years. The walls were painted a drab gray. Upstairs, she heard footsteps, followed by Germaine's laugh. She walked up the narrow staircase, pulling herself up by a hand on the well-used, round banister, her legs tired and heavy. She felt as if she were carrying Norman's body on her shoulders and was about to lay it at Germaine's feet.

She followed the voices into the front room. There she found Germaine, in a bright orange ruffled blouse and red skirt, talking to a real estate broker Abby knew from the restaurant. He worked out of an office in one of the neighboring towns and always wore a dark blazer, the shoulders covered in dandruff. Had his back been to her, she would have known him by the dusting on his jacket. The staff called him the Yeti.

Standing off to one side, and unseen when Abby first came in, was Athena, her long hair loose down her back. She was wearing jeans, with a pair of sunglasses pushed up on her head. She should have been glad both sisters were there, but instead Abby considered turning around and leaving. She could tell Germaine later that she had a stomach virus. People got stomach viruses very suddenly. And her stomach was feeling tender.

But Germaine lit up when she saw her, and even Athena smiled. The broker gave her an unfriendly nod. Abby wondered if he knew about the nickname.

There was nothing to be gained by pussyfooting around. "Germaine, I need to talk to you and Athena privately."

But before they could respond, the broker interrupted. "Look, sorry, but I really can't hang around. I have another appointment in precisely," and he flicked his wrist out of his jacket and looked at his watch, "ten minutes."

Germaine looked at her apologetically and Abby had to admit that her news could wait. She joined in the tour, staying at the end of the line, and followed the sisters as they looked inside the built-in closets and opened and closed over-painted windows.

Finally, the tour was over and they went outside. The three women waited on the sidewalk while the broker locked the front door.

"What do you think, Abby?" Germaine asked, peering into her face, as if she could read the truth in her eyes.

"It's simple. Roomy. But the carpeting—"

"Ugh, yes. I'll never be able to go barefoot. Something might crawl out of it. But I liked the kitchen, don't you?"

"Kitchen's good."

"I don't want a TV. I'll turn the second bedroom into my office, get a desk and comfortable chair—"

"That would work."

By then, the broker was standing next to them, listening, smoking. Germaine turned to him. "I'll take it."

Abby tried to slow her down. "Germaine, maybe you should wait, I have—"

"No, no, I'm sure." She waved Abby to silence. She turned back to the broker: "But I have to pull up the carpeting."

His eyes, half-shut to avoid being stung by smoke, flared open in shock. "That'll never pass muster with the owner. Oh, no, no."

"Of course it will! You'll see. That carpet's disgusting! I'll pay to have it taken up, then get the floor sanded and finished." And then, the coup de grâce: "Trust me, I've fixed up a farmhouse in Tuscany."

Germaine certainly knew how to play that trump card of hers, Abby thought to herself. By the time they said good-bye to him, Germaine made sure he had figured out how a clean, elegant, polished wood floor would add to the house's value, and was ready to pitch it to the landlord.

"Germaine, Athena," Abby said loudly, to get their attention. "I'm sorry, but I have something important to tell you. Both."

They looked at her, surprised.

Abby took a breath. Let it out. Took another one. "I went to work today, to Norman's."

Germaine nodded encouragement. Athena looked worried. As if she had a premonition, from Abby's tone, of what was coming.

"His housekeeper was out, and he was alone. I'm sorry, but—"

"What?" Germaine snapped.

"He's dead. I'm sorry."

"Oh, Jesus," she said, "*you* found him?" She sounded angry, as if Abby had stepped out of line.

"Yes. He must've died in the night or the early morning. They'll know better later, I suppose." She hesitated, but kept herself from saying anything else.

Athena stumbled, though she was standing still. As if her legs had gone weak. She gripped Abby's arm.

"Goddamn him," Germaine said. "It's not fair." She turned away.

Athena let go of Abby's arm, and sat down on the edge of the curb. She started to cry softly, head bowed.

Abby put a hand on her shoulder and squeezed it ineffectually. She apologized for the fourth time. It felt like the tenth. "I'm so sorry to be the one to give you such bad news. I'll leave you guys alone now. Let me know what I can do. If I can do anything."

Germaine nodded, her back to them. Athena didn't respond, and Abby walked to her car. When she reached it, she looked back at the two women. Germaine was squatting down next to Athena, saying something. She was scowling, and her bright skirt was spread out around her like a flower. Athena was shaking her head, still crying. Germaine started going through her purse, her movement jerky. She pulled out a tissue and shoved it into Athena's hands. She stood up next to her sister, her stance stiff.

Abby got into her car. She looked again, and now Germaine's mouth was turned down. She pulled out another tissue and held it by one corner. It looked like a flag. Like she wanted to surrender. Poor Germaine. Poor Athena. What little bit of parent they had left was now gone.

CHAPTER TWENTY-TWO

Rather than go home, Abby went directly to the InnBetween. She was early, but she thought that if Dulcie was around, they might have a cup of tea together. She couldn't help wishing Dulcie would look after her, like she'd done when they first met. When Abby and her husband had first moved back to Bantam, they were full of big plans to renovate the family farm house and turn it into a studio for avant-garde filmmakers and artists. But money was low and when Abby had first walked into the InnBetween, Dulcie had fed her and offered her a job.

However, on the afternoon of Norman's death, Abby found the kitchen and main dining room deserted. Every day, George and Sandy came in around noon to prep that evening's dishes; she knew they had been there by the dangerously high pile of dirty saucepans in the kitchen sinks. She figured they were upstairs at "church," the name they gave to their sacred espresso break on the upper porch that took place in the half hour before the wait staff came in. They sat on folding chairs, watching the street, gossiping and sipping black coffee from tiny cups. Visitors were welcome, but no one was allowed to interrupt them with work-related questions or demands.

She didn't want to discuss Norman, so she went down to the bar and over to the banquettes that lined the back wall. She pushed one of the tables aside, crawled onto the banquette, and pulled the table back in place to give herself a little privacy. She lay on her back and made herself take slow, deep breaths. The important thing was not to be caught here by anyone, especially Henry. He'd go on about it all night. She closed her eyes.

She must have nodded off, because she woke up to the sound of whispers. She had turned over in her sleep and was now looking under the table that was pushed up to the banquette. The chairs were still upturned on top of it, so she was hidden from view. Through the table legs she could see someone from the waist down, in a pair of restaurant pants. The owner of the pants was leaning up against the bar, one foot on the bar rail. On the nearest bar stool sat a woman, or at least a woman's lap covered by a print skirt. Abby didn't want to look like an eavesdropper, so she was about to sit up when Restaurant Pants put a masculine-looking hand on the woman's calf and slid it up her thigh and under her skirt. Abby heard a giggle. Who was this woman, Abby wondered? An early customer, a wife? Pants was too slim to be George, and too physical to be Sandy, who hated any kind of casual contact with anyone.

Just then, the woman crossed her legs. The legs looked familiar. For the first time, Abby could see a shoe. To her horror, she saw a brand-new, forest green Birkenstock. Dulcie. Abby ducked her head even lower. Who was the guy? At that moment, he moved closer to Dulcie, and put his hands on her knees and spread them. He moved in between her legs. Abby shut her eyes. She heard wet kissing sounds.

Suddenly, there was a loud slam from upstairs. Laughter, talk. Staff, coming to work. Abby watched Dulcie and her partner separate, and Dulcie slide off the bar stool and straighten her skirt. The man with her turned and disappeared up the back stairs behind the bar. Abby could hear his footsteps disappear. Dulcie stood motionless for a moment. Abby wished she could see her face so she could better understand what was going on. But she was afraid to move at all, in case she did something to reveal herself.

Dulcie walked carefully up the front stairs. Abby heard Henry's voice, and Dulcie murmured something in reply. Quickly, she slid out from banquette, hitting her head on the underside of the table as she did. Henry had the heaviest feet in the restaurant, and she could hear him thundering down the stairs. She sat up, leaned back against the banquette, and stretched out her legs. Henry jumped off the last step.

"Hey, Henry," she said casually.

He whipped around at the sound of her voice. "Abby! I just saw Dulcie, she said she didn't know where you were." He looked at her curiously.

Abby shrugged and stood. "I was here. George and Sandy in church?"

Henry went behind the bar. "Yeah, they're upstairs."

"Who else is here?" She stood and sauntered toward the bar.

"I don't know. Becca's here. And Fritz. He's in the kitchen, doing the pots. Where he belongs."

"Fritz, huh? Really?"

"Yeah. What's the big deal?" Henry started to set up his bartending tools, lemons, limes, cutting board, knife.

"Nothing. I thought maybe there was someone else here."

"Nope." He looked at her suspiciously before opening the beer cooler and peering inside.

"Okay, what's Dulcie wearing?" Abby leaned against the bar and asked the question as if she were testing his memory.

"How the hell should I know. Some flowery dress and those fuckin' ugly green shoes. So?"

"So nothing." Abby turned away and walked up the staircase.

Upstairs, Dulcie was filling the cash register. She glanced up and smiled when she saw Abby. "Hey, honey. Did you just get here?"

Abby couldn't make eye contact. "Yeah, I was upstairs, and just went down the back. I had to ask Henry something."

"Well, I'm glad you're here. I need to talk to you about something."

Oh, no, Abby thought, she is going to tell me about Pants. She didn't want to hear a love confession, especially from Dulcie. Not today of all days.

"Now?"

"Perfect," said Dulcie, taking her question as an offer. She looked around secretively and led Abby out to the closed porch, where she turned over a chair and sat down. Abby did the same and sat opposite her.

For a second Dulcie regarded her in silence. "This is between you and me, promise."

"Look, if it's really private, you don't have to tell me, honestly."

But Dulcie ignored her. "Someone," she said slowly, "is stealing beer."

"What?" Abby asked, frowning stupidly.

"Beer," Dulcie repeated. "Someone is stealing beer."

"Not possible," Abby said firmly, once the words got through.

"It's true, I swear. I've done the count over and over again."

"How much beer?"

"Two cases," Dulcie answered.

"You're wrong, it's a mistake." Abby pushed her chair back, moving away from the information. She didn't need to hear this, not today.

"Abby," Dulcie said firmly, "I don't like it any more than you do, but someone is doing it, and I have to find out who it is."

"What makes you so sure?" Abby asked.

"Not me, it was Fritz. He's been keeping an informal eye on the cases. He got me to do a careful tally."

"Oh, Fritz." Without thinking, Abby rolled her eyes.

"And what does that mean?"

"What do we know about him, anyway?"

"Enough. He's a good person," Dulcie said, her voice steely.

Abby stood up, upset. "Are you telling me that you trust him more than the others?"

"I'm not saying that, but—"

"They're family," Abby said angrily, "they wouldn't rip you off."

Dulcie's expression stayed hard. She stood up also and pushed her chair into the table. "We can talk again about this when you calm down. Someone's stealing from me, and I have a right to find out who it is. You act as if I'm trying to—to drown puppies in a bucket." She looked at Abby as if she were a stranger, and walked back into the dining room.

Well, if she'd had any doubts before, they were gone. Pants and Fritz were one and the same. God, how could Dulcie let him touch her? With a shudder, Abby went to work. This day wasn't turning out so well, she thought.

CHAPTER TWENTY-THREE

The morning of Norman's funeral turned out to be crisp and sunny, not a cloud in sight, as if Nature were scoffing at the idea of mourning such an old man. Its lot was full, so Abby parked down the street from the mansion that was now the Best Funeral Parlor. Painted a crisp, pure white, it sat on a slight rise, a blacktop driveway leading up to it. The original owner was Milo Best, the grandfather of the present undertaker, but the name always made Abby think of those Chinese take-out places in strip malls, with names like the Amazing Restaurant or Tip-Top Chopsticks.

As Abby walked up the driveway, she saw three or four people disappear slowly through the porticoed entrance. They were dressed in black. One was a stooped old lady with a small hat on her head.

Inside, the front entrance led into a roomy foyer. Across the way, large beveled-glass doors were propped open, leading into the main room, an auditorium-cum-chapel, with nicely padded folding chairs arranged in neat rows.

Abby felt a hand on her arm and turned around. It was Maddie. She was wearing a dark gray linen dress that ended at the knee. Her skin looked whiter than usual against the dark fabric. Her face was drawn. "Thanks for coming," she said.

"How're you managing?" Abby asked. She gave her a hug, feeling the small, thin body in her arms.

"I just took him for a checkup, you know?" Maddie said, looking at Abby. "The doctor said he was in great shape. So I just didn't expect it. But he was ninety-two, after all."

Abby nodded. "It would just have gotten harder for him, as his memory deteriorated. Already it was frustrating, frightening. Eventually he wouldn't have been able to work at all."

"Yeah." Maddie smiled wanly. "I should look on the bright side, right? It was time."

"You must've been proud of him when you were a kid," Abby ventured.

"Yes, I was. Which reminds me. I think we should still have that show of his work. As a sort of memorial. A good-bye. What do you think?"

"Sounds like a great idea."

"It makes sense. It'll also help me get organized. I want to salvage whatever I can of his work, organize it, and then decide what to do with it. I'll probably sell most of it. But I need to find someone who can help me put together some of his old pieces."

"Paul worked with him years ago, didn't he?"

"That's right."

"If he helped Norman dismantle most of the work, maybe he can help put it back together."

Maddie nodded thoughtfully. "Good idea. I don't know why I didn't think of it. I'll ask him if he has the time. Maybe you and Paul could go through the Metal Building and he can figure out what needs to be salvaged. Then we can get rid of all the junk and clean the place up. It'll help me, and you'll still have some work, at least for a while."

Abby nodded. "I appreciate that, thanks. Listen, Maddie, you should know that I saw Norman a few nights before he died."

Maddie looked puzzled. "At the restaurant," she said.

"No, later. He called me and asked me to come over, said he'd had a break-in. I called the cops but everything was fine, so I let you sleep."

Maddie looked stunned. "Everything was okay? I wish you'd called me."

"When I got there, he said he had something important to tell me, but he couldn't remember what it was." Abby smiled. "I told him to write it down once it came to him. He also offered me an apartment in his basement," she added with a shake of her head.

Maddie nodded slowly, as if she were trying to understand what she was hearing. "Okay. We'll talk more later. I should go," she gestured to the auditorium behind her, "and make myself available."

About ten people were already sitting in the main room, in random arrangements and clusters. Abby saw Paul near the front, staring blankly forward.

To the front of the room was a table with an easel on it. Propped on it was a blown-up photograph of a man. The picture had been shot outdoors, and he was squinting into the light, his dark hair windblown and long on his collar. It had to be Norman, but there was little Abby could recognize, other than the general ratio of eyes to nose to mouth. His arms were crossed and he was smiling. The focus on the background was less sharp, but Abby could make out trees and the corner of a building. Part of a door. It looked familiar, and with a jolt she recognized the Metal Building. But so different. No rust, no weeds.

Abby's eyes drifted, and she realized that the easel wasn't standing on a table, as she had first thought, but on a dark wood casket. So, Norman was with them after all. To remind anyone who might wish to forget that this was not a social event. Or, that it was a social event of a specific kind.

She walked over to one of the long windows to look out. A flash of color caught her eye. Germaine was walking gingerly on the grass, her ankles wobbling in high-heeled shoes. She was wearing black, with a bright purple top. Next to her was her sister, spartan by comparison in all black. On Athena's other side walked Cal, long hair combed neatly back in a ponytail, wearing a dark blue suit that seemed a little too short for him, black shirt buttoned up all the way, no tie. He had a slight stoop and his hands were interlocked behind his back, giving him a professorial look. Abby watched Germaine put a hand out and stroke Athena's arm, a gesture of comfort.

Abby turned away from the window. Behind a clump of people at the back of the room, she noticed Franklin. He was nodding, looking at the ground, as he listened to Mitch and Suzie Helder. There were plenty of people in the room she had never seen before. She suddenly understood that Norman's life had been very full and these were all men and women he had touched in some way.

"Norman didn't know half these people," said a hoarse voice next to her. Abby looked, and standing next to her was the old woman with the hat that she had seen when she was standing at the bottom of the driveway. Her hair was dyed an ash blonde, teased, and pinned into a bouffant. The hat was a thin, black pancake, set straight on her head but tilted forward to make room for the mound of hair, with a short veil flipped back over it, like a sheet that had been turned down at bedtime. Her lipstick was red and radiated away from her mouth through the wrinkles like a crimson starburst. She was wearing a girlish black shirtwaist dress with a wide patent leather belt. Her shoes were black flats that had stretched and cracked to make room for the arthritic joints of her toes.

Abby nodded. "You knew Norman a long time?"

"Since before the war. New York. What about you?"

"Not long. I was working for him."

"Hmm," the old lady said skeptically. "What did you do, his laundry?"

"Close," Abby said with a laugh, refusing to be baited, "I did some secretarial work, answered letters. Stuff like that."

"Aha," the lady with the hat nodded, her voice breaking raspily, "you were his whachamacallit, that word he loved—"

"Right. His amanuensis. I'm Abby, by the way." She put out her hand.

The old lady ignored it. "Good for you. I'm Bella Massicotte. Walk outside with me. I'm dying for a smoke." As if to prove her point, she broke into a deep chest cough.

"I don't think we should. The service is going to start soon," Abby said.

Bella put a hand on Abby's arm. Her knobbly fingers tightened and her painted nails dug in. Abby felt as if she had a pet raptor on her arm and had forgotten her leather arm guards.

"Norman would have sneered at all of this. I bet he wanted his body flung in the lake when he shuffled off this mortal coil. It's Maddie's idea. Come on, let's go."

There seemed to be no escape, so Abby let her new friend pull her toward the door. Anyone watching might have thought she was supporting and guiding her frail little grandmother. They'd have been wrong on more than one count.

Once they were outside, Bella directed Abby to a bench near the entrance that had a view of the street below. It wasn't until she was sitting down that the she let go of Abby's arm. Her nails had left indentations on the skin. Abby rubbed her arm as Bella rummaged through an old lizard-skin purse until she found a pack of cigarettes and a gold lighter.

She lit up, exhaling a cloud of smoke along with a grunt of pleasure. "Thank you, dear. Now sit down next to me. Tell me about you. What will you do now that Norman's dead?"

"It's okay, I have another job, and I'll be helping Maddie get the old Metal Building in order. How did you know Norman?"

Bella sighed. "You only knew him as a senile old man. Such a shame. I've known Norman since 1939, just before Europe went to war. He was studying painting, and I was a hand and foot model—for photographers and illustrators. Hard to believe that now, don't you think?" She held out a gnarled hand and looked at it in disgust.

"Hey, listen," Abby said. "I tried modeling, and got one catalog job. In two years. End of career. But you obviously had one. So, tell me more about Norman."

Bella took a deep drag on her cigarette. When she spoke, her voice was conspiratorial. "We had a fling. Went at it like there was no tomorrow. He had a studio apartment over a butcher shop on Fourteenth Street." The old lady's gaze moved from the grass on the ground in front of her to the rooftops on the other side of the street. She looked at Abby with the smile of an old troublemaker. "Norman was a fascist, did you know that?" She made a dry, undefined sound. Abby realized she was laughing. "Or he thought he was. He liked all that manly talk and the marching around. I think he craved order. I told him Hitler would cut off his artist dick and shove it in his mouth. He came around when he saw what was really happening. Disillusioned, poor baby."

Abby watched her. It seemed so incongruous, this feisty old woman from a different world, sitting there in Bantam, New York, opening a window onto the past. "Did you and Norman go on seeing each other?"

Bella flicked an ash onto the grass. "We weren't in love. I didn't believe in love. We were lovers, so we got together when it suited us. But it was over once he married Wanda and had little Maddie. Then his work became his lover."

Abby looked at her curiously. "Why are you telling me this?"

"What does it matter? You're a stranger. Who cares anymore? Who was screwing whom? It's all so old hat. *Vieux chapeau,* as I like to say. How could it matter, when Wanda is long gone, and Norman is in that room back there?" She gestured with her cigarette to the building they had just left.

"Did you know Wanda?"

"Naturally. We were friends. I would come up, sometimes for weeks at a time, to work and paint. Wanda would cook wonderful meals, and organize picnics and walks in the woods. She was a devoted wife."

"So you were a painter, too?"

"We all were. Most of us, however, were amateurs." She didn't say it the way an American would—"amacher"—but with the French pronunciation, which somehow elevated it to a more gracious status.

"Did Wanda also paint?"

"Yes, actually. She was quite good. But she lacked confidence."

"Were she and Norman close?"

"You mean, were they lovey-dovey and such?" Bella asked, her tone ironic.

"You tell me. Did Norman seem to care about her? Value her? I've heard she worshiped him." Abby wondered how trustworthy Bella was.

"She belonged to him. She was his. She was a child when they met, and she knew nothing else. Wanted nothing more than to please him and make him happy. And if what he wanted was to work, then she provided meals and peace and quiet. Yes, he valued her, in a way. She made his life very comfortable. That was her job."

"What about the sisters? Why did they take them in?"

Bella grinned, as if she had a good secret and was dying to share it. "Ah, the foster girls. The beautiful little Athena, and the dumpling—what was her name?"

"Germaine," Abby said, lowering her voice and glancing around. She felt sorry for any child thrust into this outspoken company. "You knew them."

"Of course I did. I came up from the city two weeks after they arrived."

"They're both here now."

"Where?"

"Inside, I think. Would you like to meet them?"

"Not particularly. The past is the past. I came up here to pay my respects to Maddie, and now I'm ready to get the hell out of here. I have a driver waiting for me, very expensive. The sooner I go, the less it costs me. Here, give me a hand up and help me to my car."

The claw attached itself to her arm once more. Abby helped Bella get to her feet and they walked slowly around to the parking lot.

"Norman was one of my last living friends," Bella continued, suddenly sad. "He was no barrel of laughs, but I can't stand being this close to his corpse." She brightened. "But you, my young friend, I am happy to have met. You remind me of myself about half a century ago. If you want to call me, I'm in the Manhattan book. Massicotte. M-a-s-s-i-c-o-t-t-e."

After seeing Bella off, Abby walked back to the entrance. Meeting one of Norman's contemporaries was a piece of luck. There couldn't be many left. She went inside and saw, through the glass doors, that someone in a black suit and a dog collar was standing at the lectern, speaking. Bella was right; it was time to leave. She opened the front door quietly, and slipped out.

CHAPTER TWENTY-FOUR

The InnBetween was like an injured animal, getting weaker by the day but with occasional, inexplicable bursts of feverish energy. It was late autumn, and Abby had been cut back to three nights a week. She, and whoever else was on the schedule, would lean against the wall by the cash register, waiting for customers, their shoes creating scuff marks on the pale paint. As they did, they played a guessing game. They tried to figure out what in particular was causing customers to show up, or not. Most explanations worked either way: the good weather, the bad weather, the closing of summer houses, the preparing of flower beds, the phases of the moon, leaf-peeping, George's vegetarian lasagna, the movie showing at the Kipling, George's meat lasagna, Becca's choice of music, or a new restaurant ten miles away.

But even though high season was over, there was a core of customers who came no matter what. On Friday, one couple who drove upstate, rain or shine, ate roast chicken, and barely said a word to each other. The divorced financial planner who lived in the village and came in every Saturday looking for a little conversation and a lot of wine, his laughter too loud, his loneliness too tangible. The somber Wednesday evening diners who sat alone, then walked across the circle to the village court to contest speeding tickets. Wednesday was also Father Lester's night. He would drink a Rob Roy, eat a steak, and do the crossword puzzle. The staff called him Father Les, and were working on a repertoire of knock-knock jokes about him.

Just as there were customers they could depend on, so were there rituals. And every day, no matter what the season, about forty minutes before they unlocked the front door of the restaurant, George held a staff meeting. This was when he listed the specials and their ingredients, giving the waiters time to write them down. He warned them if he was running low on a specific dish. He also gave special instructions and reminders.

That afternoon, George gave a loving description of his lamb chop special, paying special attention to the ingredients in the herb sauce. Abby watched Henry's eyelids droop while the chef was talking. It didn't matter how George described it, Abby knew Henry was just going to call it lamb chops.

Fritz was leaning up against the door jamb. He had his bandana tied low on his head, and a five o'clock shadow dusted his cheeks. He caught Abby looking at him and blew her a kiss. Abby looked away from him. She wondered why he felt he needed to be there; he didn't serve food or deal with the customers.

When George had finished and all questions had been answered, Dulcie stood up. "Everyone, I have something to say." Abby saw her glance quickly over at Fritz. His eyes were on the floor, as if studying it.

"We have a problem," she continued. "For the first time since I opened this place, something has been stolen." Abby saw Henry wake up and pay attention. "Three cases of Heineken have gone missing. I've done the count over and over, and there's no way around it."

Abby couldn't help herself. "Three? I thought you said it was two!"

Dulcie looked at her coldly. "That was a week ago. Now it's three."

"I don't believe it. When?" Henry asked. He seemed stunned.

"It started a while back," Dulcie answered, purposefully vague. "I didn't mention it before, because I hoped I was the one who had made a mistake."

"How could someone take three cases of beer without us knowing?" Becca asked, confused.

"There are ways." Dulcie said grimly, looking around at them. "I'm going to have to talk to everyone, okay? Privately."

Dulcie conducted her talks with each of the staff in a corner of the porch. Abby wondered what she thought she would accomplish, other than getting everyone upset. Maybe she hoped someone would confess privately, or squeal on a coworker. Maybe she knew the exact days and times the beer disappeared and was going to re-create the crime scene, with diagrams and little arrows—Suspect A went upstairs to the liquor supply, leaving Suspect D alone with the cases for twelve minutes, in which time she could have taken two of them, run upstairs, out the back door and to her car without being seen by Suspect B, who was in the prep kitchen peeling potatoes. In the meantime, Suspect E was taking a crap, but was he really? Or had he actually—Stop it, Abby said to herself. She's doing her best.

The beer was delivered every couple of weeks. The cases were then carried downstairs and piled up against the wall in the narrow hallway behind the bar and under the staircase, in direct defiance of the fire marshal's instructions. Then, when each case was used and refilled with empties, it was taken back upstairs and placed in the little foyer outside the back door. Eventually, when the new delivery came, the distributor would take all the empty cases away with him, and the cycle would start again. It wouldn't be hard to make off with the InnBetween's beer, or anything else, Abby thought, as she set the tables in the dining room. From where she was working, she could see Dulcie with her pad of paper. Becca sat opposite her, hunched over, her hands nervously clutched together. It was just a matter of Dulcie's deciding which of her employees might do it to her. As far as Abby was concerned, there was only one person worth suspecting, and he was washing dishes in the next room, sperm circling the top of his head like bees around a honeycomb.

After the kitchen closed that night, she was putting away the desserts in the prep kitchen when Henry walked through on his way downstairs. Fritz was noisily stacking clean and steaming dinner plates.

"Henry," Abby said in a voice loud enough to be heard over the crashing plates. "You know this other job I have, right?"

"Yeah." He stopped and nodded. "With the old guy. He died, didn't he? What'd you do, change his diapers or something?"

"Show some respect. Look, his daughter wants me to line up someone to help with some heavy lifting. We're clearing out his old studio in Bantam Center, it's full of junk. You interested?"

"Yeah, I could use the bucks. When?"

"I'm not sure yet, I'll let you know. Bring work gloves."

"Hey, you think I've never done manual labor before?"

"Easy, Henry."

He grunted and disappeared down the back stairs. He didn't seem his usual fun-seeking self.

Before leaving, Abby went downstairs. Henry was wiping down the bar. She pulled out one of the bar stools and took a seat. "What's up?" she asked.

He shrugged. "I'm trying to figure out this beer thing. I feel like I'm going to take the fall for it, you know?"

Abby nodded. He was the best candidate—young, male, and Hispanic. "I'm going to find out what's going on, okay?"

"What're you going to do?" he asked, his curiosity piqued.

"I don't really know, to be honest. But I've got a few ideas."

"Let's watch the place," he said, suddenly excited. "Come on, we'll get whoever's doing it, beat the crap out of them."

Abby shook her head. "No, that's a bad idea. You just have to go on as usual, that's all, okay? If I need your help, I'll ask for it. Okay?"

He shook his head in disgust. "You're like the little Nancy Drew of Bantam, you know? You need to get laid. I'll introduce you to my cousin. He lives in the city, but he's coming up in a few weeks. He's cool."

"I do fine," she answered defensively.

Henry smiled, as if he'd caught her in a trap. "Oh, yeah? By who? We're puttin' some money down in the kitchen. I say it's that plumber, what's his name—Sean. Yeah, my sister's girlfriends tell me he's a stud."

Abby was blushing. "Well, then maybe they should call him." She climbed off the stool. "Anyway, what do you mean, you're placing bets?"

"George thinks you're hot for the lawyer, that you've been gettin' it on with him but got pissed when he started seeing Germaine. She's tough competition, no argument," he added, wistfully.

Abby shut her eyes. She really didn't want people in the kitchen laying bets on her sex life, but if she let Henry see that she was upset, she was roadkill. And she was glad that her sex life, or lack thereof, had given him something to think about besides the beer. She looked at him with a smile that lifted only half of her mouth. It was the best she could do. "So, what does Sandy think?"

"Who the hell ever knows what Sandy thinks?"

"And what about Spermhead? He have any opinions?"

"Who gives a shit?" he sneered.

CHAPTER TWENTY-FIVE

Henry might not care what Spermhead thought, but Dulcie obviously did. The next day, she came to work wearing black jeans and a tattoo above her left breast.

The jeans were enough of a surprise. She always wore shapeless, midcalf dresses, dowdy enough to qualify her as an active member of an orthodox religious sect. So black jeans were a major change. Abby realized she had always assumed her friend was shaped like a trapezoid.

Henry did a double take. "Whoa, Dulcie, what's up?" he said, as if his boss had deliberately set out to shake up his world.

Dulcie blushed, but otherwise ignored him.

Abby found out about the tattoo by accident. She was going into the dining room to change a light bulb in one of the standing lamps, when she found Dulcie with the shoulder of her blouse pulled down, showing something to Becca. Abby stopped in her tracks. The two women hadn't noticed her come in and she could see the tattoo from where she stood. It was about three inches across and had a Native American theme—it looked like a head-dress with feathers. The skin around the design looked red and irritated.

Becca was saying: "My butterfly took a couple of weeks to heal properly. That'll be beautiful when the swelling goes down."

"What is it, Dulcie?" Abby interrupted rudely.

Guiltily, Dulcie shot her a look and covered the design, wincing as she did so.

"What's the occasion?" Abby went on, ignoring the hint. "You discovered your grandparents weren't actually Norwegian, but Navajo?"

"None of your business, Abby. Just because you don't like ink."

Ink. Abby couldn't believe what she was hearing. This was her middle-aged boss, mother of three, owner of a minivan, wearer of Birkenstocks. Ink. If she were into tattoos, Abby thought to herself, this would be the day when she would get all of her own burned off.

Abby shrugged her shoulders, went to the lamp and started unscrewing the light bulb. She took it out, replaced it with a new one, and left the room.

That evening, she and Dulcie barely spoke. The truth was, she was hurt that Dulcie hadn't told her about it first, maybe even asked her opinion. And she was stumped as to why she would have put that particular image on that particular place. But she knew it had to have something to do with Fritz.

That night, George had two specials, pasta with asparagus and a Mexican fajita with slow-cooked shredded beef. Abby promised herself she would eat one or the other before the night was out. It didn't matter which one. And she wasn't going to worry about Dulcie, her tattoo, or the dishwasher. Her agenda was simple: she was just going to think about making money and eating one of the specials.

Knowing it would be slow, she and Becca took the upstairs stations, leaving Henry to cover the bar and the downstairs dining room. To their surprise, there was a pleasant flow of customers from about six o'clock. Not a rush, but a steady stream. They had no trouble keeping up, and by eight-thirty the flow slowed to a trickle; by nine it was over. Perfect. She'd be home by ten-thirty, she thought to herself as she cleared the last table, throwing the tips into the large, plastic jar under the register.

Then, at about ten, as she and Becca were putting away the desserts in the prep kitchen, Fritz accidentally splashed a pan full of dishwater down his front. He cursed and peeled off his jacket. His T-shirt was also soaked through, so he pulled it off over his head. On his muscular, barrel-shaped chest was a tattoo. It was a headdress, nearly identical to the one that Dulcie had just gotten. Becca saw it too and stared. Then she looked at Abby, her eyes round.

"Abby," she hissed at her, as soon as they were in the dining room together. "What's the deal? Are they together?"

Abby shrugged. "Yeah, I think so."

"Wow," Becca said. "Talk about shock. It's like finding out your mom's getting it on with some random guy." Then she thought about it some more. "Yecch," she said, "how could she? He's, I don't know, nasty."

"She doesn't seem to think so."

"They're doing it, right?"

Abby felt cornered. "Becca, I don't know. She's a grown woman, she can do it with whoever she wants, right?"

"Yeah, but what about her kids?" Becca pointed out, worried.

"What about them? I'm sure she's considerate, you know—"

"Yeah, but what about breakfast? I mean, he must come out of her room in the morning," she said. She was like someone picking at a sore. She wanted specific answers, and Abby didn't have any.

"Look, Becca, I don't know anything about that."

Becca shook her head. "I've got to talk to George." She started to walk away, but Abby grabbed her by the arm.

"No, you can't tell George, it's not fair," she protested.

"I have to, it's his kitchen, he's got to know what's going on."

"Fine." In frustration, Abby went back to cleaning and filling the ketchup bottles, and upending the chairs.

When Becca came out, Abby was counting out the tip money. She looked up. "Did you tell him?" she asked, keeping her voice low.

"Yeah," Becca said, "but he already knew."

Abby nodded. Of course. Somehow George learned about everything before anyone else. He kept his ear to the rail and heard the rumble of a train before it entered the county. "What else?"

Becca looked around, as if the walls had ears. "He told me we have to be careful what we say," she whispered. "You especially," she added.

"Shit," Abby said, knowing George was right, but not sure why.

When she had finished what she was doing, she went through the swinging door, past Fritz, and into the kitchen. George was putting a container of sour cream into the fridge.

"George, do you have any of the asparagus for me?"

"Sorry, babe."

Disappointment. "What about those fajitas?"

"They ran out of here. I think I should make 'em again next week, what d'you think?"

"Shit."

He laughed. "I'm sure I got some of that somewhere."

She was hungry, but as she looked around the kitchen she felt her appetite fade away. The salad station had nothing but ends of lettuce left in the bowls; on the floor, strands of swollen spaghetti emerged like earthworms from the holes in the black rubber mats, and the linoleum beneath them was a sheen of grease and dirty water. A teaspoon stuck out of the floor drain.

"You know what? I'm not that hungry, anyway. Maybe I'll just have some ice cream." Something frozen, untouched by human hands, she added to herself. She started to leave, then changed her mind. "George," she said, dropping her voice, "why did you tell Becca I should watch my back?"

"Watch your back?" George asked, glancing quickly toward the outer room where Fritz was at the dishwasher. He began to wipe down the butcher block cutting surfaces, using a mixture of bleach and water.

"Yeah, you know, because of . . ." and she tilted her head toward the door.

He stopped what he was doing and leaned forward. Looking her in the eye, he lowered his voice. "Because if you force Dulcie to chose between you and the guy she's shtupping, who seems to be making her happy, you're gonna lose out. Simple. So don't be a dumbass about it, Abs." He began wiping again. Abby nodded. There was nothing much more to say.

In the dining room, she emptied the tip jar on the staff table. All she had left to do was divide the tips, and she could go home. With some ice cream.

She had just divvied up everyone's take for the night, when the front door opened. She glanced up, cursing herself for forgetting to lock it.

She started to rise, ready to send the new arrival away, when she saw it was Franklin. "Hey, there," she said, surprised. It was late for him; he was usually a dinner customer.

He nodded. "If you join me, I'll buy you a beer." He was wearing neat light khakis and a blue polo with a navy crewneck sweater. He looked very preppy and somehow calming. All that soothing blue.

For the first time in a while, Abby smiled as if she actually meant it. "Sure. Will you take this down to Henry? I've got to give Becca her cut." And before he could protest, she gave him a short stack of dog-eared bills and some change.

She found Becca in the prep kitchen, cleaning the coffee pots. She pushed her tips into her apron. "Forty-five. We're all going to have our cars repossessed."

Downstairs, she took a seat on a barstool next to Franklin. She let out a long, heartfelt breath.

Henry, who was cleaning out the sinks, said: "You want something?"

She looked at the bottles behind him. "Yeah. A glass of port."

Henry grunted in surprise but proceeded to pour her a glass. When he had replaced the bottle on the shelf, he said: "That's it. I'm outta here. Close up for me when you're done, okay, Abby?"

"Okay. 'night, Henry."

After Henry had thumped up the back stairs, Franklin took a sip of beer. "I hear you found Norman Smith. That must've been tough."

"Hey, I'll get over it. Poor guy. I hope he didn't suffer."

Franklin took a drink and nodded.

Abby propped her head on her hand. "Maybe he should have had a live-in person, someone to keep an eye on him. I mean, think about it. Ninety-two? That's too old to be living alone."

Franklin shook his head. "Wouldn't have one." He took another gulp.

"What d'you mean, he wouldn't have one? How do you know?"

"He was my client."

Abby stopped what she was doing and looked at him.

"I suggested he hire live-in help at the beginning of last year, but he was stubborn." He shook his head. "No one could talk him into it."

"Why didn't you tell me you were his lawyer?"

Franklin shrugged. "It didn't come up."

Abby leaned on the counter, fascinated. "So did you know him a long time? Were you friends?"

He shook his head. "No, nothing like that. For years his lawyer was this old-timer who lived in Pittsfield and collected antique cars. When he died two years ago, Maddie brought Norman to me. Everything was pretty much in order already, his estate was all set up. So we only met three or four times altogether, if he had a question or wanted to change something. We got along. I liked him."

Abby nodded. "I liked him, too. I wonder what he was like thirty years ago."

"As self-involved as he always was. Successful, too. They often go together."

"So what happened to all the money he made?"

"What do you mean, what happened to it?"

"Well, I mean, did he spend it all, or give it to charity? Was he a secret gambler or something?"

"Not at all. Norman died a rich man."

"Really? Hey, are you allowed to tell me that?"

Franklin laughed. "Borderline. And that's all I'll say."

"So you can't tell me who inherits?"

"Nope."

"It's got to be Maddie." She looked at him sideways, to see if that got any kind of a reaction.

Franklin shook his head. "Forget it, my friend."

"Another beer?"

"Sure," he answered. "Might as well. Germaine should be here soon."

She got him a second beer out of the cooler, opened it, and put it in front of him.

Cat had been right, obviously, about the power of mushroom ravioli; Franklin and Germaine had been into the restaurant together for dinner three times since that first impromptu date. Abby had not only gotten used to seeing them together, she'd decided it was a good thing. Franklin seemed to have a spring in his step, and Germaine wasn't expending as much energy working Henry into a lather.

Abby lowered her voice. "Did she come to your house the other night? Saturday, late, actually early Sunday?"

Franklin looked at her with faint suspicion. "Why should I tell you?"

"You know, there's no reason to be so secretive. There's no client privilege, or whatever. She came to see me, late, and I wondered where she had been before that."

Franklin thought about it. "Yes, she was there," he said, with a certain effort.

Abby shook her head. "Is it that hard for a lawyer to tell the truth?" When he didn't answer, she asked him curiously, "Does she know you were Norman's lawyer?"

"She does. I felt it would be strange not to tell her."

Abby nodded. "Poor old guy. He was lying on the floor, face down, as if he had tried to get up and had rolled off." Suddenly, Abby sat up straight. "Oh, my god."

"What is it?" Franklin looked at her with real concern in his eyes.

Abby stared at the back bar, her mouth slightly open. She didn't move.

"Abby? What?"

Abby took in a sudden breath and shook her head as if dismissing an idea. She spoke slowly. "It's nothing, it's just a stupid little thing."

"Come on, tell me."

"No. No. Let me think it out some more."

Just then, a pair of familiar black high-heeled sandals appeared at the top of the stairs, descending slowly. Abby started making a Stoli and tonic. Germaine looked ready to take on the world, until she got closer. She had dark circles under her eyes and she looked drawn.

She and Franklin kissed on the lips and she sat down in front of the waiting drink.

"You okay, Germaine?" Abby asked.

Germaine moved her head in a gesture between a nod and a shake, as if she were undecided. "I've been better."

"I'm sorry to hear it."

She took a long swig from the cold glass, put it down and looked at Abby. "I've decided not to take the house on Findlay."

Abby nodded. "I didn't think you'd want to, you know, after Norman—"

"You think I was going to hang around for that old goat? Forget it. Nah. I'll stay a few more weeks, and then head back to Italy. I miss my house, and it's getting cold here. But I did think I'd finally get him to tell me about Wanda. I guess I'll die not knowing."

"You may just have to accept the fact that maybe he couldn't remember," Abby said.

Germaine didn't deign to reply.

Abby, however, didn't noticed. Her mind was on other things. She went behind the bar and washed out her glass and went upstairs. For the next half hour, she did her last few chores, and as soon as she politely could, she ushered Germaine and Franklin to the front door and locked it behind them.

Chapter Twenty-six

The next day, on her way in to work, Abby pulled up in front of the Lacey Memorial, the multipurpose building in town that housed the police station. She ran up the wide, stone steps and into the marbled lobby. To her left was the oversized Dutch door marked POLICE. It was open.

"Hello," she called out, "Is the chief here?"

"Who wants him?" answered the deep voice of the man she was looking for, coming from his office off the short corridor.

"Chief!" Abby called out, "It's Abby Silvernale. I need to talk to you. Can I come back there?"

She heard a heavy sigh. "Come on in, Abigail, but just for a second. I'm on my way out."

The chief sat at his desk, a stack of papers in front of him. His name was, by some strange quirk of fate, Chief Sheriff. Or maybe he was a good example of a name influencing a child's perception of himself. He must've always played the cop in cops and robbers. Either way, Abby trusted him, even though he had a habit of always calling her Abigail, which made her feel as if she were in trouble. He looked over his little town like a stern and watchful parent. He was of medium height, stocky, and had hair that was so dark it looked dyed, though Abby could see the faint threads of gray around the temples.

He peered at her over his reading glasses. His thick eyebrows were raised, and he was waiting.

"What do you want, young lady?"

"It's about Norman Smith."

"I'm listening," he said, sitting back and crossing his arms.

Abby went to the chair on the other side of his desk and sat on the edge of it. "You know I found his body."

"Yes, I did. I read the report."

"Well, I left something out."

"Abigail, if you keep information—"

"Hear me out," Abby protested. "I didn't leave it out on purpose, I just remembered it late last night. And it might not mean anything."

He pulled off his glasses and rubbed two little red marks on the bridge of his nose. "Let's hear it."

"Before I tell you, will you answer one question?"

"Depends."

"My question is, was anyone there at the time of his death?"

The chief shook his head. "We have no reason to believe so."

"Okay. Actually, this is a two-part question: is there any chance someone might have caused Norman's death?"

He looked at her as if he were considering his reply. "No, I won't answer that question, and now you get to tell me what you suddenly remembered."

Abby looked at him resentfully. "I'm trying to be helpful," she said.

"Come on, Abigail. I don't have all day," he said, sitting up and organizing a pile of papers into a thick stack.

"Okay. When I went to work that morning, I saw the note from Saranda, his housekeeper."

The police chief sifted through some files on his desk till he found the one he was looking for. He flipped it open and looked through the papers in it.

"Right. She'd gone to the airport to pick up a friend."

"Exactly. So Norman had been alone from suppertime, when Saranda left, until morning."

"Correct."

"The thing is, his cane."

"Go on."

"After I called the paramedics and Maddie, I sat in the living room with him, with, you know, the body."

"Uh-huh. I see no mention of a cane."

"That's probably because it was there, in the room. There was nothing out of the ordinary about it."

"But now you say there is."

"Just a little teeny something."

"Out with it."

Abby hesitated. "Can I draw you a picture?"

The chief handed her a legal pad and a pencil. "Be my guest."

Abby took them and came around the desk. She stood next to him. She put the pad on the desk and on it drew a rough outline of the living room—windows, couch, chairs, doors.

"Norman always used that cane. He didn't like to walk without it. And when he lay down for a nap, he always put it right here," and she drew an X at the foot of the couch. "That way, when he woke up, he knew where to find it."

He looked at her with a little nod. "I see. So where was it?"

Abby put another X where the cane had been propped against the wall. "Over here. By the door. It means he would have propped his cane, then walked six feet to the couch without it."

"Could he do it, physically?"

Abby thought about it. "I guess so. But he didn't like to."

Chief Sheriff nodded at her, watching her all the while.

Finally, Abby said: "That's why I asked, is there any sign that someone was there with him?"

He shrugged. "There was no report of anything untoward. No strange cars or goings on." He stood. "I'm sorry, I've got to go."

Abby got up, too. "Thanks," she said, walking to the door.

"No problem, young lady. You hear anything interesting, you come back, okay?"

"Yup. Yes, sir."

He hesitated. "One more thing. There was no reason at the time to believe there was anything suspicious about his death, and his immediate family didn't request an autopsy. As far as I know, Mr. Smith's been cremated. You should have spoken up sooner, Abigail." He put on his jacket. "And as far as that cane goes, his son-in-law or his daughter might have visited him that night, maybe sat with him for a while until he fell asleep, right? Maybe leaned it against the wall?"

Abby nodded. "They could have. Did they?"

The chief lifted his hat off the top of his bookshelf. He fitted it on his head. "I'll ask them. I think we're finished here, right?"

Abby left while she was still ahead.

CHAPTER TWENTY-SEVEN

Silvernale, I met a friend of yours today." It was bowling night. Abby had managed to miss the last two, using work as an excuse. This time, however, she'd come so she could forget about the restaurant, Fritz, Dulcie, and even Norman. She was ready to focus on bowling. Not Sean. Just bowling.

Her eyes were on the small arrows on the lane. "Who was that?" she asked Mike, who was sitting behind her. Without waiting for an answer, she took four steps up to the foul line and let the ball go. She watched as it rolled smack down the center. The ball crashed into the pins, sending them flying. "Yes!" Her first throw of the day, and she got a strike.

"Good girl!" Mike clapped from behind her.

"So who's this friend of mine?" Abby sat down next to Mike and reached for her beer. She leaned back, relaxed. Feeling good.

"Nice gal. A writer."

Shit. Germaine. "Oh. How'd you meet her?"

"She was at the auto parts store. She needed some help putting a new bulb in her a rear brake light."

"Sounds like her."

"She was very friendly, loved hearing about our Monday nights—"

"Aw, Mike, you didn't tell her about this, did you?"

"Why? She thought it was great—"

"Of course she did. Now she's going to want to come bowling."

"Well, I don't think that would be so terrible. I mean, she seems lonely—"

"Yeah, she's lonely, she's a lonely—"

"Now, come on, honey, it's not like you to be so—"

"Yes, it is, Mike."

"What're you two talking about?"

Abby hadn't heard Sean come up behind them.

Mike looked up at him. "A friend of Abby's."

Sean sat down in the empty seat next to Abby, making sure there was plenty of space between them.

"So, who's this friend?" He leaned forward in his seat and looked at Mike.

Mike shrugged. "Some woman I met today, seems to love Abby and wants to come bowling with us. We could use a sub." He looked at Abby. "So what's wrong with her?"

Abby sighed, defeated. "Germaine LeClair."

Sean's smile broadened. "Oh, the *author?*"

Mike looked at him. "You know her?"

"Not personally. But I know her book. I'm a huge fan." His expression was serious. "Tell me, Mike, what does she look like?"

Abby put her face in her hands.

Mike looked a little embarrassed. Sally, who was watching the exchange, raised her hand-painted eyebrows expectantly. "Well, she's a good-looking gal," he conceded.

Sean shot a look at Abby. "She a skinny little thing?"

Mike snorted. "Not exactly."

Sean put his arm around Abby's shoulders, in a rough, just-pals, gee-whiz kind of way and said: "Aw, Abby. Come on, now, Mike and me, we'll never stop loving you, no matter what—"

"Get off me, you idiot," she said as she pushed him away. "Okay, fine. But I just wanted to keep things separate, I didn't want to mix it all up, I want . . ." and she ran out of steam, unsure of what she wanted.

The three of them looked at her in silence, until Sean sat back and said: "Hey, we don't want to put any pressure on you, believe me. But she's a hell of a writer, and boy, she's good to the working man. Speaking as a plumber, that means something."

He raised his eyebrows suggestively and laughed at his own joke.

Abby wanted to hit him.

Mike caught her expression. He took her by the arm, pulled her to her feet and made her walk to the back of the hall with him. In a low voice he said: "What's going on here, Abby? Sally says there's something up between you and Sean. Now I'm not one to go spreadin' trouble, but if you two have things you need to hash out, then maybe you should do it properly so it don't affect the league."

"Oh, I wouldn't want to mess with the league," Abby grumbled. "And anyway, why don't you talk to Sean? Has he said anything about me? Made any comments?"

Mike snorted. "Hell, no. He hasn't come for the last two weeks, and neither have you. So if there's a problem, the two of you need to work out a schedule and alternate. At least Sally and I'd know what was going on. It'd be a tad more courteous than leaving us to play alone or scramble for subs at the last minute."

Abby nodded. "I'm sorry, Mike. I didn't realize. Okay, I'll talk to him."

After that, her bowling took a nose dive. No more strikes, no spares, just what she thought of as sideswipes, when she managed to half-heartedly knock down a few outer pins. The evening seemed to drag on forever.

Finally, standing in the parking lot, she waited until Mike and Sally had walked to their cars.

"Sean, I'm not feeling great, I don't think you should come over," she said, awkwardly, unsure if he even wanted to.

"Fine with me. Just tell me," he asked, "is this because I asked you to have dinner with me?"

She shrugged. She had no idea. Maybe.

"Okay." He nodded.

"And Mike, he feels that you and I are giving Sally and him a raw deal. If we don't want to be here at the same time, we should set up a schedule and organize subs, so they aren't left with a mess every Monday evening."

He still didn't say anything, so she filled the gap. "Maybe you should go next week, and I'll go the week after. That way—"

"Forget it," he shrugged. "I've made plans already. You can have next Monday."

So if that's the way it was going to be. Shared custody of the bowling team. "Okay, fine. Suits me fine."

There was a pause, while they each waited for the other to say something, and then Sean walked away.

Abby couldn't remember how they had reached this deadlock, this place of hostility. She tried to think what he had done wrong. Or was it the other way around? Should she be asking for his forgiveness? No. She had just been honest. He had tried to coerce her into something. Dinner. And now he was sulking. She hadn't done anything wrong.

But it sounded ridiculous when she thought it out loud. And she knew she had hurt Sean. Again. One day he would walk away and she wouldn't see him again. She wouldn't blame him. Maybe this was the night.

The sky was clear, and against the endless dark background, the stars were white points of light, some twinkling, some bright and sharp. An airplane, camouflaged for a second as a star, revealed itself by its plodding, blinking trajectory across the sky. Abby watched it as Sean started his pickup, reversed, and drove away.

CHAPTER TWENTY-EIGHT

It was Thursday, and when Abby arrived at the restaurant, Dulcie had posted an announcement of more scheduling changes. Abby had lost her Sunday night shift.

"Dulcie," she said, finding her boss in the upstairs office, "what's the deal? You take me off Sundays, that means I only have two nights."

Dulcie kept her gaze down on her paperwork. "I know, I'm sorry, Abby, but we're overstaffed, there're no two ways around it, and you have another job. All Henry has is this place, I can't cut him back."

"My other job is dead, so to speak, in case you hadn't noticed."

"Yes, but you're still working there, aren't you?"

"Starting Monday, but it'll be over as soon as the studio is clear and I've helped set up the show. And how are you going to run the whole place with one waiter and one bartender?"

"It's going to be difficult, but I'll be here. I'll work." She smiled apologetically at Abby. "Look, I'm sorry, but I need to run this place like a business, not a charity." She shut one ledger, opened another and began to write. Clearly, Abby had been dismissed.

Abby walked slowly downstairs. How could Dulcie say that? She blamed it all on Fritz. Abby wasn't sure just what he was doing, but she knew he was doing it. He had Dulcie under a spell. But, as George had said, if Abby tried to go up against him, she would lose.

"She's in love," she said darkly to Henry, while they were setting the tables.

Henry saw it a little differently. There was a note of reluctant admiration in his voice. "It's all about the cock. I tell you, he doesn't have that sperm on his head for nothing. The guy's obviously an artist."

Abby shook her head in disgust. There was nothing she could do. If Dulcie wanted to get rid of her, she would.

That afternoon there was a stranger at the staff meeting. The woman was in her thirties, with shoulder-length blonde hair with dark roots. She had obviously spent a fair amount of time in the sun, because her skin was dry and brown, the lines around the eyes showing white. She leaned against the wall, her arms crossed, eyes moving between the different members of the staff.

Before George gave the specials, he looked at the newcomer, and then at Dulcie. "You going to introduce your friend, Dulcie?"

Flustered, Dulcie stood up. "Yes, yes, of course. Everyone, I want you to meet Carmen. She has just arrived from California, and we are very fortunate to have her here. She is going to be our *garde-manger*."

"Our what?" asked Henry, with a look of disbelief on his face. "Why do we need a garbage man?"

Dulcie shot him a look. "Henry, please. Not a garbage man. A *garde-manger*. George can explain."

George looked stunned. "I can explain? You hire someone for my fuckin' kitchen without consulting me?" He looked as if he was about to blow a fuse. "Dulcie, you and I need to talk. Alone." Without waiting for her, he turned and walked out of the room, his head thrust forward angrily. Dulcie gave a nervous look around the room and hurried after him. Everyone remained motionless as they listened to George stomp angrily up the backstairs to the second floor.

"We should all get back to whatever we were doing, guys," Abby suggested. She started setting the tables, ignoring the woman, Carmen, who hadn't moved from her spot against the wall.

Henry followed her anxiously, like a kid whose parents are fighting. "What the hell's going on? What's a garge-whatever?"

Abby glanced at the new hire. "I haven't a clue. Ask Carmen."

Henry looked over at her. "Yeah, okay." Without moving any closer he called out: "Hey, Carmen, what's that thing you do?"

"*Garde-manger,*" she said, and shoved her hands in her jean pockets and walked over to Henry and Abby. She had a slightly rolling gait, like she was a sailor or had just gotten off a horse. "Just a fancy French word for food watcher. I'll do salads, cold things, and help George make sure everything's running smoothly in the kitchen. Expedite." Her voice was low, and had a Western twang to it.

Henry watched her. "George doesn't need anyone."

Carmen shrugged. "Everyone can use some help."

Abby knew there was more to it than that. "How did you meet Dulcie?"

"Through a mutual friend."

"Who's the friend, if you don't mind my asking?"

"Fritzie's an old pal of mine," she said gesturing with her head toward the prep kitchen.

"Fritzie? You mean, Sp—the dishwasher?" Abby bit her tongue.

"Yeah."

"Oh. How do you know him?"

Carmen gave a short laugh. "We go way back."

Abby waited for her to continue, but Carmen seemed done. She looked at Abby with amusement.

"What's so funny, Carmen?"

"Nothing. You should take it easy."

Her tone seemed intended to infuriate. Abby put down the knives she was holding, and left the room. She followed Dulcie and George upstairs, and found them in the tiny, cramped office. He was sitting on the only chair, a sheet of paper in his right hand, and Dulcie was perched on the desk. They both looked up when she appeared in the doorway.

"Dulcie, what's going on?"

"Abby, excuse me, George and I are having a private conversation here."

"Look, I just spoke to her, she's got some little plan up her sleeve—"

George held up the sheet of paper. "Abs, she's got a hell of a résumé," he said, an apologetic tone in his voice.

Abby looked at Dulcie. "You just cut me back a shift, and now you're hiring her?"

Dulcie looked uncomfortable. "She'll only be working Fridays and Saturdays, Abby."

"There's something weird going on, she's a friend of Spermhead's—"

As she said it, she saw George look away with a grimace, as if he'd just witnessed a car crash.

Dulcie looked at her. "Spermhead? Who's—oh!" she gasped, light dawning. "Is that what you call Fritz? That's horrible, Abby. Oh, my god, I can't believe you'd insult someone I care for. I mean, his work ethic, his experience, his knowledge of the business—"

Abby tried to interrupt. "Dulcie, I'm sorry, I—"

But Dulcie had only just begun. Her voice rose. "When Fritz told me about Carmen, you know why I didn't ask anyone's opinion? Because Fritz is right. Over the years I've let the staff make all the important decisions for me."

"So now he's making them—"

"Be quiet! I've been too easy going, too democratic, so this time I made my own decision: I hired Carmen. I've explained everything to George. He realizes that, yes, he could use another person in the kitchen, under his control. He could use the help! But did *you* even bother to find out if Carmen will lighten George's load? No, you're just upset that she's a friend of Fritz's! Spermhead! Abby, that's so cruel and ugly! I feel betrayed, you know that? By you, of all people!"

What little was left of Abby's good intentions disappeared. "You feel

betrayed! How can you say that? I feel betrayed! Ever since you've been getting it on with that tree stump, you've been treating the rest of us like shit!"

Dulcie's jaw dropped. For a second, she was speechless. "Tree stump! Get
out of here, before I fire you!"

"So fire me! I don't give a flying fuck! You've cut my shifts back so much,
I don't make any money here anyway!"

And with that, Abby crashed out of the room, hitting her shoulder hard
against the door frame and jamming her finger on the wall.

Abby walked shakily down the stairs. She couldn't believe what was happening. She'd been a good friend to Dulcie, she'd helped her and stood by
her. She couldn't believe that Dulcie would talk to her like that. As she
stormed by the prep kitchen door, she glanced in. Fritz's back was to her,
and Carmen was standing next to him, looking her way. Abby knew they'd
heard every word. Behind them, in the kitchen, Sandy was on the line, and
he looked away when she caught his eye.

Abby went through the dining room and down the front stairs. Cat and
Henry were talking together at the bar. They looked up guiltily when she
appeared. She ignored them and turned right into the ladies' bathroom.

Once she closed the door, she locked it and sat down on the toilet seat.
She put her face in her hands.

She hated Dulcie. She hated the InnBetween. She didn't want to be a
goddamn waitress, anyway. She was going to walk out the door and never
come back, and they could fuck themselves. George, too, for being such a
whore that at the first sign of a little less work, he caved. Dulcie, for
betraying her. Fritz, for being a creep. And Carmen, for muscling in where
she wasn't needed or wanted. She'd show them. All of them. She brushed
angry tears from her eyes.

Eventually, she took a deep breath. She closed her eyes.

When her heart rate was back to normal, Abby tried to organize her
thoughts a little more realistically.

She had always felt that Dulcie was family. But she wasn't. She had her
own children, and she had found a man she liked. Abby was an employee,
that's all, not family. Dulcie was her boss. Anyway, it was so easy for people

to switch their loyalties. You had to watch out, not become too comfortable, because look how quickly things could change.

What did she really want to do? She could quit. But if she did, she would make Fritz extremely happy. And that was reason enough not to quit. What else? The beer. Who stole the beer? And what was Carmen here for? They were slowing down, cutting back on everyone's hours, yet Dulcie had hired a new person in the kitchen. What was going on? Had Fritz decided to gradually fill the restaurant with his cronies? Probably. If she quit, Dulcie wouldn't have anyone watching her back, not the way she, Abby, could. And though she was so mad at Dulcie she could spit, Dulcie was her responsibility. If she didn't look after her, who would?

The evening crawled by, stilted and painful. Carmen wore crisp whites in the kitchen, and during a lull Abby saw her leaning a forearm on the warmer, saying something across the stainless steel shelf to George. She saw him laugh in response. Abby moved a little to her left so she could see Sandy, and to her dismay, he looked happier than she'd seen him since the day Dulcie had given in and ordered a very expensive slicer for the kitchen. Carmen was winning hearts and minds, and Abby wasn't sure how she was doing it.

Toward the end of her shift, Abby drank a large cup of coffee. She wanted to stay awake. An hour later, she moved her car from the Dollar Store parking lot to an empty spot on the traffic circle across from the InnBetween. She sat in her Bronco, long after the owner of the Chinese take-out had turned off his lights, locked his door, and walked slowly across the circle, his footsteps audible even after he had disappeared from sight up Main Street. From where she sat, she could see all three entrances of the restaurant, albeit none of them very clearly. She also kept an eye on the police station. She didn't want some nosy cop arresting her for loitering.

At last, by eleven, everyone had gone home. The only person left in the building was Fritz.

Abby sat long enough to see Fritz bring out the garbage and put it in the Dumpster, drag out the heavy black rubber mats, and leave them in a pile for the day man to hose down. She saw him stand outside the downstairs back door and smoke a cigarette. She saw him bring out cardboard boxes to be cut down and recycled. Smoke another cigarette. And that was it. No carting of beer cases to his car. No accomplice knocking on the door, no whispering in the alley.

Two hours later, she saw him leave by the side door and walk to his car on Findlay Street.

Abby was chilled to the bone. Time to go home.

On her hilltop, the wind was blowing. In the moonlight, the bare maples stood on the edge of her first field like a somber and skeletal chorus line. She let her dogs out, and they stood near the door, barking. Dead leaves whirled around the trailer, and she wondered how strong the wind would have to be to pick it up and blow it away.

That night, Abby locked the doors after the dogs had finished their last walk. She was relieved to be home, and alone. She wanted to barricade herself in and not go out again until she ran out of food—not answer the phone, and if anyone came by, pretend she wasn't there. She curled up on her bed, fully dressed, and stared at the wall. Without Dulcie and the restaurant, she had no one. Well, Germaine was around, but she didn't count. She thought of Sean and wished he were there, lying next to her. But she had probably screwed that up. She was shocked at how fragile her sense of security and belonging was.

She rolled onto her back and looked at the cracks in the low ceiling. She examined the light fixture, a pink glass breast centered above her. She knew she was indulging herself, floating in self-pity, but she rationalized it by saying to herself that it didn't matter, there was no one around her to behave for. Just as she said it, a cold nose touched her hand. She started and looked down. Delilah was doing a slithering crawl up toward her, tail wagging, love oozing. Her delicate black lips seemed to be smiling at Abby, and Abby couldn't help it, she smiled back. She was lucky, she had her dogs, her yellow trailer, she owned land—and she could stand outside and hold up a handful of dirt, like Scarlett O'Hara. She was healthy, and she had two jobs. Well, one and a half. Actually, more like two halves, right now. But that wasn't really so bad. She could make it all work for her. She just had to stay focused on the questions. Like Fritz. He was a question. And Norman. The adoption. And Wanda. Don't forget Wanda.

She rolled over and put an arm around Delilah. Rick, afraid of being left out, came and stood on top of her. Yeah, she thought, life could be worse. She thought of Sean again, but pushed it out of her mind. It was Thursday night, not Friday, not Saturday. And yes, she was at home in bed with her dogs. So what.

CHAPTER TWENTY-NINE

Abby hadn't been to Norman's house since she had found his dead body on the living room floor. She parked in front of the house, feeling anxious and a little queasy.

Saranda's car was in the driveway. Abby knocked on the kitchen door, and when no one answered, she let herself in. The kitchen looked neat, the sink dry and unused. She heard the vacuum in the front of the house. The house seemed overheated. Her hands were balled into fists, and her palms were sweating gently.

"Damn," she muttered to herself. She had been hoping to catch Saranda in the kitchen and not have to walk through the living room.

However, she did, and whatever she was afraid of didn't happen, or wasn't there. The room was exactly as it always was, a slightly worn, well-proportioned and comfortable room. The house didn't yet know it had no master. Eventually someone else would come in, change it, paint it, rename it. Just as Norman must have done in his day. The new owners would eventually erase the old man who had lived there for more than forty years. Today, however, Saranda was vacuuming nearby, and the plaid couch was still waiting for Norman to lie on it.

In the office, Saranda screamed when Abby tapped on the door to get her attention over the sound of the machine.

"Sorry, sorry, I just wanted to say hi," Abby said, as the woman cursed at her.

"Abby, you should have given me some warning, girl. This place feels like a ghost house to me today."

"Me, too. I know, I should have called. Can I make you a cup of coffee?"

Saranda relented. "Okay. But don't make a mess in there. I'm nearly done with that end of the house."

Ten minutes later, they were sitting at the kitchen table. Abby had even scrounged up some cookies. "They're just going to go bad," she said, feeling as if she had to apologize for looking in Norman's cupboards.

"What are you going to do now?" she asked the housekeeper, when they were both sipping from their mugs.

Saranda sat back in her chair. "I'll work for Maddie a little longer, and then I'm going back to school."

Abby was impressed. "What're you going to do?"

"Nursing. I've been considering it for a good while now, and this seems like the proper time. And you?"

Abby gave a half smile. "I still have my first job. At the restaurant. I'll just stay there, maybe find something else part time."

"You should make something of yourself, you know. You're a smart person. Sometimes things happen, and you should take them as a sign. Norman died for a reason, the poor old man. Time to make a change."

"You're probably right," Abby said, paying lip service to what Saranda was saying. She didn't have plans or dreams on the back burner, ready to pull forward when a sign came along. "In the meantime, I wanted to ask you something."

"Fire away."

"Can you take a guess at how Norman died?"

·

"No, sugar. But he was an old man, and I've got to believe his heart just stopped working."

Abby nodded. "Could he have died of a drug overdose?"

"You're pulling my leg! A drug overdose?"

"What if he took too many pills?"

Saranda looked unconvinced. "I don't think so. He has one of those boxes, marked with the days, and anyway, I'm the one who reminded him about his pills, after his breakfast. He never bothered with them otherwise."

"What pills did he take?"

"Let's see, he took aspirin, then one for his memory, and something for his heart. That's it."

Abby sat still, thinking, tapping on the table with one finger. "Do you think he could have killed himself?"

Saranda shook her head, for once looking at a loss. "I don't know. It's hard for me to believe he'd do such a thing, but he was an old man, and he had a flighty imagination. Sometimes he thought people were after him, or would come over in the night. Believe me, he told me one tale about some woman who came and tried to shoot him. You see what I mean?"

Saranda sipped her coffee, watching Abby. When Abby looked less than surprised, she exclaimed: "Surely that was a fairy tale, was it?"

"It didn't happen quite that way. It was a misunderstanding. But he wasn't that far off."

"Oh, my lord! That man. So there was some truth in it, anyway."

Abby nodded. "I think there was always some truth in his stories. He told me a strange story, two nights before he died, of being abducted by priests and locked in a cellar. Maybe cellars and basements meant something special to him. Or maybe it's all some kind of code."

Saranda put down her cup. "That reminds me, he left a message for you. I don't know when he wrote it, it could have been weeks ago. But I'm pretty sure it's for you. I left it on his desk." She stood up. "I'm going to finish up in front and get the upstairs. My kids are taking me out to dinner tonight, so I want to be done early."

Abby stood, too, and took the mugs to the sink. Saranda went back to work and Abby washed out the coffee pot. She left everything as she had found it. She noticed that Norman's pill dispenser was next to the phone. Behind it were the bottles of medications. Carefully, she wrote down the names of the drugs and the dosages on the pad of paper next to the phone. She tore off the sheet she had written on, folded it up and slid it into her pocket.

In the study, everything seemed exactly as she had left it. A single piece of yellow paper lay in the center of Norman's desk. Abby sat down in front of it and picked it up. A few lines of wobbly writing crawled unevenly across it. In places the writer had pressed too hard, tearing the paper. She tried to read it, but all she could make out was:

The old woma [illegible] here, to hant me hant hant
hant hant
Lamy [?] will tomoro.
[scrawled, smeary] Nor [illegible]

Abby felt a cold tightening of her stomach. What was he talking about? She didn't understand, but she felt he was writing with urgency. To her. She read it again. The old woman was here? To hand me? Hang? Hunt me? Why had he written the word so many times? Had he suffered some kind of hallucination? She wondered what old woman he was referring to. Could he mean the girl in the field, Wanda? She'd died when she was about fifty, Abby guessed. Not really an old woman, but maybe that was who he was referring to.

She got up and went over to the low chest of drawers where she had found the drawings for the mural. This time, she went straight to the folder she had first opened, and once more turned over the drawing done so many years before of the girl in the field. Wanda. There she was, her young body open and unprotected. Abby studied it, but it revealed nothing new to her. Norman must've been about thirty-six at the time. And she'd have been, what, eighteen? It was the beginning of a long relationship. Abby knew there were plenty of successful relationships with that wide an age gap. But still.

Slowly, she looked through the rest of the drawings. Some were char-coals, and some pen-and-ink. All were done with a sure, confident hand. They covered a range of studies, from still lifes to quick sketches of people caught in a variety of poses. An old man, sitting on a chair outside a door. A woman, laughing, wearing a head scarf. Abby turned it over. Bella. But none of the sketches revealed any secrets, at least as far as Abby could see. Just the focused work of a skilled draftsman.

Abby closed the portfolio and returned it to the drawer. She sat for a few minutes, then listened for Saranda. She could hear the vacuum cleaner upstairs, so she took the stairs up to the second floor. Saranda was in Norman's bedroom, on her hands and knees, pushing the nozzle back and forth under the bed.

Abby went over to the machine and turned it off.

"Drat!" said Saranda, turning. "Oh, it's you," she said when she saw that Abby, not an unplugged cord, was responsible.

"Sorry to interrupt. I just want to ask you about this letter," Abby said, holding up the yellow sheet.

Saranda sat back on her haunches. "Yes?"

"Do you remember when you found this?"

"Just today, sweetie."

"Was it sitting on his desk?"

"No, it was behind it. Maybe it slipped back there."

Abby nodded slowly, thinking. "So you think it might have been there a while?"

Saranda put her finger on the ON button of the vacuum, ready to go. "No more than one week. I clean his office from top to bottom once a week. I rotate the house, you know."

"I see. Thanks, Saranda. And good luck, okay?"

"You too. Think about what I said. Time to make a change." And she pushed the button.

Abby walked slowly toward the staircase. Her footsteps were silent, drowned out by the vacuum cleaner.

She drove back into Bantam and out the other side. At the light she turned east, but before leaving the village, she made another left at the only drug-store in town. Part of a large chain, it occupied a building that years before had been a small supermarket. Abby usually tried to avoid it, having had a run-in with one of their employees over the summer, but she needed to speak to the pharmacist.

She walked by the racks of make-up and toothbrushes to the back of the store. Luckily, there was only one old man waiting. He was sitting slumped in the only chair, very still, looking at a flyer.

Abby went to the counter, and waited to catch someone's eye.

"Can I help you?" asked a friendly young woman. She was large and blonde, and wearing a white coat with a name tag above her left breast.

"Yes, please. I need some information," Abby said, as she dug into her pocket for the piece of paper where she'd written the names of Norman's pills. She found it and laid it, wrinkled, on the counter. She pushed it gently toward the blonde. "I need to know something about these medications."

The woman, whose name tag said L. MCGRATH, PHARMACIST, took it and glanced at it, then asked Abby: "What do you need to know?"

Abby suddenly felt awkward. The old man in the chair was looking at her, curious. "I, ah, need to know what happens if someone who is on both of these medications takes an overdose."

L. McGrath's expression changed from warm and friendly to faintly sus-picious. She looked back down at the sheet of paper. "Why do you ask?"

Abby shifted her weight from one foot to the other. "Well, because I have an elderly friend who is taking these pills, and, ah, I want to make sure she doesn't hurt herself." She had found her story, and now she could run with it. "She's forgetful, and I don't want her taking more than she's supposed to. So I want to know, in case she does, what might happen."

Ms. McGrath didn't look convinced. "First thing you should do is make sure she has a dated pill dispenser."

"A what?"

She pointed to the wall next to the counter. "One of these."

Abby saw a rack of pill containers exactly like Norman's, with the days of the week on each little separate compartment. "Oh, okay, good," she said, taking one off the hook. She looked at L. McGrath expectantly.

Reluctantly, L. McGrath examined the paper. "The heart medication could be dangerous. If she takes too many, her heart could race and she could have a problem. Especially if she lives alone."

"So it could bring on a heart attack?"

"Possibly. Depending on her condition."

Abby gave her a grateful smile. Then, realizing that might seem inappropriate, she wiped it off her face and nodded, solemnly. "Well, I'll make sure she's very careful. Thank you." She took the paper out of the woman's hand and turned to go.

"Wait, your pill dispenser," said the pharmacist, holding it up.

"Oh, sure. Of course." Abby paid for it and took the bag, trying to appear grateful. She thought the woman looked faintly victorious.

CHAPTER THIRTY

On her way back through Bantam, Abby stopped at Victor's for coffee. She sat outside, sipping it in the late-morning sun, thinking. There wasn't much she could do if someone had given Norman a few extra pills. She'd just have to keep her eyes open. At least she knew that he could've had a shove on his way to the other side. Not that it did her much good, but it helped to be informed. She thought of the people who might have done it: Germaine headed her list, for the simple reason that Abby'd watched her pull a gun on him.

In the meantime, she had something else to do. When she finished her coffee, she threw her empty cup in the tall trash can on the sidewalk. She walked down Main Street, past the old Carlson's building and stopped at a small, two-story wooden house. It was set back from the sidewalk behind an ornate black iron railing. A sign hung, gallows-style, from a post in the front garden, which in summer was filled with flowers. It read: *Franklin Delano Van Renesse, Attorney-at-Law.*

Abby let herself into the garden and walked up the path to the front door. Inside, Abby took the steep, creaking wooden stairs. Abby remembered an old story she'd heard as a girl, about a man who had kept his horse upstairs, in this very building. She wondered who was left to tell that story. She felt a flash of worry that there was no one, or that she'd imagined it. She pictured Norman, his forehead resting on his fingertips. Trying to remember.

Franklin's secretary, Mary, was on the phone. When Abby pointed to Franklin's office, she nodded.

Abby knocked. Waited.

"Come in."

Inside, Franklin was sitting at his large oak partners' desk. There was a wide bay window on Abby's left, and the wall across from her was lined with books. Franklin had an open file in front of him, and he was writing on a legal pad. He didn't look up but kept on with what he was doing as he spoke.

"Give me one second, I'm nearly done."

Abby took a seat in the comfortable armchair across the desk from him, and listened to the scratch of his pen. She picked at a loose piece of skin on her thumb.

Finally, Franklin looked up. "Well hello, Abby. What brings you here?"

Abby tilted her head to one side. "Beer."

He looked at her, questioning. "You have one? You want one?"

"No, clever man. I have to catch someone who's stealing it."

"Okay. This sounds like something to do with the InnBetween. Am I correct?"

"Yes, you are."

"Okay. So, please, tell."

"Well. You know Dulcie hired a new dishwasher, right?"

"No, I did not," he answered.

"You're kidding."

Franklin shook his head. "You might find this hard to believe, but not everyone cares that much. About the staffing at your restaurant."

"You are so wrong. Anyway. Dulcie hired this guy, his name is Fritz. We call him Spermhead."

"Nice."

"There's a good reason, but he'd be a creep even without it. The problem is, Dulcie really likes him. In fact, he and she are doing the dirty, as far as the rest of us can tell."

Franklin shook his head. "God, I hope I never have to work in a restaurant."

"You just might, you know, you hit the skids, need a little extra cash to support your coke habit."

"What coke habit?"

"The one you're going to develop if you keep going out with Germaine."

Franklin sat back in his chair. "Did you come here for advice, or to talk trash?"

"Sorry. I'm feeling a little bitter. The thing is, Spermhead has Dulcie believing that we're stealing from her."

"Are you?"

"Look, no one has ever stolen from Dulcie, ever. I mean, yeah, we take desserts home once in a while, and have a drink at the bar, but we don't steal from her. We don't rob her."

"Not outright. So, some beer is missing?"

"Yes. Thanks to Spermhead's diligence, and according to Dulcie's calculations, there are three cases of beer missing."

"She should know. I mean, empties, tallies, invoices, it all should add up, right?"

"Yes, but I think Fritz did it."

"Why?"

"It's obvious, Franklin! Because he wants to discredit us with Dulcie. Discredit me, in particular. I've been too close to Dulcie, and he doesn't like it. He has some kind of agenda. I can feel it. I just don't know what it is. And now this old friend of his, Carmen, is working in the kitchen, helping George and Sandy."

"How does George feel?"

Abby made a face. "George isn't a suspicious guy. He likes people, and this woman's good, she's making the kitchen more efficient. He's happy. Sandy adores her, thinks she walks on dishwater."

Franklin nodded. "I see. So what do you want me to do?"

"I don't know. I suppose I just wanted to talk it out with you. You're a friend, you're an unbiased third party, right?"

He shook his head. "No, Abby. If I were unbiased, I would go to the Big Sperm, or whatever you call him, and get his side of the story."

Abby was exasperated. "You don't need his side of the story. Trust me, he's a lowlife. He's manipulating Dulcie, and sooner or later he's going to hurt her. You just wait and see, Franklin!"

He looked at her steadily, as if she were a troublesome but basically well-intentioned child. "So what're your ideas? I know you've got some. Maybe not all that sound, but something."

Abby shifted in her chair. "I sat outside last night, watching the restaurant. I thought maybe I'd catch him."

"Did you?"

"Nope. I just watched him do his work and smoke a lot of cigarettes out back."

Franklin nodded. "Don't do that anymore, okay? It's not a good idea. Or if you do, at least get someone to sit out there with you."

Abby smiled. "Fine. I'll call you. You can park in front of the Chinese restaurant with me for a few hours."

He suddenly looked irritated. "Listen, I've got work to do. Let me think about it, okay?"

Abby stood up. "Fine. Thanks." She walked to the door, and then asked: "Is something wrong?"

Franklin opened another file on his desk. He looked up at her. "No, nothing at all, Abby. Just don't do anything stupid, okay?"

CHAPTER THIRTY-ONE

Monday morning of the last week in October, and the leaves along the sides of River Street were rotting in thick brown piles. Abby parked outside Norman's house, feeling that first real crisping of the air, a sign that winter was starting to flex its muscles. Not cold yet, just the season looking over autumn's shoulder and showing its sharp, pointy teeth.

Abby wore an army surplus jacket that she'd inherited from her husband. It had been handed down from her father-in-law, and the name SILVER-NALE was stenciled on a name tag sewn over the breast pocket. When she wore it she felt like a member of a clan, with the dead Silvernale men watching her back. She wondered if they actually would have, had they known her.

It was the first day of the Metal Building cleanup. In a moment of inspiration, Abby had phoned Cal and asked him if he wanted to spend a few days clearing out the abandoned studio with her. It seemed like a good way for him to learn something about his grandfather and get to know his uncle.

They would save any heavy lifting for the second day, when Henry was joining them.

A large black Dumpster had been delivered and left by the rolling iron doors of the Metal Building.

"Everything seems possible when you have a Dumpster," Abby said, as she unlocked the green door and pushed hard to get it open. Paul and Cal followed her into the cold gloom. She found the light switch, and they waited while the fluorescents flickered into life.

"Do you think you're going to know what's garbage and what's his work?" Abby asked, looking at the jumble of metal on the floor and on the shelves in front of them.

"I'll know." Paul said, surveying the work area.

And he seemed to. He spent the morning taking everything that needed to be salvaged and putting it in a neat pile outside, while Cal and Abby, both wearing heavy work gloves, took out bucketfuls of wood and metal scraps and tipped them over the high side of the Dumpster. A collapsed sofa was left to wait for Henry, but they got rid of half a dozen broken chairs and a folding table that was caked in rust. They worked around the heavy equipment designed to cut, bend, and press metal. When Paul had finished, they swept and cleaned the floor.

At one, they stopped for lunch and ate their sandwiches outside, sitting on plastic folding chairs they had found stacked in a corner.

"It's like the secret burial ground of elephants," Abby said, drinking from her water bottle, gesturing to the pile of blades and twirled metal that were the limbs and parts of Norman's work. "Maybe we should dig a hole and plant it all in the field."

"Back to where they all came from," Paul said, wiping his forehead with the back of his hand, leaving a streak of dirt to mark the spot. He seemed worn out, his long body sagging in his chair.

"Why did he stop?" Cal asked.

Abby wasn't sure what he meant. "Stop what?"

"Making these things."

"The big pieces?" Paul looked at him.

"Yeah, I heard he was pretty famous. What happened?"

"He *was* pretty famous. Pieces like these were worth a lot of money." Paul shrugged. "It was before my time, but I think he just burned out. After a while, he fired his agent and most of his staff. He became reclusive. His work changed."

"Is that when you started working for him?"

"Yes," Paul said, self-mockingly. "Just like me, to miss all the excitement."

"What did you do for him?"

"Oh, I'd do some of the work on pieces that were sent back for repairs. I'd run the machines, bend metal, solder, weld. I also helped him pull up all the pieces from the field out here, and junk them."

"Those were permanent? I thought they were just put up temporarily, for a show," Abby said.

"Oh, no, permanent. There must've been at least eight huge pieces spread out across the field. Set in cement. So delicately balanced that even the slightest breeze would move them, and during a high wind it was something to see. They looked alive, bending and waving. These ones here," he said, leaning down and touching a long, thin piece of stainless steel that was wider at one end and thinner at the other, "these were blades like enormous chopsticks, slicing and cutting. Those over there were circles within circles. You see those flat squares? They used to rise and fall, like fans. It was something."

"Why'd he get rid of them? Did you ever figure it out?"

Paul shook his head, and nudged one of the lifeless and dirty pieces of metal with his foot. "No, I never did."

Eventually, Abby put on her gloves and clapped her hands together once, making a dusty cloud. "Cal, we should get back to work before we lose steam. Let's go upstairs and check it out. Paul, shall we use our judgment, or do you want to tell us what to keep and what to get rid of?"

"Well, I might as well come up and see," he said wearily, standing with effort.

They clanged up the iron staircase that stood at the back of the studio and led up to the enclosed mezzanine. At the top, they found themselves on a small landing. To the left was a closed door. On the landing, a desk was set against the back wall under a high window, and there was a table in the center of the space.

"This was the office, and a sort of communal eating area, conference room," Paul said, gesturing to the table. Through the window, Abby could see the thick stand of trees behind the building.

A narrow corridor led off to the right. Paul went first, leading them to the kitchen at the far end.

It was more of a galley than a kitchen, with small appliances built into and around each other, a short counter, and a few overhead cupboards. All of it was filthy. The refrigerator door was open, the rubber seal around it eaten away, rust patches over its surface like mange. The stove was no better.

Abby was glad she was wearing gloves, even though she hadn't touched anything. The floor was gritty with dirt.

Paul made a face of disgust. "These appliances should go in the Dumpster, while we have it. Maybe the whole room should."

Backtracking, Abby and Cal followed Paul through a hollow-core door into a tiny bathroom. It had the bare essentials: toilet, sink, and a narrow shower. Everything was covered in grime, and the sink and toilet were stained with rust. The faded shower curtain was still in place, torn and hanging from two rings. It had a pattern on it. Abby held up one hardened edge. It was a map of the world.

"Look, the U.S.S.R.," she said, pointing to a big patch that had once been pink.

"I remember that," Paul nodded.

He turned on a faucet in the sink. Nothing happened. "Shut off. I'll turn them on once you've finished in here. We should leave these fixtures. They're fine, so long as the pipes aren't rusted solid."

The door on the other side of the landing opened into what was obviously a small bedroom.

"Who used this?" Abby asked, surprised.

"Norman used to nap here occasionally, when he was working on something. I suppose in the old days staff could sleep here if something big was going on and everyone was working late. Or if the roads were bad."

The walls, originally white, were now dull and gray with dust and age. A lightbulb hung by a wire from the ceiling. In the corner was an iron hospital bed, a small wooden table next to it. Across from the bed hung a plain mirror, discolored with black spots. A faded blanket was folded at the foot of the stained and torn mattress. The insides showed spots of the original blue but the fabric had been eaten out in a foot-wide crater through every layer, creating a foul, sour-smelling mouse habitat, long abandoned.

"Christ," Abby said, dropping the corner. "I'll go get some garbage bags from the house."

Paul nodded. "When's Henry coming?"

"He'll be here tomorrow."

"Good. I don't care what you do in here. Get rid of everything."

Abby nodded. "We'll leave the iron bed. They're indestructible."

For the rest of the afternoon, Paul stayed downstairs, bringing the metal pieces back into the studio and organizing them on the swept floor, making separate piles of like parts. Abby and Cal took on the upstairs. Using thick plastic garbage bags, they collected everything that wasn't too big or anchored down, starting with the blanket.

Cal was excited when he found a row of moth-eaten work jackets hanging on a wall. He thought he could keep one, but when he lifted it off the peg, it kept its pointed, hanging shape until it cracked apart in his hands.

"It's weird to know that my mother was here when she was a girl," he said, holding the rotted jacket. "She had a rough time, I think."

Abby looked up from what she was doing. "Yeah?"

Cal nodded. "She doesn't talk about it much, but it eats away at her, you know? She can't let it go. I wish I could help her." He shrugged and pushed the last jacket into a full garbage bag. He lifted it up and left the room.

Abby watched him, wondering. She went back to what she was doing. Inside the drawer of the bedside table she discovered a pair of worn leather moccasins filled with acorns. She hesitated before throwing them away, wondering if they were the pair that had first brought her and Norman to the Metal Building less than six weeks before. They were saturated with dark rings of mouse urine; she smiled, picturing the shoe collector in Berlin receiving them in the mail.

From under the bed she pulled out a small ivory suitcase. Inside was a plaid robe, a pair of cotton pajamas, a towel, and a toothbrush bag, its zipper rusted solid. Every item was covered in patches of black mold. She closed the suitcase and took it downstairs with the full garbage bag. It all went into the Dumpster.

The next day Abby and Cal were back at the Metal Building by ten A.M. Henry appeared an hour later, his thick black hair tied up in a ponytail, work gloves tucked into his back pocket. He and Cal began by carrying down the old stove. Next was the refrigerator, followed by anything from the kitchen that wasn't nailed down, and if something was, they used a crowbar to free it.

By lunchtime, the upstairs was bare. The bedroom was empty except for the iron bed frame and the mirror on the wall. The bathroom had been stripped of everything but the fixtures, and the kitchen was left with nothing but the sink and a capped-off gas pipe for the stove. Abby had put on a mask and swept up mounds of dirt and deadly-looking black crud and shoveled it into garbage bags.

Maddie came out to see how they were doing and to bring them a pizza. Cal set up the folding chairs in the sun. They took off their gloves and ate in silence, tired and filthy.

"I'm going home now," Abby said, standing up with a sigh. "I need to boil myself. Cal, let me give you a ride over to the house."

Cal glanced at her, nodded, and kept eating.

Henry sat back in his chair with his eyes closed. "Yeah, I'm looking forward to a hot shower, too. I feel like I've been soaking in the past, and it don't smell so good."

Maddie started cleaning up the paper plates and putting them in the pizza box. "I really appreciate this, you know. So would Norman."

"So what else is left to do?" Abby asked.

Maddie looked at the open door, trying or organize her thoughts. "Not much. Paul will take all the salvageable pieces over to the workshop. It's heated, so he can take his time over the winter finding the plans for the sculptures, and organizing the reassembly. And that's about it."

"Okay," said Cal. Abby and Henry just nodded.

About fifteen minutes later, Abby and Cal got into the Bronco. She had asked him to take a ride with her for a reason. When they arrived at the house, Abby stopped the car and turned to the young man next to her.

"Cal, I need you to be honest with me."

He blushed quickly, the color spreading up to his forehead. Abby couldn't tell if it was anger or embarrassment. "Why? Ah, sure. What's up?"

"I'm just going to come right out and ask. Did you send your aunt that anonymous letter? Back last August?"

Cal's mouth opened and closed. An expression of indignation blew across his face, but only stayed a short time, as if he'd tried it on and discarded it. His face finally opted for belligerence. "Yeah. So?"

Abby looked at him, trying to gauge why a young guy like him would do it. "Good. I'm glad you told me. It only occurred to me yesterday, when you were talking about your mother."

"What're you going to do about it?"

Abby took a moment to think about it. "Nothing, I'm not going to do anything. I think you should talk to Germaine, though. Actually, I think she's sort of grateful for that letter, it got her off her butt. But she needs to know. As does your mother. It'll clear the air."

Cal looked at her, waiting to see if she was going to keep going. When she didn't say anything else, he nodded, then took hold of the door handle as if he were about to get out.

Abby put her hand on his arm. "Why'd you do it?" she asked.

Cal slumped back into the seat, his expression unhappy. He turned and looked at Abby. "My mother's an addict." Abby's eyes widened in shock, and Cal shook his head. "No, not drugs. She's addicted to shopping."

"Oh." Abby smiled.

Cal didn't smile back. "No, it's serious. She a compulsive shopper, but only from home. Online, catalog, phone. It doesn't matter. I have to go through her mail every day and take out stacks of catalogs before she can get her hands on them. Not that it stops her. She has four different kinds of remote earphones for the TV, all in their boxes. Clothes hanging in her closet with the tags still on them. Books, so many books. Two dog beds, even though we don't have a dog. Useless kitchen appliances. She buys me things I'll never use. You don't see it, because she stores it all away in her attic, in the guest room, in the basement. It's nonstop. Ask the post office—they must get four boxes a day for her. Trust me, I know, because I spend a lot of time returning things."

Abby opened her mouth to say something, but Cal gestured her to silence. He kept talking, eyes on the dashboard. "I figure it's gotta be something to do with her past. Her family. She buys this stuff to try to fill some sort of void. That's my theory. What else could it be? I've tried to talk to her about it, and sometimes she even agrees with me. But nothing changes. She just buys another blender."

"But why'd you say in the letter that there was something suspicious about Wanda's death?"

"Last year, it got so bad my mother was like a guitar string that's wound too tight—I was just waiting for her to snap. The anonymous letter was pretty lame, I see it now, but I was desperate. From the way my mother described her, my aunt sounded like the kind of person who wouldn't be afraid to, you know, make some noise. And there was something about Wanda, something my mother wouldn't talk about, so I embellished, I guess. I was afraid if I just wrote to Germaine, she wouldn't take me seriously. So I sent the letter inside another envelope to my mom's agent in Belgium and had him mail it." Cal finally shot Abby a quick look. "I was young. I know better now." He nodded. His defense was over.

"It must be hard on you, looking out for her by yourself," Abby said.

"I'm pretty used to it," With nothing else to say, Cal got out of the car and shut the door. He raised his hand in a salute and walked away.

When Abby got home, she took off all her dirty clothes outside the front door and stood for a moment, naked, enjoying the breeze on her body and the isolation that made it possible. One of Lloyd's cows looked up from the ground and watched her, lower jaw rotating, eyes unimpressed.

She stood a long time in the shower, scrubbing off the smell of mouse urine that she was sure had saturated her hair and skin.

Her arm muscles were sore from hauling trash, but she was happy to be working. After all, it was Tuesday, and she didn't have another shift at the restaurant until Thursday.

The phone rang, interrupting her thoughts.

Abby picked it up and heard a loud sigh. Germaine didn't bother to introduce herself. "I just got a call from that woman down in Hudson, from the Department of Social Services."

"Hello to you, too. What did she have to say?"

"She says the file's in, so I said we'd be down to see her tomorrow morning at ten. Happy now?"

"Yes, Germaine, thanks. And I hope you are, too."

"I want to drive, okay? Where do we meet, Victor's?"

"Perfect. Nine-thirty?"

"Fine. Will I see you at the InnBetween tonight?"

"Nope, I'm not on."

"Come in anyway."

"Not tonight. I'm tired. See you tomorrow, okay?"

"Okay. Party pooper."

CHAPTER THIRTY-TWO

The next morning, Abby made a short detour before meeting Germaine. Maddie had arranged for the Dumpster pickup on Friday, so before it was too late she wanted to do a last check of the Metal Building. In fact, she had left a couple of bags of trash on the mezzanine floor of the Metal Building and wanted to make sure she hauled them out. She had the key in her purse and, without stopping at the house, drove across the field and parked next to the empty cinderblock building.

Inside, the studio was cool and damp. Abby went up the metal stair, the noise echoing in the silence. She looked through the grill work of each step to the cement floor below. If she slipped and fell, would she die or just break a leg or two? How long would it take someone to find her?

Upstairs, she found the last two bags where she had left them. She wished she'd brought her work gloves. The place was much cleaner, but it really needed mopping as well.

She was about to make her way downstairs, when the desk on the landing caught her eye. It was set back against the wall, under the window. Plain, wooden, and apparently undamaged, they had left it alone. Curious, Abby put the garbage bags down. She hadn't looked in the desk. She should make double sure it was solid enough to merit keeping.

It had one long shallow drawer under the writing surface, and two deep enough for files on the right-hand side. She pulled the long one first, but there was nothing but a few pencils, and a pen that had leaked on the wood, creating a large stain. When she tried the top file drawer, she discovered that the wood had swollen over the years, and it wouldn't move. Bracing herself with one foot on the desk, she pulled hard. With a harsh squeal, it gave way. Abby peered inside, but the drawer was empty. She tried the lower one, and it slid open with relative ease. Inside, a dusty pink manila folder lay on the bottom of the drawer.

"Aha," Abby said out loud, and as she reached in to pick it up she felt a shooting pain in her back where she'd strained it opening the top drawer. She lifted out the folder, and, once she'd checked it for spiders, laid it on the top of the desk.

However, if Abby had been expecting something interesting, she was out of luck. The folder contained receipts. Handwritten receipts from hardware stores, lighting stores, and grocery stores. On each receipt was a name, in pen. She looked through them and found receipts labeled John, Norman, Mike, Athena. It must have been the studio's system for reimbursing expenses incurred by various members of the staff and family. Some were dated with just the month and day, others also had the year. They seemed to cover a few months of 1982—July, August, and September. Athena's two bills were from Dunbar's Pharmacy, on Main Street in Bantam. Abby remembered Dunbar's. It had still been there when she first moved to Bantam, though it had long since moved to the edge of town and been bought out by a big chain. The articles listed were aspirin and shampoo. Nothing sinister.

Disappointed she hadn't discovered the Rosetta Stone that would unlock all the mysteries, Abby replaced the file and closed the drawer. Her back still protesting, she hauled the two garbage bags down the narrow iron staircase and outside, heaving them over the tall side of the Dumpster. It was strange, being there alone. She pictured the Metal Building as it must have been, all those years ago, bustling with people, everyone with a job or a purpose. She realized, when she thought back to the receipts, that she hadn't seen any with Wanda's name on them. And then she remembered that 1982 was the year Wanda died. So she was sick then. Not running errands for the studio.

She thought of Athena, a junior in high school, her sisters gone, living here with her parents. Her mother sick, her father working. She should ask her more about it. And what had Cal said the other day? It'd been rough? He sounded protective of her. A good son would be. Still, it was interesting.

CHAPTER THIRTY-THREE

Half an hour later, Abby arrived at the café in time to get a large coffee to go. She chatted with Victor, keeping one eye on the street. The Miata pulled into the handicapped parking space in front of the café fifteen minutes late. Germaine climbed slowly out of the low car, her eyes bloodshot. Abby met her outside.

"I need coffee, I'll be right back," she said as she walked past Abby.

She came out a few minutes later and stood on the sidewalk, took a drink of the hot liquid, breathed deep and said: "Abby, drive, okay? I'm wrecked."

Abby had to admit she enjoyed driving the sporty little car. Especially with the top up. She felt differently about herself as she sat in it, as if she were a more flamboyant, light-hearted person. Someone who took risks and lived with a little smile on her lips. She tried smiling flirtatiously as herself in the rearview mirror. Then, afraid Germaine was watching her, she glanced over. But her passenger was staring dully at the road ahead, her coffee held against her lips.

They arrived at the Department of Social Services by ten-fifteen. Reesa, the woman who had called Germaine, was busy with someone else. They took seats in the waiting area. Germaine immediately put her head back and shut her eyes.

Half an hour later, Reesa was ready for them. This time she took them into a small, adjacent office. They sat across her desk from her and watched as she pulled a file from a stack in front of her. She flipped it open, laid her hands, palm down on it, and said: "Here we are, Germaine. The file you requested."

Abby followed her gaze and looked at Germaine. It suddenly dawned on her that Germaine was not just hungover, she was terrified. She sat in the chair, pale and motionless, her breathing shallow. Abby reached over and took one of her hands. It was ice-cold and clammy. She gave it a squeeze.

Reesa flipped through the file, looking over the papers. "I went over the case file with my supervisor, and it looks like your mother left everything open. No restrictions. The adoptive family also. So why don't you ask me questions, and I'll answer as best I can. How does that sound?"

Germaine nodded, swallowed dryly and said nothing.

Abby looked at her. "Do you want me to ask questions until you're ready?"

Germaine nodded again.

"Okay." She turned to Reesa. "Can you tell us why the girls were taken from their mother?"

Reesa looked for the right sheet. "It says for neglect, endangering the children's welfare." She read on. "A neighbor complained that the two little girls, ages eight and ten, were left alone for entire days and nights. They were dirty and hungry. They'd come over asking for food." The young social worker looked at Germaine, something like pity in her expression. "Another neighbor said the mother, Bridget Gubinek, was a fixture at a local bar, The Tainted Lady down on Warren. We have a police report here. She was arrested there twice for causing a disturbance, once for assault."

Germaine's expression hadn't changed, she hadn't moved, but her face had gone from pale to flushed, and her eyes had tears in them.

Abby waited to see if she would ask something. When Germaine didn't speak, Abby said: "What about the girls' father? Was he around?"

"I don't remember seeing anything about him, but let me look." Reesa slowly turned over the loose pages. As she read, she made an unconscious sound, like a hum. The flip of the pages was the only other sound in the room.

"Ahh, here's something," she said finally. "This is in a letter that your mother addressed to this office. She is explaining why she wanted her daughters back, because their father had moved to California three years previously, for work reasons, and she was going to join him as soon as she had the girls with her."

Germaine spoke, her hand still cold in Abby's. "Does she give his first name?"

Reesa looked up. "No, I'm sorry."

Germaine didn't answer.

They sat in silence for a few moments. Abby asked: "How did you find the foster family, the Smiths?"

Reesa flipped through more papers until she zeroed in on the one she was looking for. "It was the mother, Bridget Gubinek, who requested them."

"Oh, really? She knew them?"

Reesa looked up. "Oh, sure. It was a situation I'm sure we were very happy with. We'd much rather keep children within a family."

"What?" Germaine said.

"Yes," Reesa continued, "according to this, Wanda Smith and Bridget Gubinek were sisters."

CHAPTER THIRTY-FOUR

That Friday night, Abby filled in for Cat, who was visiting family in Boston. She was late for work. She'd been doing that more often lately—not on purpose, but she'd found she no longer looked forward to going into the InnBetween, and when she was there, she worked her shift, took her tips, and left. She and Dulcie were civil to each other, but they no longer shared complaints or jokes about the customers; Dulcie had stopped keeping her up-to-date on her younger son's latest skateboarding injury, or her thirteen-year-old daughter's frightening abuse of eyebrow tweezers.

Abby had to admit that the kitchen seemed to work efficiently on the first Saturday night that Carmen had organized the flow, but she no longer felt comfortable chatting with George when she was there. Just as there was less conversation among the wait staff in the prep kitchen, because Fritz seemed to be listening to every word.

Also, it seemed the staff was arguing more, bickering about scheduling, stations, and tips. No one had discovered who had stolen the beer, so, by default, they had all agreed that it must've been a miscount, or a delivery mistake. But it was unlikely anyone really believed that. Henry had become sullen. Like a teenager, he was resentful when asked for anything out of the ordinary and rolled his eyes if Dulcie reprimanded him.

By the time Franklin came in for dinner, alone, the dining room was crowded. He asked to be seated in Abby's section. Abby was working the porch, where there was only one two-top free.

"You're lucky," Abby said as she showed him to the table.

He sat down and said in a low voice: "I've got a solution for you."

Abby didn't know what he was talking about. "For what?"

"To catch your beer thief," he said, pleased with himself.

"Really? How?" Abby asked, pulling out the chair opposite him and sitting down.

Franklin shook his head. "I think you should take my order, do whatever you have to do, and when things quiet down, come sit and I'll tell you."

Abby scowled at him, pushing herself to her feet. "Okay, fine. What d'ya want?"

"Hmm," he said as he picked up the menu and looked it over carefully. "I think I'll have the roast chicken."

"Okay," Abby turned to go.

"Wait, wait," Franklin continued, looking at her disapprovingly. "And a green salad."

Abby turned away again.

"And wine, please, if you don't mind. Red. House."

To Abby's back he called out, "I don't know about this service—"

On her way into the kitchen to drop off the order, Fritz grabbed her arm to stop her. "Abby, I need a favor."

Abby looked at him coldly. "What?"

He ignored her attitude, and spoke ingratiatingly. "I'm expecting two good friends. A couple. If you seat them, be sure to put them somewhere good, okay? Maybe the four-top in the alcove."

"If it's available," Abby said and kept going.

"And let me know when they show up, okay?" he called after her.

Sure enough, half an hour later a couple appeared at the door. Abby went to seat them.

"Hi, I'm Peter. We're here as Fritz's guests." Peter sounded as if he were from New Jersey. His silk shirt was opened at the neck, showing off a bed of white chest hair. He was wearing a black velvet blazer over pressed jeans. Up close, the blonde with him looked about forty, her skin pale and soft, her makeup heavy but skillfully applied. She was wearing so much gold jewelry that it seemed to weigh down her birdlike neck and arms. She smiled tentatively at Abby.

Abby glanced around at the tables. The alcove table was free, so Abby deposited them there with menus. She took their drink orders.

"So, Fritz, I put your guidos in the alcove," she said as she walked by him. Instead of annoyed, he looked up from the dirty dishes, pleased. She found Becca and told her she had two new customers and that they both wanted apple martinis.

It wasn't until Franklin was well into his chicken that Abby was able to sit down across from him. "I'm just lucky Germaine didn't come in and nab you," she said, as she relaxed into the chair.

Franklin looked around hopefully. "Oh, is she here?"

Abby said: "Yes, she saw you sitting alone and left. Just kidding. By the way, did she tell you about her mother?"

Franklin nodded.

"I wonder why Wanda and Norman never let the girls know they were all related?"

Franklin shook his head. "I don't know. It seems pretty heartless, but maybe they had a good reason, or somehow believed it was better for the girls."

Abby thought of how Germaine had reacted when she'd heard the news. "I don't see how. To spend your whole life believing you have no real family." Abby glanced at the door. "I don't have much time. Come on, now, I want to hear about your solution to the beer problem."

Franklin put down his knife and fork. He wiped his mouth on his napkin, replaced it on his lap and took the last sip of his wine. "Ahh," he sighed, closing his eyes.

Abby glared at him. "Franklin, have a heart."

He took pity on her. "Okay. Here it is. I have a friend," and he leaned forward in his chair and spoke in a low voice, "a private investigator. He has an office in Albany. I've hired him a couple of times over the last few years."

"What for?" Abby couldn't resist asking.

"This and that. When I needed some information during a defense case."

"What does he do, spy on people?"

"Now who's slowing me down?"

"Sorry. Go on."

Franklin cleared his throat. "Anyway, I called him, and asked his advice. And he said it was simple, you need a camera."

"Like a surveillance camera? Those ones you see in stores?"

"No, no, something small you could hide near your inventory."

"They must be expensive."

"You're a friend of mine, he'll lend you one."

"Sounds good. Let's do it."

Franklin nodded. "Why don't I call him back and you can drive up to Albany, meet him at his office, and take it from there?"

"Excellent. Thanks, Franklin."

Franklin leaned closer. "Only thing is, I wouldn't tell anyone. If Dulcie finds out, she might tell your Sperm guy. And if you warn anyone else on the staff, it'll probably leak out. I suggest you do it by yourself, and if you learn anything, go directly to Dulcie with it."

Abby felt a stab of nervousness. She nodded. "Okay. So, what's his name?"

Franklin looked a little uncomfortable. "Pinky."

"For real? Pinky?"

"Yes."

"Pinky what?"

"Pinky Smerling."

"Pinky Smerling! Okay."

He left soon after. She didn't see him go, because she was busy watching Fritz welcome his friends. He had put on a clean, dry apron, and he was standing by their table, shaking Peter's hand and laughing loudly at something he said. He even bowed over the little blonde's hand. Before he went back to work, he had a whispered conference with Carmen, who nodded. Abby could tell by their gestures that they were discussing food options. Huh. Pulling out all the stops, obviously.

Abby caught up with Becca at the cash register. "Who are those guys?" she asked, gesturing with her chin to their table.

Becca shrugged. "Friends of Spermhead's. They seem kind of tacky, but okay. They're building a big house in Goose Creek. She's sweet. She wants me to do some gardening for her, so I said, yeah, I'd be glad to. As long as she pays me, I'll do anything."

CHAPTER THIRTY-FIVE

In Abby's mind, downtown Albany was a patchwork of contrasting neighborhoods divided by invisible lines of spit. No gradual change from one to the next. Arbor Hill, burnt out and desperate, sat next to the gracious old homes on Washington Park, which rubbed elbows with the shabby charm of Lark and some of the other bird streets, which were up the hill from the capitol buildings. A quilt. Surrounded by the usual spread of suburbs. Of which Bantam would one day be part.

Pinky Smerling's office was a second-floor walk-up on a run-down block of Lark. Pinky had informed her over the phone that she should buzz three times because the intercom wasn't working.

She turned off at the Arbor Hill exit and drove by boarded-up townhouses and small corner bodegas. On Lark, she found a spot without too much difficulty in front of a small Greek restaurant. Saturday was usually a busy day on Lark, but it was still early enough for the students and night people to be sleeping. Abby locked the Bronco and crossed the street, looking for the number of the building. She found it half a block down. It was a weather-beaten gray stone townhouse, three stories high. The front steps were swaybacked with wear.

The lower floor was below street level and housed a used-clothing store. A collection of formal gowns, mostly prom and bridesmaid dresses, were displayed in the window on hangers suspended by string from the ceiling.

Abby walked up the stoop, the sag in the steps making her feel she might fall backward. She found the intercom marked Investigations and pressed the bell three distinct times. She waited. Ten seconds later, the door started to buzz and she pushed it open.

Inside, she shut the door carefully behind her, though the lock seemed so flimsy she could probably just have pushed it open. A steep staircase led up, and across from it a row of four cheap silvertone mailboxes had been attached to the wall. There were two doors, one on Abby's immediate left and one straight ahead. Abby knocked on the door to her left.

She heard footsteps in the apartment, approaching the door. A boy, who Abby guessed was about fourteen, appeared. Very pale-skinned and wearing wire-rimmed glasses, he had frizzy brown hair that looked like a bush that had been in a rainstorm and was temporarily flattened out, creating an arbitrary part on his head. He was wearing jeans and a loose-fitting T-shirt.

She smiled at him, hoping to put him at ease.

"Abby Silvernale?" he asked politely, his voice deep. Startled, she realized that he was much older than he looked. Young, but not a kid. He was shorter than Abby by at least three inches, and his frame seemed narrow and delicate under his baggy shirt. Her revised estimate put him somewhere in his midtwenties. Luckily, he had spoken before she had asked to see his father.

"Yes, that's me. Pinky, right?" Abby answered.

"Yup. Did you find the place pretty easily?"

"Piece of cake." She waited. "Can I come in?" She asked, tired of standing in the doorway.

"Oh, right," he said, and moved to one side, gesturing awkwardly with his arm.

Pinky led the way to the sofa, and grabbed a stack of papers that was lying on it. He took them to the desk and jammed them into a drawer. He shut the laptop on his desk, as if doing so would make the place appear tidier.

"You've got quite a library," Abby said, looking around the room. There were bookshelves and piles of books everywhere.

"No choice. I'm a graduate student," he said. He sat down in one of the armchairs. He blinked a few times behind his glasses.

"Oh," Abby said in surprise. "I thought you were a private eye."

He blushed, whether with embarrassment or pleasure, Abby couldn't tell. Pinky didn't clarify. "I do a little work, investigations, surveillance, things of that nature. On weekends. But I'm getting my master's."

"In what?" Abby asked politely.

"Library studies. So I don't really consider myself a *private eye*." He said the two words slowly, as if they had special meaning to him.

"Oh, okay."

"I work part time at the New Scotland Avenue Branch of the public library."

"Oh, I see," Abby said. And then she added: "That's perfect, though, isn't it? New Scotland? As in New Scotland Yard?"

He smiled, pleased. "Yes, I like it." Pinky stared at her with something like warmth in his eyes. The silence grew awkward.

To break it, Abby asked: "So, how do you know Franklin?"

"Franklin?" he said.

"Yes. How do you know him?"

"Oh, he saw my ad in the yellow pages. He was my first client. I've worked for him on and off ever since. He helped me with my, you know, problem. I have great respect for his legal skill."

Abby didn't know. But her imagination started to bounce around. She nodded. "Well, he speaks highly of you," she said, pushing the truth. "So, how do you suggest I solve *my* problem?"

He pushed his glasses up on his nose. "Let's go over it a little. Franklin explained that you're trying to find out who is stealing liquor at your restaurant."

"It's not actually my restaurant. But I've worked there for a long time and I'm close to the owner. Well, I was close to her. But she hired a new dishwasher and she fell in love with him, and now he says that one of us stole three cases of beer. I know it's not true. But I have to find out what's going on."

She looked at him, thinking that she was sounding whiny.

Pinky looked skeptical. She revised her estimate of his age. Maybe closer to late twenties. "What if there is no more theft?"

Abby nodded. "It wasn't all stolen at once. So I have to believe that if he did it twice, eventually he'll do it again."

"That's what everybody assumes," Pinky said, a tinge of bitterness in his voice. "It's not always true." He paused. "It sounds simple enough. If I lend you one of my smallest cameras, could you find a time when no one is around to attach it to a wall, so it's trained on the spot you want to cover?"

Abby thought of the hallway behind the bar. She was alone there plenty of times. And if Fritz was there at the same time, he was usually upstairs. "I don't see why not," Abby said. "But the walls are stone. Will it still work?"

Pinky made a dismissive gesture with his hand. "Oh, sure."

She suddenly remembered something. "Will it have a, you know, wide range of vision? So it can cover a corridor about ten feet across?"

Pinky thought about it. "It won't be as wide as a bigger camera, but it's a fish-eye, so you're going to get a broad picture. Some distortion, but lots of good detail. It should work fine."

"Great."

"You also have to be able to set up the transmitter. Do you have a secure area within say, two hundred feet, where you can hide it?"

Abby wondered if she was in over her head. Why hadn't Franklin told her the damn machine needed a transmitter or whatever? "How big is it?"

"Depends. Do you have a computer, or do you prefer to use a VCR?"

Abby shook her head. "My computer's really old, so I guess a VCR would be the best thing."

"Okay, so the machine will be yay-hoo big." Pinky held his small hands, fingernails bitten down low, about a foot and a half apart. He must've known by looking at her that a visual aid would be necessary. Abby stared at his hands, trying to imagine hiding them somewhere in the restaurant.

Finally she nodded. "I've got it. The wine storage. Is it a problem if it's up a few flights from the camera?"

"Shouldn't be," Pinky said. He stood up. "Hold on." He went to the back of the room and opened a deep drawer. He pulled out a small aluminum case, bringing it over to the coffee table. "So," he said, as he opened it, "let's see what we have.

"Where are you, where are you?" he said, talking into the case as he dug around, pushing things aside.

Finally, he found what he was looking for, reached in, and held up something about the size of a large button. "Here it is." He put it gently in the palm of Abby's hand. Abby studied the little camera. "Cute."

"Do you have an exit sign near the area you want to watch?" Pinky asked.

Abby thought for a moment. "Yes, it's at the end of the hallway."

"Well then, you could put this right next to it, and no one will see it. The light from the sign will mask it."

Abby shook her head in admiration. "Great."

Pinky didn't smile, but the blush reappeared on his cheeks.

"What do I owe you?"

He shook his head, making his bushy hair bounce. "Nothing. I told Franklin, it's a loaner. Here, let me put this in something to keep it safe." From the metal case he pulled a small black velvet box that looked as if it should hold an engagement ring. He put the camera in it and dropped the box into a zippered green tote bag with a logo printed above the words Surveillance Systems in block letters. "I'll get you the transmitter, and show you how to set it up and start it. Camera's motion-activated, so you won't run out of space or anything."

As he was adding what looked like a small VCR to the tote bag, Abby asked him: "How'd you get the name Pinky? You're not a redhead. Is it something to do with your finger?"

"No, no. My middle name is Pinkerton. I'm a direct descendent of Allan Pinkerton."

Feeling ignorant, Abby asked: "Allan Pinkerton?"

Pinky looked at her in surprise tinged with disappointment. "The father of the modern detective. You've heard of the Pinkerton Men, haven't you? They tracked and caught train robbers."

"Yeah, vaguely," Abby said.

He handed her the tote. "You should know that, if you're going to do surveillance."

"You're right." Abby walked to the doorway, looking forward to getting outside. The stuffiness was getting to her. "Well, thank you, Pinky. As soon as I'm done with this, I'll get it back to you."

Pinky stood at the entrance of the building. As Abby started down the sagging front steps, he said:

"Dashiell Hammett was a Pinkerton Man. Did you know that?"

"No, no, I didn't." Once she reached the sidewalk she turned to say something to him just in time to see the front door close. He was gone. She turned away and crossed the street toward her car.

CHAPTER THIRTY-SIX

Abby picked that Sunday night to install the camera. It was Halloween. They never did much business on Halloween, so there was a good chance the night would be slow and end early. She left the surveillance equipment in her car, still in the green tote bag that Pinky had given her. She looked for Dulcie, who was in her office, as usual. Abby told her she'd slept late and if Dulcie wanted her to close up, she'd be happy to.

Dulcie looked up from her desk. Abby noticed a slight tightening of the eyes, as if she didn't quite trust the motive behind the offer. "That's very kind, Abby. You don't want to go home early?"

Abby shrugged, trying to look nonchalant. "Hey, I always like to go home early, but it seems that you've been doing a lot of late nights, and I thought, you know, we've kind of been at odds lately, so I'd give you a break. But it's your call."

Dulcie, always a sucker for kindness, said: "That's very sweet, Abby.

Thank you, I'll take you up on it. Tonight's Halloween—I feel like I haven't seen the kids in weeks."

Abby started setting up her station, feeling slightly guilty.

By five-thirty, Findlay Street was filling with little vampires, Harry Potters, and princesses as they took off, squealing and laughing, swinging their plastic jack-o'-lanterns, their paper bags, and for the most optimistic, their pillowcases. Parents, wearing hats with ears, or colored wigs, strolled behind the littlest ones. Occasionally, the staff could hear overwrought shrieks and would step out to watch from the sidewalk.

Inside the restaurant, however, the evening shift seemed to take forever to grind along. Customers lingered over their meals, the clean-up was delayed by endless conversations and the meager tips took ages to count and split up. Henry and Becca were roughhousing, and they knocked over all the checks so the food tallies, which were only half done, had to be restarted.

Finally, the last ones out grunted their good-byes, and Abby was left alone in the building. With Fritz. She realized that she had always managed to avoid being alone with him by rushing through her chores and leaving when everyone else did. But tonight she had no choice.

Abby went out to her car and retrieved the tote bag. She left the checks on the staff table, so if Fritz wanted to nose around, he would think she hadn't finished up. When she came back in, he was still in the kitchen. She went down the front stairs, and behind the bar. At the bottom of the back stairs, she listened again. She could still hear the sauté pans banging in the sink.

Quickly, she grabbed a chair from the barroom and set it in front of the back door, under the exit sign. She took the tiny camera and its holder, and put them in her apron. In case Fritz came down, she pulled open the sliding door to the walk-in vegetable cooler, which stood right by the back door, and pushed the tote bag behind a box of eggplants. Taking the mount out of her apron, she climbed up on the wobbly chair. She peeled off the backing and pressed the mount to the wall, next to the EXIT sign. She gave it a few seconds then she tested it gently. Carefully, so as not to drop it, she took the camera out of its little box and snapped it into the mount, just the way Pinky had told her to. She looked at it to make sure there was nothing obviously crooked or off about it. No one would notice it, she hoped, unless they were looking for it.

Just then, she heard a sound behind her. She froze and listened. She heard the sound again, and realized to her horror that it was Fritz coming down the stairs. By the sound of it, he was near the bottom. She grabbed the back of the chair and jumped down with a loud, graceless thump.

Unable to think of anything else to do, she turned around and sat down in the chair, leaned back and shut her eyes.

"What's going on?" he said.

She opened her eyes, and he was standing in front of her, about eight feet away. She hadn't heard him approach, and he was much closer than she expected. She sat up, not needing to feign being startled. "Shit, you scared me."

"What's wrong with you?"

"Oh, this here?" she said, gesturing to the area her chair was occupying, in the dark back corridor right in front of the door.

"Yeah."

She sighed. "Just resting."

"Why here, in front of the door?"

"I was going to sit outside, but I suddenly felt a little dizzy," she said. She nearly touched the back of her hand to her forehead, but stopped herself in time. Too much. Fritz looked at her suspiciously, his gaze traveling around the confined space. The tote bag, she thought, with a flush of panic, then remembered she'd put it in the cooler. She slumped lower in the chair, and prayed he wasn't planning to make himself a little late-night eggplant parm.

When he couldn't figure out what she was up to, he looked her over, his eyes moving down her body. Suddenly aware of how alone she was with the man, Abby bent forward at the waist. "I feel sick," she said, hoping the prospect of vomit would turn off that nasty light she had seen in his eye. Doubled over, Abby could now only see Fritz's feet in their heavy, rubber-soled restaurant shoes. He walked slowly toward her. She held her breath. A damp, meaty hand settled on her back.

"Maybe you need to lie down on one of the banquettes until it passes," he said, his voice becoming soft and caressing.

She wanted to jump up and run for it, but she needed to get the bag with the receiver. She forced herself to sit still. She started to make heaving sounds. The hand on her back was generating a hot dank spot and began to move slowly down her spine. She looked up at him. "Fritz, please, could you prop open the door with a milk crate? I think I'll just stand outside for a minute, get some air."

Reluctantly, the hand left her back. He moved around her, and pushed on the panic bar of the door. It swung open, and a gust of cool air swirled around her.

"Ah," she said, standing up, "you just go on with what you were doing. I'll take a few breaths, then get out of here."

"I'm going to have a smoke. Want one?" he said, kicking a crate in front of the door so it wouldn't swing shut.

"No, thanks. But you go ahead."

Fritz turned his back on her, and moved to the sidewalk. He fished around in his pocket, found his cigarettes, and lit one, his face momentarily illuminated by the match. He flicked the match into the street and turned uphill, toward the traffic circle. Abby stood still, unsure how to proceed. If he came back in, he'd catch her going in the cooler.

Just then, as if he had decided to help her out, he began strolling up the street, the smoke from his cigarette white in the streetlight.

Quickly, Abby pulled back the cooler door, and stepped inside. She put a foot on the track to keep it from sliding closed. She felt around behind the eggplants, grabbed the green bag, and tried to lift it out. It resisted, and she pulled harder. "Come on, come on," she said softly.

But it didn't budge.

She reached back and felt with her fingers. The bag seemed to be snagged on something. She forced herself to take a breath. She needed to see what she was doing. She took her foot out of the door, and it slid shut with a clang.

There was a ceiling fixture in the walk-in cooler, and she reached up and felt around until she found the chain. She pulled it and the single bulb, protected by a wire grating, lit the tiny room with a dismal glow. Abby was surrounded by shelves filled with crates of lemons, oranges, onions and broccoli. She shivered with cold. She had to move quickly, before he finished his cigarette.

As silently as she could, she pulled the crate of eggplants toward her. Peering over, she found that a piece of wire had gouged a hole in the bag. Slowly, fingers trembling, she bent it enough to be able to release the fabric. She lifted the bag out of its hiding place and gently slid the crate back in place. When she was holding the tote securely, she turned off the overhead light.

Very carefully, she started to slide open the cooler door. She peered out. At first she felt disoriented, as if the door had opened onto a white wall. Then, to her horror, she realized she was looking at Fritz's back, in big white close-up. He was turned to the exit, and had just pulled the milk crate out of the door. The noise he was making must have covered the sound of the cooler door. Gently and slowly, Abby let it slide shut again. She stood on the other side, just inches from him, afraid to move, afraid to breathe.

She waited. Finally, she heard his footsteps on the back stairs. Carefully, she slid open the door of her hiding place, and peered out. All clear. She stepped out, slid the door closed, walked quickly into the bar room, and up the front stairs.

In the dining room, she put away the tallies she'd left on the table. What she really wanted to do was escape to her car, but she still had to set up the receiver. Making sure Fritz was in the kitchen, she moved as quickly and quietly as she could, up the wooden stairs to the next floor, past Dulcie's office, left toward the front of the building, to the room that was used as liquor storage.

She stood in the doorway, undecided. Inside, an entire wall was covered in deep wooden shelving. To her immediate right, the shelves were given over to hard liquor, sorted according to type. Next to them were stacked the cases of wine, opened ones in front, closed ones behind. House wines, reds, whites, etc. Where to put the transmitter? And then she got it. The Prosecco. No one ordered Prosecco. Well, just about no one. Dulcie had bought it hoping to educate people, which was usually a bad idea. When it came to bubbles, people knew what they liked. Either the good stuff, or the cheap knockoffs. The Prosecco just hadn't caught on.

Abby squeezed in behind the front cases. By pulling and pushing, she managed to make some room behind the last unopened case of sparkling wine and gently placed the machine on the shelf, hidden from sight. There was an outlet on the wall behind it, and if she dropped to her knees and extended her left hand, she could just reach it. When it was plugged in, she adjusted the cases and stepped back. The transmitter was small, and unless someone was reorganizing and shifting the cases, it wouldn't be found.

Her heart beating fast, she closed the door. She stood outside the room and listened. Quiet. She walked as softly as she could back down the stairs. Fritz was standing in the prep kitchen.

"I think the best thing is for me to go home," she said quickly.

He didn't say anything, just watched her. Abby grabbed her purse from under the cash register, and pushed out through the back door, into the night air.

Outside, the little trick-or-treaters were long gone. A group of teenagers, in masks and low-hanging jeans, stood on the corner, smoking. They ignored her as Abby walked quickly across the circle to the safety of her car.

CHAPTER THIRTY-SEVEN

Abby had written Bella's last name, Massicotte, on the back of a Best Funeral Home business card and stuck it in a pocket of the jacket she had worn that day. She called directory assistance for the number.

When Bella answered the phone, Abby reintroduced herself: "Hello, Bella? My name is Abby Silvernale. We met at Norman Smith's funeral, and I was wondering if I—"

"I remember you. The girl who shoved me down, right next to Norman's body."

"What? I never shoved—"

"I called my lawyer, you know, as soon as I got home," Bella went on, "and he asked me for your name, but I told him I didn't know it, so he said, well, that's no good, Bella. How can we sue her, if we don't know her name?" She laughed. "But now you've told me, it's Abby Silvernale. I'll call him *tout de suite*. Thank you so much."

"Hey, I never pushed you! I took you outside, we talked—"

"You picked my brain, more like."

"Well, I'm sorry I called you. I'm going to put the phone down now."

"Wait, wait, wait! I was teasing! Just teasing! Christ almighty, nobody can take a joke these days. I was just having a little fun with you, Missy, take it easy."

Abby took a deep breath. "Are you serious?"

Bella gave a phlegmy chuckle. "Honey, I have never sued anyone, not even my ex-husband. Just playing with you. Pretty good, don't you think? Actually, I was hoping you'd call. We hadn't really finished gossiping, and I could use a visit."

Abby wondered if she should hang up while she still could, regardless of Bella's assurances. "I don't know. Just remember, there were plenty of witnesses at the funeral, and you didn't fall down."

"Hah! Much good that would do you. They'd all say they don't know, they hadn't been paying attention at that particular moment in time. I read a lot, I know about witnesses. People are just not observant. So, when're you coming down?"

"Down?"

"To Eighty-eighth Street."

"I was hoping we could just talk on the phone," Abby said weakly.

"I don't like the phone," Bella answered firmly.

"You seem to like it just fine," Abby tried to counter.

"Hmm," the old lady said, and Abby thought she could hear pages turning, maybe a date book. "I could see you tomorrow, at eleven-thirty in the morning. Have lunch with me, then you can turn around and go home. Take it or leave it."

Abby thought she heard a note of entreaty in Bella's command. She knew when she was defeated. "Okay. Eleven-thirty. Eighty-eighth and what?"

The next morning, Abby drove to the northernmost stop on the New York City commuter train line. It was well over an hour south of Bantam, but Abby was afraid of driving into the city in her old car. If she hit traffic, it would overheat. She pictured herself, stopped in the middle lane on one of the many congested arteries into the city, all vehicles at a standstill behind her, snaking away for miles.

Her train got into Grand Central at about eleven, and Abby spent some time looking at the subway map, remembering which trains she should take for the Upper West Side. Once she figured it out, she waited on the platform, listening to the dark underground echo of the tunnels.

At Eighty-sixth she got off the train and climbed the dark, stained cement steps to the open air. She found her way to Bella's address without any difficulty. It was a prewar apartment building, gray and ponderous. In the lobby Abby could see, through the heavy, beveled glass panes of the entrance, a doorman in a maroon uniform. When he saw that she was entering, he beat her to the door, holding it open so she could pass through. Nice.

Bella lived on the fifth floor. Her front door was one of four that opened onto a sedate, marbled foyer. Abby rang the bell. A cacophony of yapping and howling broke out inside the apartment. Abby waited, and as the sounds drew nearer and more insistent, a rusty voice shouted in counterpoint: "Clam it, clam it, clam it, ya little bloodsuckers!" A shuffling of feet, punctuated by a last "Enough!" and the locks on the door began to be opened, snapping and clapping, starting from the top and moving down. Finally, the handle turned, and the door swung inward. What seemed like half a dozen small hairy creatures rushed out, barking, yipping at the air, and circling Abby.

Standing in the doorway, cigarette hanging from her mouth, was Bella. This time, her yellow-blonde hair was down to her shoulders in a flip, stiff as steel. Her lips were the same crimson as the first time Abby had seen her. She was wearing a beige cashmere sweater set, decorated with a large turtle pin, with a ruby head and emerald eyes. On her feet were embroidered Chinese silk slippers.

"Come in. Ignore my babies. They'll get over you in no time." Abby could feel the damp noses of the little dogs as they sniffed her ankles and feet, smelling Rick and Delilah. When they wanted to explore higher, they stood on stumpy little hind legs, their front paws on her knees, and rudely sniffed as far as they could reach.

Inside the apartment, the dogs quickly lost interest. Bella led her across a green marble floor to the living room. It was a nicely proportioned room with a fireplace on the left, though the walls on either side of it were thigh-high in old newspapers. Across from the door were three large windows, their panes filmed and spotted. Abby could tell that the sofa and armchairs were upholstered in what had probably once been an expensive and elegant cream brocade, but they were now threadbare and discolored, the cushions sunken. The little dogs spread out, each claiming one section of seating, until everything was taken.

"Get out," said Bella, waving a hand at one of the occupants of an armchair. Once it was free, she prodded Abby on the arm and pointed at the seat. "Quick, quick, before she sneaks back up and you sit on her."

Abby sat down on the stained and worn cushion. The little bitch sat on the floor at her feet, watching her, willing her to leave. Abby ignored her.

"Sherry?" Bella asked as she walked to a cabinet on the wall opposite the fireplace. Without waiting for an answer, she brought down two schooners from a shelf and began to fill them from a bottle on the shallow counter in front of her. The liquid was golden. She brought the glasses over, spilling a little from each as she moved. With a sigh, she put them both on the dark wood coffee table, next to a silver cigarette box and an ashtray that looked like a kidney-shaped swimming pool, and was nearly as big.

"Coasters in the drawer, darling," she said, pointing to a shallow drawer in the table. Abby found the cork circles, decorated with Audubon bird prints, each one different. She chose two and stuck them under the glasses.

Bella picked up one of the other dogs from a sofa cushion and sat down, keeping the dog on her lap.

"Drat, I should offer you crackers or something."

"No, no," Abby protested. "I'm just glad you agreed to see me." She nearly added, "and not take me to court," but thought better of it.

"Good." Bella reached for the ashtray on the table next to her drink, and ground out her cigarette. She hadn't once flicked it, so Abby imagined that the ashes just fell wherever they might. The filter was ringed in red.

"What do you want to talk about?" Bella asked, taking a sip of her sherry.

In the light from the windows, the makeup on her face accentuated the craggy lines in her face, making her small bright eyes look mysterious and all-knowing, like those of an ancient spirit peeking out from behind the bark of a tree.

Abby settled herself into the chair. She watched her hostess carefully as she spoke. "Germaine and I went to the Department of Social Services in Hudson. She was allowed to look at her old file, and she found out something she had never known before. She learned that her mother and Wanda were sisters."

Bella said nothing. Her eyes grew even brighter, Abby thought.

"Did you know that?" Abby asked.

"No, I didn't. Very juicy." She kept her eyes on Abby. "But it makes sense, absolutely."

"Why do you say that?"

Bella leaned forward and opened the silver box. When she'd lit a cigarette, she asked: "I mean, why the hell else would they have taken those girls on?"

"What do you mean?" Abby asked, trying to clarify.

"Well, look. Norman had no interest in children, from what I could see. And he was already pretty long in the tooth. Sixty, give or take."

Abby nodded. "What about their mother? Did you ever meet her?"

Bella held the cigarette near her face with her right hand. "Once. What was her name?" she asked Abby.

"Bridget, Bridget Gubinek," Abby said, hoping to jar some extra memories loose with it.

"Of course. Bridget. Bridget. Blotchy skin, I remember. Ratty hair. Nothing like Wanda, who was all peaches-and-cream. She was rude. I remember Wanda picked me up at the train, and when we arrived at the house, there was an old station wagon in the driveway. Wanda seemed upset when she saw it. She jumped out of the car and ran into the house. By the time I dragged my bag in—by myself—she was in tears. Norman had been berating her about something, I'm sure. He was sitting at the kitchen table and his ears were bright red, a sure sign he was furious."

"Was Bridget there?"

Bella let out a stream of smoke. "No. But Norman told Wanda to find her. He wasn't going to put up with it anymore, etc. etc. Wanda was a mess, poor girl. I felt sorry for her. Off she went, and Norman and I sat together. I was drinking something, I don't remember what." She seemed to be drifting off in time.

Abby reeled her back in. "Did Wanda find Bridget?"

Bella looked at her, surprised. "Yes, of course. She reappeared about half an hour later, like a duck with her ducklings in tow. She brought Bridget, who had Germaine and Athena following behind. They all stood in the doorway. I don't recall if Maddie was there."

"What happened?"

She bent her head down, shut her eyes, and made a gesture with her cigarette hand. "Don't rush me. I'm trying to remember. It was a long time ago, and I haven't thought about it in ages. Let me see. Wanda was crying, I think, and Bridget was ranting. She'd been walking in the woods. She wanted to take the girls away, they belonged with her. She was a disaster, disheveled, dirty. Norman shut her down, I do remember that. He did it without even moving from his chair."

"What did he say to her?"

"He told her he would never let her have the girls, that she had no right to them, she'd given up her rights. She was irresponsible and dangerous. A slut and a drunk. That an animal wouldn't treat its children the way she had treated hers. By the end, poor Bridget was a basket case. I felt extremely uncomfortable being there, so I got up and I took the girls outside. I didn't think they should be hearing such things about their mother, even if they were true."

Maybe so, but Abby noticed she'd stayed long enough to hear most of it.

Bella shook her head. "He was harsh, but I think the woman needed to hear it." Her cigarette had gone out, and she put the cold stub in the ashtray.

"Norman had a lot of power in his family," Abby said, more as a statement of fact than a question.

Bella nodded. "Yes, that he did."

"How did the girls seem to react to the scene?"

Bella pulled gently on the ears of the small dog on her lap. "They came with me out to the work shed. We found some paper and pencils and I made them draw me pictures. They were both quite good, as it turned out. They scribbled away, and when a voice was raised so high in the kitchen that we could hear it, they would stop and listen. The older one said: "'When Mom leaves, we have to stay here.'"

"The little one started blubbering, 'Why? I want to go home.' But Germaine said to her, 'No, this is home now. With Uncle Norman and Aunt Wanda. Mom doesn't take care of us so good.'"

"She said that? Really?"

"Yes, terrible English."

"No, I mean the Uncle and Aunt part."

"Oh. Well, I assumed she was calling them Uncle and Aunt in an honorary way. But it all makes much more sense if they were related. How did it never occur to me?"

Abby took her first sip of the sherry. It was sweet and warm.

"How long were you there that visit?"

Bella thought for a moment. "I'm going to guess about two weeks. I never went for less. I would go three or four times a year."

"What else happened during that visit?"

But Bella wasn't going to be rushed. "Not yet, I promised you lunch, and lunch it is. I hope you like niçoise salad." She stood up. "Follow me," she said, as she led the way out of the room.

Bella walked down the marbled hall, her embroidered slippers slapping on her soles, two of the dogs at her heels, their claws clicking. The next room was a dining room, and the kitchen was at the end of the hall. Abby guessed it had been remodeled sometime in the fifties. The counter was lined with small cans of dog food.

Bella opened the refrigerator and brought out a platter. She handed it to Abby and took out a pitcher that clinked with ice. Abby looked at their lunch. A ring of deviled eggs surrounded a mound of salad, decorated with small black olives. Abby could see shreds of tuna fish. "This looks nice," she said.

"Put it on the dining room table, dear, and then come back for the lemonade. I'll get us a little vodka. But guard that salad with your life. They'll be up on the table before you can say Jack Robinson, I guarantee," she said, looking lovingly at the little hairy creatures that were already circling Abby's ankles.

Bella insisted they not discuss Norman during the meal. Abby asked her what kind of work she had done. Bella told her she had worked for forty years as secretary to a publisher of high-end art books. "But I ran that business, believe me. Never mind the title. My boss was a good man even though he was a lazy S.O.B. The only thing he wasn't lazy about was sex. We were lovers for twenty-five years. He got sick suddenly—he had a bad ticker—and as soon as he died, his son fired me. No severance, no gold wristwatch or whatever. The louse. Not even a party. But he was too late, kiddo. A case of the barn door—his father had already bought me this apartment." She wiped the corners of her mouth with her thumb and forefinger.

Abby had a train to catch, so she kept an eye on her watch. "I have to leave soon," she said apologetically.

"Well, you shouldn't let me rattle on," Bella said. She got to her feet, and together they cleared the table and put the food away.

"What else did you want to know?" she said as she led the canine procession back to the living room.

"Well," Abby said, as she sat down again. "You were telling me about the time you went to stay with Norman and Wanda, the first time you met the two girls."

Bella lit a cigarette and exhaled with a satisfied sigh, as if all that food and drink were nothing but a prelude to the best part of the meal. "Ah, yes. It was a strange visit. You know why? Because everything went according to schedule. Norman worked during the day, took a break for lunch. And at dinner Wanda would prepare a delicious meal, friends might come over, we would drink too much, listen to music, discuss art. No change."

"Why was that strange?"

"Well, there were two new children in the family."

"How did they fit in?"

Bella shrugged, her shoulders up, the corners of her mouth down, suddenly looking very French. "As best they could. They played outside on good days, inside if it rained. The way children did in those days. Apart. Occasionally, if we all went on a picnic, they came along. I suppose it was Wanda who looked after them."

"So," Abby asked, "no sign of Bridget?"

"Oh, she'd show up once every few days and make a scene. Eventually, Norman called the police. They came over and remonstrated with her. She insisted that Norman was trying to steal her babies. The cops finally had no choice, they took her away. One of them told Norman he should take out a restraining order on her."

"According to the adoption file, Bridget was trying to get the girls back. She wanted to take them to California, to join up with their father."

"Pooh! Fiction. The father was long out of the picture. I think they'd lived together for a while, but as soon as the second child was on the way, he skedaddled. I doubt she even knew what state he lived in."

"So, did Norman take out the restraining order?"

"The next day. Norman always did what he thought was right. For himself and to keep peace in the house. He didn't believe for a minute that Bridget could be rehabilitated, so he didn't think he was being harsh. Tough, maybe, but not harsh. He pushed himself and expected others to do the same. He had little tolerance for addiction or weakness. And to him, Bridget was weak."

"What about Wanda? Wasn't she weak?"

Bella laughed harshly. "Ah! But she was addicted to him, and Norman didn't see that as a weakness. Just the natural order of things."

Abby sipped her spiked lemonade. "What about you? How did you fit into this happy little family? Was Wanda jealous of you?"

"Oh, no. She would often come and ask me to back her up on certain issues. And I found that easy to do. I wanted to defend her, because she didn't seem able to defend herself."

"When did Bridget have her accident?"

"I'd just come back to the city. In fact, I'd just let myself in the front door"—she gestured toward the entrance to the apartment—"when Norman called me. He couldn't find Wanda, and he wanted to know if she'd called me or told me where she was going. I said no, not after leaving me off at the station. He told me she hadn't come home yet. It was suppertime, and he hadn't heard anything from her. He was pretty cross."

Abby leaned her head against the back of the chair. The alcohol and the food had lulled her into a state of relaxation, and she imagined Wanda, behind the wheel of whatever big car Norman owned, pulling out of the train station in Hudson. Where would she go? "What about Bridget? Did he try getting in touch with her, to see if she'd seen Wanda?"

"Norman wouldn't do that. He asked me to."

"Did you?"

"I did. He had a phone number for her, in some boardinghouse in Hudson. But she wasn't there. And the woman who answered hadn't seen her or Wanda. So I called Norman back and told him."

"Was he upset?"

Bella lit another cigarette. She thought for a moment. "I think he was angry. Angry enough not to say anything more than 'thank you and goodnight' to me. And honestly, I didn't give it much thought. I assumed that Wanda had gone shopping or run an errand. She was a grown woman, for heaven's sake. She was just late. I wasn't concerned."

"When did you get concerned?"

Bella finished her sherry and put her glass down on the coaster. "I went out that evening, and when I got in I called Norman. It wasn't too late, and I had begun to feel a tiny bit guilty for shrugging it all off. The phone rang for quite a while before anyone answered. Finally, he picked up. I asked him if Wanda had come home and he said yes, and when I expressed relief, he gave me the news about Bridget. She had had too much to drink and taken a corner too fast. She was killed immediately."

Abby sat silently, imagining the woman lying by the side of the road. Germaine and Athena's mother.

"Where had Wanda been all that time, from when she dropped you off at the station?"

"He told me she'd been out with her sister. Trying to talk her into rehab or something. He thought Wanda was being a simpleton and should just have washed her hands of Bridget. But Wanda believed she could help her, I'm sure. She told me later she'd sat in some dive with her in downtown Hudson for hours."

"According to the police report, Bridget liked to go to a place called The Tainted Lady, on Warren Street."

"Well, that's perfect, isn't it? Anyway, whatever Wanda said, it didn't work. Poor thing. I don't think she ever quite got over that. She blamed herself. And Norman and the girls missed their dinners, on top of everything. What a night."

CHAPTER THIRTY-EIGHT

Fifty-nine m.p.h. on the interstate, and the Bronco was shuddering and pulling to the left. Abby held on tight to the steering wheel, to avoid ending up in the oncoming lane.

"Yes, I need an alignment," she said loud enough to be heard over the rattling and trembling of the car. Sometimes acknowledging something was as good as doing it.

Which was what Germaine had felt, when it came to telling Athena about their adoption file. She wouldn't actually do it. So Abby was driving south, on her way to see Athena. She had called ahead, saying she was passing through Woodstock on her way to visit a friend (which was not true) and could she drop in. Athena had sounded surprised that Abby would have anything to discuss with her, but she seemed perfectly happy to see her. She went over the directions, in case Abby had forgotten how to get there.

Everything in Athena's yard looked beautifully tended, all the plants cut back, and the beds cleaned up and mulched and ready for the winter. This time, there were delicate little lights wrapped around the porch posts, and a fat pine wreath hanging on the front door. It was as if Athena's early Christmas had expanded from inside the house outward, revealing itself to the neighbors only when it could no longer be contained within four walls.

Athena opened the door quickly, as if she'd been waiting for Abby. "I'm so glad you could come," she said politely, as if it had been her idea all along to invite her. She was dressed in black-black jeans and a black T-shirt. Her skin looked deathly pale by comparison. Her long hair was tied back.

"Thanks," Abby said, as she stepped into the cozy hallway.

"Why don't we go in here," Athena said, leading her into the living room. It was as Abby remembered it, warm, welcoming, perfect. "I'd offer you something, but there's nothing in the house."

"Oh, I'm just staying for a few minutes. I don't need anything," Abby reassured her, though she wouldn't have minded a glass of water.

Athena took a seat on the far end of the couch. Abby picked one of the arm chairs. Once she was seated, she let her gaze travel around the room, at the rich colors and the towering Christmas tree. It was packed with dozens of sparkling ornaments, more than Abby remembered from her first visit.

"It looks as if you've really made an effort to find unusual ones," she said. "Ornaments," she added, when Athena looked confused.

"Oh, yes. My favorites are vintage ones from the fifties and sixties, and they're getting hard to find," Athena explained, pleased.

Silence settled on them again. Abby pointed to a painting hanging above the mantle. It was of a small boy. To Abby it seemed amateurish—the colors garish, his skin jaundiced. "Didn't you used to have something different there?"

Athena glanced up. "Good memory. I just hung that. It's Cal. I painted it, from a photograph I took when he was six. Do you like it?"

Abby had no choice. "I do, yes. The colors are . . . electric. But what was there before? A woman, right? Was it you?"

"God, no, not me. It was a little austere. I like this better." She looked at Abby questioningly. "Is there something you want to ask me, or tell me? I'm happy to see you, but there must be a reason."

"Yes, actually. Did Germaine tell you that she filed a request with the Department of Social Services to look at her adoption file?"

Athena looked shocked. "No, she never said anything. I can't believe it. Why would she do that?"

Abby decided to leave out the small detail that she had bullied Germaine into it. "I think she was just trying to put to rest some long-standing fears she's had. I encouraged her. I thought it was a good idea. She needs to understand the, uh, family dynamic a little better," Abby added, "in her desire to understand your mother. You know she has some unanswered questions about Wanda's death. So the more answers she gets, the clearer it'll all become. Figuring out why she was adopted seemed like a good place to start."

"I think that's a terrible idea," Athena said, squeezing her hands together. Suddenly, she bolted out of her seat and went over to a side table. Picking up a phone, she started punching in numbers. "For god's sake, can't she just let it all go? We were family, and that's that."

Abby stood up and held out a hand. "Athena, hold on. Hear me out. She already found out, okay?"

Athena stopped and looked at Abby. "Found out what?"

"Your mother and Wanda were sisters. You knew that, didn't you?"

Athena slowly put the phone back on the receiver. "So?"

Abby wasn't surprised. "When did you find out?"

Athena shut her eyes, tired, as if the knowledge were a burden. "I've known for years. Wanda told me, about a week before she died."

"Why did she wait so long?" Abby asked, curiously.

Athena shook her head. "Norman wouldn't let her tell us."

"Why?"

Slowly, the woman walked to the couch and sat down on the edge of the seat, her shoulders slumped. "I don't know. I think he meant well. Or maybe not, maybe it was a way to erase our mother from our lives, make us think we were there through the goodness of his heart."

"Did you feel that way, as a child?"

Athena nodded, in slow motion. "It hung over our heads, though no one was crass enough to say it. We might have felt differently if we'd known we were family, not just charity cases. Instead, we were the children of the crazy woman, the drunk. They could send us back to Social Services whenever Norman gave the word."

"Did Germaine feel that way too?"

"Germaine? She just wanted to get out. And as soon as she could, she was gone. But not me. I was stuck there, with them."

"How was it, toward the end?"

But instead of answering, Athena looked at Abby, her expression hardening. "I really don't see what business this is of yours. I think you should leave now."

"Athena, I'm just trying to find out what happened."

"But that's not your place, is it?" She stood up, suppressed anger propelling her to her feet.

Abby stood up, too. "Whatever you want."

She started walking to the door, but before she left, she had one last question she had to ask. "That woman, the portrait that you used to have here, who was it? Was it your mother?"

Athena's face was tense and her voice low. "My mother? Which mother? You mean Bridget the drunk? Or do you mean Wanda the drunk? It was Wanda. Just before she died. Wanda. Now get out of here, go go go. Before I lose my temper."

Sitting in her car, Abby looked at the bungalow. She watched as Athena methodically pulled the heavy drapes on the front windows, starting from the left and working her way around the house, as far as Abby could see. She shook her head. This family had done way too much of that over the years, she thought to herself as she turned the ignition key. It wasn't until she was heading north on the interstate, that her breathing became a little less shallow.

That evening, Abby sat on her metal chair, watching the sun set over the Catskills. The dogs were sniffing around in the field near the trailer, and Abby thought about Athena. She had a lot of rage. Enough to kill the old man? Possibly. She had seen and felt him manipulate and control her and the rest of the family.

Abby thought about the portrait of Wanda. Why was it suddenly no longer there? Had Athena grown tired of thinking about her and her past, or did she feel she had finally dealt her revenge, and it was time to put it behind her?

Abby remembered the note from Norman. She went inside, and found it in her purse. She looked it as she walked back outside.

The old woma [illegible] here, to hant me hant hant
hant hant
Lamy [smudged] will tomoro.
[scrawled, smeary] Nor [illegible]

Was he being blackmailed? Abby suddenly wondered if the word 'hant' was 'haunt.' Did he repeat it so many times for emphasis? Abby sighed. Or maybe he was just trying over and over to get it right. The old woman was here, to haunt me. What was 'Lamy'? She looked at it, trying to see it as letters instead of a word. If he had made an 'm' instead of a 'w', then it would be lawy. Maybe he meant lawyer. Lawyer will tomorrow. Lawyer will come tomorrow? Or he meant his will. Maybe he wanted to do something to his will. Change it? Hadn't he said something like that to her, the last time she saw him? It was possible, but there was no way to know. Abby shook her head. Some things might never make sense, no matter how hard she tried to understand them.

Chapter Thirty-nine

It was a dead Tuesday night. By nine-thirty the restaurant was empty. Dulcie had been gone for most of the shift; George and Sandy had closed the kitchen and finished their cleaning by nine. Becca had punched out halfway through the shift, saying she'd pick up her tips the next time she was in. Henry had spent most of the evening sitting behind the bar, leafing through an old magazine someone had left on a table. By a quarter to ten he threw the magazine across the room and shut down the bar.

Soon, the only people left were Abby and Fritz. Abby was doing the tallies, and Fritz was washing out pots in the kitchen, listening to a call-in talk show. Abby could hear it from the dining room. Everyone has an opinion, Abby thought to herself as she counted up the covers. She looked over the list. Twenty-eight. Wow. Some lousy night.

She put the tally sheets away and took a videotape out of her purse. She put it in her apron and, glancing toward the kitchen to make sure Fritz wasn't standing in the doorway watching her, walked quietly to the staircase that led to the second floor. Slowly, so the boards wouldn't creak, she went upstairs. Once she reached the landing, she listened. She could still hear the pots clanging in the sink. Thank god he had a noisy job so she could keep track of him.

Quickly now, she went into the liquor room. One last look behind her. No Fritz. The case of Prosecco was exactly as she had left it and, as far as she could tell, not one bottle lighter. She made a mental note to suggest to Dulcie that she unload it as a special. If she didn't move it soon, it would turn to vinegar.

She reached behind the last case, and felt for the transmitter. She felt a flush of relief to find it was still there. She lifted it up so she could locate and push the eject button. When she did, the tape popped out, making a loud whirring sound. She pulled it out, and fitted in the new tape that she had in her apron. Her hands were shaking just a little bit. She put the receiver back down on the shelf and slid the tape into her apron. She stood still, waiting. Listening.

She heard nothing.

She stepped quickly out of the storeroom and shut the door. At the top of the stairs, she listened. Still nothing. She felt a throb of panic. She undid her apron, took out her pens and unused checks and, with the tape still in it, rolled up the apron, wrapping the strings around it as if it were ready to put away. She walked down the stairs, and when she got to the cash register, she returned her pens and unused checks to their proper places. Found her purse and slipped the bundle she had made with the apron into it. One last look around the dining room. Front door locked, chairs up, windows shut, lights off.

She walked to the kitchen door and yelled out, making sure her voice sounded slow and tired: "I'm out of here, Fritz. Goodnight!"

And without waiting for an answer, she left by the back door. On Findlay Street, she couldn't help herself. She broke into a run and raced across the dark traffic circle. Once she was in her car, she waited for her breath to steady. She looked back at the restaurant. It looked peaceful and ready for bed. Through the porch windows, she could see the tables bristling with upended chairs. The lights in the dining room were off, but the glow from the kitchen made it appear as if a night-light had been left on to keep away nightmares. Abby looked at her watch. It was eleven-thirty.

There was a full moon hanging low over the leafless trees lining River Street. A harsh wind was blowing small clouds across its yellow face, fast, as if they were late for a gathering. The last of the leaves whipped angrily around the car, slapping into the windscreen, some bouncing off, others collecting in her wipers.

Once the dogs had been out and were back inside, Abby slid the tape from the restaurant into the VCR and rewound it.

The film was black and white, and the action jerky, but Abby was surprised that she could actually see what was going on, considering the size of the camera. She watched Sandy appear at the foot of the stairs with an empty milk crate and disappear into the vegetable walk-in. He walked like Charlie Chaplin. He reappeared, his crate filled with what appeared to be broccoli and green peppers.

She saw Henry running out from the bar and up the stairs. Over and over again. She saw him take a case of beer behind the bar. Reappear immediately with the case, now clearly much lighter, because he held it with one hand. He put it back on the stack.

She saw Becca stop, put her hand up under her skirt, pull down her shirt tails, then straighten and smooth the whole thing into place.

She saw Fritz carrying mats outside.

The next frame the light was different, and Abby realized it was daylight coming in the back door.

Now she saw the day man carry the mats back in.

She kept playing the tape. More coming and going. More nights. Henry, running up and down the stairs. She saw herself walk out from behind the bar, glance up at the camera. And wave. Well, if anyone had found the tape, she had just broadcast to them that she put it there. Smart.

She saw Fritz appear around the stairs and go to the cases of beer. He was bareheaded. Abby sat up. He pulled out two stacked cases of beer. Abby held her breath. This was it. Then, to her disappointment, he sat down on them. He leaned forward with his elbows resting on his knees, his shoulders rounded. He didn't move until he looked toward the staircase, as if he had heard someone. He started to stand and Dulcie came around the corner. Abby couldn't see her expression well, but she stood in front of him. It looked as if they were talking, their heads wobbling from side to side. Fritz suddenly sat back down on his crates, and Dulcie shifted around jerkily then sat on his lap. He put his arms around her waist and leaned his head against her. She put her arms around his thick body, and her face against his bald, tattooed head.

Abby pressed PAUSE, and the image of the two of them was frozen on the television. Shit. It looked like love.

She pressed PLAY, releasing them. On and on went the routine of the restaurant. She saw plenty of asses being scratched and balls being adjusted, moves that might put her off her food, but none of them illegal. Each day went by very much like the one before: Sandy and his vegetables, Henry running up and down the back stairs for food or bottles of liquor, waitstaff walking through, visits to the ice machine, and so on.

And then, finally, something happened that interested her. She didn't know what it meant, but it interested her.

Fritz appeared from the bar. He was followed by his two guests from the week before, the ones who were building their dream house in Goose Creek. It seemed strange that he would take his gold-draped visitors on a tour of the ugly, gray dungeonlike back corridor. In fact, Abby didn't remember him taking them around the restaurant. She thought back. She would have remembered it, if they'd left their table together for any length of time. She put that thought on the back burner and watched the tape.

Fritz stood in the corridor next to the man, seeming to point out the ice machine and the walk-in cooler. He pointed at the back door, his mouth working. He gestured to the staircase. Throughout, the guy called Peter nodded, his expression serious. The blonde woman stood behind them, motionless. She might have been making sure her dress didn't touch the damp walls. When they were done, they walked in single file up the back stairs. Odd.

When she reached the end, the screen turned blue. She had seen nothing else that was different or noteworthy on the rest of the tape. Except that, after the scene in the back hallway, it seemed to cover one more shift, with Abby working. Which would have been that Sunday, the shift that had just finished. Therefore, the night the guidos got the tour had to be Saturday. Abby hadn't worked Saturday, because she and Cat had switched: the Friday before for this Saturday.

Abby rewound the tape to the beginning of Fritz's appearance with his friends. She watched it again and when it was done she reached for her phone.

Becca answered after two rings. "Hey, Abby," she sounded surprised when she heard who it was. "What's up?"

"You know that couple that came in last week, friends of Spermhead's? The people you're going to garden for?"

"Oh, right, yeah."

"They came in again on Saturday, right?"

"Yeah, I think so. Yeah, she got the scrod."

"Do you have their phone number?"

"Oh, no, gee, I'm really sorry, Abby. I gave her my number, but she didn't give me hers."

"Do you know their name?"

"Nope. I don't think they ever told me. And they don't have a mailbox."

"Mailbox? You went to their house?"

"Yeah, a few days ago. Well, it's just a rental, but then she drove me in her Jag to the place they're building. It's a friggin' mansion. They must be loaded."

"Did she say what kind of work they do?"

"I don't think she works, but Peter, he's in the restaurant business. He's got a chain of places in Westchester or something."

"This is going to sound weird, but can you give me directions to where they're living now? I think I need to discuss something with them."

CHAPTER FORTY

The next morning, Abby drove into Goose Creek at nine-fifteen. She turned left before the Dairy Queen and carefully followed the instructions Becca had given her the night before, double-checking each left or right as it wound through the woods.

Eventually, she arrived at a cedar-sided contemporary set in an open field. There were a few bare saplings planted near the house, but otherwise it sat alone on the green meadow. The elegant silver Jaguar parked next to it looked sadly out of place.

Abby knocked.

The delicate blonde woman who answered the door was already in full makeup, though she was wearing a dressing gown. Abby noticed little furry slippers. She thought fleetingly of Germaine.

"I'm sorry to bother you, but my name's Abby and I'm a waitress at the InnBetween. I met you the other night when you came in to see Fritz."

The woman didn't look as friendly as she had at the restaurant. "I remember you. You were the rude one."

Abby was taken aback. "Sorry if I came across that way."

"That's okay," she said indifferently. "What d'ya want? I don't need another gardener."

"It's kind of important. May I come in?"

The woman looked her over carefully. She wasn't going to be rushed. "Fine," she said at last.

She led the way into a high-ceilinged room, dominated by an enormous fireplace.

"Coffee?" she asked, somewhat grudgingly.

"Thanks."

On the right was an open kitchen separated from the main room by a counter. The woman opened a cabinet and found a mug. She filled it from a large coffee machine and handed it to Abby. "Milk and sugar over there," she said, pointing.

While she was fixing her coffee, Abby said: "Becca said you're renting this house while you build."

"Yes. I wanted to buy this one, but Peter says it's too small." She took a sip of her own coffee. "So, what's going on? Abby, right? I'm Gloria."

"Right." Abby paused before speaking. "I'm going to be straight with you. What I need is an answer."

"Oh, yeah?" Gloria said. "Well, we'll see. What's the question?"

"It's about Fritz. I need to know what you and Peter were doing at the restaurant Saturday night."

Her hostess looked at Abby with disdain. "We were having dinner! Anyway, why should I tell you our business?"

"How long have you known Fritz? I mean, is he family or something?"

"Not so long. And no, he's not family. Why?"

Abby knew she was taking a risk and suddenly wished she hadn't come alone. She took a deep breath. "I think Fritz is planning something. Something illegal. And I need to know what it is."

Gloria looked at Abby, weighing something in her mind. She put down her coffee, walked across the living room to the foot of the staircase and yelled, her voice escalating to a piercing screech: "Peter! PETER! Come down! Now! It's important!"

Later, as Abby drove down the hill, she tried to decide what was the best course of action. Either way, Dulcie was going to get hurt.

She could give Fritz an ultimatum: be a man, tell her the truth and get out of town. Or else. Or else what? Either way, Fritz was going to have to deal with Peter and Gloria. Peter, whose parting words had been, as he stood in his rented doorway, T-shirt showing angry patterns of sweat around his neck and arms: "He shouldna fucked with me!"

Peter had an appointment with Fritz the next morning, but Abby hoped that gave her enough time to deal with him in her own way. Back to the big question: which move was kinder to Dulcie? Abby was dying to confront the man, she realized. But wasn't it fairer to Dulcie to allow her, as the owner of the business and the person most involved with the man, to make the decisions?

Abby drove home, dressed for work, and collected the videotape. Once she was back in Bantam, she turned up High Street. The blue minivan was where it always was, on the dirt turnaround. She hesitated for only a moment, then knocked firmly on Dulcie's door.

Chapter Forty-one

Abby promised Dulcie that she would behave as if nothing had happened. Dulcie had cold-bloodedly decided that she wouldn't confront Fritz until the dishes were cleaned and the worst of the shift was over. "I'll fire him after he's done his work," was all she said, her face hard. But Abby could see her eyes were bright with tears.

It had been a tough couple of hours. First, she'd had to break the news to her boss that's she'd put a spy camera in the restaurant.

"Are you crazy? How dare you!"

"Look, I had no choice! I had to find out, for chrissakes! I knew something was going on, and there's no way you were going to get the truth."

Finally, Dulcie relaxed enough to say she could play the videotape. Abby started it up, and they watched their coworkers run nervously back and forth. When they came to the part where Dulcie kissed Fritz, Dulcie said: "Oh, god, how could you, this is private!"

Quickly, Abby fast-forwarded, until the scene with Peter and Gloria.

Dulcie watched the three, jerky figures. "So? What's so terrible about this?"

Abby pointed at the screen. "I've taken friends around the restaurant, but I've never made a big deal about the fixtures. When I saw this, I decided to go see these two and find out what was really going on."

Dulcie looked at her skeptically. "And what did you find out?" When she saw Abby hesitate, she added, "Come on, whatever it is, I can take it."

So Abby told her what she had learned.

That evening, she tried to ignore Fritz and behave as if it were a normal shift. But it wasn't easy. Each time she walked by him or brought in a pile of dirty dishes, she felt him watch her. She was sure he could smell her nervousness, and if she made eye contact with him, he would know precisely what was going on in her head. On top of that, Dulcie was doing a poor job of behaving as if nothing had happened. She was giving him orders and snapping at him when he spoke to her. The man was no fool, he was bound to figure out something was up.

At eight o'clock, just when Abby was beginning to feel that the evening would never end, Germaine and Athena came in the front door.

"Abby, we want to sit in your section," Germaine said loudly from the front door. Abby wondered longingly if she could tell them they were closing early. Looking expectant, the two sisters bustled into the dining room, talking animatedly and picking out a table right in the center of the main dining room.

Luckily for Abby, they ordered quickly. Athena asked for a glass of wine, which surprised Abby. She had never seen her take anything alcoholic. When their drinks came, the two women sat close, their heads together, talking. Abby was thankful they were busy with each other and tried to avoid walking by their table more than necessary, in case her presence broke the spell.

The evening dragged along. At about nine-thirty, the sisters began to bicker about something. Abby did her best to ignore them. A half hour later, after they had paid their check, Germaine followed Abby into the prep kitchen.

"You can't come in here, Germaine," Abby said as she slid an armload of heavy plates down on the counter next to Fritz.

"Abby, we're going out to the Metal Building."

Abby opened the swing door the wrong way and gently tried to push Germaine out. "Now? Why?"

Germaine didn't move. She shut her eyes and shrugged, as if the vagaries of human behavior were a mystery to her. "Athena insists. She wants to show me something. Something important. And it has to be tonight. So yes, now."

Abby looked over at Athena, who had followed Germaine and was standing behind her in the dining room. "Important?"

"Very. I can't leave it any longer," Athena replied, tersely.

"Well, have fun." Abby glanced over her shoulder. She wasn't far from Fritz, who shot her a dirty look as he worked at his machine. He obviously wasn't happy with her standing even within ten feet of him.

"You come, too," Germaine said suddenly.

"What's so important?" She finally managed to shepherd Germaine back into the dining room.

"It's about Wanda," Germaine said. "She swears we'll only be there for twenty minutes or so. Come on."

Abby looked curiously at Athena who was now watching them both, her expression resolute, as if she had made up her mind and nothing could change it. Abby was definitely interested.

It was bad timing, but if she finished soon, she could make it to the Metal Building, then back to Bantam in case Dulcie needed her. "Okay," she said to Germaine, "I'll meet you there as soon as I can."

She finished cleaning her station and did her closing work. She put her checks away and divided the tips. She was just starting to put on her jacket, when she heard a thunderous crash in the prep kitchen, followed by a yell. She heard Dulcie's voice, raised, though she couldn't make out the words. Abby ran across the dining room and pushed open the swing door.

A black, six-inch deep container full of gray water and dirty silverware had been upended on the prep kitchen floor. The knives and forks were spread across the linoleum, with a heavier concentration at Fritz's feet. The soupy water radiated away in a splash pattern from his thick-soled black shoes. Dulcie was standing at a distance of about six feet, her expression black. It appeared she had just thrown the bus tray at him.

"You bitch," Fritz said, as he moved out of the pool of water, shaking himself off. He was drenched from the waist down.

"No, you low-life bastard," Dulcie's voice was low and full of loathing. "You make me sick."

George came out of the kitchen, frowning. He was holding the brush he used for scrubbing down his counters. "What's goin' on here?" he said, taking in the scene.

Sandy and Carmen followed him and stood in the doorway, watching. Abby watched as Carmen took everything in; for the first time since she had arrived, she looked nervous, even afraid. Someone came and stood in the doorway behind Abby. It was Henry. "Water fight," he said. But he spoke softly, as if sensing something big was going down.

"Dulcie?" George said. "You okay? What's up?"

Dulcie shook her head. "You better call the police, George."

"Come on, Dulcie," Fritz burst out. "I don't know what you're talking about. George, she's gone nuts." He grabbed a dry rag from the counter and began rubbing at his face. Abby wondered how much was to dry himself, and how much was to try to buy time.

Dulcie stepped up to him and pulled the towel out of his hands. "You liar, how dare you."

Fritz looked like he was going to hit her. Quickly, George stepped up to them both and put a protective arm around her shoulder. "Dulcie, let us get this cleaned up, and you can tell me what's going on."

But Dulcie pulled herself away. "No, now. You know what this guy's been doing? He's been pretending he owns the InnBetween."

"What?" George's attention moved from Dulcie to Fritz. From concern to disbelief.

"Yes," Dulcie continued, nodding and smiling, furious, "and he and his *girlfriend*," she turned and pointed at Carmen, "they've been busy conning people into investing money in the business. *His* business. *His* restaurant."

George gaze moved between Carmen and Fritz. "Go on, Dulcie."

"It was Abby who figured it out," Dulcie continued. "She saw what he was up to, inviting them here, showing them around, giving them a fancy meal—which I paid for, by the way! God, I can't believe I was so stupid! Oh, and if you think *I'm* pissed, wait till tomorrow, when he has to face the people he tried to rip off."

Behind her Henry said: "Go, Nancy Drew."

Fritz heard him and turned his head. When he saw Abby, his gaze filled with a raw, unfiltered hatred. "Fucking bitch," he mouthed silently.

Abby couldn't stop herself. She blew him a little kiss.

Chapter Forty-two

There was only one other car on the road, way behind her. Otherwise, Abby hadn't seen a soul, and the few houses she passed were dark and shuttered. She was nearing the turnoff for Bantam Center when the Bronco sputtered and coughed. She cursed and gave it a little more gas, but the car jerked once and died.

Pushing away a stab of anxiety, Abby put it in neutral and got the lifeless and ponderous pile of metal over to the side of the road. She made a sound between a sigh and a groan. What if the transmission had given out? It would cost a fortune to fix. And then she remembered the gas gauge. It stuck sometimes. When had she last filled the tank? She couldn't remember. It was the gas, had to be. Stupid, stupid, stupid. She looked in her rearview mirror, hoping to see the car that had been behind her most of the way, but it was no longer there; it must have turned off somewhere.

She sat there, considering her options. She could wait until someone drove by, which might not be for another half hour. She could put her seat back and try to sleep. Or she could get out and walk. She was only about half a mile from Norman's house, she realized thankfully. Athena and Germaine would both be there, with cars.

Abby fished around her glove compartment until she found the small flashlight she kept there. She took her purse and got out. The wind took a pull at her jacket, chilling her.

The yellow moon helped her follow the road. Her mind drifted back to the scene she had left at the restaurant. After her outburst, Dulcie had coldly and brutally told everyone at the restaurant exactly what Fritz had been trying to do.

"Until Abby set them straight this morning, those people believed he owned the InnBetween. He talked them into becoming silent partners with him. They wanted to feel like part of the community, so they were going to give him one hundred thousand dollars, for improvements to 'his' restaurant! And he was going to take the money and disappear. Leaving me holding the bag." When she said that, involuntary tears started filling her already reddened eyes, until they overflowed and ran down her cheeks.

Angrily, she brushed them aside and said, "I'd like everyone to finish cleaning up, then I want you all to go home. I'll lock up. Henry, if you don't mind, you stay with me. Luckily, tomorrow we're closed. Fritz and Carmen, this is your last night. Take your stuff and get out. Don't take anything that doesn't belong to you. I'll be checking. And first thing in the morning, I'm calling the cops. Okay, that's it, back to work."

Fritz stood there, sullen and unmoving.

On the dark road, Abby kept walking. She tried to keep her mind on where she was going. Given what had happened, she was glad she was joining the sisters at the Metal Building. She was too wired to go home, and Dulcie had refused her offer of company. She wondered what kind of proof Athena could possibly have of what had happened to Wanda. She also wondered how reliable Athena actually was. Abby didn't know her well, but from what Cal had said, his mother was probably walking an emotional tightrope.

Abby thought of Athena's Christmas tree. And then, suddenly, she understood, as she walked in the moonlight, the wind gusting enough to give her an occasional push. In hindsight it seemed obvious. It wasn't a real living room, it was too perfect: it was a set. A happy room, somewhere the ideal family would live; where love abounds and Christmas is all year long, or at least from September on.

A theory that might fit in with Athena's compulsive shopping. Trying to fill an unfillable void? So what did it mean? If Athena was living in a fantasy world, did that make her dangerous?

The main street of Bantam Center began on her left. She crossed the road, and a dog started barking in the house nearest her. She walked quickly along the edge of the front yards. She was only a few houses away from Norman's, and she was glad she had the advantage of surprise on her side. What if Athena was lying? What if her fantasy entailed doing harm to Germaine?

When she reached the house next to Norman's, Abby crossed the front lawn on a diagonal. Germaine's was the only car in the driveway. Wise move. The Miata, with its low undercarriage, would not do well on the track to the Metal Building. She walked to the right of Norman's darkened work shed and started hiking across the back field, trying to follow the wheel tracks.

Could this be a trap? What if Athena went off the deep end, and had some kind of breakdown? What kind of proof could there be in the Metal Building? Abby walked as quietly as she could, grateful for the sound of the wind that covered any noises she might make as she stepped on the stones and dry grasses in her way.

The moon disappeared behind a thick mass of clouds, and the night suddenly became impenetrable. Abby's left foot hit a rock and she tripped, hitting her right shin hard against the stone. She got up and stood still, fighting the urge to moan at the sharp pain.

Suddenly, a sound behind her made her stop moving. She listened, holding her breath, and tried to analyze what she had heard. A twig snapping, maybe. Or one small stone hitting another. How far away had it been? She stood motionless for as long as she could stand it, but other than the usual busy night sounds, she heard nothing more. She must have imagined it.

Gently, she rubbed the tender area on her shin and started walking again, this time more slowly, moving her legs cautiously. She was losing her sense of distance. She glanced at the moon, and was glad to see that the heaviest part of the cloud mass had passed, leaving only a light cover.

As soon as the last few clouds were blown aside, the moon shone down, brightening the field around her. She looked behind her but saw no one. The Metal Building was closer than she expected, looming ahead of her like a ghostly cruise ship. Pale light filtered from the dirty casement windows that ran high along the sides of the building.

Colorless in the moonlight, she could see the dark shape of Athena's car, parked in front of the building. The rusted door to the studio was only partially closed, revealing a tall, narrow rectangle of light. Abby walked up to it and pushed it an inch. She listened. She heard raised voices. Female voices. They sounded as if they were upstairs.

She stepped inside the building, appreciating the hard flat smooth surface under her sneakers. Well swept. She looked up the metal staircase. She could now make out what the voices were saying. She listened.

"—oh, you didn't care. You pretended to care, but you weren't here, looking after her—"

"It doesn't mean I didn't love her."

"Don't bullshit me. You just wanted to get away."

"And you didn't want to go anywhere! You just wanted to stay here and suck up to him, that's all that mattered to you. You wanted to be Wanda's little replacement, for god's sake. Cook for the big man, look after him. Pathetic."

Abby sighed. The sisters seemed unable to leave their past behind. It was always with them, regardless of careers or present-day lives.

Abby figured that with all the noise they were making, she could walk up the stairs and they wouldn't hear her. She left the door open and started climbing, moving as softly as she could. They were still going at it when she reached the landing. She followed their voices toward the small bedroom.

She stood, unseen in the dark hallway, looking in. The room was very different from the first time Abby had seen it. The mattress was gone, and from where she stood, she could see Athena sitting at one end of the bed frame, on the edge of the iron springs, both feet planted on the floor and her head in her hands. She had on the clothes she had worn to the restaurant, jeans and a dark jacket. There was a large shopping bag leaning against the wall next to the bed. Abby moved forward silently. The room was lit only by the bulb hanging from the center of the ceiling. It cast a hard and ugly light around the small room, carving deep shadows on the two women in it.

Germaine was standing at the foot of the bed in slacks and her black fur coat. Abby hadn't noticed her wearing it in the restaurant. As far as she was concerned, the coat did not bode well.

Abby stood in the doorway, and cleared her throat. Both sisters looked in her direction.

"Abby, Christ, you scared me. What took you so long?" Germaine said.

"My car broke down and I had to walk," she answered, without moving.

Athena huffed. "I don't see why she has to be here."

Germaine put her hands in her fur coat pockets, and pulled it around her. "She's my friend. And I thought it would be better to say whatever has to be said in front of an outsider. God, it's cold in here."

Abby felt a throb in her shin. She wished there was a chair somewhere. "It sounds as if you two have already covered everything."

Athena looked up at her. She looked exhausted, very different than she had at the restaurant just a few hours earlier. "Not everything. I just wanted Germaine to see this room."

"Now I've seen it. Can we get the hell out of here?" Germaine said angrily.

Athena didn't answer. She reached into the oversized shopping bag next to her.

Given the weirdness of the moment, Abby wouldn't have been surprised if she pulled out an Uzi. Or maybe a tutu she'd worn when she was six. Instead, she lifted out a frame. She turned it to face the two women in the room with her. She didn't say anything.

Abby recognized it right away. It was the portrait of Wanda that Athena used to have hanging over her mantle. The one black-and-white article in the otherwise color-saturated room.

Abby looked at Germaine, puzzled. To Athena, she said: "So?"

Athena smiled grimly. "Germaine knows who she is, right?"

Germaine snapped at her: "Of course I do. I'm not an idiot. It's Wanda."

"Why—" Abby began.

Athena ignored her. "Yes, it's Wanda."

"Who did it?" Abby asked, confused.

"Wanda." Athena answered. "A few weeks before she died."

Abby looked at the picture with a new understanding. "She was so thin."

"Are you trying to lay this on me? Because I wasn't home?" Germaine said, petulantly.

But Athena shook her head. She turned the picture so it was facing her. She gazed at it. "Look at it, Germaine. Look at what she's wearing, look at where she is." She rotated it so it was once more facing Germaine and Abby.

They both looked carefully. Abby felt she was seeing it for the first time, as if she hadn't really looked at it before. The woman's shoulders were bones covered in skin, and the nightgown she was wearing seemed to have slipped off one of them, for lack of anything to hold on to. Her collar bones created deep pools on either side of the base of her neck. Her cheekbones were bladelike. She had a sweet smile, however. Maybe that was all Abby had noticed the first time around. Abby's eyes traveled to the background of the picture. And then hopped a few inches to the space behind the frame. That's when she saw it. The vertical lines behind Wanda weren't wallpaper but a bed frame. They were the fat bars of the iron bed. She had drawn the picture from the exact spot where Athena was sitting. Abby glanced to the opposite wall. Suddenly the age-spotted mirror took on a new significance. She had sat on the bed in her nightgown, and she'd drawn a self-portrait. Just a few weeks before she died.

"She was sleeping here, wasn't she?" Abby asked quietly, looking at Athena.

Athena nodded slowly. "Yeah. She was. In this godawful room."

Germaine sat down on the other end of the bed, as if her legs had give out. "Why? Was she upset with Norman? Were they fighting?"

Athena sat silently, looking at a spot where the floor met the wall. Her gaze was unfocused, distant. "She was terrified of the cancer, of dying, of losing Norman. Did you know she was an alcoholic, Germaine? Must have been genetic, or something about their growing up, because she and Bridget were both drunks. You should watch yourself, by the way. Why do you think I never drink? Except tonight. I needed a little help tonight." She looked thoughtfully at the picture. "In a strange way, because of the drinking, I think being married to Norman was actually pretty good for her. Kept her on the straight and narrow. She had responsibilities, people to take care of. And he wouldn't have tolerated it, she knew that. She'd seen how he'd treated her sister—cut her out of our lives without a second thought. So she kept a lid on it."

Germaine nodded. "But when she got sick—"

"Yes," Athena continued for her, "when Maddie went to school, and you went off to college, she had more time to herself. And then she found out she had cancer. I guess that's when she stopped fighting 'the drink,' as Norman called it. She got bad. Went on benders. She became a falling-down drunk."

When Athena didn't say anything for a while, Abby prompted her. "So what happened?"

"Looking back, it's obvious. Norman put up with it for a little while, and then he cut her off."

"Off booze?" Germaine asked.

Athena shook her head. "I wish. No. Off himself."

"He was cold with her?"

"Cold would have been bad enough. No. He stopped talking to her. Unless it was to give her an order, or tell her off."

"Oh, Jesus," Germaine said, her face sad. "Poor thing."

Athena's gaze was unmoving, fixed on the floor a few feet from her. "She tried to stop drinking, but she couldn't. He never hid the liquor or the wine, or even locked it up. He said she should have the character to stop without resorting to tricks."

Germaine looked sick.

Athena kept talking.

"One night, about two months before she died, she got loaded. They were in the kitchen. She was getting weepy. Telling him how much she loved him, how much she needed him. He said she was a disgrace, she should have some discipline, show some spine. I was upstairs. I could hear him going at her. He didn't really yell, but his voice was hard and flat. And then I heard the door slam, and he stomped up the stairs and shut himself in his bedroom. I heard some banging and crying outside, so I looked out my bedroom window. Wanda was half lying, half kneeling on the steps, sobbing, twisting the door handle. But she couldn't get in. He had locked her out of the house."

"Oh, god, what did you do?"

Athena rubbed a hand over her face. "Nothing. I could hear her crying and wailing, but I was afraid to do anything. Anyway, he was right. She was just so messy, so sloppy. Begging. Finally she shut up and I fell asleep."

No one said anything. There was nothing to say. The silence grew painful. Abby asked, "Was she okay the next day?"

"Nah, worse," Athena answered in a matter-of-fact voice. "I think she believed that if Norman gave up on her, then her life was over. I did try to talk to him, but he was adamant. He said she was no longer welcome if she was not going to be a productive member of the household. He said I was to take over running the house and Wanda was no longer part of the family. I packed up a little suitcase of her things—"

"A small, ivory-colored suitcase—"

Athena looked jarred by the interruption. "I don't remember. Yes, maybe."

Abby nodded. "Sorry. Go on."

Athena continued. "I moved some things out here and tried to clean it up and make it presentable. But it was terrible for her. Dismal and dark. She was so scared. At night she would beg him to let her stay in the house, but he would push her out the door and lock it. I made sure there was a flashlight near the back door, so she could find her way out here. But it was so far, and it was cold." Athena's chin started to wobble. "Oh, god, how could I do that to her?"

Germaine sat down again next to her. She put an arm around her sister's shoulders. Abby couldn't tell if she really wanted to be kind, or felt she should. "You were so young. I understand. It was too much for you, all alone. Poor little girl."

Athena started sobbing for real, her face in her hands, her upper body shaking. She turned her face into Germaine's shoulder. Germaine brought her other arm up to wrap around Athena. Then she looked up at Abby, her face unreadable.

Which reminded Abby of something unanswered, something lingering on the edge of the work area in her brain. She looked hard at the crying woman. "Athena, I have to ask you this. Did you do something to Norman? Did you mess with his medication?"

Athena looked up at her, her face blotchy, her expression affronted. "No, of course not."

"But you went to see him before he died, right?"

Germaine tightened her arm protectively around her sister. "Abby, stop it. She's told us everything."

"I don't think so. I know what she did. You showed him the picture, Athena, and accused him of killing Wanda, didn't you? He told me, he left me a letter."

Athena twisted out of Germaine's grip, and stood up, taller than Abby. She moved toward her. Flyaway hairs created a nimbus around her head.

"I didn't do anything," Athena said, her voice hoarse. Abby felt her breath on her face. "I just showed him Wanda's drawing. He needed to do the right thing, for once. He needed to do what family is supposed to do. He owed me! He owed Cal! I'd protected him all these years, never told anyone. And there he was, like royalty, being allowed to *forget* everything— forget Wanda, forget Bridget, forget *me*. Everyone except Maddie."

She moved back to Germaine, sat next to her and took her hand. "When he died, it would be like we never existed, you know? No, I told him he had to put us in his will, like real family. It's what fathers do. I showed him this picture to remind him of what he'd done to her. I'd been looking at it for twenty years, it was his turn. He had to do the right thing."

In the heavy silence that followed, a distant click reverberated in the empty space. It seemed to come from downstairs. Abby looked sharply at the women. Germaine was startled, but Athena was still too lost in her world to pay attention. Suddenly Monsieur Hulot, Norman's cat, stood in the doorway, his tail swishing from side to side.

"What the hell was that?" Abby asked the room. Or maybe she was hoping the cat would answer. But he was gone.

"Wait here," Abby said quietly to the two women. She needn't have worried. They didn't look as if they had any intention of moving.

CHAPTER FORTY-THREE

Abby walked silently to the top of the stairs and listened. All was quiet. The fluorescent strips on the ceiling made the work area below her look yellow and flat, like a lunar landscape. She walked as silently as she could down the stairs. Halfway down she stopped. She sniffed the air. What was that? Looked carefully around the room. Then she turned and moved quickly back up stairs, careless of the clanging sound her feet made on the iron rungs.

"Germaine, Athena, now, come!" she yelled as she ran.

Germaine appeared, Athena behind her, at the door of the bedroom. "What is it?"

Abby stopped on the last rung and looked at them. "Gas, I smell gas down there. We've got to get out."

Germaine looked worried. Athena said: "Can't we just turn it off?"

Abby, already heading back down, said: "I don't know, but we can't take the time to find out. We've got to leave."

Once she reached the cement floor, she looked around. The area to her left, toward the door, was clean and empty. On her right were some of the floor-mounted metal cutters and welding tools. The oversized, industrial space heater was attached to the wall on the right. From where Abby stood, she could hear a faint hissing sound coming from its general direction.

"It's the heater, it's leaking gas," she said urgently.

"But isn't that dangerous? It could blow up!" said Germaine indignantly.

"Just turn it off," Athena said, standing her ground, looking nervously at the hissing machine.

"I don't know if I can." Abby covered her face with her T-shirt, and walked carefully toward the heater. She could see a red starter button. There was no shutoff that she could see. She remembered the large propane tank against the outside wall, the one that was scheduled to be picked up in a day or two. She backed away from the machine. "My guess is it's leaking from the outside, and there's nothing we can do in here. Hurry, let's get out the door."

The sisters still seemed too startled to make a move.

"It's either a leak, because it's old, or someone's opened the valve on the outside tank. Come on!" She tried to remember what she knew about propane. Wasn't it heavier than air? Theoretically, if it was it would sink downward, forming a layer on the ground. Not that they couldn't pass out from the gas if they were standing in it. And moving through it would surely stir it up. She did know it was extremely volatile. She walked quickly to the green door.

Three things happened in quick succession as she approached it. First, she was about to grab the handle when she realized the door was closed. She came to a full stop and stared at it.

"Wait, wait," she said urgently, stopping the two women from running past her. Abby could have sworn she'd left it open.

The next thing was the floor. Just a short while before, the cement floor had been clean. Smooth. She'd felt proud of that—she'd been the one to sweep it. And now it was covered with a sprinkling of dirt granules, or sand.

And lastly, she saw something sticking out about half an inch from under the door. In the flat light from the ceiling, it was hard to see, but it was there. Something pale, about the width of an envelope. It looked like a strip of fabric. Abby leaned down. There seemed to be moisture around it.

"Look at that," she said.

"God, this smells bad. Let's go, quick." Germaine put a hand on her back and gave her an encouraging push. "Come on, go."

"We can't."

"I feel sick," Athena whimpered.

"The door's closed now. I left it open. Someone was here."

"What do you mean?" Germaine asked, her eyes widening with fear.

Abby turned and pushed them both back the way they had come. "Let's go, move gently, quickly, back upstairs. I don't want to pull the door open, I think it's some kind of trap. We need to find a window, fast."

The sisters turned, obediently, trustingly. The sulfurous smell had grown noticeably stronger, and Abby hustled them toward the stairs. She could feel a throbbing around her temples, like a bad headache coming on.

On the upstairs landing the air was clearer, and Germaine and Abby followed Athena down the corridor.

The kitchen, because it was in the back corner of the building, was at the conjunction of two exterior walls. The back wall was windowless, but the side was partially cinderblocks below, with glass blocks above. Nestled into the glass blocks was one of the casement windows that ran along both sides of the structure. Abby took her small flashlight out of her pocket and turned it on. She shined the weak light around the room. That one window. That was it. And it gave onto an approximate fifteen-foot drop, if she remembered correctly. She tried to visualize the right side of the building, but she had only looked at it once. Weeds, a few discarded tools. Were there any cinderblocks or broken furniture? She couldn't remember. She cursed herself for not paying attention.

The first thing was to open the window. Gently, she tried to crank the handle. It didn't move. She shone the light on it and carefully looked for a latch. Halfway up the window itself, she found it. A little metal arm on the window that fitted snugly into a bracket on the frame. It was stuck, rusted into place after years of neglect. She took off her jacket and her T-shirt. Her bare skin puckered from the cold. She put the jacket back on and wrapped the thin fabric of her T-shirt around the hind end of her flashlight. She tapped the butt of the covered flashlight against the tip of the metal arm. Her fingers felt huge and her movements clumsy. Finally, by the third hit, using her fingers as a guide, the tiny arm moved. She hit it again, and managed to move it enough to free the arm from the bracket. She tried the crank again, and felt a little range of motion. If only she had some kind of lubricant. She looked around the room but, unfortunately, she and Cal had made sure to clean out every old can, bottle or jar.

Germaine had a large handbag over her shoulder. "You have any kind of oil, moisturizer, anything greasy in that purse of yours? Germaine, I'm talking to you," Abby snapped, when her friend just stared dumbly at her.

"Oh, no. I don't think so."

"Dump it out, quick," Abby ordered.

Obediently, Germaine tipped her bag out on the floor. She looked at the pile of her belongings, wallet, keys, and so on. She shook her head.

"What's in those little bags? Tip 'em out." Abby said, pointing at a pair of little zippered pouches, the kind sold at department store cosmetics counters.

Germaine opened one of the little bags and let everything fall on the floor. Makeup. Athena grabbed the other and did the same. A hard plastic case fell out and a bent tube.

"Gimme that," Abby said urgently, pointing at the tube. Athena gave it to her. She unscrewed it, and made Athena hold the flashlight as she squeezed some of the clear gel on the joint of the window handle. She glanced at the label. Spermicidal jelly. Great. Just what the window needed. She worked it back and forth. Then she squeezed some on the hinges. Slowly, she noticed a little more movement.

"One of you, push on the window pane while I turn the handle."

Germaine was busy putting all her things away.

Athena began pushing.

Slowly, the window started to open. When it had opened as far as it would go, giving them about a ten-inch space, Abby let go of the handle and put a hand on Athena's, to let her know she could stop. They both breathed deeply as the cold, fresh air poured in. Athena looked at her. "Now what?"

Abby pointed at the black vertical rectangle. "Now we have to climb out."

Germaine looked at the window. She stared into the darkness. "Can't we just scream?"

"No. Whoever did this to us will be watching. We have to be quiet, really quiet. Athena, you first. I'll go last."

Athena nodded, her expression determined. "Do we have any sheets or anything I could let myself down with?"

Abby shook her head. "All thrown out." She looked around. Her eyes landed on the coat. Germaine's black fur coat. She pointed at it. "We'll use that."

Germaine hugged it around her body protectively.

"Don't even think of it," Abby warned.

Obediently, Germaine took the coat off and handed it to Abby.

Abby grabbed it and leaned out the window, pointing her flashlight toward the ground. The weak beam was absorbed by the dark night, but as far as Abby could tell, there was nothing below the window that might impale Athena when she fell.

She pulled herself back in. "Okay, you have to climb out on the sill. Then, we'll hold the coat open, and you grip it in the armpits. Otherwise, I think it'll be too slippery. When you've got yourself stretched out, we'll try to lower the coat as far as we can, and then you're going to have to jump."

Abby took hold of the coat as firmly as she could. Athena nodded. She put one long leg out the window and edged sideways out the narrow vertical space, till she was astride the ledge. She leaned back into the room, holding onto the frame, and the other leg joined the first outside. She turned over, slipping down on her stomach and gradually let herself slide out, holding on to the window frame. When she was out as far as she could go, and only her head was visible, she transferred one hand to an armhole of the coat, gripping the brown silk lining with white knuckles. She was still supporting herself with her other arm.

"Come on, Germaine. Hold it with me, as tight as you can," Abby instructed. Athena let go with her arm, and as she fell, she grabbed the second arm hole. The sudden jerk nearly pulled the fur away from Abby and Germaine. They struggled to hold on. Athena was now hanging. She extended her arms.

"Let it down, easy does it," Abby said. They began to slide the coat over the edge of the window. The short black hairs caught on the rusted frame. It was sliding out of their grip with Athena's weight.

Abby said through clenched teeth: "Athena, we can't hold it much longer."

Just then, Athena let go. They heard a muffled thump and a grunt. Germaine pulled the fur back in and leaned out the window. "Are you okay?" she whispered.

There was some scrabbling around, then Athena said softly: "Come on Germaine, your turn. Hurry."

Abby knew this one would be harder. Sure enough, Germaine was wearing soft, expensive slacks that immediately caught on the window. Abby finally helped her into a sitting position, both legs out the narrow space. Her hips still hadn't passed through and, because she was wider than Athena, the inevitable happened. She got stuck.

"I'm too fat," she said fearfully, looking at Abby.

"Shut up," Abby snapped. "You're not too fat, it's the window that's too small. But you're going to fit through, even if I have to coat you with that spermicidal jelly and push you out. So do it."

Germaine started laughing, an edge of hysteria to her voice. She hung on the windowsill, giggling.

Abby felt a surge of panic. "I'm serious, Germaine, we don't have much time. I can smell the stuff. Turn sideways. Do it. Now. Focus. Ignore the pain. It'll hurt a lot more when you blow up."

Germaine stopped laughing. "Oh, god. Okay." With a supreme effort, she twisted her hips and positioned them in the narrow space.

From outside, Athena's voice came up. "I'm going to stand here so you can put your feet on my shoulders, okay?"

"Okay," Germaine wheezed, as she pushed. Abby tried to help, by lifting and pushing.

Suddenly, Germaine popped out, her trousers making a rending sound as they came apart on the sill.

She turned around and hung anxiously by her elbows. "Help, help," she whispered.

"You're going to have to stretch out your arms so your feet can reach Athena's shoulders," Abby said, nodding at her, trying to calm her down.

Germaine kept eye contact with Abby, and slowly released her clenched muscles. Suddenly, she disappeared with a scream that was cut off by a second howl.

Abby didn't take the time to find out if everyone was okay. She dropped the fur and both her and Germaine's bags out the window, and was just about to start climbing out herself, when Monsieur Hulot appeared next to her, ears twitching, tail thrashing. He was obviously upset. Or something. Abby couldn't read cat. Abby knelt down and picked him up as gently as she could. She walked to the window.

"Look out below, cat coming," she said, trying to keep her voice low and calm. Before he could do anything about it, she held the cat out over the window. He extended his large paws, shot out his claws and clung to her for dear life. As she dropped him, he raked her hands and gave a desperate yowl. She heard him thump on the ground as he landed, followed by a cry from one of the sisters.

Quickly, Abby stuck one leg out the window, then the second and twisted around. Once she was ready to drop she hissed: "Out of the way!"

She heard a scrambling and panting beneath her. She stretched out her arms, pushed off the wall with one foot and let go. She tried to bend her legs as she landed, but one foot twisted under her body. She fell backward and her head ricocheted off the hard ground. She lay still, her eyes closed.

When she opened them, the sisters were leaning over her. "We're out," said Athena. "Now what?"

Slowly, Abby sat up. She got to her feet carefully. "Is everyone okay? Where's the cat?"

Athena pointed to the woods. "He ran away."

Germaine picked her fur off the ground with a groan. She put it on, and hitched her handbag over her shoulder as if she were going to dinner. "I think I broke my ass."

Abby turned on her little flashlight, and shined the light toward the front of the building. "Come on. We've got to get away from here."

Rustling through the weeds, she led the way to the front of the building.

Suddenly Athena said: "Wait, wait, I don't have my keys." They heard her muttering as she searched her pockets. "Where did I leave them? Oh no, no! I forgot all my stuff, I left the picture of Wanda! Abby, we have to go back!"

"We can't, Athena, so forget it." Abby said in a whisper. "If we can stop it from all blowing up, you get your stuff. What we need to do now is get into Norman's house and use the phone to call the fire department or the cops. But we can't walk across the field. We've got to go along on the edge, where we're less likely to be seen."

By now the moon was back out, and Abby was able to turn off the flashlight. The cold wind was biting into her, and she realized she had no shirt. She did up her jacket. Her hands were beginning to throb from the cat's scratches. There was no real path, so they had to walk very slowly, making sure not to stumble on rocks, doing their best to avoid the thorns from the wild roses and raspberry bushes that grew along the way.

She went over in her mind what had just happened. Someone must have turned on the gas while they were talking. Whoever did it knew there were people in the studio, because Athena's car was parked out front. They would have seen the lights, just as she did, they would have heard the voices. So it was a deliberate attempt to kill them.

She thought about the door. The dirt on the cement. It might have just been tracked in. Or, someone put it there deliberately, hoping that when the door scraped against it, the friction would ignite a spark. But what was the little strip of fabric under the door?

"Athena, when exactly did you go see Norman, to show him the picture?" Abby asked, keeping her voice low. They were now about one hundred yards from the Metal Building.

"It was the night we all had dinner together. I was upset. I'd driven up early so I could go with Germaine to pick up Norman. Cal came to Bantam in his own car." Athena spoke so softly that Abby could barely hear her over the whistle of the wind.

Abby nodded.

"When Germaine, Cal, and I left the restaurant, we said goodnight, but instead of going straight home I drove here. I waited until Maddie and Paul left, then I went in."

Abby stopped walking and took hold of Athena's arm. "You had the picture with you that night? You must've known ahead of time you were going to see him."

Athena shook off Abby's hold. "Okay, yes, I did know. I've wanted to show him that picture for a long time. It was then or never."

"Okay. So let's say you showed him the picture of Wanda, and he saw it your way, wanted to change his will. I think he did, because that night after you left, he tried to write to me about it. Then my guess is he probably called Maddie. At least for that space of time, he wanted to move on it. He told her what he wanted to do. So she knew he wanted to include you in his will. Now, who knew you were coming here tonight?"

"I thought I should ask permission," Athena said, "so I called Maddie from the parking lot at the restaurant."

"Maddie knew?"

"No, no," Germaine interjected, unable to keep her voice down. "You didn't talk to her, Athena. You left a message with Paul."

"Shh, Germaine. That's true. He said he'd tell her, but he said we should go ahead, he was sure it'd be fine."

Abby thought. So the first person who had known Athena and Germaine were going to be at the Metal Studio was Paul. He was an engineer, wasn't he? It would have been easy for him to rig the whole thing.

"So Paul wants to kill us? So we won't inherit anything?" Germaine asked, her voice rising in pitch.

Abby shook her head. "It doesn't make any sense. Norman didn't have time to go to his lawyer and write anything up."

In that second, they heard a noise from the field. In the moonlight, Abby thought she saw the outline of a person—she guessed about fifty feet from the Metal Building on the dirt road.

All at once, a blast like a sonic boom blew out the night behind them and the sky turned white at their backs. Abby stumbled and looked over her shoulder.

The Metal Building had disappeared in a cloud.

A few long seconds later, a light shower of dust and debris began falling on them, a tinkling, crackling fallout from the sky. Abby shielded her eyes with her hands and stood there, staring. A white haze and flames was all she could see of the building they had just escaped from.

They stood there, unmoving, their three faces lit by the glow from Norman's studio, or what was left of it. Athena was wailing, a thready, non-stop sound she didn't know she was making. Germaine was saying something under her breath, over and over. Abby was trying to make herself think. But all that was going through her head was amazement at so much fire. She didn't think all that concrete and iron could burn. Her ears hurt from the explosion and she couldn't think clearly. She wasn't sure what she should do now, what she should make the sisters do now. They should be careful, but she couldn't quite remember of what.

"Quiet, Athena," she said, taking her hand. The contact seemed to have some effect, because the woman stopped her noise. "There was someone there. Someone in the field." She handed Athena's hand to Germaine. "Germaine, I need you to look after Athena. We have to keep going. There's someone out there. We have to get back to the house."

Abby started walking again, faster, stumbling as she went. Her fatigue was suddenly overwhelming. All she wanted was to lie down and go to sleep; she could deal with everything much better if she could only sleep. But she knew she couldn't do that, so she plodded on, turning occasionally to make sure the sisters were following her.

They heard the first sirens before they reached the house.

Chapter Forty-four

By the time the fire trucks had crossed the back field, Abby was sitting in the back seat of Germaine's car. The two sisters were standing by the front door, talking to a police officer. Athena had a blanket wrapped around her shoulders and Germaine had turned up the collar of her fur coat.

Without realizing she was doing it, Abby closed her eyes. In all the chaos of cars and trucks, neighbors and police, firefighters and EMTs, she fell asleep.

She woke up to a hand shaking her gently and a cold breeze from the open door. "Abby, you okay?"

She opened her eyes. Sean Kenna. "Hey," she said. "It's so good to see you."

He looked at her, concern in his eyes. "Hey, sweetheart. Good to see you, too. I hear you were in that building, just before it blew."

Abby nodded. "Why're you here?" she asked, putting a hand on his cheek.

"Notice the uniform. I'm a volunteer firefighter, Tri-Village."

"You're a manly man."

"That's me."

Just then, the door on Abby's side opened, and Germaine looked in. "Abby, you passed out. Are you feeling all right?"

Just then, Germaine noticed Sean. "Hi!" she said, her voice sounding much more interested. "Who are *you*?"

Sean grinned. "I'm Sean. You must be Germaine." He held out his hand to her.

"Yes, I am." Germaine reached for it.

Before she could dissect what she was feeling, Abby grabbed Sean's outstretched hand and pulled it into her lap. "Germaine, this is my boyfriend," she announced, her voice hostile.

Sean looked at her, stunned. She swallowed hard and ignored him.

Germaine said suspiciously: "You're kidding, Abby. I didn't know you had a boyfriend."

"Well, you do now. So back off. No flirty-flirty, Germaine, or I'll come after you."

Germaine smiled slyly. "Relax, Abby. I promise." And she gave Sean her sexiest smile.

Abby shook her head in disgust.

Sean looked happy. He gave Abby a peck on the lips. "Gotta work. I put enough gas in your car to get you home tonight and to the gas station tomorrow. I'd have driven it here for you, but no key, so make sure you get someone to take you to it, when you're ready to leave. I'll see to you later."

Alone again, her eyes closed, and her thoughts flowed freely, drifting from one image to the other. She slid past the truth and on to the next thought, then did a mental double take. Of course. It was perfectly obvious, and she wondered that she hadn't seen it before. She knew who had taken the gun. Abby got out of the car.

Across the field, the studio was still burning, though the collection of fire department vehicles that circled it seemed to be winning. There were clusters of people, neighbors and passersby, standing near the house, watching the spectacle. She saw Germaine talking to a couple. Athena was sitting on the front steps, her head bowed.

Abby went to the door of Norman's workshed. She ignored the notice that warned,

Do not Enter—Private
By appointment only

and turned the handle. She fumbled for the light switch, and when the overhead fluorescents started to flicker, she stepped inside.

Everything was as she remembered it: the work table, his little cot behind the army blanket, the rows of small pieces sitting on shelves. The only difference was the pieces of twisted metal Paul had piled in the middle of the floor.

She hung her purse on the door handle and began to hunt.

Methodically, she started at the table. Next, she looked around it, in the drawer, on each shelf behind it. She moved slowly around the room, rummaging through the plastic bins of scraps of copper, and stainless steel. She noticed that the toaster she'd seen on her first visit was gone.

She looked under his cot, behind it, she felt Norman's pillow. Finally, when she ran out of hiding places, she stood, thinking, gazing around.

Like Blackbeard's wife, she had never been into the two rooms that gave off the short hallway at the back of the work area. The door on the right revealed a small, utilitarian bathroom. Ahead of her, she read the handwritten sign,

Gallery
By invitation only

Once inside, it took her a few minutes to find the light switch on the wall, and when she did, she had to wait for the inevitable strips of gloomy lighting to pop to life. Finally, she was able to see.

As soon as her brain understood what it was looking at, Abby stood there, amazed. It was as if she had discovered Ali Baba's cave, if Ali Baba were a giant magpie.

The entire room, which was about twenty by twenty, was a forest of hanging objects. All shapes and sizes and colors.

Lengths of aluminum pipe ran across the entire ceiling, at intervals of about a foot. They seemed to be built into a supporting framework of more pipes that were attached, vertically, against the four walls. Hanging from the ones on the ceiling were thin metal wires, like guitar strings, each about six inches to a foot apart from the next string.

And suspended from the wires, at all different heights, were dozens and dozens of unexpected, ordinary things. Abby saw bells, shoes, twists and curls of metal, a doll, dead flowers, books, the missing toaster, various tools, letters pierced through with wire. Abby identified toothbrushes, stones, two framed paintings and a white brassiere. She even saw an ice cream container. On the floor under it was a brown hardened pool. It looked as if it had been chocolate.

There was a standing fan at the front of the room. Abby turned it on for a moment and watched, fascinated, as the pieces swayed and bumped into each other, the heavy objects barely moving, the light, papery ones whipping and twisting in a frenzy.

Eventually, Abby found what she was looking for. Over on one side, hanging motionless next to a tea cup and behind a toilet brush was the black handgun. Small, dull, and dangerous. The wire was looped and tied around the trigger guard so that it hung upside-down. Abby looked at it. In Norman's mobile, it was just another found object. No different from a toaster or a velvet ribbon.

With a pair of tin snips she'd found, she cut the wire that held the pistol, took the weapon gently in her hand and studied it. In spite of having grown up in a military family, she didn't know much about guns. Her father, however, had made sure she knew about safety locks. It was on. Which meant one of two things: either Germaine had tried to fire it the way it was, or

Norman had secured the lock after he found the gun. The latter seemed doubtful. She turned the weapon over. She wasn't sure how to check if it was loaded, and she wasn't about to begin fiddling with it now. Carefully, she put it in her purse.

Stepping out into the night air, the smell of smoke still strong, she looked for Germaine and Athena, but they were gone. They must've assumed she got a ride. Everyone else seemed to have disappeared, too.

"Shit," she said. Why hadn't she asked them to wait for her? The fire trucks were still across the field, but she wasn't going to walk all the way back out there.

She pulled her jacket close to her body to keep out the chill wind. The gun weighed her bag down. She started walking.

The walk back to her car went quickly. The sky had lightened, and she knew that once she got behind the wheel, her bed was just a short drive away. With a sigh of relief, she did a U-turn on the dark, empty road. Headed in the right direction, she sat back comfortably.

"Home," she said out loud. First thing tomorrow, she added to herself, or actually, later today, she'd take the gun over to Mitch. Everything was falling into place. She'd done well. Definitely used her head and eyes. The cops would figure out how the studio blew up.

That was the last pleasant thought she had. The next thing she knew, someone grabbed a fistful of her hair and a voice whispered: "Don't move, cunt. You're taking both of us home."

CHAPTER FORTY-FIVE

Abby screamed.

Instinctively, she panicked and yanked away from him, terrified, but he grabbed her head with his other hand, locking her neck into place.

"Slow down, you stupid bitch! Slow down!" Fritz yelled.

Without realizing it, she was pressing down on the accelerator. The yellow center line was disappearing fast beneath the hood of her car, and the black trees on each side of the road were rushing by. Her breathing shallow, Abby forced herself to lift her foot. The car slowed to a normal pace. She steered the wheel to the right, back into her own lane.

"Let go of my hair, I can't drive," she gasped.

He loosened his grip slightly, but kept his hands tangled in it, his palms hot against her scalp. Abby tried to think clearly. If he didn't know where she lived, she could drive past the farm and into Bantam, right by the Inn-Between. Near the police station.

His hand moved against her head. She felt a ripple of disgust.

Suddenly, she remembered the gun and felt a wave of gratitude toward Germaine. She forced her breathing to slow down and put her right hand on the seat, tightening her left grip on the wheel. Cautiously, she edged her hand toward the bag.

Without thinking, her left hand pulled the steering wheel down, and they veered toward the opposite side of the road.

"Watch where you're going, bitch!" He gave her head a vicious shake, sending burning needles of pain down her neck.

"Stop that! It hurts," she whimpered.

"Not as much as that little explosion could have." She could tell by the sound of his voice that he was pleased with himself. "But you're a clever girl, I was pretty sure you'd get out. You saw the sand, huh?" he chuckled. "I didn't think that would work, but it was enough to scare you away from the door, right?"

It took her a second to understand what he was saying. So he'd done it. He'd blown up the Metal Building. She couldn't believe it. "You did it? Why?"

"You know why. You had it coming. You've been out to get me ever since I hired on—bitching to Dulcie, complaining about me, spying on me. You went to see Peter, for fuck's sake. What'd I ever do to you?"

"But the sisters—you could've killed all of us—"

"What're you whining about? You're all fine, right?"

Abby let up even more on the accelerator. Her fingers found the zipper of her bag, and started inching the pull open. As soon as she had enough space to slide her hand in, she started to feel around. "How'd you blow it up?" she said.

"Easy. A homemade fuse I leaned about in the army. Works like a charm. I blew up a buddy's vehicle once—that was a sight!"

"How'd you do it?" Abby insisted. Finally, her fingers found the hard shape of the barrel. She pulled it closer, then reached further along for the grip.

"If I tell you, I'll have to kill you," he said with a laugh, and gave her head a twist that made her vision go momentarily dark. "Simple. I brought an apron from the restaurant, a clean one, couldn't be wet. Dulcie didn't check, she said she was going to, but she didn't. The cunt didn't want to look me in the eye, she knew she'd shafted me."

Abby wrapped her hand around the gun. Slowly, she pulled it out of the bag and eased it along the back of the seat into her lap.

"I tore off a strip of the apron, tied a few knots in it—slows down the burn—dipped half of it in the gas tank of that car that was sittin' out there, shoved the end under the door and, voilà! Who says I'm not a good fuckin' chef?"

The tone of his voice changed.

"Okay, I want you take the next right, yeah, that road. We'll be up at your place in no time." He seemed to know exactly where they were going.

"I don't live that way," she lied.

"Oh, yes, you do. I heard everything I needed to know, workin' in that kitchen. I've seen where you live, all alone. Just those two little doggies. This is it, turn here."

He'd been up to her house. The thought made her sick. Abby slowed down and used both hands to turn onto River Street. The gun slipped between her legs. The road was unpaved and narrow, so she had to take it slowly. She was grateful for that; she needed the time. Her scalp was burning and her mind was racing and skipping out of control. All she could focus on was the fact that, if they got to her place, she was lost. She reached into her lap and, with her thumb, slid the safety off the gun.

She tried to picture everything that lay along the route they were taking: a few houses set back from the road, a pond, two big barns. Nothing else. Just darkness and trees, trees and more trees.

They were getting close to her turn off. She felt her panic rising in waves. She couldn't figure out any way to free herself. If only he'd let go of her hair. She thought she could smell gasoline on his hands.

She hated having him touch her.

Hated it.

As if he could read her mind, Fritz massaged her head hard with his fingers. Involuntarily, her revulsion and pain at the feel of his hands overcame her fear. She shook her head from side to side. Her voice escalating in pitch, she said: "Let go of me. Now! Let go, let go, let go!"

The car careened across the road. Frantically, she corrected it, and they ricocheted back to the other side. Fritz was forced to shift both hands to the back of the seat, tearing out a clump of her hair as he did. Even holding on, he was still bucked from one side to the other.

That was when she realized that, of course, he didn't have a seatbelt on. So she did it again, deliberately now, faster, and then another time, both hands firmly on the wheel, cutting an erratic S down the country road. She had no idea what she was doing, except that as long as she kept doing it, he wasn't able to touch her. And as long as she didn't roll the car, she would keep doing it forever.

They reached the Silvernale farm. Two things crossed her mind: one was Jonah's face, flashing so fast it was subliminal. The second was the prayer that, for once, Germaine had been full of shit when she swore the gun wasn't loaded.

She swerved the car hard to the right, pulled the hand break and felt and heard as Fritz was thrown full force against the left side of the backseat. Before they had rocked to a stop, Abby wrenched open the door and turned to face Fritz, pointing the gun at him.

He shook his head as if to clear it, and began to climb out after her.

She backed up, trying to keep an even distance between them. He moved toward her, and Abby felt a surge of powerful rage—at that moment, all she wanted was to zap him, erase him, and leave nothing behind but a pile of ashes. She jerked her arm up and pulled the trigger. A small explosion blew out of the weapon.

CHAPTER FORTY-SIX

Abby slept well into the afternoon. Sean had gotten up before her and called Mike, asking for the day off. His boss had willingly shifted schedules around so Sean and Abby could have time together, feeling that a reconciliation would be good for bowling. Which was why Sean was in the kitchen, making pancakes.

She lay there, listening to the sounds of cooking through the thin wall. The noises from the kitchen were a warm, comforting blanket.

Abby got out of bed and walked the short distance to her kitchen.

She let herself take pleasure in the sight. A sexy man, in boxers, making pancakes for her. It might never happen again.

Abby was without a car, so the next day she left the house with Sean. In town, she dropped him off at work and drove his pickup to Norman's house.

Maddie's car was in the driveway. Abby walked over and rapped on the kitchen door.

Maddie peered out nervously. "What're you doing here?" she said rudely.

"I called your house, and Paul said you were here. There was something I wanted to discuss with you."

Maddie was playing with her car keys. "Fine, but I'm late for work."

"I hope you're insured for arson," Abby said, trying to keep her voice neutral.

"I don't think I'll even try to claim any, I'm sick of all the drama. I just want to get rid of this place and move on with my life."

Abby nodded, watching her. "Do you want to know what the three of us were doing out there?"

Maddie dismissed the question with a wave. "I don't care, honestly." She didn't make eye contact with Abby.

"It was interesting. Can I come in?" Abby persisted.

"I'm leaving in just a few minutes."

Abby stepped into the kitchen and shut the door behind her. "Athena told Germaine how your father treated your mother in the weeks before her death."

"Oh please," Maddie said scathingly. She stood awkwardly in the middle of the room. "That's taken on urban myth proportions. Or should I say, exurban myth? My father did nothing to my mother."

Abby pulled out a chair and sat down at the table. "That's not entirely true. He was angry with her for drinking, and was probably afraid of her illness, so at night he locked her out of the house. She spent the last weeks of her life sleeping alone in that cold, filthy building out there. And Athena, who was sixteen at the time, went along with it. And has been blaming herself ever since."

Maddie's face was pinker than Abby had ever seen it. "That's ridiculous, completely ridiculous. My father wasn't like that—he wasn't some kind of crazy sadist."

"Athena had a self-portrait your mother did. She was in her nightgown, sitting on that iron bed. All skin and bone."

"That doesn't mean anything."

"It must have, to Norman. Athena showed it to him. So what happened,

Maddie, the night he died? I'm sure you were with him. You had spent the day with him, taken him to the doctor. I'm guessing he told you about Athena's visit, about the self-portrait she brought of Wanda—thin and wasting away, on that bed. Exiled. It was a haunting image, believe me. Did he describe it to you? His guilt over the way he'd treated Wanda caught up with him, didn't it? He was going to do what Athena wanted, make things right and include your sisters in his will—"

"They're not my sisters! I never even liked them!"

"Yeah, but that's tough, isn't it? I mean, you can't choose your family, right? And they may not have been your sisters, but they were your cousins."

"What do you want, anyway?" Maddie had tears in her eyes, though Abby guessed they were more from anger than anything like real grief.

"The truth. Do you know, at first I thought Paul or you tried to blow us up?"

"Are you crazy? I wouldn't blow up the Metal Building! All I did was listen to Norman and do what he wanted. That night, he called me after supper and I went over. He was miserable. He wanted to die. That greedy little cow Athena had reminded him of all the pain he went through when my mother died. He was obsessing about it. He wanted to end it, told me he was going to kill himself. He was weeping. He never said anything about a will, he just wanted to die, to run out into the road, to shoot himself. He was ranting. He told me he had a gun, he could do it. He was completely insane. Honestly, it was heartbreaking—his mind was unraveling. Oh, god, you should have seen him in the old days! He was the smartest man I ever knew.

"That night, I sat with him for a long time, until he calmed down. That's when I decided I had to do it. Do what he wanted. I mean, better to go now than a few years later, a total drooling idiot in a wheelchair, right? Or bedridden and fed by strangers? Don't you think? He wanted me to do it, I know he did. So I helped him. Then I sat with him until he fell asleep."

Abby was disgusted. She didn't believe that Norman had wanted that kind of help. Maybe for an hour or two, in the most dismal hours of the night. But he wouldn't have felt that way in the morning. In the morning he would have forgotten everything. Wasn't that the upside to his kind of mood swings? She thought of that extraordinary giant mobile in his backroom gallery. That had not been assembled by someone who wanted to let go.

"And this "help" you gave him, it had nothing to do with his will?"

"Of course not, he wasn't going to change his will. What I did, I did because I loved him. And there's nothing you can do about it. There's no proof."

"Oh, but you're wrong. There is," Abby lied. "Sometime after Athena visited, he wrote me a note, telling me what he wanted to do. You must've missed it. And I bet that, given the fact that Germaine and Athena are his legal daughters, and he died within days after writing the letter, the police'll pay attention to it. Or at least look into it. Either way, it'll certainly make a stink."

Maddie wiped her eyes. Her face was still flushed, but her expression was stony. "What do you want from me?"

Abby sighed deeply. She stood up. "I've had a lot of time to think about Norman's letter. I'm going to keep it safe, don't worry. But you have to fulfill his last wishes, which were to include your sisters in his will. I want you to give half of the inheritance, divided three ways, to Germaine, Athena, and his grandson, Cal. I think he would have liked that—he took a shine to Cal. What d'you think?"

Maddie looked angrily at Abby. "You've been manipulated just like he was. He didn't love them or want them. They were forced on him."

"Maybe so, Maddie," Abby said, "but Wanda loved them, just like she loved their screwed-up mother. And people seem to measure their parents' love by how much money they get. Athena feels that if she gets some money, it will finally prove that Norman loved and valued her. And look at you, you're no better. You feel that by giving up some of his money, you're being forced to give up some of his love. You should be glad you know he loved you. Your sisters never did."

But Maddie wasn't interested in Abby's pie-in-the-sky thoughts on parental love and inheritance. When she pulled out of the driveway, her tires skidded on the gravel. Abby watched her rear fishtail once on the road before she disappeared.

Maddie wouldn't give her sisters half of Norman's wealth, but she might give them some of it. There wasn't much more Abby could do. Certainly, the letter carried no legal weight.

The Metal Building looked like nothing but a charred pile of debris. She walked around the shed to the dirt track and started toward the ruined studio. It felt like the right thing to do, as part of her farewell tour.

The blackened remains of the building grew as she approached. A thin column of smoke was still rising from the heart of it.

Abby stood on the gravel, now muddy and dug up from the fire trucks. She looked at the twisted metal beams. Funny to think that, under the debris, somewhere, was what was left of the metal bed.

Suddenly, she saw the cat, tail high, tiptoeing carefully through the grass. He was giving the smoking heap a wide berth. Abby called to him, and he looked up, startled. He began cautiously coming toward her. She waited for him, and when he reached her he rubbed against her ankles and kept going along the path to the house. Abby turned and followed.

Chapter Forty-seven

At the InnBetween, no one was happy. It was Friday night. The sign had been back in the window for nearly a week:

DISHWASHER WANTED
inquire within

When the black-bottomed pans piled up in the kitchen sink, Sandy and George took turns scrubbing them with steel wool. Dulcie gloomily worked the floor and supervised the staff, her depression palpable. Abby spent the better part of each shift in the prep kitchen, wrapped in a long white apron, scraping plates and running the dishwasher. It seemed fitting that she had the job last occupied by a man she had fired a gun at.

She thought back to that moment. Luckily, when she had shot at Fritz, the bullet had missed him. A branch had exploded above and to the right of his head. She liked to think that was what she intended, but maybe she had done it to protect her car, or because she was a terrible shot. She would never know for sure.

At the sound of the gun, the farm dogs had spilled out into the road, barking frantically. Lloyd ran out of the house in his bathrobe, carrying a shotgun.

Fritz froze for one moment, then flung himself into the driver's seat, started the engine and released the handbrake. Abby barely managed to roll out of the way of the wheels as he peeled out in a cloud of dust.

He was caught before he could leave the next county. The state police gave a lot of the credit for his capture to the blue-and-white Bronco, which was slow and heavy, and very recognizable. It also made their work easy by running out of gas on the interstate. As Abby said proudly, the tank was nearly empty and the gauge was broken.

Chief Sheriff, on the other hand, was not happy with her. She had fired a handgun that wasn't hers, and all she could tell him was that she had found it that same night among Norman's possessions and had borrowed it for self-protection. And no, she honestly hadn't known if it was loaded.

By the end of the shift, when the dishes were clean, Abby sat in the empty dining room with Germaine and Franklin. They were having a farewell dinner for Germaine, who was returning to Italy the next day.

"Mitch and Suzie must be glad to see the end of you," Abby said with a smile.

"No, they're devastated," Germaine said, affronted. "Why would you say that?"

"Come on, Germaine, you've been parked with them forever."

"Oh, they don't care," she said, dismissing her friends' need for privacy. "The important thing is that Franklin's going to visit me in the spring. Aren't you?" she added, looking coyly at him.

He looked fondly at her and raised his glass. "If the crick don't rise."

Germaine pointed one red-tipped finger at Abby. "When are you coming?"

Abby shrugged. "I don't know. We'll see. It depends on my bowling league. Can't let them down."

"Oh, stop it. You just don't want to leave your sexy firefighting plumber."

Abby looked around the room. "Which reminds me, I've got to get back to work. But before you go, tell me something. Your book. Sean wants to know, and so do I. It's all fiction, right?"

Germaine smiled secretively. "You'll have to do some on-the-spot investigating, won't you?"

And that was that. Abby went back to finishing the dishes, knowing that there was a good chance neither she nor Sean would ever learn the truth about Sabatini. And they'd have to live with that.

As they was leaving, Franklin stuck his head into the prep kitchen and said: "Did you get Pinky's stuff back to him?"

Abby nodded. "Yesterday. I still haven't looked at the second tape. I'll probably just delete it. There's only so many times I can watch Henry run up and down the back stairs."

"Good idea. Spying on your friends is demoralizing."

"And I never found out how Fritz took the beer."

"You know for a fact he took it?"

Abby frowned. "No, but—"

"Couldn't someone just have walked in off the street and helped themselves?"

"Yeah, but—"

Franklin smiled, pleased with himself. "Oh, by the way, you have a job applicant out here. A potential dishwasher, I think." And he gave her a last wave and let the door swing closed behind himself.

"Hallelujah!" Abby said, pulling off her thick, elbow high gloves. Inside them, her hands were slippery with sweat.

She walked out into the dining room. Bailey was standing by the front door, all six-foor-four of him. His brown teeth were showing. Which meant he was trying to smile.

"You still need a dishwasher."

Abby's heart sank. She looked around for help. No one.

"I have to talk to the boss," she said, starting to make excuses.

And that's when a little voice in her head whispered: *Maybe it's not such a bad idea, just until you find someone better. Anyway, he's not that bad. He's just ugly. So he drinks a little too much. Who doesn't? Forget all the other stuff you heard. Probably just rumors. You'll keep an eye on him, right? No big deal. And you know he'll have no problem with the floor mats. It's so hard to find someone strong enough to carry those rubber floor mats.*

Slowly, reluctantly, she said: "Can you start tomorrow?"